Baptism of Fire

LINDA GRANT DE PAUW

Baptism of Fire

With star-spangled good wishes!
Linda Grant DePauw

The MINERVA Center
Pasadena, MD

ISBN 0-9634895-0-X

The MINERVA Center
20 Granada Road
Pasadena, MD 21122-2708

You say there are no words to describe this time, you say it does not even exist. But remember. Make an effort to remember. Or, failing that, invent.

Monique Wittig, *Les Guérillères*

CHAPTER ONE

"Lord Nelson was exactly her height." Admiral Thanatos beamed at the young cadet who stood braced for inspection. "Five foot two and at the top of the class this year. *Lafayette* is lucky to get her. She's our very best."

Lieutenant Elizabeth Costello, second officer of HMS *Lafayette*, to whom he addressed this comment, did not smile. Poor woman, Thanatos thought, she's obviously exhausted. He looked her over sympathetically. Lean, as most of those long in space tended to be, her face was angular and tanned. Her ship's medical/life support team must believe in large doses of artificial sunlight. Her eyes were red-rimmed and glazed over in an expression Thanatos could not decipher.

It was odd to see an officer on Academy grounds in mufti. Costello wore civilian clothing — a pale green silk sari to be precise. That garment was more practical for travel on Earth in early June than the heavy Navy space uniform, and it travelled well in a duffel. Of course, Costello had said something about having spent the morning in India. That must be why she's so glassy-eyed, Thanatos concluded. She's still rolling from space and jet-lagged on top of that.

In truth, the glassy eyes were not a consequence of Costello's travels. The lieutenant was still rolling and jet lagged all right, but the biggest shock to her system was the Naval Academy itself. Since her last visit to Annapolis, the school had undergone one of its perennial shifts from Spartan to Athenian. Out in space, where the war was, the Navy was Spartan — always Spartan. Cadet training, however, lurched from one thing to another every time the Admiralty sent in a new Superintendent.

Spartan meant cold showers and forced marches, emphasis on mathematics, astrophysics and engineering, all in an atmosphere that crackled with tension. Athenian meant meditation and yoga, emphasis on history, hominid psychology and languages, in an atmosphere as peaceful as a church. Thanatos's Academy set Costello reeling in a fog of unreality.

She forced herself to attend to the inspection. She would accept Thanatos's statement that Cadet Margaret C. Steele was Nelson's height. The great hero of the English Navy in the age of fighting sail had been short. But what she saw standing on the Admiral's desk was a figure straining rigidly to the maximum of its unimpressive stature, which could be no more than ten inches.

Every thread of the cadet's dark blue service uniform was exactly in place and the expression on her face was grim — what the sailors called "a quarterdeck face." Costello had stood for inspection like that when she was a cadet. It was a lot harder to look so band-box fresh and inhumanly emotionless braced under a hot sun with an inspection team hovering at your neck and bellowing in your ear. This was a holograph posed in a studio.

The cadet was a good-looking youngster — big blue eyes, and pale blond hair that revealed a tendency to curl even in the short regulation cut. She looked to be about fifteen, although her papers said she would be eighteen in September. In these days of desperate shortages in the officer corps, that made her quite old enough for command in space. She did not look ready for it. It was unsettling to think of going to war with this kid.

The holograph began to fade. Thanatos hit a button to rerun it. Costello flinched. On Earth the amount of energy required to activate a holograph was negligible; and the sun, only a few light minutes away, was always pumping out a new supply, not to mention what could be pulled from wind and water movements, matter conversion, and the gravitational field of the planet. In deep space, once the light barrier was crossed and the tachyonic inertial effect took hold, power was precious. Sailors hoarded energy and did not treat holographs as toys.

Thanatos continued to smile at the image on his desk. "Perhaps you'd like a more thorough inspection, Lieutenant," he said, punching keys on the computer control. "We can show you practically anything you want to see in a cadet." Steele's image wavered slightly, the dress uniform disappeared. Now clothed in exercise gear, the cadet performed a calisthenic drill.

"I can give you an X-ray if you'd like one." Steele's image shifted again; clothing dissolved, skin came off, organs and muscle groups and then the bare skeletal system danced on Thanatos's desk. "I've got the Kirilian analysis in here too," the Admiral continued enthusiastically. "You really ought to see that. Steele has a remarkable aura."

"Please, sir," Costello interrupted sharply. She was sickened by the sight of the dancing skeleton. How could Thanatos play games like this! Out where the war was, sailors risked flaying at the hands of Delphinians every day. *Lafayette* recently lost an officer that way. The last thing she needed was a ghoulish demonstration of how quickly a vibrant young meritocrat could be reduced to meat and bones.

Thanatos looked up from the display, suddenly concerned. "Is something wrong, Lieutenant?" He switched off the holograph. "Come, sit down. The weather must be warmer than you're used to. Let me get you some water." He led her to a visitor's chair and poured water from a pitcher.

"Forgive my insensitivity. Here I am forgetting what it's like to be just back on shore. Sometimes it's hard to remember that even meritocrats are only human." He handed her a glass of water and poured one for himself.

Now that the tiny cadet was gone, Thanatos's office seemed less alien. Very large, of course, by shipboard standards, but plain and modest. Except for the lavish use of artificial power—hardly a sin on Earth where it was so plentiful—Thanatos kept his vows of poverty and simplicity. The blue and white flag of the United Earth and a portrait of the reigning monarch dominated the room. The only other ornament was a framed needlepoint rendering of the meritocratic coat of arms with the motto "I serve." It was the sort of thing relatives gave to a son or daughter who entered the order.

The meritocratic order drew from the numerous, although imperfect, manifestations of selfless service that had appeared sporadically throughout Earth's history: traditions of samurai warriors of feudal Japan, the Knights Templar of Christian Europe, the Platonic ideal of philosopher kings. Nevertheless, the order was clearly distinct from all of these, since its members embodied without flaw the pious ideals of their precursors. Incorruptible, able, and faithful to death, meritocrats were something entirely new under the sun.

Meritocrats combined great talents with a compulsion to use these for the benefit of others. In addition, they had unusual physical stamina, strong immune systems, and a slew of character traits, including courage, compassion, loyalty and integrity, traditionally called "virtues." When scientists discovered that meritocrats could be positively identified by objective analysis of chromosomal patterns and brain waves, the nations and peoples of Earth had, by common consent, contracted to abandon their imperfect forms of government and unite under the rule of the aristocracy of merit.

Meritocratic characteristics appeared randomly, with no link either to heredity or to environment; meritocratic children appeared anywhere and everywhere. Occasionally an adult spontaneously developed meritocratic traits; and here, too, there was rarely any indication of how or why it happened.

In the great Age of Peace that had endured for almost half a century and ended only with the beginning of the First Galaxy War, meritocrats were estimated to make up about one-one millionth of the population. The wars reduced their numbers. Meritocrats led in war as they did in peace, taking upon themselves the greatest risks and inspiring others by example. Military leaders suffered a disproportionate share of casualties. How much meritocratic potential might exist in Earth's children, no one could tell, but adult meritocrats who had accepted the call and who had both training and experience were agonizingly scarce. Earth was now sending the very youngest of its very best off to war with the fervent hope that they would serve well and survive long enough to make the universe safe for hominids and bring a time of peace again.

"You know, Lieutenant," said Thanatos, "Most people would say I have the best job in the Navy. Training these young meritocrats is a delight, and I know that what I'm teaching them will help save lives — theirs and those of the sailors they will command over the years. I confess I find it a blessed relief after twenty years in space. But it has a downside. I haven't forgotten — can't forget — the horrors of this war. When the sun comes up in the morning and I've taken my post-trauma medication, it all seems like a dream. But I never take those little blue pills unless I've had a screaming nightmare; and when that happens

I remember it all, and I think about my brigade of cadets, and I don't much like my work."

Costello nodded and shook off her own memory of the dancing skeleton. Still, she couldn't rouse much sympathy for the admiral in his snug harbor. "Sir, I need to know more about the cadet training. I was told the entire class is to be commissioned directly as lieutenants. That's fine; *Lafayette* needs an officer ready to pull her weight; we're not a training vessel. But as far as I can tell from Steele's records, she has absolutely no experience in deep space. She hasn't even done an ensign's cruise."

"That's true, but she's had the equivalent. The Admiralty studied the Academy curriculum thoroughly and approved the direct commissioning."

"Sir, I don't question this woman's physical fitness or her academic qualifications either, for that matter, but . . ."

"Fine! Then I'll cut her orders and you can have her right after the commissioning ceremonies tomorrow."

"Admiral, please!"

Fleet officers, Thanatos thought. They were all paranoid. Here he was giving *Lafayette* the top cadet in the graduating class, the very best new lieutenant on the planet, and the escort officer was fussing about details of training. Training was his job; the war in space was hers. Well, you had to make allowances for the people in the fleet; long cruises tended to scramble the brain.

"Very well, Lieutenant, I can see you're still not comfortable. The cadets are on a minute-by-minute schedule today. Everything they are doing is essential to complete their training. But if it's that important to you to interview your new shipmate in person and question her about her experience, I can cut some slack. Usually I discourage outside contacts of any kind during the final year, especially during the final month. I don't want anyone accidentally saying something that's going to erode a cadet's self-confidence because that's what I build on." Costello made it clear she wanted the slack cut.

Thanatos began to push buttons again. Costello sighed. An electronically powered communication system of some sort: he even used one of those. When she was at the Academy, the school followed shipboard practices and used runners to carry messages. How could an officer trained in this idyllic environment ever adjust to the austerities of space? And this business of not eroding a cadet's self-confidence! What kind of real self confidence could be eroded by a little conversation — even by vigorous verbal hazing? Until you broke down that phoney, superficial self-assurance that passed for confidence among civilians, how could you even begin to build up the true gut-deep kind needed for command in space? Annapolis, Costello concluded, had definitely gone to the bow-wows.

Unfortunately, there was no choice. Annapolis was the only training school for Navy officers, and Thanatos was running the place. *Lafayette* was fortunate to be getting a replacement for Shankar at all; every ship in the fleet was short of personnel.

"There, now." Thanatos rose from his desk. "It's all set. Cadet Steele will meet you for dinner at Olde McDonald's at 1800 hours and answer all your questions. The Navy's buying. Relax a little. Enjoy yourself. That's what shore leave is for."

* * *

Cadet Steven Decatur Benjamin, wrapped in a white terrycloth bathrobe, sat glumly on a wooden bench, staring at the door marked SOCRATES. After SOCRATES finished with Maggie, it would be his turn. Decatur groaned. This session was a long one. He could see the digital clock through the glass panel. Whatever the experiential time frame for the exercise, the clock showed more than two hours elapsed time. Unless Maggie had got into trouble in the egg and was getting extra treatment in the debriefing sequence.

Maggie get into trouble? It seemed unlikely. She was really good at this stuff. It had taken the technicians a while to stabilize her personalized warrior mode, even longer than it had taken for Benjamin. But once it clicked, Maggie had it down cold. She actually became enthusiastic about going to sessions with SOCRATES when she found that she had a chance to beat Chuck Cabot and set the cadet record for dry runs in the simulator.

Cabot was the star athlete in the class. It surprised no one that he had stabilized in warrior mode early in the year and made the first dry run in the class early in November. He built up his record of successes in SOCRATES slowly. Then in April, after her slow start, Maggie began to catch up; and for the last two weeks, she had been on a streak. Coming into the last exercise of the term, the biggest cadet in the class and the smallest were tied with twenty-eight dry sessions each. If Maggie made it through this one, she'd break the tie. She'd also have accomplished the awesome feat of making six dry runs in a row.

The door banged open, and Maggie Steele charged out wrapped in a terrycloth bathrobe, grinning broadly as she towel dried her hair. "A dry run, Steve!" she shouted. "I did it! Six in a row! More than anyone did this year. More than anyone ever did seeing that ours was the first class through it!" She held her arms up to the man who towered over her by nearly a foot. "A hug for luck," she said. "Hug the record holder, and you'll get through a dry run yourself."

"You look pretty wet to me," Benjamin said, giving her a squeeze and a pat on the back. Cadets were warned about forming "particular friendships," but of all his brothers and sisters at the Academy, he was fondest of Maggie. She reminded him of the real older sister he had left at home when he was ordered to the Academy four years ago right after his twelfth birthday. "Is all that really from the shower?" he asked tousling her wet curls.

"Absolutely."

"What? Not even a few tears? No sweat?"

"No tears," she said, pulling the towel around her neck and shaking out her hair. "Sweat was within acceptable limits."

"And me still worried about shitting my pants or puking," Benjamin moaned. "Any chance they eased up a little on this exercise, seeing it's the end of the term?"

"SOCRATES ease up? Never. The rule is each one is worse than the one before. Anyway, they coded in a lot of debriefing time for the memory wipe, so it must have been pretty grisly. I think they expected heavy sweating; I came out real thirsty. Oh, and there was an extended adrenaline surge at some point; they made me swallow a neutralizer."

"Thanks for the hints," Benjamin said wryly. "I hope I enjoy the experience as much as you did." For someone who had just gone through a simulated day in hell, Steele couldn't have looked happier.

"I love having had a chance to beat out Chuck," she said. "It's not often a shrimp like me can match him in anything physical. But there's something else, too, Steve. There was a message for me from the Supe when the medics pulled me out of the egg. I'm excused from the Baccalaureate tonight; I get the blessing without the sermon. And he's buying me dinner at Olde McDonald's."

"The Supe's taking you to dinner? Is this the prize for proving nothing else he could invent could make you throw up?"

"No, you clown," Steele laughed. "The Supe's not coming. He made the reservation for me and an officer from HMS *Lafayette*."

"Maggie! Does that mean . . ."

"Yes! I got it! A berth on a dreadnought! One of the big ones! The biggest! She's in the Mars orbit; I've been watching her every night since she came in. *Lafayette*'s sure a beauty! They must have drifted in on the solar winds with their batteries drained, because they've had their black sail plates out to pull in solar power every time I looked. It wouldn't take near this long if they were just topping off the charge. We'll be picking up some sailors at Fort McHenry and going out to her on a shuttle catching the sunset tide tomorrow. Oh, Steve, I feel so happy! I never imagined I could be so lucky. I've got everything I ever wanted, and it's all coming together in one week."

This was what he loved about Maggie. She found joy in everything. He was going to submit to SOCRATES one more time because that was his duty. Tomorrow he'd take his commission and go to war because that was his duty. This was definitely not the way he'd be spending his teen years if he had a choice.

Unfortunately, for meritocrats there was no choice. You got your call, and then you served where the Crown sent you. Cheerfully. Whether you felt cheerful or not.

"Cadet Benjamin!" The lab door opened again, and a scowling medic came though it. "Get yourself in here! You're a full two minutes behind schedule, and that time's coming out of my prep allotment. Hustle it!"

Benjamin gave Steele the dumb sailor's hand signal that loosely translated meant "Pardon my abrupt departure; duty calls," smiled at the commoner who was about to cover his body with wires and needles, and strode into the lab.

He was glad Maggie was getting the assignment she wanted, but he'd been hoping they'd both travel to the war zone together by transport before being split up among the ships in the forward fleet. As it was, Steele would have to leave Annapolis immediately after commissioning ceremonies to join her ship. Navy service being what it was — and war being what it was — Benjamin knew the odds were against his ever seeing her again.

* * *

Liz Costello sipped ice water and peered uneasily into the cool darkness of the restaurant. Olde McDonald's was a tourist trap that served good food but was outrageously expensive. Admiral Thanatos made reservations here as a gesture of respect and kindness; Costello appreciated that, but she found the decor of the place disturbing.

Olde McDonald's occupied an historic site on Church Circle in the center of town on which a series of restaurants or inns had done business for close to three hundred years. The current owners had taken possession in 2053 and remodeled at that time to recreate what they chose to advertise as a typical eatery of the twentieth century, which was now popularly known as the Century of Wars. Recently, in an effort to freshen up the image, the restaurant had redecorated to emphasize a military motif.

The creators of the new ambience chose to interpret "twentieth century" loosely. The reproduction "antiques" artfully displayed near the entrance to the restaurant, on ledges near the ceiling, and in the rest room shared a martial theme, but they covered every war between Napoleon and the meritocratic Age of Peace. An elaborate oil painting entitled "Victory at Sea" depicted a scene including both a three-masted frigate with all sail spread and a partially submerged nuclear submarine.

There had never been an actual McDonald's Restaurant on Church Circle, but late in the twentieth century a similar establishment called The King's Burger, or some such thing, had done business a block away. That was close enough for Olde McDonalds to capitalize on the historic tradition.

Wooden tables and chairs sparkled with white lacquer so they resembled plastic, a synthetic prohibitively expensive on Earth after the exhaustion of fossil fuels. Cloth napkins displayed the quaint double-arch logo in elegant hand embroidery. Costello's white porcelain water goblet bore similar markings, and a large porcelain bowl, vaguely triangular in shape and painted with the logo and the words "French Fries" in old English lettering held some cold, thinly sliced potato chips.

In place of a tablecloth, the table was set with cloth mats, textured to resemble paper, and bearing a piece of embroidery urging the diner to "follow the dots." From her study of military technology, Costello identified the underlying design as a Sherman tank. She was certain none of the well-dressed commoners in the restaurant, who would never dream of putting a pen to the fine linens, had any idea of what the connected dots would reveal. Maybe if they did, it would spoil their appetites.

Probably not, she decided, watching the parties of civilians at the other tables talking, laughing, and enjoying their food. War, which was so much a part of her life, was a romantic fantasy to them. So far the meritocrats had successfully limited its impact on the home planet.

She inspected the prints on the opposite wall. It was too dark to see them clearly, which was probably just as well. They were reproductions of recruiting posters from the Great War of 1914 to 1919. The one she was facing bore the legend, "Bayonet the Boches!" and depicted a soldier engaged in disemboweling an enemy who presumably deserved it. Costello found it disgusting.

Costello rubbed her forehead and mentally explored her body to pinpoint why she felt so godawful. Maybe it would help if she could position herself in time and space. She focused gritty eyes on her chronometer and did the calculations in her head.

Almost 1800 here, which would make it close to 2200 in Greenwich, which was also the standard for ship time. That would be four bells. Right. Halfway through the first watch.

So yesterday . . . Was it yesterday? Yes, yesterday was June 1, 2080 in Greenwich and on HMS *Lafayette* and the chronograph said it was now June 2. So it was only yesterday. Twenty-four clock hours ago, she was on the bridge . Right after the watch changed, she boarded the shuttle for Earth.

That was the last time she had been able to sleep. The shuttle touched down in the Bay of Bengal at what time? Well, the sun was just rising. She could remember how good that first breath of cool morning Earth air smelled. There was some slight delay at the dock, but once she boarded the water taxi, the trip upriver to the little town fifty miles from Calcutta where Shankar's family lived seemed to take no time at all.

The condolence visit seemed to last forever.

Abruptly Costello came fully alert. Cadet Steele had entered the restaurant. Costello recognized her immediately and watched her speak to the *maître d'*. She wore the kilted dress uniform issued to both male and female cadets for warm weather. The stiff officer's tunic did not conceal her rounded figure, considerably more conspicuous now than it had been in the holograph taken earlier in the term.

The Academy deliberately fattened up the graduating class during their final months. It was an essential precautionary measure. They tried to put some weight on the common sailors too when there was sufficient time between impressment and embarkation. Spacesickness affected almost everyone going out for the first time. A little extra body fat could keep them going until they got their space legs.

The cadet looked good in her uniform. Costello watched the *maître d'* melt in the face of Steele's meritocratic charm. What constituted that special charisma, no one could quite finger — it differed in form from meritocrat to meritocrat — but it inevitably triggered the natural submission of the lower orders. For Steele, that charm seemed to include, of all things, dimples.

In place of the rigid expression in the inspection holograph, Steele displayed a radiantly happy face. The bright blue eyes twinkled over a dazzling smile. It was infectious. Costello realized she was smiling herself.

As Steele was led to the table, both officers switched off the smiles. Steele snapped into a brace. "Cadet Margaret C. Steele reporting as ordered, *ma'am.*" So, thought Costello, Thanatos's Athenian Academy still taught cadets the traditional courtesies of the Royal Navy.

"Sit," Costello said. "This is informal." Steele sat, her face breaking out in another flourish of bright smiles and dimples.

"I'm awfully glad about my orders, ma'am. *Lafayette* would have been my first choice, if we had choices, that is."

The cadet had an unusual voice, Costello noted, a musical voice, low-pitched and resonant. It was an odd complement to the big blue eyes, ringlets and dimples, but it was reassuring. Steele sounded like a Navy officer even if she didn't look like one.

"Did Admiral Thanatos tell you why he set this up?" Costello asked, waving a hand over the table and eyeing the gruesome poster on the wall.

"Yes, ma'am. He said you needed to know more about my training and that I should answer all your questions."

"How do you feel about that?"

"Relieved, ma'am. That is, of course I have full confidence in the Admiralty and everything and I'm sure SOCRATES is everything Admiral Thanatos says it is. Only . . . ."

"Go on. Your orders were to answer my questions. Only what?"

"Ma'am, ours is the first class trained by SOCRATES. We're sort of like a new experimental weapon that hasn't been field tested. I feel like I should come with a warning label or something so the officers I work with will know what to expect."

"And do you know what to expect?"

Steele frowned. The dimples disappeared and the blue eyes clouded. "Only the theory, ma'am. All of the instructors kept telling us it's very important that we have complete confidence in SOCRATES because it would help us get programmed faster. I probably shouldn't even be saying this. But if there's any chance that I'm going to bilge on this assignment, I think my superiors should know in advance."

"Do you think you're likely to bilge?"

"No, ma'am. If SOCRATES takes in any of us, it's going to take in me."

"You seem very sure of yourself."

Steele blushed bright red. "It isn't arrogance, ma'am. It's been confirmed by objective testing. I completed more sessions with SOCRATES at a rating of 'superior' than anyone else in our class; and in the last two weeks, when they threw the absolute worst at us, I finished every single one of them at a 'superior' rating. If SOCRATES hasn't made me into a fully qualified lieutenant, our whole class is a wipeout."

If that's the case, God save the fleet, Costello thought. "We'd better order," she said deciding it would be wise not to dwell on this possibility. "Service has always been notoriously slow in this place. I assume the redecorating hasn't changed that."

"No, ma'am," said Steele. "Olde McDonald's is still the slowest food in town. At these prices, people come here to stay awhile and enjoy the ambience, not just gobble and go the way cadets do."

"So, we'll order now, and then you can deliver your briefing on cadet training 2080's style." Costello looked over the menu. "I see they feature a lot of pig products — ham, bacon, pork roast. I suggest we stay away from those since pork is the only red meat we'll get in space, and I suppose you've also had your fill of it recently." She looked at Steele sharply. "They have been feeding you red meat, haven't they? I hope Thanatos didn't try to adjust your stomach to a heavy meat diet in a simulation."

"No, ma'am," Steele grinned. "Thanatos is big on dietary theory and has us gorging on contractive food — the warriors' diet, he calls it. In fact, after Christmas break, he totally banned fruit as too expansive and likely to interfere with our training."

"Well, forget your diet for tonight. Two things you'll really get to miss in space are beef and fish. Cattle are too much trouble, and we can't spare the water to keep seafood. I had fish for lunch, so I intend to order steak. What appeals to you?"

"Hey, just having a choice is exciting." Steele looked over the menu with obvious pleasure and finally settled on crab cakes.

Costello signaled the server, who bustled over in a dither. The boss bragged to everyone that Admiral Thanatos had personally made reservations for two meritocrats, and the *maître d'* had made it very clear that they were to get deluxe service.

The server wore a mixture of contemporary civilian fashion appropriate for Annapolis on a warm spring day and an assortment of other articles that symbolized the twentieth century in the mind of the average citizen. Starting at the top, the young man wore a green beret with paratrooper insignia, a necktie over a bare chest, a two-holster six-shooter belt, a kilt in the McDonald tartan, and white sandals that had the word Nike painted in black on the back strap. He pulled a portable communicator from his gunbelt, prepared to send an order directly to the kitchen.

Costello interrupted him as he rattled off the list of chef's specialties and ordered a sirloin medium rare and the McCrab

Cakes. He chattered into the communicator, bowed, smiled, saluted, told them to have a nice day and backed off into the shadows wondering whether meritocrats, who had taken an oath of poverty, might still leave a good tip.

"Very well, Cadet Steele. Let's get down to it. Brief me."

Steele dug into the leather sporran at her belt and pulled out a computer disk and a thick stack of papers. She folded her hands on the table and began to speak. "The definitive description of the Simulator of Combat: Retinal/Aural/Tactile Stressor, hereafter referred to as SOCRATES, is an article by Admiral Theodore H. Thanatos published in the September 2079 issue of the United Earth Naval Institute *Proceedings.* For later reference, I have secured copies of the disk publication for that volume and also made a paper printout for the convenience of shipboard personnel." She glanced at Costello. On Earth the paper printout would be considered a waste, but on ships in deep space, she had been taught, the waste was in booting up a computer.

Costello reached for the papers, glanced at them briefly, and stuffed them into the folds of her sari. "You can recycle that," she said indicating the disk.

Steele grinned. Well, she'd got that right. She continued her lecture. "SOCRATES is programmed to reproduce a series of representative Navy and Marine combat experiences from the perspective of officers functioning in various command roles. They were retrieved from deep hypnotic debriefings of meritocratic veterans hospitalized for post-traumatic stress disorders. The subjects of SOCRATES training receive full mind wipes at the conclusion of each training session to prevent development of PTSD due to exposure to the simulated stress."

Costello interrupted. "You're telling me that Thanatos put you kids through what was emotionally and psychologically indistinguishable from experiences that broke the stability of veteran officers?"

"I suppose you could put it that way, ma'am. We don't remember any of it, and it doesn't seem to have hurt us. They were very careful to get our bodies off the stress reactions right after the episode played out."

"Still sounds dangerous to me. Did any of you developed any physical symptoms?"

"Well, I don't know if you could call it a symptom, exactly," said Steele running her fingers through her curls, "but you can see if you look close that I've got a lot of grey hair. It doesn't show that much because I'm so fair. My mother got very upset she saw it in our class picture; she wants me to dye it."

"Premature greying doesn't run in your family, then?"

"Not so far as I know. I'm greyer now than you are, ma'am; and there wasn't any grey at all until last fall."

Costello had a good deal of grey shot through her hair. She was going grey much faster than anyone in her family; but she was almost forty and had been in the wars for over fifteen years. Now that Steele mentioned it she could see milk white curls intermixed with the pale blond.

"I don't know what to make of that," she said. "Was this contraption tested at all before they ran a whole class of cadets through it?"

"The SOCRATES hardware is extremely complex. I don't understand it well enough to explain. Admiral Thanatos developed the primary plans himself, but all members of the Admiralty reviewed them, and they were approved by the Crown before being tested on commoners."

"And what were the results of those tests?"

"The tables are in the back of the Thanatos article. Basically, it seems, that, as you'd expect, the commoners were much easier to train to acts of violence. Many of the test subjects came from the prison ship, and they already had a natural streak of cruelty so the SOCRATES training was redundant. None of them had any measureable bad effects from it.

"The chief who ran the simulator for us was in on some of the testing aboard *Good Hope*. He was always complaining how hard it was to work with us 'gentlefolk.' It does seem sort of a paradox — trying to teach people certified as having abnormally high levels of compassion how to cause pain and take life. The chief used to say he'd rather teach cats how to swim."

"That brings up a nice point. How do you know this training hasn't damaged your compassion? If you lose that quality, you're no longer fit for command."

"We got tested regularly on that. In fact one of the brain wave sensors was keyed to that specifically. The warrior subpersonality is an undamaged meritocrat. She feels compassion — and they say this was the worst part of the stressing — but she does what needs to be done anyway."

"Back up. What's this about a subpersonality?"

"That's how the training is supposed to work. They put us in the simulator. It's shaped like a big egg, and after they get you wired up, you climb in and curl into a fetal position. Then they close it up, and it's a total sensory deprivation environment. They start the hypnotic sequence, and that's the last you remember until a medic pops open the door and starts cleaning you up and feeding you electrolytes or something to restore the physical balance.

"While you're out — like totally unconscious — the stressor cuts in and after your usual personality tries unsuccessfully to cope with the situations, a second personality appears. We call it the warrior mode. It's different for everyone, of course, because it is born out of the dominant personality."

"This sounds to me like induced schizophrenia."

"It is, but Thanatos doesn't like using the word."

"So you're telling me that the entire Annapolis class of 2080 is potentially schizophrenic."

"I guess so, but that's not necessarily a bad thing. Thanatos says that all meritocrats who are successful combat leaders have to have split personalities. They have to be able to operate as cold-blooded killers one moment and then flip back to being nurturing parents to their troops the next." She looked at Costello, hoping for confirmation. "That's what he says; is that really what it's like?"

"Close enough," said Costello, remembering a few episodes she usually kept safely out of mind. "So you've got this subpersonality inside you. What's it like?"

"I don't know, Lieutenant. That's what feels really scary because it *seems* like she's super-competent judging from how she takes over in SOCRATES, but I don't have a clue what her personality is like. It's supposed to be very close to what I am now; just enough different to take the pain. And she knows everything about me, so when she takes over there shouldn't be any problem."

"And when, can you tell me, is 'she' going to take over?"

Steele stirred uneasily and clasped and unclasped her hands. "I don't know exactly. She's set to move in when I need her. The best case scenario is that she'll move in gradually. The deep space environment is familiar to her; that could be enough to get her awareness to leak over to me. But she could come in bang — all at once. If I'm conscious when she does . . . Well, it's scary."

"Yes, it certainly is that." Costello leaned back in her chair and drummed her fingers on the table. "I'll be frank with you, Steele, *Lafayette* needs an experienced officer to take over Shankar's berth in navigation, needs one badly. But I am scared shitless to be going into space with an officer who's been hatched out of that oversized egg you call SOCRATES."

"Frankly, ma'am, I'm scared shitless too. But I've got my orders, so I've got to ignore that."

"And I have mine." Costello smiled. There was plenty to be terrified of in space; this bright-eyed young officer was not the most terrifying thing she'd ever confronted.

"That's enough business discussion," she said briskly. "Where on Earth is our dinner?"

The server appeared at the table as if by magic. Olde McDonald's prided itself on presenting the meal unobtrusively without intruding on patrons' conversation. Porcelain plates, scalloped at the edges to resemble the paper throwaways of the late twentieth century, were set before them.

Costello breathed in the delicious odor of perfectly broiled beef, an odor that brought back memories of June evenings long past when she and her family indulged in wonderful backyard barbecues. She carefully cut a piece, put it in her mouth and chewed it slowly. The flesh was tender and the juice slightly salty. The memory of earlier days intensified. She quickly took a swallow of water to clear them out. She couldn't afford an attack of homesickness.

Steele, enjoying her crab cakes, watched her dinner companion curiously. She'd rarely seen a meritocrat close up before except for her classmates and Admiral Thanatos. Lieutenant Costello was tired, she thought, very tired. So her first job as the junior lieutenant of *Lafayette* would be to pitch in and help her get through whatever else they had to do on shore before they took off for the ship.

"Ma'am, will you explain to me what our orders are? What has to be accomplished tomorrow?"

Costello pulled herself away from memories of backyard barbecues. "Nothing complicated really. The press has given us another two hundred, a double issue; we'll be taking them aboard the shuttle at Fort McHenry. We're also going to top off our meat supply there. Our work is just to supervise loading."

She smiled. "As for the morning, I believe you are expected to participate in a commissioning ceremony."

"Will you be attending, ma'am?"

"I expect so," she said, her smile softening, "that is if my children are still as wild about Navy pageantry as they were when I last saw them." Her eyes misted slightly.

Costello was one of those officers who had decided against taking the vows of chastity. The cadets talked about those vows a lot among themselves, although they would not be allowed to take a binding oath until they reached the age of twenty-one. Most of them had already decided that when the time came they would take it. The pleasures of having a family, they thought, must be outweighed by the awful pain of separations that were inevitable if you had a Navy career.

Costello pulled two miniature photographs from a fold in her sari and passed them to Steele. "I've got some new pictures to take back to space. Admiral Thanatos got them for me from the Navy Orphans' School." She pulled out a locket that hung from a chain under her clothing. "These are my old ones," she said.

Both sets of pictures were of freckled, red-haired children — a boy and a girl. The set in the locket displayed gap-toothed grins. The children must have been about seven or eight. The new set showed even white teeth and faces marked distinctly with the character of children on the brink of transformation into adults. Had they been meritocrats, they would have been old enough for assignment to Annapolis.

"As you can see, they're twins," Costello said, "Lizzy and Andy. The carrot hair is from their father, Andrew Carline." Costello liked to talk about her family; it made them seem more real. "Andy senior is the signal officer on *Peacock.* At least he was last I heard," she said, her voice darkening. "*Lafayette* picked up a signal from *Peacock* about eighteen months ago, and it was

Andy's fist." Was he still out there with the flagship of the forward fleet, she wondered. Was he still alive?

"That's enough of that," Costello abruptly interrupted her reverie by changing the topic. "Since this is a last meal for both of us, I suggest we have dessert. The order from Doctor Gordon, our chief medical/life support officer, is to keep a twenty-four hour fast before setting foot in his nice, clean quarantine ward. "I'm going to order brandy because I like it, even though it's something I can get in space. If you have any fondness for sweets, I'd suggest that you order the chocolate mousse. Gordon put chocolate on the controlled substances list because of its high caffeine content; you can only get caffeine by prescription, and then he'll give it to you in coffee. Also, we have no cream in space, so if you like chocolate and whipped cream, this is your last chance."

"Then I'm ready to say goodbye to my favorite dessert." The server mysteriously reappeared, took the order and vanished.

"You read Bengali, Steele?" Costello asked abruptly.

"Yes, ma'am." She was glad Costello hadn't asked if she could speak it. She could, but she hadn't qualified at the native level. It had been her lowest score in Earth Languages.

"Well, that's good," said Costello. "We've both got some prescriptions here," she continued pulling some glass vials from the folds in her sari and squinting at the labels. "I had them filled at the Navy station in India this morning while I was waiting for transport here. Thought it would save some time. They labelled them in Bengali."

She passed two of the bottles across the table to Steele. "This is for your hair," she said indicating the larger one. "Don't use it until just before you report to Fort McHenry tomorrow. It will kill and inhibit regrowth of any bacteria or virus yet discovered on Earth or in space, but it will also dry out your hair so badly that it will look and feel like a pile of hay. The sailors will be shaved, but for officers on *Lafayette* hair is part of the uniform unless you can manage to go bald naturally. Personally, I'd rather be shaved than use this devil's brew, but Captain Brook won't have officers aboard who look like part of the press."

Costello pointed at the second bottle. "Swallow this as soon as you get back to Bancroft Hall. You'll cramp like hell for half an hour, but then you'll be able to get through the night and sit through your graduation ceremonies tomorrow."

"What is it?" Steele asked trying to make out the handwritten prescription that served as a label.

"One of Richard Gordon's weird concoctions. It's heavy on castor oil and tastes positively vile. Gordon believes in old-fashioned remedies, and he doesn't want any unnecessary trouble coming onto the ship. So his rule is to go into quarantine with empty bellies and empty bowels. For Doctor Gordon, that means fasting and castor oil. There are other ways to get the same results, but this is Doctor Gordon's way."

Dessert appeared, the brandy in a crystal snifter and the mousse in a dish intended to resemble styrofoam. Steele looked at the elaborate concoction and realized she had lost her appetite. Costello took a sip of brandy. "I'm sure you're well aware that infectious disease is the number one danger in this war," she said. "It kills three times as many sailors as accident or hostile fire. Gordon has an outstanding record in keeping our people alive, so we can't complain too much about his methods. But he is a real fanatic about quarantine. I'm convinced he'd have us all totally submerged in carbolic acid for a week before letting us into his quarantine bubble if the treatment wouldn't have the bothersome side effect of being fatal. Still, I know the prospect of having to swallow a dose of castor oil can really ruin a good meal. Sorry I had to bring it up."

Costello warmed the brandy snifter in her palms and leaned back in the elegant lacquered chair. "Well, I've covered my agenda, Steele. Anything you want to ask me?"

"Yes, ma'am. I know this is probably an indelicate question, but could you tell me something about the officer I'm replacing? I think it would be good for me to know."

Costello flinched. Steele had just torn the scab off a raw wound. She didn't want to think about Lieutenant Shiva Shankar. Memories began to well up, many of them happy ones. One an ultimate horror.

"You'll hear all about Lieutenant Shankar eventually, Steele," Robert said carefully, willing her voice not to crack. "But I would prefer not to go into it tonight. I spent all morning with his family. I had to bring them his personal effects and the two posthumous decorations the Admiralty authorized. They took it very hard. I'm just not up to going through it all again."

She sat silent for a few moments. Steele waited quietly. "On second thought," Costello said abruptly, "I may as well give it to you now and get it over with. Just spit it out quick and simple. It's never going to be any easier." She paused again. "Never."

She set down the brandy snifter, pulled herself erect, and folded her hands as if she was delivering a briefing. "Lieutenant Shiva Shankar, Annapolis Class of 2064, former second officer and navigator of HMS *Lafayette*, killed in line of duty at the age of thirty-four. What else can I tell you about him? A fine officer, superb navigator. Got us out of hellish situations dozens of times, and we were operating right there in the middle of that god-forsaken two-star Delphinian ring.

"A really sweet guy," she continued. "A great sense of humor. Tough when he had to be, but the crew loved him. He had . . ." Costello groped for the word. "He had a gentleness about him. He was a gentleman in the oldest, truest sense. He was in a violent profession, and he didn't shrink from violence. But he was a man of peace. Am I making sense to you, Steele?"

"I think so, ma'am."

"So. I'll cut to the end of the story. It was a small planet. We called it Little Emerald. It was on our charts. Inside the Delphinian ring. We thought it was uninhabited. No artificial structures; nothing we could pick up from orbit. But it was green. It had plenty of water, which meant we could set a launch down easy.

"We needed to land. *Lafayette* was in bad shape; we had heavy hull damage. Three sail plates were too beat up to turn, and most of the top gun ring was held together with spit. We needed to dig up some metal. Shankar took a launch down with a few dozen specialists to pick up what we needed. We ran the usual tests. There was good air on Little Emerald, moderate temperature. The oxygen component was high, but that never hurts, and it was a bit hot. It looked like a really easy straightforward operation. Our people went down in their space liners and boots — no armor, no helmets.

"Well, it turned out that Little Emerald wasn't uninhabited. It wasn't a Delphinian fortification — we couldn't have missed that even if they'd been dug in five kilometers underground. We ran all the tests. We'd been careful. But there were intelligent beings down there, and they were hostile.

"The launch set down neatly in the largest ocean about half a kilometer from a volcanic island. It looked to be exactly what we wanted. They sent a still picture back to *Lafayette*: heavy green vegetation beyond a narrow beach. No movement. No sign of life. Shankar left one sailor with the launch and took the others ashore with all their equipment in rowboats. A few meters into the woods, they discovered they had company.

"They were Delphinians all right — pig people — snouts, tusks, thick pink skin, short curly tails. They were primitives. Naked. Their only weapons were spears and stone knives. They had the same dietary needs as their 'civilized' relatives." Costello spat out the adjective.

"So! No sophisticated weapons but an appetite for hominid meat. There were at least fifty of them. Practiced hunters, apparently, who'd been short of game recently just as all the Delphinians have been since we set smallpox loose in their system during the last war. We'd landed a small team of technicians, metallurgists mostly, and a few bluestripers from recycling to help with the digging. Only incidental armament. No Marines. We never suspected the presence of intelligent life." Costello seized her glass and quickly downed the rest of the brandy.

"I'll finish this story fast," she said. Her voice took on a toneless quality. She spoke quietly, without emotion, clipping her sentences short. "Our people were out of weapon power pretty quick. When they first started firing their heat pistols, the pigs were frightened, but not for long. The undergrowth was too damp to do more than smoke and too thick to aim through. Our party retreated toward the water trying to hold the pigs back by throwing rocks, sticks, whatever they could pick up off the ground. Shankar had a long metal detector he used as a club; he managed to brain two or three which slowed the others down.

"He told his people to get to the launch, not to wait for the boats, just to inflate their space liners and swim for it, while he bought them time. He kept turning around to see how they were doing. He knew he wasn't going to make it.

"By this time we had a holograph coming back into *Lafayette*. The sailor on the launch panicked and powered up holographic communications with some wild idea those back on the ship could help. Shankar's head was bleeding, and his left arm was broken at the shoulder. He was swinging that metal detector with one hand. He had a lot of heart, but that wasn't enough. Finally, he fell. The pigs rushed in. Killed him."

Costello paused and swallowed hard before continuing. "Then they butchered him. Very professionally. Skinned him neatly, took off his head, his arms, his legs. Eviscerated him. Quartered his torso. Packed it all up in woven baskets and disappeared into the woods. No one else in the landing party was hurt. Nothing any of them could do. Nothing anyone on *Lafayette* could do. We just watched it happen. A chief out of recycling took command and brought the launch back to *Lafayette*. Only one casualty to report: Lieutenant Shiva Shankar."

Costello's eyes glazed over as she relived the nightmare. Suddenly she recalled that she was not alone.

"That's it," she said stiffly. "That's the end of the story of the officer you're replacing. And that's the end of this dinner party too." She stood abruptly and slapped the chit signed by Admiral Thanatos on the table.

"Good night, Steele," she said. "Report to me at shuttle launch 117 at Fort McHenry at 1930 hours tomorrow." She strode rapidly toward the door, her sari flapping around her ankles.

Steele remained seated for a few minutes. Costello's tale was not the first such narrative she had heard. That was what the war was about: Dolphinians hunting hominid food and Earth resisting their expansion into planetary systems inhabited by hominids.

Steele put a cash tip for the server on top of the chit Costello had left. It was about the last of her money, the last she would ever have. As a Naval officer, she would work for subsistence. Tomorrow she'd take the first vows of poverty, obedience, and allegiance to the Crown. The money still in her pocket would be thrown into the air with her cadet cap and epaulets for the children at the commissioning ceremony to scramble for. She'd hold on to one silver dollar a few minutes longer and give it to the cadet who was the first to salute her as a lieutenant.

CHAPTER TWO

The citizens of Annapolis always put on an extravagant show for Naval Academy graduations. Everywhere you went on June Day there were commoners dressed up in old-fashioned military uniforms and medleys of martial music filling the air, as if Olde McDonald's had spilled out into the streets and taken over the entire town. The graduating Class of 2080, the excuse for the party, participated only in the brief commissioning ceremony; but the related festivities continued for hours, and courtesy demanded that the new officers not depart until every bit of ritual was played out.

It was late afternoon before Lieutenant Steele carried her duffel to the Annapolis dock and boarded the East Coast Clipper for the trip to Baltimore. The other passengers smiled when they recognized her uniform but kept their distance. Steele climbed to the open upper deck and took a place at the forward rail. That was where she liked to be on a sailing vessel. Most passengers preferred the covered lower decks where there were entertainment lounges, swimming pools (both fresh and salt), and a choice of dining facilities. The commuters could look at the water through the portholes should that be of any interest to them.

Steele's tastes were simpler. She wanted to savor every bit of the pleasure of being under sail on the Chesapeake Bay on a brilliant June afternoon. It would be years before she might again set foot on Earth, inhale salt air, and feet the tingle of salt spray on her face. These were among the sacrifices Navy life required.

It felt good to face the cooling rush of wind as the tall ship sped across the bay, canvas shifting as the computer controls adjusted spread and tack to maximum efficiency. The basic space uniform she wore in place of the summer kilt was hot and uncomfortable — a heavy dark blue wool tunic with plain shoulder boards, high collar closed up to the chin by two rows of polished brass buttons, and sharply creased trousers, precisely tailored, hanging to the heel of leather boots.

Every meritocratic officer in the fleet wore this uniform; the only variable feature was the collar insignia, two small gold pins. One pin was Steele's permanent identification number — 80-01 — indicating her year of commissioning and her class rank. The same number was permanently marked on her back, just below the neck, positive identification for medics — or a burial detail. The second pin was a miniature sextant inscribed with the name of her ship, her current assignment pin. There was no mark of rank, for none was needed. Every meritocrat outranked any commoner and meritocrats were equal in honor.

Military assignments required hierarchy, but it was simple and functional. Cadets or ensigns, those undergoing training, were not qualified to exercise an independent command. Lieutenants were so qualified and could assume a command in any setting at any time, but as lieutenants they served under direct supervision. Whoever was in command of any Navy vessel of whatever size held the rank of captain. Thus a lieutenant might become a captain and a captain might become a lieutenant again as the needs of the service dictated. The highest rank, that of admiral, identified those senior meritocrats who made policy, oversaw grand strategic planning, and saw to the administration of the Navy as a whole.

Naval officers exercised authority over both sailors and Marines in the fleet. In deference to Marine Corps traditions, the Admiralty gave the commanding meritocrat of a shore-based Marine installation the rank of general. Diversion from a career in space to one on the ground, whether in some remote sector of the galaxy or on Earth, was a hazard of service. The Admiralty appointed those best suited to the job at hand. Personal preferences were irrelevant.

Steele looked around and confirmed that no one else was on the forward deck. Then, with a sigh, she pulled off her stiff visored cap and savored the feel of wind rushing through her hair, dry and spiky from the disinfectant shampoo. Knowing that the trip would soon end intensified the pleasure of sailing on the bay. As the East Coast Clipper sped toward Fort McHenry, Steele savored the anticipation of taking up official duties for the first time. Just a brief stop at the Marine installation, then out to space to join *her* ship, the Patriot class dreadnought HMS *Lafayette.*

* * *

Fort McHenry supplied personnel for all Navy vessels operating in the English language under Christian rituals. Captains chose their ship's official language and official religion, and so far as possible sailors were sorted out for assignment in a congenial environment. That was the traditional way to build cohesion.

Located on the Chesapeake Bay, Fort McHenry spread over much of what once had been the city of Baltimore. The original outbreak of Gordon's Pox devastated the urban center in 2055; the authorities ordered it razed to the ground after quarantine was lifted. Only the old stone fort on the Bay was saved.

Old Fort McHenry stood near the main gate of the modern military installation bearing its name and housed the central administrative offices. It flew an archaic banner with red stripes and white stars on a blue field below the blue banner with a white image of United Earth.

Most of Fort McHenry was functionally a jail where those forced into service were held pending their delivery to Navy warships. Marines were all volunteers; that was their proud tradition. Partly for that reason, one of their primary duties was to enforce the press.

Despite vigorous recruiting efforts, few citizens of Earth volunteered to join the Navy. For most of the first war, the Admiralty avoided conscription by giving the Navy criminals already condemned to lose their liberty. Growing needs for personnel and a low crime rate forced imposition of a more extensive system of impressment from the very beginning of the second war.

The Admiralty's conscription was as fair as such a system could be, taking those individuals least likely to be missed by a family or by the community. Civilians supported it one hundred percent — except for those who got orders to report, and they were not expected to cooperate.

It was an ugly business, but it was an ugly war. Meritocrats alone could not protect Earth from invasion. Since selfless impulses did not impel commoners to volunteer, force supplied what virtue could not.

Costello had arrived at Fort McHenry early. Two hundred sailors should be no more difficult to board than one hundred, but there were annoying gaps in the personnel records. She'd used the Annapolis computers to run off a paper copy and found an entire section missing.

Costello went directly to the office of Fort McHenry's commanding meritocrat. Her plain blue uniform was the only identification she needed. It cleared the way for her as she entered the gate of the old fort, crossed the inner yard, and passed into General Susan Sparrow's outer office. There her path was obstructed by a desk occupied by a middle-aged man wearing the dress uniform and insignia of a Marine sergeant major.

His was a gaudy outfit with a scarlet tunic, heavy on insignia, braid, and patches. The taste of commoners for such marks of personal distinction was indulged for Marines. The hierarchy of meritocratic officers had only four levels. Sailors had only two. But Marines had twenty-four. Sergeant Major was at the top. Pride in rank was a strong motivator for Marines.

The name plate on the desk indicated that its occupant's name was Pollard. Sergeant Major Pollard had the usual career Marine look about him. He wore his steel-grey hair in the long, full style favored by Marines. He had a handsome face, impeccable grooming and rigidly erect posture. Since he did not come to his feet when Costello entered, she assumed he must be disabled in some way. It would be in character for Susan Sparrow to put a wounded veteran on some kind of assignment where he could still feel useful if he wanted to continue in the service.

"You must be the escort officer from *Lafayette*," he said pleasantly. "It's unusual for us to have an officer visit Fort McHenry these days. The ships we've serviced recently have all requested a Marine escort to supervise delivery."

Costello smiled coolly. Commoners normally did not presume to chat with a meritocrat, certainly not on official matters. Pollard probably had more than a physical disability.

"I have business with General Sparrow," she said. "Is she in her office? If not, I'll want her paged."

"If it's about the records on the new Lafayettes, ma'am, perhaps I can help you. I understand you have been enquiring about transition reports."

"That's right." Costello was surprised that Sparrow would have shared such information. Perhaps she had tasked this man with clerical chores. "I have background histories and physical reports, but some of these people have been held here for several weeks. I have no information on how they've spent their time or what has been done to help transition them into the Navy."

"We've stopped keeping that record, Lieutenant. You may have heard that the Corps has had some trouble meeting its recruiting goals recently. Not every one has the courage to volunteer for service when we get so many reports of high casualty rates." He said this with obvious self-satisfaction. He, after all, was one who presumably had such courage, though judging from his age, he had volunteered long before the wars had reached their current desperate stage and was now safely ensconced in a shore berth.

"The fleet has had first call on the Marines," he continued, "so we have had to absorb the personnel shortages primarily in our embarkation installations. We've tried to adjust here at Fort McHenry by cutting down on record keeping. Practically everyone we've got is doing guard duty on twelve hour shifts. It's been hard enough for us to keep the individual physical reports current."

Very peculiar, Costello thought. Every officer would agree that the physical reports were important, but Navy doctors in space could fill in and fix up anything missed on the base. The first contact psychological records were irreplaceable. It would take depth therapy to dredge them up if they were needed later. She said as much to Sergeant Major Pollard.

"I'll tell General Sparrow that that is your opinion, Lieutenant," Pollard said smoothly. "Perhaps she will change the policy."

Costello willed her face to remain expressionless. It was her intention, after spending far too long in conversation with this commoner, to continue on her way into General Sparrow's office. And there was no question the policy would change. If, indeed, it was policy. Her snap analysis was that Pollard, the file clerk, had been indulging in a bit of corner-cutting to save himself work — corner-cutting that Sparrow would move swiftly to eliminate once she knew about it.

But how could she not know about it?

Despite her efforts to maintain an unreadable expression, Pollard appeared to know what she had been thinking.

"I trust you will forgive my presumption, Lieutenant, but I know you've been away from Earth for quite some time. Security problems on this base have grown enormously with the increased call for personnel. We have too many raw conscripts and not enough Marines to process them. Some procedures have been changed, and General Sparrow has been obliged to delegate work that she once did herself to some of the senior non-commissioned officers." Again, as one of those NCO's, Pollard preened himself.

"I have been proud to accept the additional duties the General has assigned to me, but I would not like you to think that she is responsible if I've failed to meet your expectations."

Costello's facial muscles strained with effort to keep her jaw rigid so it would not drop from astonishment. Whatever anyone did at Fort McHenry, General Sparrow was responsible! That was what it meant to be a meritocrat! If the work load was too heavy, you called the Admiralty and demanded reinforcements. You did not surrender meritocratic functions to members of the lower orders.

"I am that sure General Sparrow will take careful note of your failures, whatever these may be, Sergeant Major," Costello said stiffly. "Now I suggest you return to your work, while I speak to the General."

"These are not her stated office hours, Lieutenant Costello," Pollard interrupted.

One had to indulge the weaknesses of the lower orders, but even meritocrats had limits to their patience. "Are you challenging my presence here, soldier?"

"Oh, certainly not, ma'am. I would just like to point out, if you'll let me, that . . ."

At this point, the door to Sparrow's office opened slowly, and Costello got two simultaneous shocks. First, the man she had assumed to be paraplegic sprang to attention. Second, General Sparrow seemed to have aged thirty years since Costello had seen her last.

When Costello had an Earth-based assignment in the years between the wars, she had worked closely with General Sparrow. Costello had been sure that Sparrow was one of those meritocratic women who would keep her ageless good looks forever. But Sparrow had grown shrivelled and old. Her body gaunt and bent, Sparrow's silver hair was lank and thinning. Even her eyes, usually the last feature to loose the mark of youth, had the barest trace of their former bright sparkle.

"Liz!" she said. Her voice had lost its vibrancy but retained its warmth. She reached for Costello's hand and gave it a bony squeeze. "I thought I recognized your voice. You're here to pick up the new Peacocks, I suppose."

Costello winced. Wherever *Peacock* might be, it was far, far from the solar system. "No, General," she said. "It's my husband, Andrew Carline, who's aboard *Peacock*. I'm assigned to *Lafayette*."

"I see," said Sparrow. "Well, I know you have a lot to do, so I won't hold you up. But I'm glad I had a chance to say hello and goodbye. Please forgive me if I don't accompany you to the dock. I've had a little trouble getting around lately." She hobbled back into her office and closed the door.

Costello spun on her heel and exited rapidly, deliberately ignoring Sergeant Major Pollard. Something was seriously wrong here at headquarters, something she devoutly hoped would not involve her or her sailors.

Primrose, one of the Mars Navy Yard tug and transport shuttles, was docked at station 117 exactly as she should be. When Costello arrived, she found Steele watching a dozen sailors struggling to load pigs into the hold under the direction of a Marine corporal.

The pigs travelled in slings holding them clear of the deck to prevent injury. Although it was designed for their protection, the pigs resented the arrangement. The sailors, newly enlisted

Lafayette volunteers, had no experience managing livestock. The boars, especially, resisted their efforts. Fortunately, most of the pigs were sows — doubly useful in space as source of both food and piglets. They were also less given to fuss and bluster and had, on the average, less weight to throw around.

Another party of sailors loaded chickens. Each hen had a private basket lined with feathers and straw and liberally dosed with a synthetic barnyard odor intended to keep the birds feeling secure and in the mood to lay eggs. The contented clucks coming from these baskets indicated the efforts to provide satisfactory quarters met with the occupants' approval.

A few roosters were packaged securely in similar baskets, but the Navy saw no reason to provide them with expensive interior decoration. The occasional sounds emanating from these containers were plaintive and questioning. The question no doubt was "where's dinner?" On Doctor Gordon's orders both pigs and chickens were as empty inside as the sailors.

Steele flashed her bright smile as Costello greeted her. She was going to be a good shipmate. There was always something magic about a newly minted meritocratic officer. Costello supposed she had once looked that young and eager and fresh. Like their uniforms, which would be patched with synthetics in space as the natural wool wore thin, Navy officers tended to loose their sparkle over time. But not always. Costello had a premonition that the magic surrounding Lieutenant Steele would last a while. And as long as it lasted it would bring luck to any ship she served. There was nothing a ship needed more.

"Well, shall we get to work? Our people won't be brought to the shed for another hour, but we'll check it over now. It's important that the sailors feel secure and comfortable while they're here. They're certain to be scared witless at this point no matter how much indoctrination was done in transition. A good preembarkation environment will prevent trouble later."

Steele nodded. Her psychology professors had spent considerable time explaining the weird ideas that went through the heads of civilians pressed into the Navy. Many strange superstitions about space travel in general and Navy service in particular circulated among civilians. Almost everyone pressed into the

Navy seemed to believe that even if you didn't get killed while you were in space, you would come home all bent out of shape because of time twisting at velocities greater than the speed of light. You'd come back still about the same age you started at, but all your friends would be old or dead.

Dealing with this one, Annapolis professors said, was analagous to the challenge Christopher Columbus faced with his sailors who thought they were going to fall off the edge of a flat planet. Real fears, they said, can spring from false beliefs. Officers have to take them seriously. Cadets were required to work with random samples of civilians to test methods of countering fear of space, which was technically known as hyperagoraphobia.

"Another thing we need to check out is the heads and the medical facility," Costello went on. "I expect a couple of *Lafayette*'s veterans to show up drunk and dirty ready to take the reenlistment oath just in time to catch the boat. No sense lecturing them about it. It always happens. They take off like a shot as soon as their tour is over. Then they remember every close friend they have is still in the Navy and that there are not many jobs for gunner's mates in the civilian world. When they find out *Lafayette*'s about to move out again, they have one final blowout binge and then come staggering in here at the last possible moment. It's a traditional sailor's game, and no real problem so long as the medics are ready for it."

Costello headed for the shed with Steele at her heels. As they rounded the corner toward the single entrance, Costello was surprised to find it guarded. If the Marines were as short of personnel as Sergeant Major Pollard claimed, how could they spare people to guard an empty building?

It wasn't a question she could ask the sentries, who were behaving in approved Marine fashion, standing rigid as wooden Indians with eyes to the front no matter what passed across their line of vision. You could tell they were alive only when they rattled their rifles in salute.

The Marines rattled their rifles. Then one performed a series of clockwork movements and opened the door. From the sound-proofed structure there issued a roar of crashing surf. Costello frowned. The horrendous noise was some kind of subliminal, being played at too high a volume to be of any use. The effect of the amplified sea sounds was irritating, not relaxing, and an occasional breathy word was audible under the masking noise.

Costello peered into the dimly lit room and sucked in her breath. In a space designed to hold one hundred for a brief period, two hundred people were crowded, some on benches, some squatting on the carpeted floor. They were naked and completely hairless. Even through the roar of the subliminal surf, she could tell many of them were crying. The scene was powerfully reminiscent of POW descriptions of the Delphinian stockyards where the enemy kept its captured hominids.

Choking down nausea, Costello took a hard look at the Admiralty's gift to *Lafayette*. The group seemed a typical press — approximately equal numbers of men and women of various ages, most between fifteen and forty and in assorted sizes, shapes, and colors. About a third of them, she knew — though you couldn't tell from looking — would be dumb sailors, mute aliens, immigrants from the third planet in the Mantu system known in their telepathic language as the Colony. They were a hominid species, classified as *homo mutus*, and it was polite to call them Colonials. Navy people called them dumb sailors.

A woman wearing staff sergeant's stripes hurried over and formally reported. "How long have our people been confined here, Sergeant Larkin?" Costello struggled to keep any tone of criticism or reproach from her voice. Larkin might be in charge, but the meritocrat commanding the base was responsible. The shocking appearance of the shed meant a failure of leadership. She was not officially part of this chain of command, although she could pull rank if she chose. But God knew she wanted no part of this if she could avoid it.

"Two hundred for *Lafayette* were signed in at 1800 hours. They've been here about an hour and a half, ma'am."

"Was there a reason for bringing them over so early? Departure is scheduled for 2100."

"Well, ma'am, we had orders to keep the Lafayettes fasting, so when they started serving dinner in the barracks . . ."

"I see." The sailors should have been kept in a recreation area until the last possible moment, but it was too late to change that.

All that could be done now was assess the damage.

"Tell me, Sergeant, to your knowledge has anyone at any point explained to these people where they are going and why?"

"We've had a subliminal on, ma'am."

"Exactly what is it?"

"It's got the enlistment oath the Navy's volunteers take. The thing that goes, 'I am a sailor in the Royal Navy . . .'"

"Yes. Well *Lafayette* usually likes to have a bit more than that."

Larkin turned red. "I'm very sorry, ma'am. I wasn't told."

"Never mind. Lieutenant Steele and I will take care of it." Not easily, but they'd take care of it.

"What about uniforms? Why haven't they been issued?"

"We'll ma'am, since they were over here anyway, we decided to put them through the showers right away. And then, since we knew they'd be sitting around for a while, we thought we'd keep the uniforms until later. Otherwise they'd get them dirty."

"I see." Sergeant Larkin had given no thought to how the sailors might feel sitting around shaved and naked with people they barely knew. About all the sensitivity you could expect from a commoner, which was why Marines were required to follow specific procedures for every assignment. So what had happened to the usual drill for embarkation?

"We have everything they need ready to go, ma'am. We didn't expect an escort to come for the Lafayettes this early."

"Very well. Suppose you get those uniforms distributed now."

Within moments the Marines were moving through the mob of sailors, distributing white pull-on pants, long sleeved blue and white striped t-shirts, and white dixie cup caps embroidered with the ship's name.

The sailors were glad to get them. Most put on the cap before they put on anything else. Baldness disturbed them more than nudity. After all, most people went without clothing at the beach. But no one went totally unadorned. You styled your hair, wore some jewelry or body paint, or at least had a pair of sunglasses and a hat. As they dressed they whispered to each other remarking on the unusual quality of the clothing, the deep pockets, and the strange feel of the cloth that meant a mix of expensive polyester in the cotton fabric.

The dumb sailors were probably discussing their uniforms too, Costello thought grimly. She could identify them now; they were not moving their mouths. But they were making eye contact and smiling. None of them were using the regulation sign language. It was disgusting to see them engaging in intimate telepathic communication in public. It was bad enough that they probably did it constantly when they weren't being watched. Personnel at Fort McHenry should have strictly enforced the Navy rules against obscene behavior. In the close quarters of a warship such conduct was intolerable. Now training the Colonials to meet civilized standards would be another job for overworked Navy personnel during quarantine.

Costello wondered what impression this perversion of embarkation protocol was making on Steele. Not a good one. The young officer wore the impassive expression she displayed in her inspection holograph.

"It's time we split up, Lieutenant," Costello said. "What's going on here is not typical. I promise you, I've never seen anything like this. I'll deal with it. But I have an awful feeling that there may be problems on the dock as well. You get out there and have a good look around. Talk to the sailors and the crew of *Primrose*. See what you can find out."

As Steele left, there was a disturbance at the doorway. Here were the lost sheep returning to the fold. Two very big men, one black and one white, both wearing sheepish expressions, were escorted by four Marines who watched them suspiciously.

"Well, good afternoon," said Costello, nodding first to one and then the other, "Chief Newcastle, Chief Dover. Am I to conclude you two fine citizens have decided to reenlist in the Royal Navy?"

They grinned and nodded at her. Newcastle burped loudly, and both giggled. High time she took them home, Costello thought. God, they looked awful — as if they'd been sleeping in the street. They stank and their red striped t-shirts were covered with food stains. Drunk certainly, and heaven knew what else they had ingested. She rattled off the oath; the two men swore; and that was the end of their liberty.

"You two know what you need to do, so get to it."

"Yes, ma'am," Newcastle groaned.

“Stomach pump, shower, shave . . .” Dover recited.

“Ma’am,” Sergeant Larkin interrupted, “the medical facility is in use.”

Costello went rigid. If there was active disease in this group, quarantine boarding ceased to be routine. Psychological damage, they could hope to reverse; infection could force *Lafayette* to reject the entire press.

“Hit the showers first,” she said to the latecomers. “Then come back to the medic.” The pair lumbered off to the head dragging space duffels behind them. The Marines would have searched them at the gate; she hoped they contained clean uniforms.

“You should have told me about this before,” Costello said carefully. “When someone is sick, it alters all of our routines.”

“I know that, ma’am,” Larkin answered, reddening. “No one’s sick. We just had one great big guy who was hard to control, so we put him in restraints back there in the medical facility. I asked the medic if we could give him a sedative, but he said we’d have to get your okay first.”

At least the medic had it right; sailors didn’t get shot full of drugs just to make things easy for the Marines. “Then take me to this ‘great big guy’ that a company of Marines can’t handle. What did the press pick up? Paul Bunyan?”

“No, ma’am,” said Larkin. “Waldo.”

“What?”

“His name is Waldo Bunyan, ma’am. Not Paul Bunyan.”

"I stand corrected, Sergeant. Let me see him, whatever his name is."

Waldo Bunyan was on his back strapped on a table with a sheet covering him up to the armpits. He was a big man, heavy and close to seven feet tall; but he was no bigger than Newcastle or Dover and certainly no legendary giant. He looked thoroughly frightened and whimpered when he caught sight of Larkin.

Across the room, a civilian medic sat with his feet up watching a holograph through a portable player. The top of his head was covered by the device, which looped down over his ears leaving nose and mouth exposed. The mouth was chewing a sandwich.

“Does General Sparrow know you’re using base medical facilities for this kind of thing?” Costello demanded. The medic jerked off his headset, took note of the meritocratic Navy uniform, and shrugged. "Ask her," he said, indicating Larkin. "I just work here."

"Well, Sergeant?"

"I don't know, ma'am." That was an odd answer, Costello thought. Her question had been rhetorical. If the general knew of any Marine — or civilian — who had used a medical facility as a substitute for a lockup that person would be in the stockade.

"What do you mean, you don't know? Hasn't General Sparrow been down here to inspect?" Costello had hoped to avoid this question, but now it had to be asked.

"Not since I've been assigned here, ma'am. I've been here since the beginning of April, and she's never been to 117 while I've been on duty."

"Are you telling me that you've worked this station for over two months and have never been inspected?"

"Sergeant Major Pollard inspected a couple of times, but I've never seen the General."

Costello eyed the Marine narrowly. Lying to an officer was a court-martial offense. If she pursued this, she'd have to finish it. No thank you.

Waldo Bunyan was something else. He was one of her people, her responsibility. "Unstrap him," she said to Larkin. Larkin hesitated. "I've given you an order, Sergeant," Costello said. "I want this man set loose." Larkin reluctantly obeyed. Waldo Bunyan did nothing more dramatic than to sit up with the sheet wrapped around him and rub his wrists.

Costello wasn't surprised. Ninety-nine percent of violent people fought because they were frightened, and there was plenty to frighten a pressed sailor who was hustled through embarkation procedures with no explanation. Costello could imagine that Bunyan had put up a good fight against being stripped, scrubbed, shaved, and branded between the shoulders with a Navy ID number. But he was quiet now. No one was threatening him.

The next question was whether he would board the shuttle under his own steam or would have to be forced. Costello didn't like to see sailors dragged into space in chains. She knew perfectly well that virtually all sailors went up the ramp against their wills, but there was some dignity left to them if they could be persuaded to submit without fighting. Usually they could be.

"Do you know where you're going, Waldo?" she asked, facing the man as he sat on the table.

"Yeah, I guess. Some ship up in space."

"The ship is HMS *Lafayette*. How do you feel about going aboard her?"

"I don't want to go."

"But you are going," said Costello. "Now, the easiest way for you to get there will be by walking up the ramp at the dock on your own two feet. That's how all of your shipmates are going. Do you know any of them? Do you have any friends out there?"

"No. I don't know none of them."

"Do you think you'd feel better about going into space if you had a buddy?"

"What do you mean, a 'buddy,'" Bunyan asked suspiciously.

"Another sailor who's going out for the first time. Someone to talk to while you're waiting to board. Someone to climb the ramp with. Someone to sit next to on the ride out." Costello paused to let him think about it.

"I'm afraid the alternative is to put you in handcuffs and assign you a guard. I'm giving you a choice — a buddy or a guard. Which will it be?"

Bunyan didn't answer.

"Let me introduce you to the buddy I have in mind. If you'll agree to go aboard quietly with her, you'll have a much more comfortable trip." She turned back to the sergeant, who was staring warily at Bunyan as though she expected him to explode. "Go out to the boarding area, and get a sailor named Kathleen Clark. She's a volunteer. I saw her helping to load the pigs. I want her here on the double." Larkin was glad to get away; she bounded toward the door. "And get a uniform back here," she added glancing at Bunyan. "It looks like a triple extra large."

Larkin went off fast, and a moment later a Marine private came in with a bundle of clothing. Costello checked the size and tossed it to Bunyan. "Get dressed."

Bunyan winced as he climbed off the table. Costello hated to think of how long he'd been tied up. His muscles must be painfully stiff. She watched as he pulled on his clothing. He was a good looking man, rather old to be going out for the first time — probably in his mid-thirties — and appeared not overly bright. She recalled from the personnel records that there were several sailors on the list who had been pressed from a detox center. She checked. Sure enough, Waldo Bunyan was one of those. A tranquilizer was just what he didn't need in his first contact with the Navy.

"Hi, Lieutenant Costello!" said a cheerful voice. "A Marine told me you wanted to see me."

Kathy Clark was a plump black girl with a smile that wouldn't stop. Costello knew that of everyone at Fort McHenry, she was the happiest about going out into space — the only possible exception being Lieutenant Steele. Kathy was just twelve years old and a resident of the Navy Orphans' School. She had petitioned for special permission to enter the service at the minimum age for volunteers. She knew Lieutenant Costello as "Lizzy and Andy's mom."

"I see you've been eating like a sailor," Costello smiled at her.

"Yes, ma'am," Kathy said happily. "I read every book about space there is in the school library. And there are *hundreds*. They all say, sailors should get as fat as they can because we're sure to be sick for the first few weeks."

She said this as if she were looking forward to it. Bunyan was staring at her. Costello introduced them.

"Kathy, this is Waldo Bunyan. He's never been in space before either. I'd like you to be his buddy on this trip."

Kathy held out her hand for a shake. As Bunyan took it, it was clear from his expression that Kathy Clark was not what he had expected. "You going to be my buddy, kid?" he asked looking at the shiny dimpled face smiling up into his from two feet below.

"If Lieutenant Costello says so, I guess I am," Kathy said. "If you got any questions, I know all sorts of stuff."

Bunyan laughed. He'd been given a twelve year old baby sitter.

"Are you willing to go along quietly with Kathy?"

"Yeah, I guess so."

Sergeant Larkin watched warily from the doorway. She still expected Bunyan to start breaking furniture again.

"You two go out to the boarding area, then, and be sure you stay together."

"OK," said Kathy — then quickly added "ma'am" and held out her hand to Bunyan. He laughed again, took it and followed his buddy into the shed.

"Are you going to get the other body out of here too, Lieutenant?" The medic didn't like Marines or the Navy invading his work space, but no one ever asked for his opinion.

"There's another?"

The medic nodded toward the head. Costello opened the door and saw a small naked figure on the floor — a girl child, perhaps nine or ten years old. She was gagged and handcuffed to a pipe. She lay hunched up, her knees under her chin, sound asleep.

"And what is this, Sergeant?"

"She's your grommet, ma'am," said Larkin looking at the small body with undisguised distaste.

Robert's knew *Lafayette* was due for a grommet. Warships had a quota: for every thousand impressed sailors, the ship must take one or two of these children, youngsters between eight and twelve who were judged to be dangerous and incorrigible. The Crown usually issued a stay of execution for those under twelve on the chance that they might reform given strict discipline and a wholesome environment. A tour in the Navy seemed just the thing. Costello wasn't enthusiastic about the system, but the Navy didn't have a choice.

"Navy policy is to give everyone a fresh start. Manacles and gags are only for someone who is violent and dangerous."

"She is, ma'am," said Larkin. "Both of those." It really was not fair, she thought, having a Navy officer coming in here and acting as if Fort McHenry Marines knew nothing about the law.

Costello looked more closely at the sleeping child. "What did she do?" The eighty-pound body hardly looked as if it had enough muscle for any serious violence.

"She won't sit still, ma'am, unless she's tied down. She kicks and screams and tries to bite. And she spits."

"She seems to be sleeping very soundly. Are you quite sure no one slipped something into her water or maybe accidentally hit her across the neck?"

Sergeant Larkin stiffened. "The Marines in this unit know the rules, ma'am. We restrained her, that's all. This brat . . . that is, this *sailor*, ma'am, was delivered to us from Lorton Reformatory early yesterday and she has been kicking and screaming and fighting us ever since. When we got her over here with the rest of the press, we had to stop the spitting and the screaming so we took her in here and gagged her. Then she fell asleep. She just exhausted, herself, ma'am. No one did anything to her that's outside regulations."

"What's her name?

"Rebecca Petrie, ma'am."

The child woke suddenly. A pair of mean, green eyes snapped open, then narrowed and surveyed both the sergeant and the lieutenant suspiciously.

"Get her a uniform," Costello ordered. "This one looks like a triple extra small." Larkin came back with the clothing and two more Marines as reinforcements. It took all three to get her into pants and shirt.

Petrie's blazing eyes showed that she didn't care what the odds were; she was going to do everything in her limited power to make it hard for them. She kicked and squirmed as they pushed her legs into the white pants and rolled them up over her ankles. When her hands were set free so that they could force her head and arms into the shirt, she did her best to punch and scratch. If she hadn't been a nail-biter, she certainly would have drawn some blood.

Finally the Marines had her dressed. Breathing hard from the battle, they cuffed her hands behind her back. Then two of them held her on her feet as Sergeant Larkin disgustedly plopped the dixie cup on her bald head. Her green eyes flashed ferociously.

Costello was beginning to sympathize with Larkin and her troops. Bathing, shaving and branding this miniature volcano must have been a challenge. Meritocratic charisma would obviously have been helpful. General Sparrow should have been called in. It was odd that she had not been.

The Marines had a firm grip on her, but Petrie was still struggling as hard as she could. "If you promise to stand still for me, I'll have that gag removed," Costello said.

The girl's eyes turned on her suspiciously. She seemed to consider for a moment and then nodded. "Do it," Costello ordered. Larkin approached warily, but Petrie stood quietly as the gag was unknotted. She put out a pink tongue and wet her lips. "Water," she croaked.

"Get her some."

The Sergeant filled a glass and held it against the girl's lips. She guzzled greedily; Larkin tipped the glass until it was empty. "Do you want more?" she asked. Petrie's eyes flared mischievously and suddenly she spat out the last mouthful of water. The front of Larkin's immaculately starched and pressed uniform was soaked. Petrie emitted a nasty cackle as the sergeant, frowning angrily, looked to Costello.

"Put her out," Costello ordered. "You were right, Sergeant; this one's a lot worse than she looks." There was going to be some tiresome work to do with this spiteful child in quarantine. There was no time for it now. They'd have to take her on board unconscious. The medic had a syringe ready. In this case, he agreed with the Marines. Larkin dragged the kicking, cursing girl over to the treatment table. Between the two of them, they held her down and got a sedative into her. In a few moments Petrie was again sound asleep.

Out at the dock, Steele made her own discoveries. An initial reluctance to talk to an officer because of the traditional sailors' taboo against "snitching" was overcome by the traditional sailors' dislike of Marines. The crew of *Primrose* answered her questions and told her exactly what they thought of Marine procedure for loading sailors' gear and livestock.

"If I were the sort looking to build myself a retirement nest egg — which, of course, I am not, Lieutenant — I could see some nice opportunities for myself at Fort McHenry." This from the senior sailor who drove *Primrose*, a red-faced chief named Margolis who wiped sweat from his face with the sleeve of his red striped t-shirt. "The Marines' idea of searching sailors' gear, from what I've been seeing, seems to be to run it through the sterilizer and heave it into the hold. I'd bet a month's pay that if you looked into some of those duffels you'd find plenty of contraband stuffed in under the shirts and shorts."

Contraband was anything banned in space. Sailors were allowed to bring personal items to a set limit of weight and volume, so long as none of them were on the forbidden list. Since pressed sailors had rarely given any thought to space travel before they got their notice, they had no sense about what to pack. Their baggage always needed weeding through.

Normally both the sailors and their baggage were searched thoroughly long before they reached the boarding area. Nevertheless, it was a standard security practice to conduct another search before final loading. Steele agreed with Margolis that a run through the sterilizer was not enough.

"I don't think I'll try to cover your bet, Chief, but since the Primroses have nothing to do right now, why don't you just have another look through those bags. Anything you find that shouldn't be going out, you can keep."

That was a fair offer. Sailors couldn't be expected to do extra work for nothing. Not that items on the contraband list were worth much on Earth. But you could never tell. There might be a nice holograph viewer or a paid-up calling card mixed in with bottles of patent spacesickness remedies and electric blankets.

"Don't like the looks of the livestock loading either, ma'am," Margolis added. This was more serious. The contents of the livestock area were, for obvious reasons, not sterilized. Anything coming aboard ship that way could be carrying something deadly.

"All right. Give me one person to help, and I'll do a search."

"Same deal?"

"That depends on what we find. Just what do you think was stowed in there?" Searching through the livestock area was going to be a dirty, smelly job. There was a limit to how clean you could get pigs and chickens. Yet Margolis seemed to be thinking of volunteering for this duty himself.

Margolis shrugged. "All I know is the livestock loading looked like a Colonial fire drill," he said. "Bunch of amateurs chasing around. Seemed like most of them couldn't tell the difference between a hen and a hog. Marines running in and out of the hold, rearranging things, changing their minds about what was to be stowed where. In all that racket and confusion, a live parrot could get through."

Now a live parrot would definitely be valuable. The colorful birds with their raucous voices and talent for mimicry became almost extinct before the end of the twentieth century. What motive anyone could have for smuggling one onto a warship, was hard to imagine.

No parrot was found aboard *Primrose*. But something almost as unexpected was. Steele explained, as she displayed the collection of contraband to Lieutenant Costello. "This stuff from the duffels is about what you might expect, ma'am," she said. "Though I don't understand how it got as far as the dock."

Costello had some ideas, but was not about to expand on them here in earshot of the curious Primroses. She poked at the assortment of unauthorized objects and wondered at the thinking behind their selection. The liquor and drugs, even the perfumes and cosmetics, were understandable. But why would anyone insist on packing an electric pencil? Or a box of powdered prunes? It was amazing what some commoners believed they could not leave home without.

"There were two things in with the livestock. I thought this was probably all right," she said poking a wooden box with her foot. "Still, I wanted to clear it with you." Costello looked at the crate and smiled. It was wine. That was why it was packed with other living things.

"It's all right, Steele. It's a gift to the wardroom. Doctor Gordon will be all over it when it's unloaded to be sure there's nothing toxic inside. Assuming it passes inspection, Captain Brook will get custody. Until it runs out, we can expect to have a vintage Cabernet Sauvignon on special occasions."

"This other one I know is really bad news." Steele lifted the lid of a chicken basket. Inside a half-grown silver tabby cat lay curled in the straw and feathers.

Cats were common on Earth, but to Costello this softly breathing fur ball seemed exotic. There was no food, water, or air to spare in space for an animal that did not earn its keep. If the medical/life support officers discovered a kitten aboard *Lafayette*, it would be destroyed and its body recycled. But the animals were certainly beautiful. She understood how sailors might long for such a pet.

"A lot of palms were greased to get this kind of contraband this far," said Steele.

Costello nodded. No individual sailor would have the money to arrange for this; it must have been a whole group chipping in — messmates planning to hide and feed a feline companion on the sly — or, perhaps, some of those pagan Colonials whose religion recommended communication with animals as a path to the Divine. Brook tolerated these peculiar theological notions, but the Marines had orders to keep them from practicing telepathy on the pigs and chickens - it put the livestock off their feed.

No matter who was behind it, a path of bribery lay between *Lafayette* and the Fort McHenry loading dock. Whoever had put up the cash had been fortunate that no one in the chain of this deal had simply taken the money and split. They had somehow connected with a band of "honest" smugglers.

The kitten seemed healthy. It had been altered — which meant it had probably had a full range of inoculations too — and it appeared to have been professionally tranquilized. Not too much, not too little; enough to keep it sleeping until after it was recovered by whoever was planning to take delivery in the animal quarantine, but not enough to kill it.

"Are you going to take this to the general, ma'am?" Costello could tell from Steele's sober expression that the young officer knew exactly what "taking it to the general" meant. Putting this problem on Sparrow's desk meant fixing the responsibility.

"There isn't any choice, is there?" she said. "I'll have to leave you in charge of our people. We need them lined up and cheerful before we can take them out. They've been badly mishandled so far. You saw what it was like in the shed." This wasn't work Costello would have left to the new officer had there been an alternative. "Are you up for this?" she asked.

"Yes, ma'am!"

"You sound very sure of yourself. Is this SOCRATES?"

"No, ma'am. Navy Orphans' Summer Camp. I was a volunteer camp counselor for three years."

Costello nodded. It was certainly related experience. "Go on in and take over, then. I'll be back as quickly as possible." She lifted the kitten in its basket, climbed aboard one of the electric carts parked at the dock and drove down the cement roadway toward Old Fort McHenry.

Costello would have preferred to walk, not just because her sailor's soul was offended by lavish consumption of artificial energy, but because she wasn't looking forward to the duty facing her. She considered General Sparrow a friend, a very old friend; and she admired the woman as a hero of two wars and of many years of service in hardship posts. But friendship and admiration didn't count when it came to the question of meritocratic fitness.

The sun was low in the sky as she reached headquarters. A gibbous moon, nearly full, already glowed ghostlike in the east. The long twilight of a June evening was beginning. Earth was so beautiful, Costello thought. Every time she visited, it was harder to leave.

With a sigh, Costello parked the cart and crossed the inner court of the old fort. She was certain she would find General Sparrow still on duty. Most of a base commander's problems occurred at night. What Costello did not expect was to see Sergeant Major Pollard still at his desk. She was not in the mood to exchange pleasantries with him.

"Tell the General, I'm here," she said curtly.

"General Sparrow really is extremely busy, Lieutenant. Can you explain your needs to me? I'll take them up with her for you just as soon as she has some free time."

Costello's eyes narrowed. "You do this frequently, soldier, don't you."

"Do what, Lieutenant?" Pollard asked blandly.

"Put yourself between someone bringing a matter to the top of the chain of command and the officer who represents meritocratic authority at this installation."

"Lieutenant, I'm only trying to do my job."

"That is not what you're doing. You're trying to do the General's job. You're playing with fire, Pollard, and if you know what's good for you, you'll quit this game right now while you still have a chance."

"Are you threatening me, Lieutenant Costello," said Pollard coolly.

"That's precisely what I'm doing. And it's a threat with teeth in it. Willfully usurping meritocratic functions is a criminal offense. The penalty is death by hanging. Now is that explicit enough for you? I'm here to talk to your boss. I'm not asking your permission. I'm telling you."

Pollard pursed his lips and signaled the inner office. "Lieutenant Costello is here to see you again, ma'am," he said primly. Costello shot him a dark glance and went through the door.

"Well, Liz," said Sparrow, as she leaned forward across her desk pulled herself to her feet with an effort that was clearly painful and then struggled to stand straight and tall. "I didn't expect to see you again before you left. No trouble at the boarding area, I hope."

Costello set the basket on the desk. "This was discovered in the course of a search of the assigned transport vessel after the Marines at station 117 had all signed off on it."

Sparrow frowned. Providing security for the Navy was a prime Marine mission. For something unauthorized to pass through Fort McHenry meant a security breakdown of the first magnitude. She raised the lid of the basket and looked inside. Not a bomb, but definitely contraband.

Sparrow gently lifted the kitten from the straw and examined the small mammal. It did not appear to be diseased. Soft gray and white fur with darker patterning in stripes and dots, shell pink pads on dainty paws, pink tipped ears, and a small pink triangle nose. A very handsome creature.

"I suggest you sit down, Susan," Costello said. Without thinking she had dropped the formal forms of address.

Sparrow sat holding the warm sleeping body on her lap. As she stroked the silky ears, her mind began to wander. She began to think how nice it would be to be to sit like this, on a warm summer evening, perhaps in a rocking chair on a porch, with a sleeping cat on her lap.

"Susan!"

Sparrow snapped alert. Costello was bending over her. "Have you been having blackouts frequently?"

"Did I black out just then? Yes," she answered herself, "I suppose I did. Frequent? Well, I don't know. I certainly don't concentrate and remember things as well as I used to. I thought of asking the Admiralty for sick leave last winter, but I know how pressed they are for personnel . . ." She paused as she saw the worried expression on Costello's face.

"I should have demanded sick leave," she said slowly, realizing the implications of her statement. "As a meritocrat, it shouldn't have mattered to me what the reaction of the Admiralty might be. That I hesitated to follow my intuition should have been a clear sign to me that I might be unfit."

A silence hung between the two women. Sparrow was the one who broke it. "You're here to challenge my fitness, aren't you."

Costello nodded gravely.

"Well, go on then. What are you waiting for? Do what you have to do and get it over with."

"Susan Sparrow, it is my considered opinion that you have developed a meriotocratic flaw. This is a formal challenge." Costello spoke the words firmly. The appropriate phrasing had been taught to her on her first day as a Navy cadet as part of honor system indoctrination. She had never had to use them before; she had never served with a meritocrat in whom she suspected a flaw. "You can respond to this any way you want to. Call in a team from the Admiralty to investigate your command, voluntarily turn yourself in for retesting, or simply decide for yourself that you're unfit and announce your retirement. If you decide to do that you'll want to run your own investigation first. This animal wasn't the only problem down at 117, and the sergeant there said you haven't inspected recently."

"Very well," said Sparrow, stroking the kitten in her lap.

"I expect that Captain Brook will take *Lafayette* out of the Mars orbit as soon as we've boarded the new crew tomorrow morning. We'll be out of light signal range in less than two weeks. I can't give you any longer than that. If you haven't taken satisfactory action on your own by then, I'll have to report you to the Admiralty myself."

"Yes, of course." Strange, thought Sparrow, she had always thought it would be dreadfully humiliating to be charged with loss of fitness. What she felt now was more like relief. She had well over fifty years in service. As a meritocrat, she was bound by her oath to serve for life. She had expected to die with her boots on. But if she declared herself unfit, the Admiralty would give her the nice little pension any commoner with equivalent service would receive. If she declared herself unfit, no one would argue. Not even if she herself suspected she might be lying when she said it. Because no true meritocrat would lie. It could be very nice. Live in the country. Rock on the porch. Watch the sunsets.

Sparrow did not black out this time. The pleasant fantasies could wait. She was not so flawed that she would grasp at keeping a command she was clearly unfit to exercise, but she had enough sense of honor to want to clean her own house before turning it over to the Admiralty.

"One more thing, Susan." Sparrow looked up questioningly. "That Sergeant Major you have sitting in your outer office . . ."

"Yes, Lieutenant, I know. He's the obvious suspect."

"That wasn't what I was going to say. Actually I doubt very much that he'd be involved in smuggling. He has too much to lose. There's the matter of usurpation."

"Dear God — has he been . . . "

"I don't know. I don't want to know. I'm shipping out and whoever deals with this, it won't be me. But you might bear in mind that a subordinate could have been drawn into usurpation of authority through a misguided attempt to protect you. Throughout your career, you've had a powerful charisma, Susan, and your troops have always loved you. I'm not saying that Pollard didn't succumb to temptation once he had power in his hands. Maybe he did. He's been inspecting in your place, and that's bad enough, but the authorities won't punish him for it if you accept responsibility. Do it before you resign if you think he deserves it. Otherwise, he'll hang."

"You don't think he's connected to the smuggling?"

"No," Costello shook her head emphatically. "He has too much to lose. At the minimum, they'd take his stripes and his pension for that. And you know how much that means to commoners."

"Yes," said Sparrow, "I think I do." She lifted the sleeping cat onto her desk and painfully pulled herself to her feet again. "I'll say goodbye again, then, Liz. Don't worry; I won't force you to file a formal challenge. I had to do it once, and I wouldn't wish the experience on anyone I cared about. You'll receive a signal before you're out of range. Good luck to you and to the — and to the Lafayettes."

The seven hour trip to Mars was uneventful. Liz Costello slept the whole way. Maggie Steele looked out the porthole and watched the stars.

CHAPTER THREE

It was two bells in the morning watch, dawn for those in the controlled environment of HMS *Lafayette. Primrose* drew alongside and prepared to dock at the air lock of the quarantine bubble. The great ship, visible to those heading toward her for much of the night, gleamed in battle dress displaying her readiness to leave orbit. Silver sailplates replaced the black ones, reflecting radiant energy rather than absorbing it, protecting her batteries from overcharging.

Costello woke as *Primrose* made her initial deceleration. She stretched and smiled at Steele. "That's the first good sleep I've had since I left this big tub," she said, raising her eyes to the overhead window and the shining bell shaped ship. "Shore leave isn't all it's cracked up to be."

Ignoring the flashing signal warning all passengers to keep their harnesses fastened, Costello unbuckled, stood and stretched again. "I'm going to call Captain Brook," she said. "If I do it now, it's *Primrose*'s power. Once we're in quarantine we won't communicate with the bridge except in an emergency. While we're sealed off, there's nothing we can do for them and nothing they can do for us."

Costello was gone just briefly, but long enough for Steele to look carefully at the quarantine bubble that hung beneath the hull of the ship. The bubble had always seemed a minor appendage to warship design. What it would be like to be sealed inside it for a month was something she was just beginning to think about.

Costello returned to her seat smiling. "Captain Brook very formally instructed me to convey to you his pleasure at having you aboard *Lafayette*. Our captain is very much the old-fashioned gentleman." She refastened her harness. "You won't be meeting the captain for a while," she said. "But I think I'd better tell you something about Doctor Gordon." She sighed. "I've known him so long, I'm used to him; but his appearance can be very upsetting if you don't know what to expect.

"Gordon was a pioneer in space epidemiology, Maggie, and in his time he's picked up a dose of practically everything loose in space. He's got a meritocratic immune system all right because he's still alive. He survived both the Pox and the White Death, but they took their toll. He's in remission from Venusian Malaria, but he's still taking maintenance medication for it that lost him all his hair. What else is wrong with him, I don't really know; he probably has the longest medical record of anyone on the ship. But I do know he has chronic pain. It hasn't done much for his disposition."

"It's all right, ma'am. I've seen Pox victims and some who survived White Death too."

"Was this in SOCRATES?" Costello had never seen anyone who was grotesquely deformed until she went into space.

"No, ma'am. In real life. The cadets all spent a summer on *Eagle*, the academy training craft. We didn't take her farther than the moon, but we had to do two weeks' service there aboard the Navy hospital ship. It was hard at first to see anything in the patients except their scars. After a while we got used to it, and they seemed just like other people."

"Well, Doctor Gordon is not just like other people. He is a remarkable man. Some say he's the greatest scientist of our time; certainly he's the greatest physician. He's the current holder of Galen's Ring. *Lafayette* is very fortunate to have him. But he can be a trial, Maggie. Believe me, he can be a trial."

Primrose thudded to rest against the bubble's hull. A moment later the harness sign went off and Margolis came out of the control center. "Thanks for the ride, Chief," Costello said. "Hold our crew in the aft cabin for a bit, will you? Doctor Gordon may have some special instructions."

"Sure thing, Lieutenant Costello." Costello moved toward the exit. "Good luck to you, Lieutenant Steele," Margolis said. "It was real nice meeting you, real nice."

Richard Gordon was a hideously ugly man. He knew that just as he knew he had once been strikingly handsome. In his youth, his 6'6" skeletal frame had supported a heavy, muscular body covered with golden olive skin and crowned with a mass of black curls. His beard had been equally black and curly, and many young women had remarked on the attractiveness of his dark, deep-set eyes. Now his eyes were all that remained of his former good looks.

When Gordon came down with the White Death, surgeons removed his retinas in a desperate attempt to save his sight as his body lost the ability to produce melanin. After the crisis passed, they were reattached, but no one would call them attractive anymore. As for the rest of his body, the alphosis was permanent. Black eyes in a stark white skull that lacked even eyebrows or eyelashes might be striking, but few people had the stomach to return his gaze.

Captain Brook insisted that medical/life support officers wear dress uniform when *Lafayette* received new hands. He said it showed respect. Gordon snorted. It would show more respect, he thought, if he appeared with a bag over his head.

Nevertheless, Brook gave orders on the uniform of the day, so Gordon wore the dark blue tunic of a meritocrat in service with the Royal Navy. His service number and function insignia — a caduceus over the double ringed cross that indicated command — was silver rather than gold. Medical/life support officers held equivalent rank with other meritocrats, but it was always made quite clear that they were not in the line of ship command.

Fine. Gordon only wished it worked the other way round as well so that line officers refrained from butting into medical/life support business. As it was, Brook insisted that Gordon adhere to all the tiresome, traditional rituals of the Navy during quarantine as if the bubble were a ship in itself rather than a medical facility.

Gordon saluted Costello as she came through the airlock and announced that she now had the con. What use was having the damned con, he thought, when the bubble was firmly anchored to the hull of the larger vessel. The only conning the bubble commander could do was to order the craft jettisoned if infection became uncontrollable.

Steele looked at the tall man as he spoke to Costello. He was certainly as badly deformed as anyone she had seen on the *Mercy* during her summer cruise. He seemed freakishly tall, his body so badly emaciated that the bony structure of his skull was visible through waxy white skin, and every part of his bald head was pitted with the deep black scars of the Pox.

The ugly man, moreover, wore an ugly expression. He barely acknowledged Costello's introduction of her except to look her over keenly from head to foot with a pair of piercing black eyes. She called up her quarterdeck face and willed herself not to flinch.

Doctor Gordon focused his attention on the senior officer. "You're not looking good, Costello," he said harshly. "I want you in for a full examination just as soon as you've got the sailors unloaded."

"Gordon," Costello said with a sigh, "I'm sure that in the three days since I left the ship I've developed symptoms of everything from beriberi to bubonic plague. But give it a rest. You know perfectly well that even if I were sick enough to bury, the crew get taken care of first. When I've got them assigned to squad leaders and you've taken the lab samples you need so we can feed them, then you'll get a crack at Steele and me."

Gordon glared at her.

"Don't sulk, Gordon. Just give me the duty roster so that I can get to work. And I hope you've got breakfast on the fire, because if we don't feed these people pretty soon, they're going to start chewing on their shirt-tails."

Gordon handed over a clipboard. She glanced at it and nodded in approval as she inspected the list of names. With the mess the Marines had made of transition at Fort McHenry, squad leaders were going to have to pick up an extra training burden. She was glad to see Gordon had brought in some of his best. She went off to inspect the berthing area.

"Did she sleep at all on the way out, Steele?" Gordon asked in a milder tone, his eyes fixed on Costello's retreating back.

"Yes, sir," said Steele. "The whole way," she added not quite understanding the physician's intense concern but hoping that this information might help Costello's case.

"At least she had that much sense," he grumbled. As Costello disappeared, Gordon gave Steele his full attention. She looked to be in fair condition. Reasonably plump. Losing pigmentation in her hair; that would bear watching. Didn't look as well-rested as he'd have liked in someone about to start a shift working with a newly pressed crew.

"You didn't sleep, did you, Lieutenant," he demanded. "You probably got to bed late your last night ashore, maybe even stood vigil over your sword. Then instead of sleeping in, you spent the morning involved in those idiot June Day ceremonies, headed straight for the shuttle — probably without a nap — and then you stayed up for the whole shuttle trip staring out the window. Now you're here, it's dawn, and you've got a full day of hard work ahead of you." Steele was startled at how accurately Gordon had reconstructed her activities over the past two days apparently from simply looking at her face.

"Just because you've got a young, healthy body, don't think you can get away with abusing it," he scolded.

"That's enough, Doctor Gordon." Costello was back at the airlock. "Get off Steele's back. All of us have work to do. Steele can set up for the livestock if you'll give her a chief to help."

From his height, Gordon had a clear view into every corner of the reception area where his crew waited for orders. He spotted the person he wanted. "Greene," he bellowed. "Get over here!"

A short, pleasant-faced woman, wearing a white smock over the yellow striped shirt of a chief in medical/life support, fell out of her at ease position and moved briskly toward Gordon.

"This is Nancy Greene," Gordon said to Steele. "She's a veterinarian's mate. Poultry specialist. If you get into trouble and need someone for pigs, I'll give you another vet. But I'd rather keep the vets for the sailors this morning — they're more trouble than pigs. If you need muscle, help yourself to Marines. There are always more of them around than I have any use for." Steele nodded and took off with Greene toward the aft hatch through which the livestock would disembark.

"Before we take in the sailors, we have to decide what to do with the grommet," Costello said.

Gordon groaned. "Not another one of those already! I had one in here with the first press!"

"You've taken three hundred sailors through our quarantine since then. This load makes it five. So *Lafayette* is due for another. Grin and bear it, doctor. I don't like it any better than you do."

"The last one was a crybaby. I thought the damned kid would dehydrate himself before we got him under control. What charming habits does this little darling have?"

"Several you won't like. It looks like she bites her nails. She spits. And she's violent. I had her sedated."

"Sedatives are bad for children."

"Yes, and so are straitjackets. My charisma didn't work on her; but you're welcome to try yours."

His charisma wasn't good for children either, Gordon thought. The ability to frighten people into hysterics was all that seemed to him to have lingered of his former meritocratic charm.

"Is she still out?"

Costello nodded. "I wanted to be absolutely sure she wouldn't wake up until you could get her into an isolation berth. She could panic the whole crew if she started acting up again."

"All right. I'll put her in isolation. She'll probably wake up screaming, but she'll have to wait her turn. Anything else I should know about?"

Costello decided against mentioning the matter of the cat among the chickens. It was sure to send Gordon into a tizzy, and there was nothing to be done about it now.

"Nothing that can't wait."

"Then get them aboard. I'll stay out of sight until they've been fed."

It was 0900, two bells into the forenoon watch before Costello and Steele could take time for breakfast. Bowls of unseasoned vegetable stew were brought to them in the tiny wardroom that constituted officers' country in quarantine. Gordon slept in his surgery and Steele and Costello would be hot-bunking in the cabin that was designated as sleeping quarters for the commanding meritocrat.

"Better be sure you don't get too sick to come up for watch, Maggie," Costello warned as the two dug into their first meal to break a fast that had lasted well beyond the required twenty-four hours. "Gordon will slap you in sickbay with the commoners if he thinks both of us need the berth, and it won't help build your command image to have your sailors see you puking. Much better if you can confine that to the officers' head."

Steele nodded as she gave her full attention to the bowl of vegetables. Not even this talk of puking could damage her appetite this morning. Her insides felt empty as a black hole.

Costello poured out two mugs of synthetic coffee and pushed one over to Steele. "Did you learn to drink this at the Academy while Thanatos was training you on the Navy diet?"

Steele took a sip and made a face. "No, ma'am. We had synthetic coffee, but nothing like this. What is it?" The liquid was thick, almost syrupy, like Turkish coffee; but it was bitter, not sweet, with a flavor reminiscent of iodine.

"It's the med/life universally prescribed daily dose. We call it mudd. You have to drink at least three cups every day. What exactly is in it doesn't bear thinking about too closely. It's whatever the med/life officers decide everyone needs to swallow on any particular day. It's got some kind of contraceptive in it — everyone jokes about that in the wardroom — but it also has nutritional supplements and sometimes oral vaccines when the exact dosage isn't too important. Everyone thinks it tastes foul when they first try it, but it grows on you. Some of us suspect the med/life folks of having slipped in something as addictive as caffeine." Costello sipped her drink as she studied a clipboard.

Steele tried another sip, then held her breath as she took three deep swallows, released her breath and gagged. Costello raised her eyes. "Take it slow, Steele," she suggested. "It's easier that way, and you've got until midnight." Steele forced herself to take another sip anyway. She did not want to be faced with a large mug of this at the end of the day.

She watched as Costello finished her vegetables and then poured herself a second cup of mudd before returning her attention to the clipboard. Although she'd been working since dawn, Costello appeared more relaxed and at ease than she had at any time since Steele had first met her. In this cramped cabin, eating hydroponically grown vegetables and drinking this disgusting liquid, Costello felt at home.

Doctor Gordon came into the wardroom carrying his breakfast. It was some kind of hot grain cereal. He banged it down on the table, pulled out his chair roughly and sat. Costello looked up quizzically and poured him a mug of mudd.

"Having a bad morning, are we, Doctor?" Gordon grunted and swallowed half the drink at once.

He looked at Steele's mug. "How much of that have you got down? Is that still your first cup?"

"Leave her alone, Gordon. She's doing the best she can, and if she doesn't get it all down today you can give it to her through a feeding tube. You'll have give it to most of the new sailors that way anyway."

"I've got enough to do without that, Costello. The medics will do the feedings on the press; if a meritocrat needs it, that's one more thing on my work sheet. Which reminds me," he said, draining his cup and pouring a refill, "I'm still waiting to do a physical exam on you."

Gordon's brusque manner didn't seem to bother Costello, Steele observed. Indeed, she seemed amused by it as though it were somehow an endearing trait in an old shipmate that she had missed while on shore.

"You know, Doctor Gordon," she said thoughtfully, regarding him over the top of her mug, a hint of a smile playing on her face, "I'm considering having you put all your personal communications to me in writing."

"Now see here, Liz, just because Captain Brook . . ."

"No, no," Costello interrupted, shaking her head, "I really think it would be a good idea. Save us both a lot of time and aggravation." Steele could tell that Costello was teasing and that she was missing part of the joke.

"Let me tell you how the chief medical/life officer of HMS *Lafayette* communicates with the captain when he feels that our commanding officer is abusing his health." Costello's eyes were twinkling. Gordon scowled.

"The doctor prepares a written memo — there's even a special form for it — which must be carried to Captain Brook by a third party, preferably by a mute Colonial. Doctor Gordon may not carry it himself, and he is strictly forbidden ever to discuss the captain's health with the captain until he has first sent a memo and received formal permission."

Gordon snorted, drained his mug, and filled it for the third time. "I hate this stuff," he muttered. "It's worse than quinine. But then, my taste buds are all shot anyway, so what difference does it make."

"Now, don't change the subject, Doctor," Costello broke in. "Would you like to explain to Lieutenant Steele why we have such an unusual standing order on our ship."

Gordon gave up. "Heavens no, Liz," he grumbled. "You tell the story so well."

Costello nodded to Gordon formally, acknowledging his permission to proceed, and then launched into her narrative. The talent for telling a story well was a valued trait in a messmate. Despite his determination to keep a scowl on his face, Gordon listened attentively as Costello settled back in her chair.

"As sometimes happens during a war, Maggie," she began, "we had a battle alert one day — around lunch time. Captain Brook was eating in his day cabin, but when the alert sounded, he bounded off to the bridge. Without," she added ominously, "cleaning his plate."

"You know that wasn't really as trivial a matter as you're making it sound, Liz."

"Shut up, Richard. You said I could tell the story." Gordon muttered something to himself and to Steele's surprise poured himself a fourth cup of mudd.

"Now Captain Brook is not actually so rebellious a patient as the good doctor here might have you believe. He does not routinely defy the Navy clean plate rule or any other medical regulations. It just so happened that with a battle alert and a subsequent engagement involving two hostile craft, our captain grew a bit absent minded and forgot that he'd left most of his lunch uneaten. As a commissioned line officer, Maggie, I'm sure you can sympathize and understand how the captain might have become a bit forgetful under those circumstances."

Steele almost felt sorry for Gordon. Costello was needling him pretty sharply. But Gordon didn't seem to mind. At least his face registered no change of expression.

"Well Mickey — that's Brook's steward — finally clears away the captain's tray. The galley chief discovers that it contains uneaten food and follows the standing rule to report that fact to the med/life director. The next thing you know, Doctor Gordon, here, zooms up the main ladder, charges onto the bridge while the captain is still getting damage reports, and starts to dress him down for endangering his health."

Costello straightened herself in her chair, lowered her head, and pulled her eyebrows down in what Steele recognized instantly as an imitation of Captain Brook, whose holograph she had often seen in news broadcasts. "Doctor Gordon," Costello said, affecting a slow deep voice with a trace of Virginia accent, "I am perfectly willing to obey your medical orders, but it is bad for discipline for me to accept a public tongue lashing. Go below and put what you have to say to me in writing. And kindly remember, as you write, that you are addressing your captain and not one of your loblollies."

Steele laughed at the imitation. It really did sound just like the holographs of Brook. Even Gordon smiled sourly.

"So about ten minutes later one of Gordon's mates is on the bridge with this formal memo. Brook reads it, puts it in his pocket, dismisses the mate, and then goes off to his cabin to eat the reheated remains of his lunch. But as he's polishing off the chicken and rice, Brook looks at the memo again and decides that he's discovered a dandy way to keep his blood pressure down. He can just avoid spontaneous conversation with our genial resident physician. So now Gordon has to send Brook a memo every time he wants to discuss his health."

"It hasn't helped his hypertension," Gordon said. "Most of those memos are still orders for him to report in for a blood pressure test or to make a blood bank deposit. You and Steele may laugh about it, but to me keeping the captain from having a stroke is as important as keeping the ammunition dry or whatever it is that you line officers worry about when you're between battle alerts."

"Nobody's going to argue with you about that, Richard," Costello said. "But your obsession with the health of the officers is just a teensy bit wearing."

"Your health is vital to the ship," Gordon snapped. "Six line officers are all we have out here. You are not replaceable. I can't build a new meritocrat out of recycled chicken feathers, and keeping the ones we've got functional is my responsibility."

"All right, all right, Gordon. Steele and I are not bent on suicide. We have every intention of cooperating with you. Just try to remember that we've got a bubble full of sailors who are sure to present more disciplinary problems than usual. One of them is that sweet little grommet you've got tucked away somewhere who will get a lot worse than she is now if she'd not shaped up fast. You need at least one of us on hand to deal with those problems round the clock. There's more to be done in quarantine than help you with your war on microbes."

"My war is fundamental down here. You'll get no use from a well-disciplined corpse."

"Work on Steele after she's cleaned her plate and then let her get some sleep," Costello said, trying to end the argument. Gordon would always have the last word unless someone clamped a muzzle on him. "I'll have the crew bedded down by 2000 hours. Steele will take over on the first watch and you can examine me then. Good enough?"

"I'd rather have you come in first, Costello," said Gordon. "You look godawful."

"Gordon, I'm warning you. I will pull rank on you and make you report in writing if you push me much more. The three of us are going to be cooped up together for thirty days, and I won't tolerate this constant back talk. I don't have half the patience Brook does. Steele is going to take the first watch tonight. Until then, I'm on duty. Now have you got that straight?"

"Yes, Lieutenant," said Gordon. He always stopped arguing once he'd had a direct order. No sense in arguing after that. But he'd always do his damndest to make his point while a final decision was still up in the air. It was the only way for med/life to influence command decisions in the Navy, and he made the most of it. Screwed-up priorities, the line officers had, he thought. What use was all their macrocosmic warfare, if they lost on the microcosmic front? But that was the Navy for you, and he had sworn the meritocratic oath of obedience.

"You," he said pointing a bony finger at Steele. "Report to the surgery when you've finished your meal. And don't bolt it down; it's bad for your digestion." He bused his dishes to the galley window and stomped from the cabin.

"Is he always like that, Liz?"

"Except when he's in a bad mood, and then he's worse. It's something you'll adjust to." She looked at Steele sympathetically. Going in for a physical was never a fun experience. When your physician looked like one of the living dead and had the disposition of wet hen, the prospect had even less appeal.

"You have to realize that Gordon is starting his third boarding quarantine with only a few hours break for him in between. When new people and animals are brought aboard, that becomes the major threat to the ship as far as med/life is concerned and as senior medical officer Gordon always takes the quarantine duty himself. I'm not sure whether you noticed, because they were taken in through the forward hatch, but there were a good number of body bags loaded aboard *Primrose* before she left. Gordon must have had a rough time with the press that went through just before ours. He'll be easier to live with once he's sure that neither of us is going to die on him."

Steele had let both her vegetables and her mudd grow cold as she listened to her fellow officers argue. She finished what was left in her bowl and had another try at the mudd. It was, incredibly, even worse at room temperature. She decided to give it up and try again at lunch.

As she was about to leave, there was a knock on the door. Costello looked up from her clipboard again and sighed. "Trouble," she said. "And I still haven't finished the duty roster." She put aside the paper work. "Come," she called in a louder voice.

A dark hulking man with heavy eyebrows and a lantern jaw entered the wardroom. Steele recognized him as Otto Schmidt, the veterinarian who specialized in pigs. He was doubling as a squad leader.

"Excuse me for interrupting, Lieutenant. I have a discipline problem."

"What is it?"

"There's one of my sailors, ma'am. He told the steward he won't eat his vegetables."

"One of those already! Have you put them on the mudd yet?"

"No, ma'am. This is a very raw crew, ma'am. Nobody seems to have taught them anything. It's not just my hard-case squad either. All the squad leaders are having the same problem. We're trying to ease them into things, but there's sure to be a line out here when you hold mast."

"But this is one that can't wait because he's the first and you need an example."

"Yes, ma'am. I can't make sailors swallow medicine and obey the medics, if I can't make them eat their vegetables."

"Right. Let's go take care of your fussy eater." She detached a sheet from the clipboard and handed it to Steele. "Take this to Gordon when you go over. It's my plan to tame our grommet. Tell him I want it in place before the sedative wears off."

"All right, Schmidt. What's our problem's name and where are you holding him?"

"Charlie Ames, ma'am. He's still in the mess hall. I told the galley chief to hold the second shift until I brought you."

Charlie Ames sat alone at a table in the otherwise empty mess area. He was a lanky kid about sixteen or seventeen. His face was covered with a slightly green-tinged gel; the medics had made a rapid diagnosis of the rash on his face and started him on treatments for acne. Costello thought he looked like the type who, when he had a choice, lived on potato chips and root beer. Two Marines stood guard in their usual wooden manner as a steward waited impatiently to clear the table.

The evidence was on his plate: a mash of hydroponically grown vegetables unsalted and unseasoned as the bland diet Gordon and prescribed for sailors about to undergo a series of inoculations required. Ames had eaten his portion at breakfast. He'd been ravenous then; but when the same stuff appeared on the table at lunch, he'd told them he wasn't going to eat any more slop.

From the reactions, you'd have thought he'd said he was going to blow up the ship. The galley chief examined his dish to be sure there was nothing in there that shouldn't be, then called in his squad leader who had called in the Marines. Now Lieutenant Costello was here too.

"Clean your plate, sailor," she ordered.

Ames picked up his fork and began to pick at the food. It really tasted awful, especially now that it was cold. He left some of it spread around the dish where it didn't really look to him like so much and put down his fork.

"I told you to clean your plate, Ames. You are attempting to evade an order. That won't be tolerated."

Ames gloomily picked up his fork again and ate the last scraps. He was actually wishing he could get hold of a bag of potato chips somewhere to take the taste of the stuff out of his mouth.

"Now stand up," Costello ordered. Ames rose awkwardly from this chair and stood slouching by the table. "Straighten up and look at me."

Ames lifted his head and Costello locked her eyes onto his. "In the Navy, you eat what you are served, and you do not attempt to cheat on a clean plate check. You are going to be punished for disobedience to an order from a mate and for violation of these rules." Schmidt stood waiting for her order. "Rap his knuckles," she said.

"Hold out your hand, Ames." Ames took one look at the flat ferule Schmidt held and put his hands behind his back.

"You were given an order, Ames," Costello said. "Orders are to be obeyed whether you like them or not. You do not have a choice. Hold out your hand now, or you will have to take additional punishment."

Ames tentatively brought his hand from behind his back. Schmidt moved rapidly, seized the boy's wrist, brought his hand into position and hit him once smartly across the knuckles.

Ames cried out, jerked his hand back and put his fist into his mouth. Tears ran from his tightly closed eyes.

Costello watched him. Pain from this punishment was intense but brief. In a few moments Ames opened his eyes and began to rub his bruised knuckles with his other hand. Now that his fist was out of his mouth he sobbed audibly. Costello waited until the tears flowed quietly.

"In the future," she said slowly and deliberately, "you will clean your plate."

Ames looked at her mournfully, still rubbing his sore hand.

"Your answer to me is 'yes, ma'am'," she said.

"Yes, ma'am," said Ames tearfully.

"Very well. You're dismissed. Join your squad." Ames left with Schmidt behind him. The galley mate picked up the fork and the empty plate and carried them off. Seconds later the second shift of sailors poured into the cabin and trays of steamed vegetables began making the rounds again.

* * *

"Every hour you use that thing is going to cost the ship one sunny day, Costello."

"If Petrie has the IQ of a cocker spaniel, I won't need to use it for as much as five minutes. I've explained this to you. I need the collar for the threat it represents: a certainty of swift punishment for a limited range of misbehavior — violence and spitting. And since I am going to explain this to her very carefully, as only one of the dumb sailors could explain it to a cocker spaniel, she will take one sample of what the collar can do and then figure out how she can avoid a repeat." Gordon was a brilliant man. Why did Costello feel she was trying to get through to a two year old? "She may try a few tricks, but they won't work and then she'll start to figure out how she can get out of the collar. And we'll have explained that to her: stop fighting and spitting — and stop biting her nails if you want me to add that."

"No," said Gordon. "No, leave out the nail biting. It's dangerous to tinker with that kind of habit; whatever function it serves gets diverted to something else. I'll put Doctor Parker on Petrie's case when we get back upstairs."

"And for now, we use the collar for the other behaviors," Costello persisted, "and you give me your full cooperation. Damn it, Gordon, I'm doing this for you. Do you want to do a Pox inoculation on a sedated patient confined to an isolation bunk?"

"I want her out of there," Gordon said. "A medical facility isn't a brig."

"Fine. I want her out too."

"And I don't want her working in anything involving hominid organics — not with the spitting and nail biting. No cleaning the heads and no KP."

"Will the chicken yard suit you? If you'd read to the end of the memo I sent you, you'd see that was the assignment I put her in. I don't want her in the galley either. Too many knives around."

Gordon glared.

"You're wasting my time, Gordon. Let's go wake up Petrie."

Gordon examined his chronometer and made some calculations. "Ten more minutes. I want her to wake naturally."

Damn it, Costello thought. He'd done it again. He'd sucked her into an argument just to pass the time.

"Take me into isolation," she ordered. "We'll wait there."

The isolation ward consisted of a tier of closed bunks that medics reached with ladders and catwalks. Each was sealed with a transparent sheet through which the occupants could be cared for without direct contact. Petrie was the only occupant of the ward, and her bunk was open. Gordon picked up her hand and put his fingers on her pulse.

Petrie woke at his touch but did not open her eyes. She felt sort of strange and wasn't sure where she was. If she just stayed quiet and pretended to be asleep, maybe she could learn something. Petrie liked to learn things, especially when they were things nobody wanted her to know.

"She'll come round in a moment," a harsh male voice said. Two people, Petrie decided.

"Perhaps you should try a stimulant." A familiar voice. The Navy officer from Fort McHenry. The one they were calling Lieutenant Costello.

"Don't need one." A hand gently patted her face. "Come on, Becky. Time to wake up." Petrie considered whether to respond. The pats turned to slaps, and Petrie slowly opened her eyes.

Patients waking to find him hovering over their cot usually reacted with a scream. Gordon had persuaded himself that it was good for them. Got air into their lungs. But Petrie didn't scream; she looked him over carefully as if she found him interesting.

"You had the Pox, right?" she demanded.

"You can leave now, Doctor," Costello interrupted. "The Marines and I will take it from here."

Petrie sat up and looked resentfully at Costello. She didn't look like much fun, and she'd sent the ugly man away. The

Marines with her were not the same ones she'd seen at Fort McHenry; she was sure of that even though there'd been a lot of Marines there. These were different. But they were still Marines. No fun there either.

Petrie rubbed her neck; it felt funny. Her exploring fingers discovered the fine mesh collar. She tried to pull it off, but it wouldn't come loose.

"What's this thing?" she demanded.

"It's a training collar."

"I don't like it. Take it off."

"I'll have it removed as soon as you are trained."

"What does that mean?"

"We have serious work to do aboard this ship and no time to play nanny to spoiled children. When you learn to behave like a grownup, you won't have to wear the collar. You will continue to make mistakes and to misbehave from time to time. Every sailor does. But you will have learned to respond to verbal warnings and to take punishment like an adult, without fighting — and without spitting."

Petrie spat. "Punish her," Costello ordered. "Five seconds." The Marine checked the code on the box he held and pushed a button. Petrie had a high pain threshold, but Costello had anticipated that. The girl tried not to show it hurt, but it did; she writhed and finally screamed.

When the pain subsided, Petrie whirled toward Costello, her eyes flashing. "Give her a warning." Petrie felt the collar tingle at her throat and sat still.

"Now you understand how it works. The control box goes everywhere you do. Your squad leader — Chief Schmidt — will have it during prayers, drills and meals; your work supervisor — Chief Greene — will have it during your duty hours; and a Marine will have it when you're in your bunk. I've given these people the authority to administer up to ten warnings and up to three punishment shocks on their own authority within any one hour period. If they think you need more, they can get authorization to increase the limit by going to me or to Lieutenant Steele."

Costello was sure Petrie had brains enough to understand the choice: self-control or pain. Now to give her a positive goal.

"As soon as you can go through one full twenty-four hour period without requiring either warning or punishment, we will remove the collar and you will thereafter be disciplined exactly like every other sailor." Costello allowed her a few moments to think it through. "Do you understand me?"

Of course, she understood, Petrie thought. She wasn't stupid. This Lieutenant had all the power, at least for now. Petrie didn't enjoy pain, at any rate not her own, and there was more than one way to skin a cat. Petrie smiled to herself at the thought of skinning cats and decided on a new strategy. "Yes, ma'am, I understand," she said sweetly. "I won't spit anymore, I promise. You can take the collar off right now."

"I think not," said Costello. This was one creepy kid, she decided. Creepy and sneaky. But she already knew that.

* * *

Steele woke in the second dog watch, surprised to have slept so well. She sat up in the berth — four feet high, four feet wide, seven feet long — exactly like those of the sailors except that instead of tiers of bunks above below and on both sides, this bunk was set in the bulkhead of a private cabin. It was barely big enough for one, but for now it was serving two. Steele washed, dressed, and went out to see if Costello could use any help.

She found her in the wardroom eating dinner. "You're a welcome sight," Costello said. "Usually the officer who gets the quarantine command works without a relief."

"What's left to do on this watch?" Steele dug into another bowl of vegetable mash. Costello poured her a mug of mudd as she refilled her own.

"I've got to hold mast, and then read the evening service. Has spacesickness got to you yet or can you help out?"

"I'm feeling great, actually. I'm glad Doctor Gordon let me have a long sleep."

"If it hasn't got you yet, you'll probably do all right — at least until we cross the line and go to full acceleration." Costello picked up her clipboard and flipped through the pages. "You can help out at mast, then," she said. "I've never had one this bad in quarantine before. More than two dozen sailors on report for one thing or another. Every one of them will have to be paddled and a meritocrat has to witness to make sure it's done right. With both of us on it, we can get through twice as fast. After that, I won't mind reading prayers."

"Really bad day, huh?"

"I expected it; but I never get used to it."

"Is it likely to go on all night?"

"No, no. They're exhausted by now. You should have a quiet watch. The medics will deal with the spacesick ones. Tomorrow night is when all hell will break loose, and since we're dogging the watches, I'll take the duty then."

"If you say so, ma'am."

Costello looked up, amused. "You think I'm coddling you, Steele? Well, perhaps I am. Unless SOCRATES programmed a mast with a new press in quarantine among the horrors of wartime Naval service, you'll probably have trouble holding on to your dinner this evening."

Steele blushed. "I don't think SOCRATES did."

"That's what I figured. Maybe everyone doesn't feel this way, but as far as I'm concerned quarantine duty with a new press is the worst job in the Navy. I'm not complaining about the cramped quarters and the awful food," said Costello. "And this time, I'm not complaining about the company. Thank God I've got someone besides Gordon to talk to. But I'd rather take one sailor through a full-dress flogging once a year than supervise minor punishment for a dozen or so every day for a month."

Steele had been warned about the strain meritocrats would experience in the role of disciplinarians. It wasn't the intense stress SOCRATES was designed to simulate, but everyone knew it would be difficult. The desire to nurture and care for the lower orders came naturally to meritocrats. When nurturing involved inflicting pain, however, it wasn't so easy.

Survival in space meant obedience. Meritocrats obeyed because they had sworn an oath. The lower orders obeyed because they feared their officers. Discipline on a warship rested ultimately on threat of punishment. On a well-run ship the threat was enough. In quarantine, with sailors new to the system, it was not. Breaking the sailors to discipline required a lot more physical coercion than simply maintaining order once the crew had the right habits.

Fortunately, sailors didn't have the opportunity to get into very serious trouble during quarantine. They were too closely supervised for that; and the new crew, who had to take the whole range of immunizations, felt sick much the time. So punishments were frequent but moderate.

"It's going to get worse before it gets better," Costello said. "By tomorrow most of the sailors we have to punish will be sick. Gordon will stick them needles and make them swallow stuff they hate, and God knows what else. If they fight it, we'll have to punish them. I'm sure you understand, just as I do, that it has to be done; but that doesn't make the job any easier."

The necessity was obvious: it was never more important that the sailors respond to orders with absolute automatic obedience than when they were sick. Most sailors would never face the macrocosmic enemy directly, but any one of them could become ill. The most important rule in space was that requiring a sailor to report at sick call at the first sign of illness even if everyone knew the treatment would be unpleasant. A sick sailor wandering around outside the isolation ward threatened everyone's survival.

* * *

The sailors slept in berths stacked six deep in rows of ten each. Marines berthed separately and slept the same hours, except for those who patrolled during the night watches. The Marines on the night watches worked, as always, by the book. Using ladders and catwalks, they looked into every berth twice an hour, staying alert for unusual sounds between inspections.

A sailor who wanted to visit the head got a Marine escort. One cough or sneeze was okay, but two meant an escort to sickbay. Discreet visiting in other bunks was okay so long as it didn't disturb the neighbors; if Marines could hear it, it was too loud. And finally, even if you had a visitor in your bunk, you slept within twenty minutes of lights out or went to sickbay.

Becky Petrie was alone in her bunk but restless and awake during the first inspection. Consequently before Steele had been on watch long enough to study the full set of night orders, a Marine corporal brought the grommet to her.

"I took her to sickbay first, ma'am. But they told me she wasn't to get any sleeping pills. They said to bring her to you."

Steele had already heard and read a great deal about this little girl. The files on the case for which she had been sentenced to death were sealed after the Crown pardoned her, but she had already built up quite a history for herself in the Navy. Besides the disorder at Fort McHenry, Petrie had got herself on report twice during the day. Greene had complained of deliberate slowness on a work assignment for which Petrie had been rapped on the knuckles, and Schmidt had her on report to Lieutenant Costello for insolence and unnecessary noise — which probably meant screaming and cursing — for which she had been paddled. The training collar, however, had not been used at all, which meant that Petrie was making some progress.

The small pouting figure stood dejectedly on the deck, eyes red from crying, sniffling and wiping her nose on her sleeve. Her escort fingered the ferule. A sleepless sailor who didn't get pills usually got punishment.

"I don't think this is a disciplinary matter, Corporal," said Steele. She dropped to one knee and put her hands on Petrie's shoulders. "Tell me what's the matter, Becky," she said kindly. "Why aren't you asleep?" Petrie raised her head and met a clear, warm, meritocratic gaze.

For all her pride and bluster and homicidal history, Becky Petrie was, now, just a very lonely nine-year old. She threw her arms around Steele's neck and began to sob. Steele quickly reviewed everything she had been taught about disciplining both children and sailors, then decided to go with her intuition and returned the hug.

After a bit, the sobbing subsided, and Steele disentangled the thin arms from around her neck and held the nail bitten hands in her own.

"Just tell me what's wrong, Becky. No one can help you if you won't talk to us."

"Everything's wrong," said Petrie. "I hate this place; I hate the Navy; I hate this collar."

"The collar is for your own good, Becky. And you've been doing very well with it so far."

"But nobody else has to wear one. It looks like a dog collar. All the other sailors in the chicken yard were laughing at me. I could tell. And at dinner, one big guy called me a little bitch; and when I called him something back, I got paddled."

"And what happened to the big guy?"

"He got paddled too."

"Well, that's fair, isn't it? Look, Becky, practically everyone hates the Navy at first. It's a lot different from civilian life. But you have to give it a chance. Look on the bright side. Would you rather be in a penitentiary?"

"Maybe I would. They wouldn't care if I didn't sleep."

"Why aren't you sleeping?"

"Because I've been sleeping practically all the time since the Navy got me! I was sleeping on the floor in some bathroom at Fort McHenry, and then some guy there gave me a shot, and I didn't wake up again until it was after lunchtime here. Then Chief Schmidt made us all get ready for bed practically right after supper. I like to stay up late."

"All right, Becky. That makes sense to me. You'll have to get on schedule with everyone else, but we can work on that tomorrow. I think the best thing for you now is to do another shift in the chicken yard. Get some exercise and tire your body. When the watch changes at midnight you can try to sleep again. How does that sound?"

Not very appealing, Petrie thought. She liked being awake when other people were sleeping, but she didn't like the chicken shit job she'd been given in animal quarantine. She'd been assigned with a bunch of other sailors — most of them dumb ones — to scoop the sand that covered the deck in the chicken yard. It was like cleaning a cat litter bowl, Greene had explained, except that you scooped it three times with different scoops and buckets. The first time you sifted for feathers, the second time for chicken droppings, and the third time for left over feed.

Petrie had done some interesting things with cats, but scooping their litter had not been one of them. She didn't like this assignment, especially when she found out that the chief in charge weighed the buckets and could tell to the minute how much a scooper had slacked off. But she didn't want to go back to her bunk either.

"It's okay, I guess."

"Of course, it is. It's all in your attitude. Just see if you can't find something good in it."

* * *

Otto Schmidt made a visit to animal quarantine at seven bells, thirty minutes before midnight. Some of the pigs were showing signs of spacesickness, and he had to dose them every six hours.

The moon, which crossed the simulated sky designed to keep the animals functioning on regular cycles, was almost full. Instead of going straight to the pig sties, he paused at the chicken houses and looked around a moment before entering one.

The chickens slept soundly on their perches, soothed by a gently circulating breeze of warm summer air and a recorded lullaby of night insect sounds. Schmidt bent to examine the straw under the roosts, patting it with his hands.

"Looking for something, Butcher?" Newcastle and Dover stood in the open doorway.

"What should I be looking for?" Schmidt stammered bolting upright. "Chickens. And eggs. That's all that's here."

The chickens stirred. Newcastle jerked his thumb in the dumb sailor's gesture that meant "move out before you raise an alarm." Schmidt returned to the chicken yard and the two big men closed in around him.

"Coal and me thought maybe you'd be looking for a cute little kitty cat."

Schmidt stiffened. The gunners' mates knew. And it was not a good idea to get on the wrong side of the formidable pair. Just like the chicken sheds, *Lafayette*'s third deck had a pecking order. The gunner's mates as a class, and Thurgood Newcastle and Donald Dover in particular, stood at the top.

Newcastle was a dark black man, and Dover was one of those pale Nordic types who looked as though his mother had washed him in bleach. Except for their color, however, they were as alike as Tweedledum and Tweedledee — tall, heavy men who swaggered when they walked, slouched when they sat and snored loudly when they slept. They liked to fight — both prided themselves on their unarmed combat skills, picked up in barroom brawls in liberty ports across the known galaxies — and sailors who crossed them either deliberately or accidentally usually ended up in a lot of pain.

"What do you want, Chalkie?" Schmidt said anxiously. "You want part of the action?"

"No, stupid," said Dover. "There is no action. There was; but there isn't any now. That new lieutenant — Steele — found your little pet down at the dock. Now the whole bumboat operation out of Fort McHenry is closed down. Do you know how hard it was to get that set up? Years it took. Now the cover is blown and who knows when the Navy will have anything that sweet for sailors again."

"Chalkie and I had packed some nice presents for folks to buy from us," said Newcastle, "used up a lot of our leave time and spent most of our cash shopping the East Coast malls; but before we could get our bags passed through as carryons like we planned, the Fort McHenry Marines got hyper strac, turned them out and took all our good stuff. Left us with nothing but our clean underwear and used toothbrushes."

"And you know why, Butcher?" Dover hissed, poking Schmidt's chest with his finger, his face red with anger. "Your goddamn cat is why. It was a special order for the dumbos, wasn't it? Didn't come from any of us."

"Why'd you do it, Butcher?" said Newcastle. "I'd have thought you had more sense than to get mixed up with the dumbos. What did they promise you? A love charm, maybe? Anyone ugly as you are, magic won't help."

Schmidt was sweating. He hadn't talked to any dumb sailors himself. He wasn't the sort that did that kind of thing. But when the scuttlebutt came down that a med/life mate with access to animal quarantine might get some favors from the Colonial coven in return for a little cooperation, he decided to risk it. He was pretty ugly, and there was a special someone he wished would find him more attractive.

"You wouldn't snitch on me, would you, Coal? I'd get busted for sure, and I'm too old to go back to working in the bilges. I've got a few coins set by . . ."

"I'm no snitch," said Newcastle contemptuously. "But I want you to tell your dumb friends that Chalkie and I are real sore about the way they messed up the pipeline from Fort McHenry. A lot of sailors are going to be real sore when they find their supplies of little luxuries got cut off. If the dumb sailors want to avoid 'accidents' on the gundeck when the moon is full, they shouldn't make private deals in the gumboat trade."

"Especially not in organics. Especially not in live organics," Dover added. "Christ, Butcher, no one with any brains deals in that dangerous shit."

Petrie, squatting in the sand a few feet away, did not understand much of this conversation but found it of great interest nonetheless. She watched as the two big men lumbered out of the area. Schmidt let out his breath with a heavy whoosh, wiped his face with a handkerchief and started toward the chief's station by the pig sties.

Petrie coughed discreetly to get his attention. As he whirled in her direction, she dug the scoop into the sand and smiled. He stared at her crouched in the moonlight; her narrowed green eyes glittered. "Meow," she said sweetly.

CHAPTER FOUR

The first business of quarantine was to immunize the new sailors against the Pox. The procedure was far too dangerous to carry out on Earth or, indeed, in any environment that wasn't microbiologically secure. Immunization with a live vaccine produced a real case of the highly infectious disease. By deliberately exposing the crew to it in a controlled environment, cases would be relatively mild and, with good nursing care, most of the patients could be expected to survive it.

When Doctor Gordon was in charge, inoculations were done the third day out after seventy-two hours on a bland vegetarian diet. The day before inoculation, he put his patients through an elaborate preparatory protocol concluding at bedtime when they were required to drink a cup of what he called an "opening mixture." This was the first real test of shipboard discipline.

As usual, Costello used mealtimes for briefing. Already immune herself, she stayed on the bland diet for just a single day coming off a fast and breakfasted on oatmeal with soy milk and honey. Steele faced yet another bowl of vegetable mush. An unappetizing meal accompanied by unappetizing conversation.

"We'll bed them down at the regular 2100 hour lights out. That's when the real trouble will start. The squad leaders have to get their dozen or so charges to swallow Gordon's brew. I don't know what he puts in it, but it really is nauseating stuff. He insists that it has to be taken orally and there is not time to give it to a hundred or more people through a feeding tube. So we have to guarantee that he has cooperation.

"The rule is that the sailors can vomit up the mixture if the medics can't figure out a way to hold it down, but they have to swallow it. If they drink it and vomit, the reward is tube feeding on the second try. If they refuse to swallow it, they get a tube feeding, a lecture on obedience, and a paddling. Gordon insists that this system cuts down on his mates' work significantly and forms good health habits."

Steele, quite aware that she was expected to end her day with the same disgusting dose, worked at finishing off her required ration of mudd. She wondered what could be worse than this. She grimaced as she set down the empty mug, having barely managed to get down the last swallow withoug gagging. Costello mistook the reason.

"Cheer, up, Maggie. Today's going to be pretty ghastly, but if we get through tonight, disciplinary problems will be way down for the rest of quarantine. In a few days, the new sailors will be sick, which takes most of the fight out of them.

"The next challenge, the really painful shots — intramuscular and intraperitoneal injections — and most of Gordon's most disagreeable procedures, aren't scheduled until after the sailors are immune to the Pox. That means after the fourteenth day. Gordon says he sets it up this way because there is no sense in making anyone suffer through the other interventions who isn't going to survive the one genuinely dangerous treatment.

"That's what Gordon says. But there is another advantage for him to this schedule that he's not likely to give us any credit for. By the fourteenth day, if the squad leaders have done their job right, the crew will be accustomed to obey automatically. That's crucially important because it takes extra time and ties up personnel when a sailor has to be forced to take treatment. The med/life staff can't spare either if we're to get out of here on schedule. And believe me, no one wants to stay in quarantine one hour longer than necessary."

Steele would not quarrel with that statement. By the end of the day, she had set up a personal countdown calendar. On her honor as an officer and a meritocrat, she was permitted to take her cup of opening mixture into the officers' cabin and work on getting it down privately. It took every ounce of her self-control and ten minutes of yoga breath exercises. She had even more sympathy than before for the sailors who were having to take their medicine under the stern eye of a squad leader. She was glad it was on Costello's watch. The rest of quarantine would have to be an improvement; she could not conceive how it could get any worse.

The following day was a bit better — but not much. The Pox inoculation was more frightening than painful. The real difficulty was that Gordon would not delegate this duty. The dosage had to be precise; any mistake could be lethal. Consequently, each sailor had to take treatment directly at the hands of the grotesquely disfigured medical/life support officer. Fear was no excuse for a failure to cooperate, so a fair proportion were released from Gordon's clutches only to be confronted by either Costello or Steele waiting with their squad leader holding a ferule to punish them for disobedience. All in all, it was a long day. And at the end of it, Steele had to go in for the immunization herself.

It was late in the evening before Steele got her turn in Gordon's surgery. When she reported, she found Gordon examining the hands of two of his mates who had been working with him on the final shift. One of them was the veterinarian's mate Nancy Greene. The other, Paul Gabriel, was a physician's mate, a commoner who had completed medical training.

Steele recognized him; she had matched names to faces for most of the crew, and Gabriel was easier to remember than most. He looked about fifty, with a fringe of wispy pale gold hair around a bald pate. She'd understood at once when she heard Greene address him as Angel. Gabriel had dreamy pale blue eyes; and although he did his work competently, he gave the impression of usually having his mind on something else. Considering what his work was, Steele couldn't say she blamed him.

"Thank God, here comes my last patient," Gordon growled. "You two can go to bed. I can take care of the lieutenant alone."

The two mates smiled at Steele and started to leave. "Scrub again and rub in plenty of cream" he barked at their retreating backs. "If you don't take care of your hands properly, I'll have to put you in gloves, and those should be saved for surgical cases."

Steele waited for instructions. "Sit," he said indicating a chair drawn up alongside a low table. He put down a basin and emptied a pitcher of yellow liquid into it.

"Soak your left hand in this. It will feel cold at first, but then your hand will go numb. If you press your palm down firmly against the bottom of the basin and hold your fingers still, it will work faster."

Steele dipped her fingers into the basin and then jerked them back reflexively. The liquid was not just cold; it was well below freezing. She took a deep breath and deliberately submerged her hand as Gordon had directed.

Gordon watched approvingly. "That's what I like about working on meritocrats. You're the only patient I had in here today whose hand didn't have to be held in the bath. If you think soaking once is bad, you should try dipping into that stuff a few dozen times and getting splashed with it besides. All my mates have dishpan hands tonight. So do I. And I think it's more from exposure to the numbing bath than from scrubbing."

Gordon picked up a bottle of lotion, poured out a small amount, and began to rub it in. "Patients have enough to put up with without being touched by hands that feel like sandpaper."

Several minutes passed in silence as Gordon worked on his hands and Steele soaked in the numbing bath. Steele hesitated and then decided to satisfy her curiosity.

"Doctor Gordon." The physician looked up. "Are you related to the Gordon of Gordon's Pox?"

Gordon laughed bitterly. "That's another thing about working on a meritocrat. Every sailor in here today was dying to ask me that. You're the first one who actually had the nerve to do it." He examined his hands and poured out more cream. "Not that I appreciate the question, Lieutenant," he said and lapsed into silence again.

Steele decided he didn't mean to answer her. Of course it was an indelicate question. She regretted having brought it up. Then, not looking at her, his head bent over his hands, Gordon whispered, "I am the Gordon of Gordon's Pox."

They resumed sitting in silence. Then Gordon set aside his hand cream and began to speak. "You're much too young to remember the Baltimore epidemic, Maggie. It was a long time ago; I was only a few years older than you are now when it hit."

Gordon paused and sighed, probing a memory he'd worked hard to keep buried. "I was doing my residency at Johns Hopkins when the first cases came in. There must have been at least four or five commoner physicians who saw them before I did. The arrogant bastards were afraid to admit there was something they didn't understand. They listed the cases as *varicella gangrenosa* — a variant of chicken pox. Damned fools should have known three cases of something that rare would never show up in the same hospital in one day.

"I came in with the night shift. By that time dozens of people on the hospital staff had been exposed and all gone cheerfully off to their homes. Then I came into the ward. I wasn't afraid to admit I couldn't put a name to what those kids were sick with. It sure as hell wasn't chicken pox. So I blew the whistle." He shook his head sadly. "All three of those little ones died before morning."

Gordon raised his head and met Steele's eyes again, anticipating an expression of horror or disgust. He was surprised to see sympathy there. As though her kind eyes had power to draw the story out of him from the where it had been buried for a quarter of a century, Gordon found himself continuing his tale.

"The Ministry of Medicine had the whole greater Baltimore area under quarantine before dawn. It wasn't as if this was the first time something totally new had attacked us. We'd been stumbling over new viral diseases for decades, though none of them killed as fast as the Pox. Fortunately, no one from the hospital or from the kids' families had taken that evening to go for a jaunt down to Washington or take a ride over to Tokyo. They just did their normal little things. Shopping for groceries. Picking up their kids from day care. Stopping at tofu bars for an evening snack. Every one of them, as we know now, were carrying contagion within minutes of the time they were exposed to the cases in the Hopkins hospital.

"They spread infection through Baltimore good and proper. But by God's grace, they spread it only in Baltimore. The Ministry of Medicine successfully confined the epidemic."

Gordon slammed his palms on the table and jumped to his feet turning Steele's bath into a rolling sea. "And since I'd blown the whistle," he howled, "they named it for me. I got a reward. They named the vile thing for me." Gordon noticed some liquid had splashed from the pan. His emotional outburst behind him, he fetched a sponge and carefully wiped the table before depositing the sponge with others in a recycling bin. Then he returned to his chair.

"By the time I went down with it, it was officially known as Gordon's Pox." Gordon leaned back, crossing his arms across his chest. They extended scarred and bony from the short-sleeved medic's smock.

"I was the only physician on the Hopkins' staff who survived the epidemic, one of that small minority in the city with an immune system powerful enough to fight off the attack of the new virus with no help but simple nursing." He looked at his scarred arms with disgust. "This body has fought off a lot. It was only twenty-three years old when it took on Gordon's Pox."

Gordon's black eyes flashed and he barely restrained himself from pounding the table again. "Gordon's Pox! They named it after me like it was some kind of honor! You know what I kept thinking about all that summer I was doing my time in hell? I was thinking about a kid I was in grade school with. He was an obnoxious little brat; no one could stand him. His name was Arthur Spitzenburg. He became a botanist — not a meritocrat, but he was a good botanist. In the spring of 2055, a few months before the epidemic, he'd come out with a new rose hybrid. It's a really nice flower, deep purple, as close as anyone will ever get to black, with an unusually rich perfume. It has some medicinal uses too; I've got some growing in the hydroponic bay upstairs. Anyway, they named the flower after him — Spitzenburg's Rose. If there were any justice in the world," said Gordon, his voice rising in intensity, "if there were any justice in our goddamned meritocratic system, it would have been Gordon's Rose and Spitzenburg's Pox!

"I kept thinking about Arthur Spitzenburg that whole summer. They told me I was calling his name while I was delirious with the fever. Some hospital nurses contacted the Marine Corps air lift and had some of Spitzenburg's Roses dropped for me." He shook his head and smiled sadly at the memory. "Not a single one of those nurses survived."

Gordon glanced at Steele. She seemed enthralled by the story. He supposed there probably was something morbidly fascinating about hearing the story of the Baltimore epidemic from a survivor, just as there was in hearing line officers tell their old war stories. Still, he wondered that Steele could enjoy listening to this, sitting as she was with her hand submerged in the numbing liquid waiting to take the inoculation. Well, if hearing the story could keep her mind off it, she might as well have the rest of the saga of the Last Days of Baltimore.

"Once the Minister of Medicine had the word, Baltimore was sealed off fast and tight as a drum. Three divisions of Marines cordoned off the area. All the meritocrats inside turned out to supervise emergency treatment centers. We got as many of the common folk as possible involved in that work too. It made them feel that they were doing something. Not that it helped much."

The statistics were the same in 2080 as they had been in 2055, Gordon thought glumly The death rate for the Pox taken the natural way was 97% — except for meritocrats, where it was steady at 73%. There was no cure; the only weapon against the Pox was inoculation. Everything else was window dressing.

"The treatment centers prevented wild panic. They also guaranteed that anyone who died, died of the Pox and not of starvation or neglect when they were too weak to care for themselves. Toward the end, even that was a close thing. By the time the virus had attacked every hominid it could reach, there were hardly enough of us immune survivors around to carry water to those who were dying."

He checked his chronometer. The mates had been doing the soaks for him all day, getting patients into him and out again at regular intervals since early morning. Steele was the only patient he had sat with during the long preparation period. He was quite sure she was the only one who had sat so still and stayed so calm. He returned to his role as storyteller.

"Doctors were absolutely useless in Baltimore. The virus was immune to those stupid anti-viral pills Rejik developed. In fact, it's my firm belief that it was those damned pills that triggered the Pox mutation. I don't believe these stories of infection from outer space; not back then. Not before the wars. It was Marines, not doctors, who were the heros in Baltimore. The Marines kept the Baltimore epidemic from becoming a universal catastrophe. They had an awful assignment. God knows my job inside the city was bad enough, but theirs was worse. Anyone who tried to leave the area had to be shot. They tried to persuade those who ran to turn back, to go to the treatment centers. But if they couldn't be persuaded, the Marines had orders to shoot to kill. Most of those who tried to run were parents with babies or small children."

Gordon began to rub his hands again. He'd had nightmares about Baltimore for years after the epidemic. He still had them occasionally. Why was he dredging up these memories? He met Steele's eyes again and decided to continue.

"The Marines had a young general in command, still in her forties. You've probably heard of her — Susan Sparrow. She's been commandant of Fort McHenry since the last war. It was amazing how she sustained troop morale. She communicated with those of us inside the city several times a day. She even made me feel better. And that was a neat trick. Whatever it was she had worked on the Marines too. They did what had to be done. If they'd let just one cute little kid who'd been exposed out of that quarantine area, the Baltimore epidemic — Gordon's Pox to give it its accepted name — would have wiped out our species.

"If it hadn't been stopped at Baltimore, it couldn't have been stopped at all. It killed 97% at Baltimore; it would have killed 97% everywhere, our whole home planet inside two months. The meritocratic government would have fallen in the panic — even meritocrats have limits when it comes to controlling the primal fears of the lower orders — and the virus would have spread to all inhabited parts of the galaxy on ships taken over by commoners thinking they could escape. We wouldn't be at war now, of course," he concluded, "which the pacifists might say would be a good thing. We wouldn't be at war because we would be virtually extinct. There'd be too few hominids left in the galaxy for the Delphinians to hunt."

Gordon sighed, put his hands on his knees, and pulled himself to his feet. "But we're not extinct," he said unlocking the virus storage vault. "There are enough of us for the Delphinians and for the Pox virus too."

Gordon had carefully prepared the material to be used in inoculating every individual who needed the treatment. He took into account weight, general physical condition, and peculiarities of body chemistry. The Pox inoculation was Gordon's specialty. A victim himself, he had eventually perfected — as far as such things could be perfected — an immunization procedure.

The packet tagged with Steele's number was cold from the vault. One thing that was cheap in space was refrigeration. Anything that wasn't heated would stay at absolute zero. Even that extreme of cold could not kill the Pox virus, but it did slow it down. In the days since leaving the Mars orbit Gordon gradually warmed the cultures he needed to above the freezing mark. Now he set the packet on a tray next to a scalpel and allowed it a minute to come up to room temperature.

Gordon had a ritual he went through while waiting for the culture to warm. He prayed for the grace of a healing touch, crossed himself, and asked a blessing for himself and his patient in the name of the Holy Trinity. He didn't know if this prayer was essential to the procedure; he'd never dared to do an inoculation without it.

He brought the tray to the table and set it down carefully, not concerned, for once, that a struggling patient might send it crashing to the deck. He sat next to the young officer, lifted her hand from the bath, and dried it with a towel.

"Palm up, Steele. This goes in under the loose skin between your thumb and forefinger. That's how I've done it since early in the last war, so you'll get the old salt's insignia. It takes as well by the thumb as any place else, and since you're going to get a scar it may as well be an ornamental one.

"No scars on my hands," he continued as he slit open the packet with the scalpel. "Since I took Gordon's Pox the natural way, I've got scars on every inch of me except my feet and my hands. Lots of scars — no status."

Steele looked at Gordon's hands. They were indeed scarless. In fact, she noted with surprise, they were handsome. Long, very slender fingers were tipped with smoothly filed nails, buffed to a sheen, with the ghosts of clear half moons barely discernable against the snow white skin.

When he touched her, the skin of his hands was soft, and it was obvious that Gordon devoted considerable attention to keeping it that way. Steele had no doubt that he did so, as he said, to make the ordeal of submitting to his treatments no worse for his patients than necessary. It was impossible to think of Gordon as having any personal vanity. Nevertheless, the horribly ugly man had exceptionally beautiful hands.

"Don't watch, Steele," Gordon said as he gripped her wrist. "Just hold your hand steady, close your eyes, take a deep breath and relax. You won't feel a thing."

And he was right. Once Gordon had assembled his materials, he worked rapidly, made the incision, pressed in the live culture, and applied a waterproof dressing. When it was in place, he stood up abruptly. "You'll be sick in seven days," he said. "Dismissed."

Gordon was used to patients who were off like a burst from a laser cannon as soon as they had permission. He turned away and began to clean up his station. Steele watched him carefully empty the basin into a holding container, then wipe it with a sponge that went into the recycling bin. He filled a bucket with disinfectant and took a mop from a rack on the bulkhead. Since he had dismissed his mates, this was how the senior medical officer of HMS *Lafayette* would finish his day's work.

"Good night, Doctor Gordon," she said. Gordon looked up surprised to find her still there. "Thank you," she said.

And that's another thing about working on a meritocrat, Gordon thought. "Good night, Lieutenant," he said flatly and began to swab the deck.

* * *

On the tenth evening out from Mars, *Lafayette* approached the outer limits of the solar system, the line defined on Admiralty charts by the intersecting orbits of Pluto and Neptune. Beyond this point, although the Sun still exerted its power and held a variety of small satellites in its orbit, these became notably fewer. Once over the line, a ship captain could safely take a vessel into above-light acceleration.

The Pluto-Neptune line was an imaginary construct useful only to celestial navigators, and both of the planets for which it was named were far away from the point at which *Lafayette* was actually leaving the solar system. Nevertheless, the act of crossing the line, especially for the first time, was an event of momentous significance for twenty-first century sailors.

The commoners marked it with portentous rituals in which meritocrats did not participate. Indeed the absence of meritocrats during the crossing the line observances was necessary to their proper performance. This was a ceremony of, for, and by the lower orders; and it was conducted by their own popularly chosen cacocrats of misrule.

Nevertheless, meritocrats could watch provided they stayed discreetly out of sight. And it was too good a show to miss. At least that was Costello's opinion. While the sailors completed their preparations with a much laughing and clowning during the second dog watch, she brought Steele over to the mess hall, which doubled as a recreation deck.

"You have got to see this, Maggie. It's really wild. The only ceremony you'll get to mark crossing the line is the formation of the Pox pustule by your thumb. You'll start feeling that in a few hours even though you won't be tossed around and paddled first. But the sailors believe they have to hold this ceremony to make the scar meaningful. I think they even believe the inoculation won't work if they don't have this charade. Everyone who was inoculated while we were in the Mars orbit is getting the same treatment on *Lafayette's* gundeck tonight. They laugh a lot, but they actually take it very seriously."

From one thing or another they'd found in the bubble or dug out of the small bags of personal possessions sailors were permitted to bring into space, two members of the crew had been provided with elaborate costumes. At this distance, Steele couldn't even tell whether the two strangely garbed figures were male or female. One was tall and pale, representing Pluto, the god of the dead, and was made up to look like a Pox victim. Pluto wore a long white medic's smock and nothing else; arms, legs and feet were bare. The figure's head was bald, as were the heads of all newly boarded sailors; and with the painted scars, Pluto bore a distinct resemblance to Doctor Gordon.

"That's Donald Dover," Costello laughed. "They always give him the role when he's around because his skin is so fair. Doesn't he look convincing? He'd be a dead-ringer for our dear Doctor Gordon if he were just about half a foot shorter and a hundred and fifty pounds lighter."

Pluto's companion was Neptune, god of the oceans. The crew had dressed this personage as a Navy captain wearing a full display of decorations. Indeed, the decorations extended from the top of the ill-fitting tunic all the way down to the character's knees. The finishing touch was a wig and beard made out of a tangle of salad greens. Most of the medals seemed to have been fashioned out of chunks of brightly colored fruit. The bubble's galley chief was part of the costume committee, which did an impressive job. With the limited resources available, covering Neptune with decorations had been made easier to accomplish by choosing one of the shortest chiefs in the bubble to play the part.

"Don't you recognize her, Maggie? That's Nancy Greene! Oh, this is wicked!" Costello clapped a hand over her mouth. "She does look like Captain Brook in full dress."

Pluto and Neptune had climbed onto a table and were striking pompous attitudes while the other sailors who'd crossed the line before cavorted around them, giving mock salutes and otherwise aping the gestures of courtesy usually given to officers.

This show went on for a while, and then Pluto and Neptune began giving orders. Six of the old salts, wearing the bright red robes issued to patients in sickbay, gave a stumbling imitation of a Marine honor guard and brought in the first group of initiates — three sailors who had never been in deep space before.

"Originally that business of taking them through in threes probably had some reference to the Trinity," Costello whispered. "Now it's just tradition and so, of course, it's even more holy to the sailors."

The first contingent ordered to bow down before the cacocrats of misrule was certainly the weirdest trio that could have been joined together. They were all from Otto Schmidt's squad. Becky Petrie, the shortest and youngest sailor aboard, was in front and very clearly enjoying her position of prominence. Next came Waldo Bunyan, feeling conspicuously tall and stooping his shoulders to compensate but grinning nevertheless. Last in the group was Charlie Ames, skinny and awkward, trying to look bigger than he was and bouncing as he walked.

The old salts formed an *a cappella* choir and sang a mildly obscene parody of familiar hymns, in which the imitation of the usual evening prayer service was only slightly marred by occasional giggles from the tenor section. Steele recognized Gordon's mate Gabriel as the lead voice. He looked very much in character with his pale blue eyes rolled upward and was not one of the gigglers.

The Neptune and Pluto duo put their heads together the best they could given the two foot height differential and after completing their consultation gestured imperiously to a group of sailors who ran to the galley entrance and came back escorting a mate carrying three of the familiar white pottery Navy mugs on a metal tray.

The cacocrats of misrule waved their arms over them dramatically and then ordered the three initiates to drink. The giggling in the *a cappella* choir now spread to the alto section, but the sopranos and basses carried on valiantly.

Petrie, Bunyan and Ames took up the mugs and drained them. From their expressions Steele could tell that whatever was in them must have tasted awful. The three sailors got it down, but their faces all reflected disgust in one way or another. That made all the old salts roar with laughter, and the soprano section cracked up. The basses alone persisted with a strangely unbalanced musical line to accompany the ceremony.

"It's castor oil," Costello whispered. "For some reason, the crew find that terribly funny."

Pluto and Neptune consulted together again with further dramatics. The tall Pluto figure jumped up and down on the table and waved its arms about while the Neptune figure folded its arms and shook its head back and forth. Finally they appeared to agree and ordered the trio to get down on their hands and knees and crawl across the deck. They obeyed and made as much speed as they could because as they crawled, the old salts lined up along their path and paddled them vigorously.

The choir accompanied this portion of the ceremony with a parody of the *Kyrie Eleison* from some nineteenth century mass in which, at least, the giggling was evenly distributed among all four sections.

Petrie, Bunyan and Ames disappeared at the far end of the deck. Pluto and Neptune waved their arms about again, and the whole performance was repeated with a new set of sailors. Eventually the ceremony became boringly repetitious; and although the crew seemed to have lost none of their enthusiasm, Costello and Steele left.

Gordon was already in the wardroom eating his dinner. He gave his two fellow officers what was, for him, a warm greeting. "I thought I was going to be left alone tonight," he grumbled. "These crossing ceremonies make me enough trouble without having to be stuck in here listening to all that hooting and howling with nothing to take my mind off it."

"Why do you say it makes you trouble, Doctor?" Steele asked. "They're kind of noisy, but I can't see they're doing any harm." She really enjoyed seeing the sailors having a good time for a change. They didn't have much chance for that in the bubble, between the line officers teaching them discipline and Gordon giving them medicine. "Are you sure you're not just jealous because someone else is getting to give out the castor oil tonight?" she asked mischievously.

Gordon gave her a black look. "You think I enjoy that part of my work, Steele? That's the one good thing about this idiotic ceremony. I'd have to dose them in the morning — as I'll have to dose you — if they weren't getting it tonight from their mates. And Costello would have to paddle them if they fussed about taking it. It just shows how basically irrational the lower orders are. They'll be at it for hours, paddling each other and dosing each other with castor oil. When that's done to them by Costello's orders or mine they moan and groan about it. But with those Neptune and Pluto freaks giving the orders, the same thing is great fun. A lot of damned foolishness is all it is."

"Drink your mudd, Maggie," Costello interrupted. "If you encourage him he'll go on forever. Crossing the line with Doctor Gordon is always a rough passage."

Gordon was not to be deterred and continued his harangue. "The sailors connect the onset of the Pox symptoms with leaving the solar system, and they treat it as if it were a joke. Well, they will come down sick tomorrow, but that's because I inoculated on the third day out and there is a seven day incubation period. It's just a coincidence that we cross the line then. The odds are that twenty or thirty of the sailors I inoculated will be dead inside a week. This fussing around with a fake god of death and a fake god of sailors won't save anyone whose body can't produce the antibodies fast enough."

"Do you really expect that many to die?" Steele asked. Counting herself and the new volunteers, and subtracting the part of the press going out for a second or third time, there were two hundred and eighty-three people in the bubble who had been inoculated. If twenty or thirty were going to die from it, that was a mortality rate of more than ten percent. Although she knew her chances would be better because of her meritocratic immune system, Steele couldn't help but find this statistic disturbing.

"What the hell is wrong with you, Gordon!" Costello banged down her mug and turned on the physician. "One of your patients is at this table! The right to blow off steam in the wardroom is not open-ended!"

Gordon bit his lip and his face reddened, white skin taken over by a tide of dark blood. He turned toward Steele and seemed about to speak, but Costello cut him off with a dumb sailors' sign and did the talking herself.

"Listen, Maggie," she said using the calm controlled voice that Steele recognized as her charismatic tone, "If patients are carefully prepared so that they're in top condition before they take the inoculation, and if they get good nursing while they are sick, the risk of anyone dying from the Pox in quarantine is very small. There are ships where they lose ten percent. That, to be quite honest, is what is considered normal. But Gordon has never lost that many. Though you'd never guess it from the casual way he approaches his duties," she added with a black glance at the physician, "this officer does know his business. A good part of all that testing he does the first three days and the reason for making you eat this dreadful bland food and swallow his opening mixtures and castor oil cocktails is directed toward making sure that the risk of taking the Pox is minimal."

Costello glared at Gordon, whose scarred face was still blood red. "Fortunately this man is not the only medical officer on board. Doctor Parker, who's running the medical/life support station upstairs while we have the pleasure of Doctor Gordon's company in the bubble, is a psycho-neurological specialist. When she's around, *Lafayette* personnel have some protection from the psychosomatic symptoms I'm sure this man's abominable bedside manner regularly produces."

Costello's outburst was unlike her. Steele couldn't recall her giving anyone a tongue lashing this severe. It was equally surprising to see Gordon submitting to it so meekly.

Costello and Gordon exchanged a look. What both of them knew and Steele did not was that the psychological as well as the physical condition of patients who were inoculated with the Pox had a lot to do with whether they survived it. Discussion of mortality rates was not the best way to instill an attitude of cheerful optimism in a patient.

Gordon knew he should try to say something to repair the damage, but he couldn't think of anything. He muttered a brief, "Sorry, Maggie," and lapsed into an uncharacteristic silence.

Costello, not surprised that the job was left to her, picked up the conversation on a lighter tone to cover the awkward gap.

"The old salts in quarantine have other reasons to make a party of crossing the line, Maggie. Once the new sailors come down sick, Gordon takes us off this strict vegetarian diet. While they're sick, the new sailors are fed separately. If Gordon's done his work as well as he usually does, they won't actually feel too bad. Except for you, of course, everyone who's been inoculated will be off all work details and can spend the day playing cards or doing jigsaw puzzles or just sitting around gossiping."

Steele knew she would have no time off. Because meritocrats had stronger constitutions than ordinary people, they were expected to function even when they were sick. If they carried dangerous contagion, they would be isolated. But the Pox was not dangerous to anyone who had been inoculated, so there was no reason to isolate her.

"Another thing," Costello continued. "By tomorrow, the pigs and chickens will have finished their ten day quarantine and so will be approved as fit to eat. Sick or well, everyone will start to get some meat and eggs on the menu. Unfortunately, you will have a few days when you won't be able to keep down much more than chicken soup."

"That sounds delicious right now," said Steele. "Almost worth being sick for. I've always been told that Navy food takes some getting used to, but this stuff is even worse than I expected." She took a mouthful of the vegetable mash that had been her diet staple for ten days and made a face.

"You're going to be surprised at the improvement," Costello laughed. "Actually, Gordon is a good life support officer as well as a good physician. He has a very talented group of cooks at work in the galley. Once we're upstairs, where Katie McDougall is chief, we are going to be very well fed indeed."

Thinking about food was a favorite preoccupation for sailors, commoners and meritocrats alike. Memories of dinners past and the promise of others to come put Costello in a good mood.

"There's something else too," she said and gave Gordon a smile to show he was forgiven. "When we go to full acceleration, medicinal alcohol gets added to the ration. Most hominids need a mild tranquilizer if they're going to spend a long period in deep space. Our ship's doctors decided that except for those with special sensitivities, alcohol is the best drug for the purpose."

Costello leaned back in her chair, anticipating future pleasures. Steele knew she liked her bit of brandy. "In deep space, all sailors are entitled to what the crew call their 'grog ration.' Most of them take it as beer, but they can have just about anything they want within the limits of the prescribed dose. That means that you and I can have wine with dinner or brandy at bedtime. Gordon even has some sweet liqueurs in his pharmacy, if your tastes run in that direction. Captain Brook actually drinks rum and water — real grog. None of the rest of us can stand it."

"What about you, Doctor Gordon?" Steele asked, trying to bring the med/life director back into the conversation. He was still looking glum, and she was sorry to see that Costello's sarcastic scolding had upset him so much. "What will you drink when medicinal alcohol is added to the menu?"

Gordon shook himself out of his musing. If he'd done Steele any harm with his thoughtless reference to mortality statistics, obvious brooding about it would only make it worse.

"Alcohol isn't included in the clean plate rule," he said in what he hoped sounded like a jovial manner. "I have to eat my spinach and drink my orange juice with the rest of you. But I do without alcohol. The only thing in stock on *Lafayette* that makes me feel good is laudanum. Since I can't have that, I stick with quinine."

Gordon's attempts at light conversation were the despair of everyone who was exposed to them. Costello rolled her eyes to the deckhead. Damn that man! He was trying, but now their junior lieutenant was staring wide-eyed at the ship's senior medical officer who had just casually confessed to a craving for opium.

Gordon, realizing too late that he had clumsily created another awkward situation. Not knowing what else to do about it, he excused himself and left the table, explaining that he had to check his Pox cultures to make sure they were still virulent in case anyone had to be reinoculated.

Steele watched him go, her eyes round and her mouth open.

"We have to make allowances for him," Costello said. "He's in a lot of pain. He's very close to burnout, and he knows it. Any commoner in his position would have been retired on a pension years ago. As an officer, he's bound by his oath, and the Admiralty will work him to his limits until he's dead. Just as it will do to you and me. Get used to it, Steele, it's part of the job."

"Can't anything be done for him?"

Costello shrugged. "Not by a line officer. He's the doctor. Parker works on him when he'll tolerate it. I won't let her near me if I can help it. Parker's a Colonial, you know. Doesn't give us much choice in health care providers — a dumbo doctor or Richard Gordon."

Costello got up and bused her dishes. The raucous sounds of the crew laughing and singing as they celebrated crossing the line by beating and dosing their mates still echoed through the bubble.

"I've got to monitor the signal station now. Captain Brook will give us a signal when he's ready to accelerate so we can prepare our people for it. You'd better get to bed; it's easier if you can sleep though it, and you'll be sick in the morning anyway."

Costello checked the navigation instruments at the bubble's emergency helm control and did a series of dead reckoning calculations in her head. *Lafayette* was a good two hours from the line, but that was cutting it close. Time was running out on the unfinished business she'd left behind at Fort McHenry.

There had been no message from Susan Sparrow. If none arrived by the end of the watch, she would have to open communication with *Lafayette* and relay a signal to London. Once *Lafayette* was in deep space, communication with Earth would be slow and dangerous. She had given Sparrow as much time as she could.

Costello sat at the small signal console in the bubble and fingered the keys lightly. The apparatus looked like a child's toy compared to the elaborate equipment on *Lafayette*'s bridge. It was capable of transmitting only to *Lafayette* unless she reprogrammed it to send out radio waves. Such transmission had little use in space — the waves were slow and spewed out in all directions, where they could be picked up by any curious ear. The radio was for signaling when one wanted to be heard, for sending out a warning to keep away if the bubble were set adrift while carrying contagion. The message Costello needed to send was confidential. She'd either have to code it or have Captain Brook forward it for her, which would be awkward.

A Marine whose duty it was to strike the bell came to the signal station and looked at her curiously. Costello ignored him as he pounded out seven bells and left her alone again. Thirty minutes to the end of the watch. Costello took a pencil and a sheet of paper from the recycle basket and began to work on a coded message to the Admiralty.

Engrossed in her writing, she was startled when the signal apparatus whirred to full power. Captain Brook had activated it from the bridge. His image appeared on the screen, and he was equally startled to find her already sitting there.

"Something very strange just came in, Lieutenant," he said. "It's a copy of a recent issue of *Navy Times*. It came with an attachment designating it as urgent and directing it to your attention. I hope it was not too urgent; it appears to have been routed through Mars."

Brook obviously wanted some explanation, but Costello put on her quarterdeck face and gave him just a plain, "Yes, sir."

"Do you need paper copy?" That meant powering up the printer as well as consuming supplies.

"Yes, sir. I'm afraid I do."

"Well don't let Gordon recycle it. Save it for the wardroom when you get out of quarantine. None of us have seen a newspaper in a long time. This one is only a week old."

The printer powered up and began to spew out sheets of paper. "I glanced at it on the screen when it came in," Brook said as they waited for the printout to be completed. "The lead story is on Fort McHenry. Do you know this Melnitski fellow?"

"Who, sir?"

"Edward Melnitski. He's taken over command of Fort McHenry."

"Oh, no, sir. I don't know him."

"But you do know General Sparrow."

"Yes, sir."

"I assume there must have been some very good reason why *Lafayette* was ordered to break signal silence in order to get this to you."

"Yes, sir." Brook clearly expected more, but Costello held on to her quarterdeck face and said nothing. Brook frowned, and then his eyebrows flickered.

"In that case, I won't ask you what it was." He knew, Costello realized. And he knew it was a subject that she was bound by honor never to discuss. Her interview with General Sparrow was now as if it had never occurred.

"I hope they're still running the crossword puzzle," Brook said. "I always enjoyed those. I'll signal when I'm ready to take us over the line." The screen and the signal apparatus went dead. Costello scooped up the sheets of paper, folded them, and began to read.

The change of command at Fort McHenry was the lead story for the week and there were profiles of both Edward Melnitski and Susan Sparrow in the center section.

Costello smiled at the photograph of Sparrow; she was looking remarkably well. In the photograph, she was wearing some kind of frilly, flowered thing that was about as far from a Marine uniform as you could get. But she still sat tall — the hypererect posture that old Marines kept from habit. On her lap sat a silver tabby, also sitting tall with alert eyes facing directly into the camera. The photo caption read: "General Susan Sparrow,

UEMC (Ret.) and her cat Contraband relax at the Old Sailors Home in Newport, Rhode Island."

Costello flipped to the back of the paper where long columns of small type recorded transfers and reassignments. As she expected, there had been a good bit of activity in and out of Fort McHenry. Both Sergeant Major Pollard and Staff Sergeant Larkin were on the list. Whatever had happened at Fort McHenry, there would be no scandal in the Marine Corps. Before she resigned her command, General Sparrow had cleaned her house.

CHAPTER FIVE

During the last evening in quarantine, Steele and Costello had the unusual experience of sharing a meal with a cheerful medical officer. Since Doctor Gordon's usual manner was morose, it wouldn't take much to brighten up the atmosphere. But Gordon wasn't simply less gloomy than usual; he was downright ebullient. He bounded into the wardroom, a broad grin on his face, and ostentatiously added a twist of lemon to his usual glass of tonic.

"A little extra something to spike up the quinine," he announced, stretching out his long legs and giving every appearance of intending to enjoy himself.

"Well, well," said Costello. "It's Doctor Gordon in a merry mood. To what do we owe this gleefulness? Has one of your viruses had babies?"

"No, my dear Lieutenant Costello," Gordon chuckled. "No little mutants today." The idea of virus babies amused him. His original medical specialty was pediatrics. The needs of Earth had forced him to take up a career in epidemiology, and the wars had forced him into a life aboard Navy ships. He'd never spent much time with babies. He supposed he never would.

"No virus babies," Gordon repeated. "In fact, Lieutenant Costello, I have the pleasure officially to report to you that we are clean. Absolutely, one hundred percent clean. There is no disease at all. No one is sick. No one is about to be sick. There are no sick sailors, no sick chickens, no sick pigs; no sickness at all.

"And let me add to my report the interesting statistic that in this entire quarantine period, no one has died. Except for the fool who broke her arm clowning around when we crossed the line, I don't even have anyone listed as injured. I just finished analyzing the last set of blood tests, and I am now absolutely certain that everyone's shots for everything took. I can lift the quarantine on schedule tomorrow and release a full complement of healthy sailors into *Lafayette*."

"That is good news! Even Lillian Shaper is going to make it then?" Shaper had been a matter of concern from the beginning. The middle-aged Colonial was a true test of the Navy recruiting slogan, "The Navy can use anyone." In the wake of a failed relationship and frustration with a dead-end job, the flabby-muscled woman with flat feet and a heart murmur had impulsively decided to run away to space. The recruiters promptly signed her up, and before she had time to think about it, she was on her way to HMS *Lafayette*, with an aptitude profile describing her main talents as sculpture, flower arrangement, and holography. She had motion sickness aboard *Primrose* and had never been entirely well since.

"That's right. Even Shaper." Gordon preened as though he had just perfected a cure for death. "Blood tests showed the malaria immunization took full effect days ago. Temperature, blood pressure, everything normal. But she kept hanging onto her blanket and cried when anyone tried to take it from her and get her out to work. I finally got so frustrated with that case that I sent a Colonial orderly back to think-talk her." Costello wrinkled her nose in distaste.

"Don't go prissy on me, Liz," said Gordon. "I do many things in sickbay you might not like to watch. The Colonials are used to think-talk. It doesn't bother them to submit to it."

"Sorry, Richard. I suppose it's no worse than pumping out her stomach. Especially if it worked."

"It did work. First thing Shaper does is pick up some elementary sign and start shaking her hands — 'I feel cold.' So I decided to go after the symptom, issued her a winter uniform even though it's July, and — behold! — now she's in the galley in a watch cap and sweater, chopping veggies and arranging salads, happy as a pig in mud."

"So you've got a perfect score! That's damned near unbelievable! Congratulations!"

"Unbelievable," Gordon chortled, "definitely unbelievable! I've had clean quarantines before but never from a port as infected as Earth, and never with a new press. Somebody or something brought some magical good luck into the bubble." He gave Steele a huge grin and a wink, a truly macabre display of ivory teeth against white lips below a flashing coal-black eye.

"Why, Captain Brook ought to put me in for a commendation, maybe get the Crown to give me an oak leaf cluster for Galen's ring." He inspected the large silver ring on the middle finger of his left hand with satisfaction.

"Well, how about that, Maggie! Doctor Gordon's come to dinner wearing a display of decorations. Does that mean we get an extra bottle of wine on the table tonight?"

"No way," Gordon growled, sounding more like his usual self. "I'm not feeling so self-confident that I'm going to permit substance abuse." He examined his ring fondly and gently rubbed the stone with his cloth napkin. "I just felt I deserved to have this thing out where I can look at it for a change. A ring is a damned impractical award for a physician. I usually wear this lump of metal on a chain." He rested his hand on the table where Steele could see it.

"Old Doctor Galen didn't know about microbes and probably never washed his hands. He used this ring the way I use chemicals and a microscope. It helped him diagnose illness and gave his hand a healing touch. The stone is supposed to stop hemorrhaging." Steele studied the deep green stone flecked with red and engraved with the figure of a man wearing a bundle of herbs around his neck.

"I've been tempted to try it a few times," Gordon said. "But if the magic in Galen's ring doesn't work, I don't want to know."

"Did that ring really belong to Galen?" Steele asked. The Greek physician had lived in the second century of the Christian era. There was something awe inspiring about being in the presence of an object so old.

"He definitely had one that matches this description, Maggie; but the experts say they can only confirm its provenance back to the sixteenth century. Queen Elizabeth I of England presented it to her court physician Doctor John Dee. It was lost for several centuries and then returned to the collection of crown jewels. I'm the third physician to receive it as a royal award. When I die, it will be returned to the reigning monarch and awarded to someone else." He pulled the ring from his finger and passed it across the table. "You can hold it if you like."

It was a thick, heavy ring and deeply engraved. There was something ironic about awarding such an ornament to a man who spent much of his time up to his elbows in infectious materials. She looked inside the band where three sets of initials were etched into the metal.

"D.M.M.," she read. "Dolores Magdalena Mendez," she said looking up at Gordon. "Right?"

"Very good," he said. "I'm glad the schools are still teaching medical history." Actually, Mendez was an easy one. She had found the generic cure for cancer. Her research, the first all-resource design, had been prompted by the late-twentieth century AIDS epidemic. Concluding that the presuppositions of so-called "scientific medicine" were blocking progress, she deliberately surveyed all healing modalities ever known in any Earth culture for possibly effective forms of intervention. From acupuncture through blood-letting, chemotherapy and on to reiki, rolfing, sorcery and zen meditation she tabulated what had once worked for someone somewhere. The result of her research was an all-source computerized prescription which any particular individual could use to find the most probably effective program to follow.

Once sufferers began to test the Mendez cure, it seemed so obvious, straight-forward and simple, that it made the painful, mutilating, and only partially successful treatments used to treat cancer victims in earlier years seem barbaric. History teachers had a hard time explaining to children that twentieth century physicians were generally well-meaning though ignorant people and not vicious sadists.

"Can you identify the next one, Maggie? Who was S.C.R.?"

"Stephen Calvin Rejik," Steele answered promptly.

"You're pretty good at history, aren't you? Yes, good old Stephen Calvin Rejik. Given some hindsight, Queen Anna Maria should have had him shot instead of giving him a decoration. Cure for the common cold! That's what he got the ring for. He didn't just cure the common cold, he came up with an all purpose virus killer. Just great. It killed all known cold-producing viruses. And because everyone who got a sniffle started swallowing the damn Rejik pills, we suddenly had a planet full of mutating viruses. It was worse than the penicillin resistant bacteria that were already killing us. One of the new viruses killed Rejik. The ring stayed in the vault for a while after that." Gordon lapsed into silence.

"Until Richard Gordon came along," Costello prompted.

"Yes, until Richard Gordon came along," the doctor said with a sigh. "Richard Gordon with his primitive program of quarantine and inoculation." He held out his hand, and Steele returned the ring. Gordon closed his fist around it, feeling its weight.

"Back there in Baltimore, waiting for the Marines to lift the quarantine and raze the city after everyone who was going to die was dead, I passed the time reading medical history in the Hopkins' library. That was what we did in those days when faced with a problem that seemed to have us licked. I learned what techniques had been used to control smallpox before cowpox inoculation had been discovered and before those damned pills of Rejik's were around. After Baltimore, everyone was alert for signs of the Pox, and victims got slapped into quarantine fast; but there was enough slippage to show the need for immunization in high risk areas. So I experimented. I learned to minimize risks. And when the Delphinians started mining our space lanes with the Pox, I worked in Navy quarantines."

Gordon held the ring in the tips of his fingers, his eyes focused on the figure engraved on the stone. "I killed a lot of people," he said. "I saved a lot more. So Queen Anna Maria took the ring out of the vault again, and just before the end of the last war I got a decoration. I guess I deserve it as much as Rejik did, though I'm no Doctor Galen. I'm no Doctor Mendez either, for that matter — never had that kind of imagination. Haven't had the kind of computer support she had either, not since I've been doing my work in space. But I do what I can."

"And we all love you for your sweet disposition," Costello smiled, "and for bringing us through a clean quarantine."

Gordon returned the smile. It was a surprise to Steele to see that the deep black eyes could still radiate warmth.

"That's right," he said replacing the ring on his finger. "No one died in this quarantine. For once there's been no blood on my hands." He darted a mischievous glance at Steele. "Only figuratively speaking, of course."

Steele smiled at him and rubbed the scar that had formed at the base of her thumb. She might still die in space; but thanks to Doctor Gordon, it wouldn't be from the Pox.

"If your war on microbes gets too dull on this voyage, maybe Captain Brook can find something for you to do on the gundeck," said Costello.

"No thank you, Liz," said Gordon. "As a physician, I am bound by my oath never to wage war against anything my own size." Abruptly his manner darkened.

"And my war won't get dull. It's going to last much longer than your war against Delphinus. There will never be anything more than a temporary truce in my war. Rejik proved that."

"How early can I take the crew out of here?" Costello recognized the signs; the doctor's victory celebration was over. It was time to make arrangements for the morning.

"Any time after 0530. But you won't make yourself popular with the people upstairs if you start that early."

"All right. Let's plan on giving the crew one last meal down here, and we'll unseal the hatch right after morning prayers."

Gordon nodded, stood up, and left without saying goodnight.

* * *

Costello never dawdled through prayers. On the morning quarantine was to be lifted, she read through the service at an even faster clip than usual. She slammed the book shut, dismissed the crew, and fired up the signal console to request permission to leave the bubble in what seemed one unbroken movement.

"All set," she announced cheerfully to Steele and Gordon. "Hall has the duty and is on his way down to unseal the hatch. Last one out's a rotten egg!"

Gordon snorted. He'd be the last one out. He'd spend most of the day in the bubble, making sure that it was properly cleaned, refitted and sterilized for the next time it was needed.

"Officers first, for a change," said Costello. "Hall will take charge of the crew. After you've reported to the captain, I'll give you a complete tour of the ship, and neither of us will have to stand a watch for twenty-four hours. What a beautiful day! Just so we don't get a battle alert to spoil it."

Lieutenant Henry Hall had graduated from Annapolis with the Class of 2077. Steele knew him slightly and didn't like him. Of course, he'd been a firstie and she'd been a plebe. His job had not been to make himself loveable.

The only way into the ship from the bubble was through the main hatch, the vessel's central mast, which ran from the bubble to the bridge, a ten foot diameter tube of weightlessness, through which sailors could propel themselves to any level of the ship. For most purposes, sailors used ordinary ladders or ramps that connected decks and levels within decks. Costello went up first, and gave Steele a hand through the few feet of weightlessness before the hatch opened into the isolation bay on the lowest level of *Lafayette*'s third deck.

Superficially the decor in isolation resembled that in the bubble, but the few differences were striking. First was the presence of sunlight, simulating that of a bright July day, streaming through the thin curtains covering artificial windows. In the bubble's independent life support system, the energy needed to produce sunlight was not expended except in the animal quarantine where it was needed to keep the livestock on accustomed time cycles.

The second difference was the air. It smelled sweet! The odor of disinfectant permeated the bubble. The fresh air was like perfume.

Hall gave Costello a hug and Steele a handshake to welcome them aboard. Steele looked him over, hoping to find him more appealing than she remembered. Hall was of medium height, medium build and medium complexion. Steele thought his eyes were too close together, his nose too long, and his lips too narrow. She knew it was wrong to judge people by their appearance, but she just didn't like his looks. Now that they were serving together, she'd have to make an effort to overcome that prejudice.

"I'm glad I'll be senior to someone now," Hall grinned at her. "I've been junior to everyone since I came aboard."

A joke, Steele decided. Meritocrats never took pleasure in superior rank; their pleasure was to serve. Now she remembered something else she disliked about Hall. He had a very strange sense of humor.

She forced herself to return the grin, and Hall got a flash of blue eyes and dimples that he had rarely seen but had always hoped to tease out when he was at the Academy. The last time he had seen Steele, she had been just short of fifteen. Growing up sure hadn't done her any harm.

"Let's get out of here," said Costello. "I'll take you through the whole med/life station this afternoon, but right now I'm dying to get out under the open sky." She thrust her clipboard at Hall. "They're all yours," she said. "Watch out for the grommet. She's more trouble than she looks."

Costello led the way back into the main ladder and, grasping rope handholds, the two officers propelled themselves toward the gundeck. On the way, they passed two sealed hatches that gave access to the most secure area on the ship, the 'tween decks, which housed the arsenal, the main engines and the brig.

The third hatch opened at the center of the gundeck. The immense chamber gave the illusion of being open under an Earth sky. It was flooded with the brilliant sunshine of a July morning at the latitude and longitude of Greenwich, England.

"Nice, isn't it," said Costello. She lifted her arms, turned up her face toward the synthesized sun, and stretched with unconcealed pleasure. "It isn't always like this, of course. The light changes with the time of day and with the seasons. We get our share of bad weather both to save energy and to make sure we can readjust to Earth. And when we go to general quarters, all the amenities go. But the aerographer's mates have standing orders to give us perfect weather when a crew comes out of quarantine."

Steele was speechless. It was one thing to read about shipboard weather control in a textbook and something else actually to stand under a blue sky with a flock of fluffy white clouds and breathe what seemed for all the world to be naturally ionized fresh ocean air.

Costello laughed. "When you get your head out of the clouds, have a look at the rest of it. Since this refitting at Mars, *Lafayette* is more beautiful than I've ever seen her. Brook made sure we got nothing but the best. He think's it's important for morale to have a good-looking ship, and Gordon agrees with him. So we've got what is probably the handsomest home away from home in the whole Navy. After a few engagements, we'll have to patch in here with the same synthetics in use on the other decks, and some of the glitter will be gone from this big tub. But just look at her now!"

Steele glanced around and got the impression of polished metal, bright paint, and smooth wood. The main mast, which besides the gravity-free ladder contained the ship's gravity stabilizer, heat controls, and air filtration system, was painted blue and gold on its outer surface and disappeared through the "sky" into the top deck. An alcove was built into the mast about a third of the way up, and in it was a huge, vividly painted bust of the young Lafayette, Lafayette as he must have looked on the day Cornwallis surrendered at Yorktown. The head was thrown back and the mouth was open and laughing.

A broad, royal-blue circle was painted on the deck between the central mast and the circular bulkhead. The numbers of the weapon sections were painted on it in gold so they could be read from the command station at the mast. The spaces between the numerals were filled with bands of gold stars. Six ramps outside the circle led to the engine bays. Four ramps inside the circle, barred with metal gratings, led to the armory and magazines.

The bulkhead itself, between the weapon banks, was also decorated with blue and gold paint. The gundeck had a strangely cheerful appearance for a chamber designed for the work of death and destruction that was *Lafayette*'s mission in space. If Steele hadn't known exactly where to look, she would never have noticed the tell-tale bulges in the bulkhead that indicated where the heavy armament was stowed.

Gun bays ringed the circular deck. They were arranged in nine sections, each of which contained nine weapons banks stacked in tiers nine high connected by ladders and catwalks. Each bank was equipped with a full assortment of artillery pieces, from short-range anti-asteroid guns to long range lasers with a killing range of up to ten light minutes.

When the crew was at full strength, two dozen sailors went to each bank when at general quarters. At the moment, there were sailors at only three sections. Most of them were on their hands and knees buffing the deck while others were on the catwalks and ladders repeatedly running out and stowing the weapons, drilling for speed.

"It's a little gaudy," Costello said, "but it's just the thing for the commoners. And I have to admit I love it too — especially that big bust of Laughing Boy. It's an antique a group of grateful citizens purchased for *Lafayette* near the end of the last war. I don't think there's another ship in active service with anything like it."

"Look at this," she said, squatting to rub the deck. "We even have real oak planking here on the gundeck. Brook likes it because it's traditional. Gordon likes it because it's a healthy surface for bare feet; and the Admiralty likes it because they could shuttle out the planks from Earth and get them cheap."

"And I like it," a voice broke in "because hand buffing it every day keeps the deckhands out of mischief."

"This is Lieutenant Roderigo Rivera," said Costello, coming to her feet and holding out her arms to the new arrival. Just as Hall had, he welcomed her back with a hug. "Rod's our first officer and gunner and expert in beating the devil to the punch by inventing ways to fill idle hands with useful work."

"That's nine tenths of a gunner's job," said Rivera cheerfully. "While eighty percent of the crew is below decks slaving away under med/life's indulgent command, doing the work that keeps us all alive, I have to keep our fighting force occupied."

Rivera was a big, heavy-set man. No hint of emaciation here: space travel obviously agreed with him. Steele admired his coffee-colored skin, warm brown eyes, and thick black hair with a cowlick that fell onto his forehead. Rivera pushed it back with what was clearly a habitual gesture.

"And you must be the new navigator," he said with a grin. "We've been reading all about you. If you're half of what they say you are, we can expect good hunting on this voyage."

Steele blushed. "Our instructors at Annapolis set high standards for us."

"I don't mean your grade transcript, Lieutenant. I mean this SOCRATES stuff. Costello faxed out the Thanatos article for us.

Brook took it on paper and had it bound. We've been passing it around the wardroom. Very impressive piece of work Thanatos did there. Looks very promising."

Rivera kept an eye on his sailors even as he seemed to be giving Costello and Steele his full attention. Catching sight of some impending problem on a ladder, he flashed the "duty calls" sign and ran over to attend to it. A moment later a roar of laughter rose from the group gathered around the officer.

Steele was surprised by the sound. Except while crossing the line, sailors in the bubble had few occasions for laughter.

"Don't be fooled by Rivera's casual style of command," said Costello. "He's got that lot broken. He's not like that in the bubble. He's a lot tougher than I am, really scares the hell out of them. But once he's got them tamed, they eat out of his hand. By the time they're released from quarantine all he has to do is let that big boyish grin fade out slowly, and it's as effective as a ten-minute tongue lashing from any of the rest of us. He took most of the people he's working with now though the quarantine just before ours. You can tell by the clipped hair."

"Will our sailors laugh like that?" It hardly seemed possible.

"Believe it! They'll react to the sunlight and fresh air just the way you did. Compared to what they had in quarantine, they'll be very happy with their berthing arrangements and work assignments. The Navy has something for everyone, as they say. They'll tuck away a couple of Katie McDougall's good meals, and then they'll muster up here with everyone else for evening prayers. By the time Brook has got them singing 'Eternal Father,' the new people will be feeling as if they'd gone to heaven and joined a force of the heavenly host under the command of the Archangel Michael. Even Brook can't hold morale constant at that pitch, but he'll get it up there this evening. If you want to see a miracle, watch the Colonials. Going from Gordon in the bubble to Brook on the gundeck always gets to their kind especially."

Costello took a last look around. It felt good to be back home. "Time to get you topside. The captain has very precise ideas as to exactly how long it should take an officer to get from quarantine to the bridge."

Passing from the gun deck to the bridge was like going from day to night. It was always night on the bridge. The dome that covered it was an observation window looking out into the cold blackness of space. In order not to interfere with visual or telescopic observation, and to conserve energy, lighting was restricted to small red lamps. Costello and Steele passed the sentry and halted at the hatchway to allow their eyes to become accustomed to the change and saluted the aft section where they knew the flag would be.

Lieutenant Hall was on the bridge. Apparently he'd made quick work of turning the crew from quarantine over to Doctor Parker and her mates on the third deck and returned in time to confirm quarter hour log entries.

It all looked very familiar to Steele. Top-deck mockups of all classes of Navy ships were used in training at the Academy. "I suppose my berth is on the third level behind the wardroom in with all the spare parts and canned goods."

"That's the tradition, Number Five," said Costello. "The more junior you are, the farther from the bridge you bunk. Think you can find the way? Hall has the cabin under the captain's gig. You're over by the escape hatch."

Steele needed only an instant to orient herself. The main ladder opened only onto the bridge. Access to the two lower levels of the top deck was either by ramp or by straight metal ladders. Steele crossed the bridge toward the extreme right, letting her fingers brush the metal railing to guide her through the darkness. She swung herself onto the ladder and slid down to the second level.

Costello was right behind her. "I've got the middle cabin," she said pointing. "Lamashtu is behind me, and Rivera's over there, behind the captain's day cabin."

The second level was brighter than the bridge. The deckhead had the appearance of a translucent skylight spilling sunlight into the narrow corridor. "It's a little darker on your level," Costello nodded toward the second ladder. "Let's go check it out."

The third level of the top deck was dominated by the wardroom, the largest open area in officers' country. With the officers' galley, it filled half the space. Most of the rest was allotted to docks for launches, the small craft used to rendezvous with another vessel or to go to ground. The larger part of *Lafayette*'s fleet of launches was docked on the top level of the third deck, but three, including the captain's gig, were stowed on the top deck below the bridge.

The third level's deckhead, like that on the second level, was a translucent skylight, but scarcely any light came through because the top two feet of the corridor were used by the galley for storage. Nets filled with foodstuffs from Earth that could not be produced or obtained in space hung in every bit of spare footage on the ship. Similar conditions, Steele knew, prevailed at the beginning of a voyage on the third deck, although there the need for security required that food be stowed only in guarded areas. As the months passed, sailors ate themselves into more head and elbow room.

Steele could walk upright along the corridor; but Costello had to stoop. Steele easily found what she was looking for — a narrow door built into a cranny between a launch bay and the galley. "Mine," she said.

"It's either the junior officer's cabin or a broom closet," Costello responded. She pushed open the door. "Funny," she said. "Inside it looks just like mine."

Officers' cabins were all identical. This one was virtually indistinguishable from the one Steele and Costello had shared in quarantine, except for the lighting. When the door opened a small round porthole lit up. It displayed not only sunlight and clouds but a holographic recreation of an Earth sea.

Steele's space duffel had been unpacked and the contents stowed in a concealed wardrobe that also held a commode and washstand. The bunk folded up into the opposite bulkhead. Beneath the porthole stood a small desk and a single chair.

Somewhere above, a Marine pounded out three bells.

"I'm going to report to the captain now. He'll be expecting you to report as soon as he's finished with me — I'd say half an hour. He's probably in his day cabin at this time of day, but when you get to the bridge, Hall will tell you where to find him."

"Any wise advice, Liz?"

"I'm sure you've seen Captain Brook in the holographs. That's exactly what he's like in real life. He always talks as though he's dictating his memoirs—very formal, calm and serious. He's a stickler for traditional courtesies, so do a good checkout of your rigging. And don't smile unless he does."

Steele's dimples flashed.

"I know what you're thinking. Our captain has the reputation of being a first-class tartar, but he's really not like that. Sometimes when I watch him deal with Doctor Gordon, I think he has the patience of a saint. Anyway, the Thunderer's bark isn't as bad as it's made out to be."

The more sensational reporters of war news liked to refer to the commanding officer of HMS *Lafayette* as George "The Thunderer" Brook, and everyone knew how he had acquired the nickname. Enormous passion was concealed under Brook's chillingly formal exterior; and, especially in his younger days, occasionally it had burst forth in Jovian rages. Such outbursts were extremely rare, because Brook worked hard to control what he viewed as a weakness of character. Nevertheless, those who witnessed Brook in a rage never forgot it.

The best-known incident had occurred on a troop hospital ship in Moon orbit near the end of the First Galaxy War. Brook had gone aboard to visit Lafayettes who were undergoing treatment there. He had a quick look around and that was enough to convince him that the hospital director was deficient both in compassion and in respect for human dignity. Doctor Antonio Lear, Brook concluded, was a flawed meritocrat unfit to serve in a position of authority.

Without hesitating, Brook prepared to perform his duty under the meritocratic code of honor. Halting in the middle of a ward through which Lear had been escorting him, he told him he wished to speak with him alone. Brook's fierce expression was a clear signal of what he had in mind, and Lear had tried to put him off. As a result, Brook had delivered his challenge then and there, demanding Lear's resignation right in front of a ward full of commoners, at full volume, and using language that made the Marines and even some of the younger sailors blush. The medical staff had cheered.

Doctor Lear had refused to resign voluntarily and his subsequent retesting for meritocratic fitness had been a memorable scandal. Lear failed the examination and when last heard from was working as a veterinarian in the Ukraine. Queen Anna Maria formally censured Brook for conduct unbecoming a meritocrat, since he had done in public what he should have done in private. And Brook, a deeply religious man, spent the entire period of his shore leave on Earth — his first in many years — in a monastery in Antarctica doing penance for the sin of anger.

The commoners connected with the hospital, both patients and staff, hailed the Thunderer as a hero. They took up a collection; and, knowing that meritocrats could not accept gifts from members of the lower orders, purchased some valuable antiques as a gift to the ship. These included the bust of Lafayette now in a position of honor on the gundeck.

Steele took the ramp from her cabin across the lower level up to the captain's quarters on the other side of the ship. A Marine stood guard at the head of the ramp. Close by, the captain's runners sat cross-legged on a bench. The three Colonial sailors, two boys and a girl in their early teens, had hair grown in enough to show they had been in space for a while, and they wore their dixie cups as top deck etiquette demanded. Their fingers flashed in rapid conversation until they heard the Marine rattle her rifle in salute. Then they put on sober faces, dropped their legs over the edge of the bench, and sat on their hands, their eyes following Steele curiously as she entered the captain's day cabin.

The captain's work quarters were wedged-shaped, with two full sun windows forming the angle opposite the door. On this bright day, sunlight was reflected from the polished surface of his desk, which was bare except for a thin leatherbound book, a pen, and a model of *Lafayette* supported by a silver spike that ran through the bulging bell-shape and defined top and bottom for the model just as the central mast did for the ship.

Brook stood to greet his new officer. He was a man of average height and build but gave the impression of being taller because of an upright posture that fell just short of the Marine brace. Thick, wavy white hair and a neatly trimmed white beard were both soft and lustrous, clear evidence that it had been a long time since Captain Brook had been through quarantine and an equally long time since he had set foot on land without a space liner. He carried his seventy-three years with a flair that made men of forty seem callow.

With a gracious gesture, he invited Steele to sit in one of the two visitors' chairs which, with the desk, filled most of the deck in the cabin.

"I am uncomfortable with this, Lieutenant. Very uncomfortable." Brook settled himself in his chair, lowered his heavy eyebrows and picked up the book in front of him. It was neatly bound in pigskin with gold lettering identifying it as an article by Admiral Theodore H. Thanatos reproduced with permission from United Earth Naval Institute *Proceedings*. The instruction manual, as Costello called it, that came with his new officer merited special handling.

"Lieutenant Costello described to me a conversation concerning your training that you had with her prior to your embarkation. It was her opinion that you yourself have some misgivings about this innovative procedure. Is that correct?"

"Sir, misgivings is too strong a word. I have confidence in the Admiralty and in the instructional staff at Annapolis."

"As she reported the conversation to me, Lieutenant Steele, you declared yourself to be 'scared shitless.'" Steele blushed scarlet. Brook reached for a bell pull to summon a runner, who bounded in a moment later knuckling her forehead in the approved gesture of respect.

"Return this to the wardroom," the captain said loudly handing the book to the girl. Although Colonials usually had excellent hearing and no difficulty understanding English, Brook could never rid himself of his conviction that anyone unable to speak must have difficulty hearing. The girl took the book, nodded, knuckled again and dashed out.

"It is my opinion that the wisest course will be for us to work around your innovative training. It is quite difficult for me to imagine what it would be like to have a subpersonality come on line in an officer I had become accustomed to working with. I would prefer to train you myself in my own way to my own standards. We have a very close relationship on the bridge, as I am sure you know. We are so familiar with each other's character and habits that we respond as a unit during emergencies, each confident of how every other officer will react in any given situation. I wish to be certain that the Lieutenant Steele who is reporting this morning is the one who will be serving at navigation when we go in harm's way."

"Sir, I would promise you that if I could. Though I respect Admiral Thanatos, you are my commanding officer and if you say forget something I learned in school, I want to obey you. But the training was very thorough. We were told what we were learning was set so deeply into our personalities that even Delphinian torture couldn't root it out."

Brook frowned. "Then we have a problem. Or, I should say, I have a problem." Brook steepled his hands and regarded Steele over the tips of his fingers. Aside from her eccentric training and unusually youthful appearance, the new lieutenant seemed promising. He'd had a very favorable report on her from Lieutenant Costello, and Costello was not easily impressed.

"Have you had any sense of the presence of this subpersonality of yours since you've been aboard?"

"No, sir."

"Are you quite sure of that?"

"Yes, sir. It feels like there is someone else with us when it happens. That's what we were told. And it won't surface unless we're under high stress."

"Many officers find duty in quarantine stressful."

"Yes, sir. It was stressful, sir. But it wasn't stressful enough to trigger SOCRATES."

"Then, if I understand you correctly, you will know with absolute certainty that you are operating out of a new personality when your training has, as you put it, been triggered."

"Yes, sir. That's correct, sir."

"In that case, we will consider your condition to be a potential psycho-neurological problem. We can cope with that. Whenever you detect the presence of another personality, in however faint a degree, you are to inform me and report immediately to Doctor Parker — no matter what you may be doing, no matter what the hour, day or night. Badly as I need an officer at navigation, I would rather have you in sickbay than behaving erratically on the bridge during a crisis."

"Aye, sir."

"Am I correct in assuming that your subpersonality is equally bound by the oath you took at commissioning and will not act in any way in disobedience of orders?"

"The oath is sacred to both of us."

"Then we should manage well enough. It may well be that after medical/life support personnel evaluate your subpersonality in a clinical setting, there will be circumstances under which it may safely be utilized on the bridge." Brook stood. "We will meet again at the evening service, Lieutenant. Dress uniform is worn at prayers and at dinner. The watch bill is posted in the wardroom."

* * *

When soft chimes woke her shortly after three bells in the third watch, Steele thought for a moment that she was back at the Naval Academy. Swinging out of her bunk, she began breath control exercises and set her sidearm to charge, reflexively performing routines she'd performed repeatedly in a battleship mock-up. As she came fully alert, the brief surge of stress hormones triggered by being startled awake was followed by a stronger one as she realized that this was not an Academy drill.

Her movements remained automatic as Academy training meant them to be. While her personal weapon charged, Steele continued controlled breathing and pulled open the wardrobe in which her space liner hung ready. The thin material, clear, elastic, and strong as a second skin, created a complete biostatic environment. It was a one-size-fits-all garment that stretched over the wearer's ordinary clothing — except boots. Officers and Marines shed their footwear at general quarters. If ordered to the launches, whether with a boarding party or following an order to abandon ship, space armor with boots was ready at the air lock.

Within the ship, unless there was biological contamination, the liner was only partially sealed. Steele's fingers moved over the pressure clasps and buckles, following the drill: stockings, jumpsuit, face mask hung in front, helmet hung behind, pistol belt, and finally the seven-point safety check of the belt and weapon before it was strapped in place.

As Steele performed these actions, both her body and mind were preparing for combat. The body sensations were automatic and unpleasant but familiar: increase in heart rate and blood pressure, surface constriction of blood vessels as blood left the skin to provide the muscles with more sugar and oxygen, a queasy stomach and an urge to evacuate. The mental preparation, designed to soften the impact of the stress hormones, was to detach emotionally and intellectualize.

Steele felt her body's increased nervous-system activity as her clammy hands worked rapidly over a final check of her rigging. Stuffing the gloves into her belt, she deliberately tightened her sphincters and continued to force her breathing into a deep slow rhythm as she felt the temperature in the cabin fall.

Steele considered how the ship reacted to the alarm just as her own body did. The cabin porthole blacked out, replaced by dim red emergency lighting. On every deck, energy was diverted from non-essential life-support activities into the engines and the weapons banks.

This abstract train of thought had the desired effect. As Steele bounded from the cabin her stress response was already fading. Before she reached the bridge, her hands were dry.

Costello was working all three bridge stations — signal, navigation, and helm. Such versatility was expected of every lieutenant. In theory, one meritocratic officer alone could drive and fight the ship — there was a saying that so long as one officer remained alive, the ship would be alive. In theory also, one well-trained sailor could handle a full bank of weapons. In practice, it was better not to push to theoretical limits.

Costello slid over to the signal station; Steele, whose place at navigation was between signal and helm, picked up the other two. The three officers' bridge stations worked together: signal found the target, navigation figured out how to get them to it, and helm, in cooperation with the engineering station in the 'tween decks below, took them there.

Steele checked out her two stations and found them both in "wait" status. "What are we hunting?"

Costello shrugged. "Don't know yet. There's nothing on the scopes. Whatever it is may have gone to cover."

Neither officer considered the possibility that whatever it was might have been readying for an attack. No ship in space would challenge *Lafayette*. She was always the hunter, never the prey. Nothing would dare challenge the behemoth of Earth's Navy.

Indeed the recurrent tactical problem for a battleship commander was to ferret out enemies and force them to stand. Self-protection was never a primary consideration in action unless *Lafayette* should by some fluke find herself pitted against a fleet. And in the vastness of space, fleet activities were confined to staging areas or regions close to inhabited planets of high strategic value. Fleets did not cruise randomly.

The soft chime that signaled a general alert continued to sound. In the dim red light, half a dozen captain's runners at their assigned position by the mast waited for orders. Around the periphery of the bridge, sailors on duty for the watch recorded external hull and space conditions for the regular quarter-hourly log entries.

Captain Brook stood at the rail by the main hatch studying his chronometer and occasionally glancing into star-streaked space through the dome overhead.

"Probably pirates," Costello said as she watched the captain. She couldn't tell from his apparently random observations through the dome where he expected to find their target. "We have to go after those pests every time we spot what looks like a renegade merchant vessel."

Extermination of piracy was part of the Navy's mission from the earliest days in space. Even in the midst of a war for species survival, the selfishness of common hominids from all the inhabited systems tempted some to go into space to make a dishonest profit. For them, the wars were just another opportunity to steal and sell. In recent years the most tempting trade was with the Delphinians. The enemy found hominid pirates agreeably willing to hunt and barter their own kind.

"I hate pirate chases, especially this deep out. A bunch of cowards, mostly. Don't have the guts to stand and fight or to blow themselves up. So we have to run them down and board them. Then there's all the tedium of putting on a prize crew and taking them in convoy to a prize port. Thank God I won't get this dirty job. Someone else will take command of the prize crew; I've just put in my time in quarantine."

Costello was awfully talkative, Steele thought. Pre-battle nerves. It reassured her to see the lieutenant felt it too. At least she wasn't alone.

Navigation was still in wait status. Steele called up an update from engineering and confirmed readiness at the helm. Hall arrived on the bridge, his gloves in his hand, stuffing them into his belt as he slid into the helm position.

At once, the chimes stopped. Brook said something to his runners and all of them disappeared down the hatch.

Brook approached the control center. Holding his chronometer in one hand, he pointed at Hall with the other.

"Too slow," he said.

"Sir, I was in the head. I'm sorry sir."

"I did not request an explanation, Lieutenant, and an apology is inappropriate."

Costello and Steele kept their eyes on their equipment, running the protocols to secure from general quarters, pretending they hadn't heard the exchange between the helm officer and the captain. If the captain planned to reprimand someone, it should be done in private.

Hall, however, was off the hook. Brook dismissed him and released the con to Costello. It was Steele who was required to accompany him to the privacy of the day cabin.

The windows came on as he opened the door. Dawn was breaking. It would be another fine day. By the main mast, a Marine hammered out three bells.

Brook motioned Steele to a seat and stood for a few moments watching the first rays of the sun illuminate the gentle motion of a calm sea. He was puzzled by the results of his drill. Running this kind of exercise was expensive. He didn't do it often, and he didn't do it without a good reason.

Now that all new sailors had cleared quarantine, Brook wanted to confirm that the ship was prepared for action. On the third deck, the waisters, who had no direct combat functions, nevertheless had battle stations. An early-morning drill would give the medical/life support officers and Marines who operated under their supervision an opportunity to check out their readiness. But there were less costly ways to do that. This drill had been to confirm the readiness of Lieutenant Steele.

Steele made it to her position as rapidly as any of the senior officers, a shade under what might be expected factoring in the location of her cabin and the timing of the drill, intended to wake her from deep sleep. Her rigging was in order, and she had gone about the business of handling a double station calmly and without fuss.

Perhaps that should not have surprised him. This kind of performance was what the Naval Academy promised to deliver. It was not, however, what he had gotten from the Academy in the past. More specifically, it was not what he had gotten in the case of Henry Hall.

Hall had been on board for three years now, starting as an ensign and earning promotion to lieutenant, Brook had to admit, only because Brook had relaxed his standards. Hall's time on the drill was only fractionally worse than usual for him. The bridge had become accustomed to function with only two officers at command and control in the early stages of an action. Since the tragic loss of Lieutenant Shankar, Costello had handled all three stations alone, occasionally even after battle had been joined.

Brook had anticipated that Steele would reach her station in approximately the time that Hall had managed when he first reported to *Lafayette*. It did not seem possible to him, despite her lieutenant's commission, that she could actually pull her full weight on the bridge immediately. And yet she had.

He turned to face her. "I am forced to ask you a difficult question, Lieutenant, which you must answer on your honor. I expressly forbade you to undertake any duty on this ship while you were under the influence of SOCRATES. Have you violated that order?"

"No, sir."

"Very well, Lieutenant. You are dismissed."

CHAPTER SIX

Days aboard *Lafayette* blended into a pattern of shipboard routines. The unexpected happened at night. Why this should be the case in space, where night was endless, could only be explained by the determination of the ship's designers and the medical/life support teams to maintain an illusion of natural Earth cycles.

Hominids — officers and crew alike — were diurnal creatures. Accordingly, work was scheduled for daylight hours; only a few people rotated into night shifts. These included Marine sentries, sickbay personnel, sailors who stood watches on the bridge, and, of course, the officers. Except for the officers, everyone who worked nights got double time off to compensate for the stress.

For officers, stress was the job. The captain and the medical/life support officers were on call around the clock, and the five line officers stood either the first or second watch two or three times every week. These watches were either very dull or filled with unpredictable activity.

As a result, the breakfast hour in the wardroom was a favored time to share scuttlebutt. So it was at seven bells on a morning late in September; Maggie Steele had the watch when four of her messmates gathered around the table to share a meal and the story of how Charlie Ames had almost gotten himself defenestrated during the night.

"He must have been planning this break in for quite a while," said Rivera, digging into a plate of bacon and eggs. "When the Marines grabbed him and hauled him to me on the bridge, he had a nice collection of burglar's tools on him."

"I don't like to search folk at engineering after a shift." Martha Lamashtu shook her head and poked at her cereal. "Seems like I let this boy down by leaving him too much open to temptation."

"Don't be silly, Martha," Costello broke in, pouring herself a mug of mudd. "None of us wants to run a station like a prison. It would kill morale if we did that. And you especially! Daily strip searches would definitely be out of character for Big Mama."

Lamashtu chuckled and sipped her mudd. She'd done plenty of searches in her time, but her preferred method of managing sailors was to let them know how much she loved and trusted them and how very disappointed she would be if they ever let her down. For her, it worked.

A heavy black woman with snow-white hair, Martha Lamashtu had been in space since she was sixteen, and she had been tending the machinery on *Lafayette* since the battleship was first commissioned during the First Galaxy War. But she had been an ordinary sailor, taking orders from meritocrats, until, to her surprise, she got the call to meritocratic service and was returned to *Lafayette* as a commissioned officer.

When Lamashtu first joined the Navy, the "Old Navy" as they called the pre-war service now, she had been flunking out of school and been arrested twice for vehicular theft. The meritocratic authorities gave her a choice between the Navy and a reformatory. Her parents encouraged her to join the Navy, hoping some time in space would straighten her out, and, for once, she'd taken their advice.

It seemed that the Navy did straighten her out, and far beyond her parents' expectations. She'd gone from blue to red stripes on her first tour. She'd been the black sheep in a family of seven children, and they were all pretty surprised when Martha came back to Earth with commendations from her meritocratic officers and announced that she meant to reenlist and make a career in the Navy. She often wished her parents had lived to see it. Both had died before Lamashtu returned from her first tour.

Lamashtu had been back to Earth only once since her commissioning, but it had pleased her a lot to see how much pride her brothers and sisters took in her qualifying for the meritocracy. As a meritocrat, Lamashtu felt no personal pride. But it was good to know she was no longer the shame of the family.

Lamashtu never broke the strong emotional ties to her kin on Earth. Although she had only erratic contact with them through ship-to-ship mail drops, she thought a great deal about her brothers and sisters, her nieces and nephews, and now a flock of great-nieces and nephews, many of whom were already old enough to have children of their own. To her, the growing Lamashtu clan symbolized Earth's people, for whose benefit she had spent almost half a century in space.

"It's the Marines' job to search lockers and the bunks," said Rivera. "After they picked up Ames, they were all hot to turn out all hands in the middle of the night to make sure nothing else had got by them. But we all know that complete security is impossible on the third deck. There are lots of places to hide things. Ultimately it wasn't Ames's tool collection that was the problem; it was how he decided to use it."

"Did he really go for the ship's store?" asked Hall, spreading honey on a muffin. "I can't believe anyone would be that stupid. Break in anywhere else, and the sailors wouldn't give a damn. That's an officers' problem. But risk contamination of the store? You'd have humans and Colonials fighting over who got to push him out an airlock."

"He isn't real bright," said Lamashtu. "Rod roused me up to check out the lock. Looks like he was after the cakes and pastries. Probably nothing on his mind but the sweets he can't have until he's earned them."

"But all the sailors know there's a lot more than that in the store," Hall persisted. "There's the supplement to the grog ration, for one thing. Those who've got the clearance to buy extra on Saturday nights would kill anyone responsible for cutting off the beer for the rest of the cruise. And how about those Colonials who got clearance to burn candles and incense once a month? Gee, they might not toss him out the airlock outright for getting their supply of weird stuff confiscated, but they say they've got these curses . . ."

"For God's sake, Henry," Costello interrupted. "You sound like some superstitious sailor."

"Henry's right about the ship's store being something the third deck powers agree on," said Lamashtu. "Ames may not be thinking so right now, but he is real lucky that the Marines caught him before he broke through the seal. Gordon would have shut down the store for sure, and the whole crew would be out to get the sailor who was responsible."

"And the Marines who failed to stop him," Costello drained her mug, and reached for the pot of mudd. "So what else happened on your watch, Rod?"

"What do you think?" Rivera grinned. "I sent runners to wake up Martha to check things out below, and I called the captain. Brook decided that since everyone involved was awake, there was no reason not to hold mast at three in the morning. Twenty minutes later, Ames was in the brig with instructions to consider the state of his soul and to meditate on the punishment he'll take at noon."

"And who's going to get that dirty job?" Costello reached for a muffin. "I've lost track. Is it you, Henry?"

"I think it's going to be Maggie," Lamashtu interrupted.

"What makes you think that?" Costello set down her mug.

"Captain told me he was thinking of giving it to her. Asked my opinion. I said I thought it was a good idea."

"Martha, how could you!" Costello pushed her plate aside. "Maggie hasn't even witnessed punishment worse than paddling. She's nowhere near ready for something like this."

"Captain Brook asked me what I thought. Didn't ask me to speak for the wardroom, just for my own self. I'm the one whose been training her at a secondary specialty. She's been doing real well, even supervising the sweepers out on the hull. I think she's fit for every job on the ship right now, and I don't think it's good for her to be over-protected."

"I agree," said Rivera. "We've had her on board for two months now. I, for one, would like to get a look at what SOCRATES has produced."

"Brook ordered Steele to keep the lid on that." Hall finished off the last scraps on his plate and drained his mug.

"That's not it exactly," said Lamashtu. "She's under orders to report to sickbay when it surfaces. She says she won't be able to control it, anyway. When it's triggered, it will take over no matter what she does."

"This whole business is just too spooky for my taste," said Costello. "I don't see how you and Rod can be so enthusiastic."

"I expect it to be a lot like what happened to Martha," Rivera said. "Maybe it was spooky, but it sure was a good thing for the ship."

"What was it like for you?" Hall asked. He knew that Lieutenant Lamashtu had become a Lieutenant just recently. She only outranked him by about a year. But she seemed so much a fixture in the wardroom that he could scarcely imagine her serving as a common sailor.

"It came over me gradually about five years ago." Lamashtu cradled her mug in her hands. "I already had almost forty years toward my pension but didn't feel like retiring, and I'd drifted into doing volunteer work with some younger sailors who were having trouble adjusting in space."

"What she means, Henry," Rivera chimed in, "is that she was involved in shaking some sense into the grommets and other trouble-makers who seemed hell-bent on getting themselves hanged as quickly as possible."

Martha shrugged. "It's not a bad hobby for a middle-aged sailor with frustrated maternal instincts. Anyway, the med/life folks were the first to realize something was going on. I wasn't getting sick as much. In fact, when they started analyzing the records, they found I was on sick call as infrequently as officers were and was having much faster recovery than average when I did go down with something."

"So Doctor Gordon ran a chromosomal analysis," Rivera interrupted. "And when he saw clear signs of a meritocratic pattern he booted up the computer, produced a full report with schematics, and trotted it up to the captain."

"Who then sent a runner to trot down to engineering and fetch me," said Lamashtu. "Can you imagine what that felt like?" Of course, they couldn't, she thought. There were some things these early hatching meritocrats would never understand.

"Officers don't just invite you in to chat when you're a common sailor." she continued. "When you get a personal invitation to report, it means big trouble. And here it was the Thunderer wanting me. A summons from the first officer is bad enough, but to get one from the captain! You better believe I was one real scared sailor!

"I hot-footed it up the ladder, wracking my brains to think what awful thing I could have done and thinking I was probably going to be busted to blue-stripes and thrown in the brig. Then, when I get to the top deck, I realize it couldn't be anything like that because I'd climbed up under my own power without an escort. If I'd done anything bad enough to get busted for, it would have been a squad of Marines, not a Colonial blue-striper who came after me.

"So I calmed down a little, but I sure wasn't relaxed. And then when the captain gets me in his cabin he asks me the strangest question. He says to me in that rumbly voice of his, 'Chief Lamashtu, if I were to arrange for you to have a fortnight leave in New Australia, how would you spend the time?' That's some question, huh?"

"If I ever heard those words, I'd be sure I'd died and gone to heaven," said Costello. "Nobody gets two weeks' shore leave in the middle of a war. Two days even doesn't come very often. And New Australia! The playground planet of the Pleiades! I guess I could find some ways to pass the time!"

"So could I, if I ever got asked again," said Lamashtu, "which, of course, I won't. But back then, when I tried to think of an answer, I found I wasn't coming up with visions of ice cream parlors and tropical beaches. When I opened my mouth, I told the Captain that if I had two weeks, I'd turn myself in for the meritocratic examination."

"He didn't divert us to New Australia, of course," said Rivera. "But he put in to the Naval Station at Stormy Rock where they had a testing facility, and two weeks later we had a new meritocrat and a new officer. Damndest thing I ever saw happen, and awfully good luck for *Lafayette.*"

"Do you think it might go that easily for Maggie?" Costello asked thoughtfully.

Eight bells sounded, and Hall left the wardroom for the bridge. A moment later, Steele appeared. Her watch had been uneventful except for one course change to avoid a dust cloud, and she was hungry for breakfast.

She picked up a plate of eggs and bacon and took Hall's place at the table. Costello poured her a mug of mudd.

"The captain wants me for something," she announced as she dug into her food. "Told me to eat first and then report. Anybody here have any idea what it's all about?"

"Drink your mudd, Maggie," Costello said.

Steele took a swallow and grimaced. It was more acid than usual. Doctor Gordon must have decided to dose them all with extra vitamin C again. Someone on board probably had a cold.

Steele took two more swallows and set down the mug. The other occupants of the room watched her as she began eating again. After a few moments, she became aware of the unaccustomed silence.

"What is this? Watch Junior Lieutenants Drink Mudd Week?" she demanded.

Costello coughed, picked up her dishes and excused herself. Rivera stood and followed her example.

"So you all do know what the captain wants with me," she said, taking a muffin. "Only you're not telling." Lamashtu reached over and gave her hand a squeeze before clearing her dishes.

"All right, I go in with no hints in advance," Steele said as her messmates left her alone to finish her breakfast.

Ever since Steele had been identified as a meritocrat at the age of seven, she had been told a lot about what she could expect in her adult life. It would be a life of sacrifice and dedication and never-ending work. What no one had ever even suggested was that some of it might be enjoyable.

Meritocrats were expected to embrace their duty cheerfully, but they were not expected to be happy. The biggest surprise Steele had after entering Annapolis and joining the Navy was that she genuinely enjoyed the training and the work. It was no hardship at all to maintain a cheerful attitude. She assumed that all that would change once she went into space, but it did not.

She did not enjoy all her work, of course. Much of quarantine had been dreadful, especially during the last two weeks when she had worked in a fog of fever and nausea. During that period, Lieutenant Costello took over more than her share of the watches and of unpleasant duty. Perhaps if she'd forced Steele to do a larger share, she would have discovered the secret about Navy life that she seemed so far to be entirely missing. This life was not supposed to be enjoyable. It was not supposed to be fun. But for Steele it was.

A few weeks earlier, Steele began to think that if this apparent abnormality didn't disappear pretty soon, she ought to turn herself into the captain to have her fitness retested. Somehow even that thought did not depress her, and when she asked Costello about it, the Lieutenant only laughed.

Steele was actually relieved to learn that the captain intended to give her a special assignment. That meant one of the ship's dirty jobs. Costello did two of them in return for a brief shore leave and a chance to visit with her children for a few hours. She made a condolence call to notify next of kin of the death of a fellow officer, and she took command of the bubble during quarantine.

Usually, Brook assigned dirty jobs as they came along according to a rotating schedule that he would modify only under unusual circumstances such as those that got Costello the missions on Earth. Hall and Rivera each had a turn in quarantine while *Lafayette* took on new sailors in the Mars orbit. Lamashtu had a special assignment of some sort between the time that Costello went to Earth and the time they left the bubble, but Steele didn't know what it was. The senior officers didn't tell her everything. She was still being babied.

Steele sipped her mudd and made a face. This disgusting drink was the only thing so far she really hated about the Navy. Below the predominant flavor of iodine she was now also aware of an undertone of licorice and garlic, substances that Doctor Gordon praised for their medicinal properties. Steele didn't mind garlic, but she loathed licorice and the two in combination produced something indescribably awful. She took a deep breath, drained the mug, and went topside to see the captain.

"I am extremely particular about this procedure, Lieutenant. I will not inflict pain without purpose. If flogging is to be more than a useless torture, it must be carried out with dignity. Strict observance of our rituals and traditions when punishment is administered is a matter of great importance to our sailors; it is their guarantee that punishment is neither arbitrary nor capricious but will be precisely the same for every sailor in every equivalent circumstance."

Brook meant to take his time briefing the new officer. Such briefing would not have been necessary had he chosen to give the assignment to Lieutenant Hall. Brook decided to involve Steele for two reasons. First, he could measure her capacities only by testing them; and, second, he was reluctant to trust Hall with something this sensitive.

Since acquiring his newest officer, Brook had made up his mind to get rid of Henry Hall entirely at the earliest opportunity. Despite his meritocratic certification, Hall appeared to lack the capacity to become an effective Naval officer. Either that, or he was not willing to put out the effort, which came to the same thing. Brook preferred being short-handed to being burdened with an unreliable lieutenant.

When *Lafayette* reached the Pegasus station, Brook would see to it that Henry Hall transferred off. Perhaps another captain would have better success with him. Meanwhile, he would keep Hall on routine assignments where he could do no damage.

He was confident that his new officer was reliable. All she lacked was experience, and he could take care of that.

"There are three challenges facing an officer assigned to supervise punishment. The first is the personality and psychological condition of the offender, the second is the emotional response of the commoners to the offense, and the third is Doctor Gordon." He sighed. Gordon's inevitable involvement in a flogging case was a strain on both the physician and the captain.

"Doctor Gordon must certify an offender fit to receive the punishment. He always raises objections. Matters of discipline are clearly outside his circle of authority. Nevertheless, before certifying fitness, he feels it necessary to point out, at tedious length, that flogging does not promote physical well-being. I then point out that flogging is not prescribed as a health tonic but for the psychological and spiritual benefits it may be expected to bring both to the offender and to the sailors who are required to witness it. None of this need concern you. Gordon and I have this conversation every time I order punishment. I suppose you could say it has become part of the ship's tradition.

"There is an additional complication in our dealings with the medical/life support station in this case, however, because of the nature of the offense. The physicians suspect that Charlie Ames may have a pathological craving for refined carbohydrates. That, of course, in no way reduces Ames's culpability or requires any mitigation of his sentence. Nevertheless, Doctor Gordon felt it necessary, for his own purposes, to run a series of metabolic tests on Ames as close to the time he made his attempt to secure access to sweets as possible. Doctor Parker and a series of med/life mates have been in and out of the brig, drawing blood and whatever else they needed, at intervals throughout the night.

"I would have preferred that the offender's time of confinement be uninterrupted and solitary," Brook continued. "A period of enforced solitude and silence prior to punishment encourages introspection and a narrow focus of attention. Unfortunately, in this case, the medical concerns appeared to me to be valid and to take precedence. My apprehension now is that the extensive involvement of the med/life station may confuse the offender. Whatever his impressions so far of his time in the brig, it is important that he understand that he is primarily the subject of disciplinary action, not of medical intervention. I assume that from your experience with Doctor Gordon during quarantine you will have developed your personal style for dealing with him."

Steele had learned during quarantine that managing the medical/life support director was no easy matter. He would push to get his way until he exhausted you, if you let him. The only solution, so far as she could see, was for the line officer to be clear and persistent and not allow the physician to fog the issue.

"Fortunately, except for his possible confusion about the significance of his preliminary contacts with med/life personnel, I see no difficulties arising from the mental state of the offender," Brook went on confidently. "I easily brought him to a state of repentance and contrition during mast. He made a good confession. It will not be necessary for you to break a rebellious spirit, which means that your task will be considerably easier than it might have been."

That was certainly true, Steele thought. There had been some nasty cases in the bubble in which sailors being punished had been stubborn or insolent under correction so that she — or more usually Costello — had to keep at it until they submitted. The mere memory of these scenes made her stomach churn, and she regretted that she had been required to eat such a large breakfast.

"Another favorable circumstance is the outrage the lower orders feel toward the perpetrator of this crime. There will be no need to convince them of the justice of the punishment. Rather, you will be obliged to guard against a possible excess of enthusiasm in those commoners who will be directly involved in its administration. Do you understand why the ship's store is so important to our sailors?"

"Yes, sir. It represents their liberty, their freedom to choose." That was the textbook explanation, and it summed it up pretty well. By allowing an oasis of free choice in the tightly controlled environment of a warship, sailors had an approved focus for their exercise of personal will — and the officers, by their power to permit or deny access to that privilege, had an effective and unobtrusive means of discipline.

To enjoy the privileges of the store, sailors needed appropriate approval forms from med/life support and enough cash to pay for what they wanted. The chief source of funds was their Navy pay, gold and silver coins handed out twice a month by the officer of the day. These metals were the common currency of the known universe. Pay could be supplemented by private barter for goods or services.

Pressed sailors served without pay and had no access to the store for their first three months in space. Then they were offered an opportunity for early reenlistment as volunteers. Rarely did anyone refuse to take the Queen's coin, for taking it meant the end of their stigmatized status and admission to all the rights and privileges due to free volunteers, including access to the store.

The sailors voted on what the store would stock, and the meritocrats laid in the items selected provided that they were not on the contraband list. Most of what the sailors wanted was things to eat and drink beyond the standard ration. Some of these were brought to the ship and stored frozen; others were produced aboard the ship from ingredients purchased for the purpose.

The store also stocked clothing authorized for wear off duty and on shore leaves, writing and craft materials, playing cards and puzzles, and musical instruments. These last were especially popular with the Colonials, who spent a disproportionate amount of their pay on such things as bells, harmonicas, dulcimers, and ukuleles. A few of the Colonials also demanded candles, incense, and an assortment of exotic items from their home planet.

Profits from the store subsidized other luxuries for the crew; most of it went to draw energy for Monday night football holographs. To the third deck, the ship's store represented all the innocent pleasures possible in space.

Brook resumed his briefing. "It is traditional on *Lafayette,* to have formal punishment administered by our gunner's mates rather than by Marines. It reenforces for the sailors the perception that serious crimes for which they are punished are offenses against their fellow crew members not against a superimposed authority structure.

"I have already informed Chiefs Dover and Newcastle that they will be wanted for disciplinary duty this morning. In that way, I have also assured the insertion of this information into the third deck scuttlebutt. This will quiet any grumbling that might otherwise occur if the sailors suspected that the culprit in this case would receive more leniency than matched their impressions of justice. The chiefs will already have begun making preparations on the gundeck where they will be highly visible at this hour." Brook lowered his eyebrows and stroked his beard.

"Before you go to take charge of them, I feel it necessary to make reference to one other matter." Steele clasped her hands together uneasily; she was afraid she knew what was coming.

"Lieutenant Costello told me about the physical problem you had during quarantine when it was necessary for her to punish a sailor for stealing a weapon." Just what she was afraid of. Steele felt herself redden. Of course Costello would have to report it, but it had been horribly embarrassing.

The sailor involved was Becky Petrie, who, even when she should have felt too sick to do anything, retained a taste for malicious mischief. Having discovered a ploy by which to evade nighttime surveillance, Petrie had managed to take possession of a knife, slaughter a chicken, and use the blood to write rude remarks on the decks and bulkheads in the messhall during the graveyard watch. The Marine who discovered it happened to be a firm believer in ghosts and ran to Costello, reporting in near hysteria that the bubble was haunted.

When Petrie was punished, the theft of the knife was a small part of the charge. Costello was most concerned about Petrie's stubborn persistance in trying to pin the blame on Kathy Clark in whose bunk she chose to conceal her new toy.

Costello expressed her exasperation to Steele. Petrie required severe punishment but there were few options in the bubble. Everyone in the bubble was already in confinement. The food could hardly be worse. And since she weighed less than a hundred pounds, Petrie was not fit to take as much chastisement at one time as Costello believed was appropriate. So Costello had spread it out over a week.

Steele's "physical problem," as Brook expressed it, had come during the third and final session, which Costello insisted she witness. The girl's buttocks were by then a mass of bruised flesh, still swollen and inflamed from the earlier paddlings she'd received. She was substantially less able to bear chastisement than she had been before, but Costello was determined to have her case done with and made her take the whole balance due.

When it was over Petrie was in agony. Costello decided that she would allow Petrie to spend a few days out of uniform and sent Steele to pick up a red robe from sickbay.

Gordon got a look at her on her way through his station and didn't like what he saw. As soon as Petrie was dismissed, the doctor had stamped into the wardroom carrying a basin and a hypodermic syringe, and grumbling that he hoped he wasn't too late to save Steele's breakfast for her. He'd ordered Steele to drop her trousers and take up the position Petrie had just abandoned.

Costello was furious. She shouted at Gordon that line officers had to learn to control nausea without drugs. A lot of their work was nauseating. War was nauseating. Steele would just have to get used to it.

Gordon shouted back that he was giving Steele a medical order. Vomiting could lead to dehydration, and Steele was already vomiting more frequently than was good for her. She could get used to the nauseating aspects of command in space after she was out of his quarantine.

Without intending to, Steele put an abrupt end to this debate by actually getting sick in the basin. Gordon then put away his needle, and Costello told her curtly that she needed to work on deep breathing techniques to keep her physiological responses under control.

Brook paused and observed Steele as she remembered this event, relying on her memory to make his point for him.

"I am aware that you were undergoing a series of inoculations when that incident occurred, and I will assume that was the explanation for your loss of control. Nevertheless, I want to emphasize to you, Lieutenant Steele, that there is no place in the modern Navy for an officer who is squeamish about pain and blood. Naval warfare isn't what it was before we went into space. This isn't an old-fashioned push-button war we're fighting. When we engage an enemy it means close action. I am not one of those who will wastefully destroy a ship that might profitably be taken as a prize. When you take out a boarding party, the pain and blood and death won't be coming from some invisible enemy so that you can hardly distinguish the situation from some peacetime accident such as an explosion in a mine or aboard a merchant tanker. What your sailors suffer and the suffering they inflict will be face-to-face all the way. The deliberate infliction of suffering is what war is about. I will accept no excuses if you lose control of yourself in such situations. Do I make myself clear?"

"Yes, sir."

"Very well. The most important thing for you to remember is that you are preparing Ames to participate in a ceremony. It is appropriate for him to fear punishment. Indeed, the more he fears it, the more effective it will be and the less physical suffering it will be necessary for him to endure in order to achieve the desired results. But his fear must be controlled. I want no displays of mindless panic.

"Anything that can be done to help him maintain his dignity should be done. But if he cracks at any point — and he probably will — you must take care to observe the formal routines described in *Naval Regulations* that are designed to preserve an illusion of dignity. May I assume that you are acquainted with the governing articles?"

"Yes, sir." Experience only came with service in space, but *Naval Regulations* could be studied on shore. The cadets at Annapolis virtually memorized what had grown, by a process of accretion, to several hundred thick volumes of law, tradition, and advice. Some of it, unfortunately, was contradictory or outdated. In deep space captains had blanket authority to overrule most of it if they judged it "necessary or convenient and in the best interests of Earth" to do so. But Brook with his strong sense of tradition respected *Naval Regulations* almost as much as he did the *Book of Common Prayer.*

"Very well, then. Newcastle and Dover are waiting for your orders. Have Ames at the forward ramp on the gundeck at noon." He took a last look at the young officer. "Dress uniform is appropriate for this assignment, Lieutenant."

* * *

The weather was partly cloudy and an early chill of fall hung in the air on the *Lafayette* gundeck. The aerographer's mates were saving energy in preparation for an October Indian summer. At four bells in the forenoon watch, deckhands could be found at their usual assignments, some drilling on the ladders as others buffed the deck.

A party of hullsweepers stood for inspection in their heavy armor, then moved off linked together by a lifeline, already walking in the shuffle prescribed for safety during outside work. As the sweepers entered the hatch leading to the 'tween decks airlock, each sailor paid close attention to the pair of gunner's mates sitting crosslegged on the platform surrounding the mast, bent over work that was not part of the ship's everyday routine. Newcastle and Dover were knotting together the tails of a whip.

The two did not look like the type who would choose macramé as a hobby, and they were not. Their handicraft work was for profit. The chiefs who did the dirty work when the officers ordered a flogging got extra pay for providing the whip. By tradition, the gunner's mates were permitted to design whips to their taste so long as they kept to the prescribed limits laid down in *Navy Regulations.* Every offender was entitled to a fresh hand

and a fresh whip. Once it had been used, the individual flogged had a right to claim ownership of the whip since he or she would be charged for it. The fee was passed on to the mates who had performed the extra duty. Few wanted the souvenir; ordinarily the instrument of punishment was put into a recycling bin.

When Steele arrived on the gundeck, she became the object of curious inspection; every hand on deck knew why she was there. Her first task was to examine the whip.

The mates handed it over, proud of their craftsmanship. The rope handle had been worked over a leather core and included a variety of fancy knots and decorative touches. Eight tails were bleached white like the handle, with the blood knots that would "scratch like a cat" made tight and evenly spaced. A ninth cord was made of braided pigskin, dyed dark red.

Steele fingered the knots in the white tails to be sure no metallic wire had been worked into them, and then examined the red "cut deep" cord. "A thieves' cat," she said.

"Yes, ma'am," Dover replied.

"Ames did not steal," she said. "His offence is 'attempted burglary.'" The mates turned down their mouths, expressing their opinion that the distinction was hardly worth making. "Take it out," she ordered. "Nine plain cords — that's it."

Dover took back the whip, traced the red cord to its root in the handle and reluctantly began to work it out of the design.

"Which of you has the duty?" The chiefs had their way of dividing up the work when a sailor was to be whipped. Newcastle indicated it was his turn to use the cat, so Dover would be responsible for preparing the gundeck, coordinating with Marine security personnel, and supervising cleanup of the area afterward.

Newcastle would stick with Steele and supply any physical force that might be needed to keep Ames compliant. Steele took him down to the brig. It shouldn't take two hours to get Ames ready and have Doctor Gordon sign off on him, but Steele couldn't be sure. Med/life operations had a way of taking far longer than any line officer anticipated; and she had no idea of what was involved in what the captain called "metabolic testing." Weighing the advantages and disadvantages, she decided to get an early start; if Gordon finished with his "patient" early, she could let her "offender" serve out a little more time in solitary. That was better than having Ames show up late for his "ceremony."

Ames was sitting on the bunk holding a Bible, the only non-utilitarian object permitted in the brig. Presumably, that was a good sign. He pulled his lanky body upright and jerked it to attention when Steele entered the cell. He looked pretty bad, she thought. His eyes were red, he was unshaven, and his uniform looked as if it had been slept in although Ames clearly hadn't had much sleep. He stared at her, nervous and frightened. When he saw Newcastle standing behind her, he started to cry. She stifled the urge to speak to him gently.

"Take him to the head; he needs a shower and a shave."

Newcastle took Ames by the arm and marched him out of the cell, muttering something Steele couldn't quite hear but which stopped Ames's crying as if he'd turned a switch.

"We need a clean uniform here," Steele said to the Marine on duty. Ames stumbled into the head.

"Wet down, soap, rinse," Newcastle growled at him as he entered the shower. "You've cost this ship enough today; don't let me hear you wasting water or you'll take a dry shave."

Ames did as he was told, and cleaned himself with two short bursts from the showerhead. Newcastle handed him a razor and allowed him another half cup of water. As Ames shaved, Newcastle stepped out into the corridor to pick up the bundle of clothing. Steele was talking to the sentry; she must be trying to find out what had been going on in the brig all night. Newcastle already knew. A flock of clucking medics, probably oozing sympathy, had been bustling around as if this were the bloody sickbay. As far as he was concerned, this was not a good start for his morning's work.

When Newcastle brought Ames out of the head, Steele inspected him again. He looked better, although he probably felt just as bad.

"All right, sailor," she said. "Let's go. Put your hands behind your back." Newcastle pulled out a pair of handcuffs; Steele held out her hand for the key.

Ames looked at her mournfully. "Lieutenant Steele, do you have to use these things on me?"

Steele ignored the question and checked to see that Newcastle had not closed the cuffs too tightly. He'd been tempted to do just that, but remembering Steele's insistence on removing the cut-deep tail from the cat, he changed his mind.

Doctor Gordon met them at the foot of the main ladder. He barely glanced at Ames. The boy looked about as he'd expected him to — godawful, and he'd soon be looking worse.

He studied Steele more thoroughly. He could tell his inspection annoyed her. She slowed her breathing and relaxed the muscles of her face. When he looked into her eyes he met a cool steady gaze.

Nice try, Lieutenant, he thought, but you're wound up tight as a spring. Damn Brook. Did he have to push his officers to the limit? Steele shouldn't be on an assignment like this for at least another month. Physiologically, she just wasn't ready for it. Her stomach couldn't even handle mudd yet. If she got through this morning without retching, it would be on pure grit. The cool blue eyes still met his levelly. She was going to prove she could outstare him. Steele had plenty of grit. She might make it.

Gordon glanced at Newcastle. As usual, the big black man looked fine. He had the constitution of an ox, and after twenty-five years on the gundeck, he could be shaken by nothing and could stomach anything.

"Gabriel's waiting in my surgery, Newcastle. Take this sailor in to him and give him a hand."

Newcastle turned to Steele. He was under her orders. She hesitated a moment. Newcastle wasn't a nurse. On the other hand, in the battle for control that was shaping up between the line and med/life, Newcastle represented the line.

"Take him inside." She handed Newcastle the key to the cuffs.

Gordon turned his black eyes on Steele again. She might make it. But she might not. "I can give you something to keep your gut steady," he said.

Steele's eyes flashed. "I am not the patient, Doctor," she said icily. "And I don't want that sailor kept waiting for you. I'd appreciate it if you just get to work on him and finish what you have to do as quickly as possible."

Gordon shrugged. "All right, Lieutenant. Whatever you say. You're running this show."

Gabriel and Newcastle came to attention as the officers entered the room. Ames tried to stand as well, but Gordon put a hand on his shoulder and pushed him back down onto the stool.

"Stay there," he barked and turned to Newcastle. "Get out," he said. "Wait in the corridor."

Newcastle again looked to Steele to confirm the order. She considered. The room was very crowded, and Newcastle took up a lot of space. Furthermore, she was now present to represent the line. She nodded to Newcastle and he left.

Ames was stripped to his skivvies. He sat huddled on a low stool looking cold, skinny, and thoroughly frightened. When Gordon approached him, he began to whimper.

It really was too bad that *Naval Regulations* required the chief medical/life support officer to perform this examination. Most of the lower orders were terrified of Gordon. She wished Gordon would curb his abrasive personality. This job was going to be difficult enough without Gordon frightening Ames into a fit.

She noticed Gabriel smile at her shyly. Gordon frowned at him, and the smile disappeared. Gordon picked up a stethoscope.

"What I'm primarily interested in," he said, addressing Steele as if her were speaking to medical students during hospital rounds, "is three things: heart, lungs, and spine."

He warmed the stethoscope briefly in his hand and began methodically working over Ames's chest and back. Occasionally he ordered him to take a breath or release it, but otherwise the doctor ignored him and continued his lecture.

"Anyone who's fit for duty is usually fit to take a flogging, but punishment could trigger an attack in someone with a weak heart. Newly pressed sailors are all checked out at their embarkation point and, of course, my mates examined this man repeatedly during our own quarantine, so I'd be much surprised to discover any heart defect now."

Steele looked at Ames. That was a mistake, she instantly decided. Tears ran down his cheeks, and he was trembling. She wondered how Gordon could work like this, taking the information he needed and ignoring the obvious trauma in his patients. "Intellectualize and detach emotionally" she repeated to herself. She forced herself to listen to Gordon's clinical observations.

"The condition of the lungs is important because the whip well laid on by the full force of a strong arm will knock the wind out with every stroke. A pulmonary weakness could result in serious distress after only five or six blows."

Gordon pushed Ames forward and ran practiced fingers down the length of his spine, palpating each vertebra. He had halted his lecture. Probably he considered the reason for this procedure to be self-evident.

Steele noticed that Ames no longer seemed to feel cold; on the contrary he was sweating now, and he flinched from the doctor's touch. She was annoyed to find that she was sweating a little herself. She repeated the deep breathing routine and tried to relax.

"That's it, sailor. Stand up," Gordon ordered. "My mate is going to give you an enema and finish up the tests we started last night. Try to cooperate." Gordon turned away from his patient and began to rummage in his desk. Gabriel guided Ames into the adjacent treatment room.

"You can watch if you want to," Gordon said to Steele as he continued to search through the desk drawers, "but I wouldn't recommend it. If you get him tensed up any more than he already is, all this will take a lot longer." He shot her a sharp look. "Won't do you any good either; you're already pretty green."

Steele was not about to admit it to Gordon, but she was feeling sick. She smelled the fear on Ames, and even knowing that Gordon was more the cause of it at this point than she was, it still turned her stomach.

"Is all this really necessary?"

Gordon stopped shuffling through his papers and glared. "You think I do this for my own amusement? If this series of blood tests isn't completed, everything we put that poor kid through during the night will have to be redone. And I'll tell you something else. There's no way I'm going to let a sailor take a flogging until I've cleaned him out. It's bad enough I'm going to have to deal with blood and probably vomitus contaminating the deck without having to clean up feces."

Gordon opened another drawer, peered inside, and slammed it shut. "Just in case you think this is some kind of personal whim, I'll have you know that Captain Brook doesn't care for it either.

It interferes with the dignity of the occasion." Gordon snorted. Reaching the last drawer in his desk, the doctor finally narrowed his search. He opened a thick file folder, going through the contents sheet by sheet.

"Damned waste of clean water, too," Gordon muttered. "Wouldn't be necessary if the officer in charge didn't insist on scaring the victim into fits before you even get started."

Steele was about to respond that it wasn't she who had been frightening Ames. Then she remembered that was only because it wasn't her turn yet. The thought made her stomach heave again.

"Goddamn Navy has a form for everything." Gordon finally located what he had been looking for, slammed the paper on the desk, picked up a pen, and began to fill in the blanks.

"He's fit to take punishment," he said. "Not that it's going to do his health any good. How much does Brook intend to order? Did he tell you?" Steele shook her head.

"Well, he's fit for anything up to five dozen, which is over the Biblical maximum, and I doubt that Brook will want to give him anything near that much." He pointed his pen at Steele. "But if he decides to go that high, you can tell him from me, that I've certified him fit for punishment now, but he won't be fit for anything afterward if he takes the maximum."

He scribbled his signature on the form and held it out to Steele. "As for you," he said, "I still think . . ."

"We're finished, Doctor." Gabriel brought Ames back to the office. "I got him dressed again, Lieutenant, but Chief Newcastle has the handcuffs."

Ames looked marginally better with his uniform back on, but the remark about handcuffs shattered what was left of his self control, and again he burst into tears.

Gordon slammed his palms on the desk and got to his feet. He seized Ames by the shoulders and spoke to him roughly. "Don't act like a baby," he barked. "Every hand on the ship is going to be watching you when you're taken up for punishment. You'll be thoroughly ashamed of yourself later if you start to cry before you've been hurt, and you can be sure that your mates will never let you hear the end of it. Now stand up straight and hold your head up."

Ames made an effort to pull himself together. Gordon left him for a moment and returned with a damp towel. He sat Ames down on the stool and spoke to him firmly as he wiped his face.

"I'm going to give you some advice. Try to listen to me now. If you can remember what I tell you, you can make this a lot easier on yourself.

"You deserve what's coming to you, so don't waste your energy fighting it or feeling sorry for yourself. Concentrate on getting air into your lungs. If you must scream, go ahead. No one will hold that against you. But whatever you do, don't start cursing."

Steele watched as Gordon locked his eyes to Ames's. The sailor was listening as if hypnotized. Despite all his deformity and his bluster about corporal punishment, Gordon still had meritocratic charisma and could use it when he chose.

"Blasphemy is offensive to God," Gordon continued echoing what Steele knew to be the captain's sentiments more than his own. "If God is offended, our ship is endangered. So never curse where God or an officer can hear you. That you hurt is not an excuse for profanity. If you take God's name in vain in front of the whole crew, Captain Brook will have you punished for it on the spot on top of what's already due you. So hold it until we get you below again. God doesn't listen on the third deck."

* * *

When the order came for all hands to assemble on the gundeck, most of the crew was already there, some sitting on the catwalks between gun stations or clinging to the ladders, others gathered on the deck in the hemicircle facing the main hatch. Unlike prayers, in which every sailor had an assigned place, mustering to witness punishment more closely resembled Monday night football when the first to arrive got their pick of positions.

Some came early to get the worst possible view while still obeying the order to attend. Others enjoyed watching a shipmate writhe in pain and made sure to get close to the action. Still others were forced into front and center places because their mates thought they could use a close look at the consequences of anti-social behavior. Becky Petrie was in the front row.

Most of the ship's Marine force was also on hand early. Instead of mustering together as they did at prayers, the Marines deployed around the deck, ready to deal with any disturbance. Also deployed at intervals through the gundeck were yellow stripers from med/life whose orders were to watch the crowd for signs of faintness or nausea — especially the later — and to make appropriate intervention.

Otherwise, the gundeck appeared much as it did when it was set up for morning and evening prayers. The captain's lectern stood on the platform surrounding the main mast, in front of the hatch through which he would enter. The four-part choir stood on the platform to each side of the lectern. Below them four Colonials with accordions set up stands for their music and practiced the more difficult passages. Near the musicians stood two Marine drummers. They had their backs turned to the others to make it clear they were part of operations and not entertainers.

Marine sentries guarded the barred forward hatch that opened from the ramp leading to the brig; and behind it, Steele stood with the two gunners mates and Charlie Ames, waiting in the wings to enter on cue.

A piping signal called all hands on deck. The remainder of the crew spilled out of the hatches and found themselves places in the crowd. After a suitable interval, the captain and the ship's officers exited from the main hatch and took their places, the captain at the lectern and the officers lined up in order of rank, standing at ease off to one side in front of him.

The officers left a space for Steele between Lieutenant Hall and Doctor Gordon. At the end of the officers' lineup stood the tall, thin Colonial woman who was second in command in med/life.

Waiting behind the gratings, Steele could feel Ames's growing anxiety. The two gunners' mates had him wedged between them, and his breathing was shallow and rapid. She hoped she had not brought him up too early. Her goal was to achieve a delicate balance — allowing Ames enough time to anticipate, but not enough time to push him into panic.

Fortunately, the cue came right on time. The choir broke fortissimo into the opening bars of the *Dies Irae* that had been the basis of the crossing-the-line parody in quarantine. The Marine stationed at the hatch unchained the grating. Newcastle and Dover pushed Ames through it. So far so good. Steele quickly crossed the deck to take her place in the officers' lineup. The captain was in charge now.

Newcastle freed his prisoner's hands and marched him to his position directly below the captain's lectern. The captain waited for the choir to finish its performance, and then, with appropriate solemnity, read the governing articles from *Naval Regulations* and delivered a five minute sermon on a text from the fifty-first chapter of Psalms 51: "A broken and a contrite heart, O God, thou wilt not despise."

The clouds programmed to gather over the gundeck earlier in the morning thickened. There was no breeze. It seemed to Steele that the still air was too warm; she was finding it hard to breathe.

The captain concluded his sermon, and Ames was moved back to the grating. It seemed to Steele it took the gunners' mates a long time to get him ready. When Ames was firmly bound spread-eagled against the grating, Newcastle stepped back. Dover picked up the cat and stood running his fingers through the tails, waiting for the captain's order.

Steele felt her eyes stinging, and despite her efforts to control her breathing, it was growing rapid and shallow. In desperation, she found the accupressure point on the inside of left wrist and pressed it hard. It helped some, but not enough. As the captain intoned orders to commence punishment, Steele, blood pounding in her ears, could not distinguish the words.

Then Marines responded with a roll of drums, the whip cracked against vulnerable flesh, and Ames threw back his head and gave a full-throated scream that pierced her heart.

Another roll of drums. It was just beginning.

Then, abruptly, as she fought nausea and tears, Steele felt another even more powerful physical sensation that made her suck in her breath sharply. A feeling of piercing cold ran up the length of her spine as if someone had traced a line with a piece of ice. The chill intensified at the base of her skull.

Although Steele had never experienced it before, she knew what that icy touch meant. A Colonial — and it must be Doctor Parker — was initiating telepathic contact. Under *Naval Regulations,* to do such a thing without permission was a felony. Steele had had virtually no contact with Doctor Parker, but the woman was an officer and a meritocrat and non-consensual telepathy was a criminal act. She could scarcely believe this was happening.

A gentle soprano voice spoke as if into her left ear. "Here is a navigational problem for you, Lieutenant Steele. Calculate the fastest course from Mantu to Gibraltar by way of the Point of Storms. The tide is high and the month is December."

Of course! That would do it! If she could shut this gruesome ceremony out of her consciousness, her body would steady itself. And a tough navigation problem was the ideal distraction.

For Steele, space navigation was not merely a professional specialty; it was also an absorbing personal interest. She relished the challenge of plotting a course where all directions were equal and nothing at all was fixed. In space there were no fixed stars, no fixed speeds, no fixed ports. Everything moved — matter, light, gravitational forces, time — all must be balanced when a ship was maneuvered toward a targeted destination.

Most of this work required a computer. Only a miracle could save a ship in deep space without the power to boot up electronic aids to navigation. But navigational problems in coastal space were on a human scale. Difficult to solve without a computer, but not impossible. A good knowledge of the charts was sufficient if you had a head for mathematics.

In an instant, Steele had the slowly rotating Mantu tide charts for December in focus. The sounds of the drum, the lash, and the screaming faded from her awareness as the whole grisly scene on the gundeck disappeared.

CHAPTER SEVEN

A bolt of lightening split the sky above the gundeck and was followed by a deafening crack of thunder. Steele jerked back to reality. Ames's punishment was over. Captain Brook solemnly intoned a concluding prayer.

Both of the medical/life support officers had crossed the deck. Steele watched them examine Ames and consult together, Doctor Parker touching her throat to activate her artificial vocal cords. In a moment, the captain would direct the musicians to play the exit voluntary, and he and the other officers would leave the deck.

Steele hesitated as to where to go when the captain dismissed them. On the one hand it was she, not the medical/life support officers, who bore primary responsibility for Ames. She ought to get to him fast before the attentions of the medics got him thinking of himself as a patient rather than as an offender. He was supposed to reflect on his pain, not seek relief for it. On the other hand, she needed to get out of her hot dress uniform and to wash her face. She was feeling a lot better now — the few minutes of concentration on the course to Gibraltar had done her as much good as an hour's sleep — but she was sure she looked less than professionally sharp, and she was supposed to set an example.

The sky began to clear as the accordionists struck up a curiously cheerful fugue by J. S. Bach, and Steele decided to compromise, making a quick stop in the officers' head to wash before heading down to sickbay. When she got there, Doctor Gordon was waiting for her.

"Hold it right there, Steele. My mates can finish without you." She could hear Ames moaning in the treatment room.

"My orders are to stick with Ames until he's back in the brig."

"My orders to you take precedence now," Gordon snapped back. "I'm declaring you unfit for duty. You don't need to watch this. We're cleaning him up and applying antiseptics. It won't take long. And, since I know this is what you really care about, I'll make sure no one slips him any painkillers."

"There's nothing wrong with me, Gordon, and you damn well know it!" She'd gotten through the roughest part of this assignment and wanted to wrap it up. Med/life had no business interfering at this point.

"I'm not interested in your self-diagnosis, Lieutenant. I say you're on the sick list. Now get yourself over to Doctor Parker. She'll take care of you. I'll see to it that Ames gets back to the brig. I assure you getting iodine worked into the cuts on his back won't deprive him of any pain. He'll have plenty to hold his attention for a few hours. You do as Parker tells you, and you'll be back on duty in time to let him out."

"This is ridiculous! I'm as fit as you are!"

A sardonic smile spread over Gordon's scared face. "That may be, Lieutenant, but I have had long experience functioning in this condition and you have not. Now don't waste my time. Go!" He pointed a bony finger toward Doctor Parker's office at the other end of sickbay.

Steele pressed her lips together, whirled around and strode toward Parker's station. The Colonial officer was perched on a stool at a laboratory bench working with an array of test tubes. When Steele called her name, she turned abruptly. Steele was surprised to see that she looked frightened.

The Colonial touched her throat to activate her artificial larynx and spoke in a toneless metallic voice. "Not be angry, please. Much apologies. Not meant harm you. Only try help."

The painfully articulated words contrasted sharply with the pleasant, fluent voice that Steele had heard telepathically on the gun deck. Steele recalled that the Colonials, because of some peculiarity in the evolution of their frontal lobes, lacked the mental capacity as well as the physical ability to produce articulated speech. They could not master grammar, syntax or diction, nor could they easily remember the patterns that determined how words must be arranged or pronounced to produce meaning. They could understand spoken speech easily since they received the thought behind it. But unless they communicated telepathically, which they were rarely permitted to do with humans, they could make themselves understood only with enormous effort. Few had mastered a voice box as well as Doctor Parker. Few even tried.

Steele was instantly sorry that she had burst in on the Colonial so abruptly. She realized that she must look pretty grim. If she were to report Parker for communicating telepathically, the doctor would be court-martialed. But Steele had no intention of preferring charges.

"I'm not angry with you, Doctor Parker. Doctor Gordon just ordered me off duty and told me to report to you for treatment. But I know there's nothing wrong with me, and that's what I'm mad about. Actually, I'm very grateful to you for what you did for me on the gun deck."

Parker smiled. A pretty face, Steele thought, with a broad forehead and small cleft chin. Her hair was deep chestnut and she wore it pulled back from her face and twisted at the nape of her neck with some kind of elaborate plaiting. Her eyes were her most striking feature; they were an unusual shade of hazel that seemed to shift from green to brown with her mood. Her gaze carried the same unconscious charismatic power Steele had come to recognize in other meritocrats.

"Glad you not mad." The smile carried the warmth absent from the synthesized speech. "I see you have distress. Think-talk only way can help. Need do even be you not want. Think you be fine now. Sit. I check. Be sure."

Steele sat in the visitor's chair by the doctor's desk. Parker put a thermometer into her mouth, felt her pulse, and then returned to the lab bench where she put some liquid in a retort on to boil.

Steele studied her curiously. She'd never really looked closely at a Colonial before, she realized. Actually, there wasn't much to see. Except for their telepathic abilities and failure to develop vocal apparatus, the Colonials were physiologically identical to the hominids of Earth.

Scientists believed that many millennia ago, before any of the hominid spiecies of Earth evolved into speaking creatures, the ancestors of the Colonials lived on the planet. How they ended up on a world in the Mantu system in a distant part of the galaxy, science could not explain. The Colonials had a tradition which the Academy course in Comparative Religion compared to the Biblical account of Noah's Ark. Only instead of just taking two each of every animal species, the captain of the Colonial "ark" had taken two hominids from every established genetic pool then on the planet the Colonials called "Home." However absurd it sounded to non-Colonials, this myth did explain why the Colonial hominids had as much racial and cultural diversity as those on Earth — and such eerie similarities to humans.

Parker withdrew the thermometer. "You all right now," she said smiling. "Not bother do blood pressure. You and me, we know. Symptom that worry Gordon not serious. I have something fix you all up good." She brought the retort of boiling liquid and a box of coarse, dark, flaky material over to her desk and sat opposite Steele.

"What is that stuff?"

"Tea," said Parker, setting two mugs and a plain white teapot on the table. "Fix you up good. Fix me too. Bad to stand on deck, hear person scream." She began to prepare the tea. "I must watch careful, listen good. Be doctor job if sailor need help."

Steele hadn't thought about Doctor Parker's job on *Lafayette* before. Her contacts with the med/life section were all though Gordon. But Gordon did not run the section alone. As his second in command, Parker had responsibilities in med/life comparable to those Rivera had as Brook's first officer.

Parker had the skill and training to take over full control of med/life should Gordon be disabled. In addition, as the work was divided up, the Colonial physician took primary responsibility for most of the medical activity that involved direct contact with patients. She was in charge of the daily sick call; and, with the exception of Gordon's private surgery and laboratory, the entire sickbay complex, including the recovery and isolation bays, was her domain.

As senior medical officer, Gordon bore direct responsibility for the health of the meritocratic officers. But the crew were cared for by Parker. They seemed to have the best of it, Steele thought. She couldn't imagine that Gordon would have realized that what she needed was exactly what Parker had prescribed — a nice cup of tea. She felt sure he'd have given her a shot of something; or if he gave her anything to drink, it probably would be an extra dose of that disgusting mudd.

Parker poured. The tea was a pleasant herbal blend. Steele detected traces of peppermint and camomile as she raised the mug to her lips. She took a sip and flashed a brilliant smile at the Colonial, who was enjoying her cup of the brew. There was a trace of something sweet in the mug; the drink was delicious.

It suddenly occurred to Steele that Doctor Parker must feel very isolated aboard *Lafayette.* As a Colonial, she had no social contact with the other officers, and the rule against "inappropriate intercourse" with commoners meant she had no social contact with the Colonials in the crew. Although there were more than five thousand people aboard the ship, no one ever spoke to Anne Parker except on professional matters.

"May I call you Anne, Doctor?" Steele asked impulsively.

The Colonial's eyes danced with pleasure. "That be nice, Lieutenant," she answered.

"Then you must call me Maggie," said Steele.

Parker stared in astonishment. Humans often called Colonials by their first names, but it was unheard of for a Colonial to be invited to reciprocate.

"It's all right," said Steele, who had never thought much about the social barrier between the two groups. "After all, here we are drinking tea together. I know I was sent into you for medical treatment, but this doesn't seem to me to be a doctor-patient relationship right now. All the other officers call me Maggie. I don't see why you should be an exception."

Steele saw Parker's hand flutter at her throat as she struggled to use her voice box to express what she felt. The box gave her only limited control over tone, pitch and inflection even when she could manage to produce appropriate words.

"Why don't you just go ahead and think-talk me." Steele didn't really want to feel that icy touch that preceded contact a second time — it wasn't at all pleasant; but she was curious to hear Parker's real voice again.

The chilling vibration moved up her spine, more rapidly this time than it had on the gundeck, and she flinched from it. Then a musical vibration that seemed to come from just behind her left ear flooded through her mind.

"Lieutenant Steele — Maggie — I deeply appreciate your friendly overtures to me. I thank you most sincerely for these magnanimous gestures. When I communicated with you on the gun deck, I was prepared to be punished for it. You have not only forgiven that intrusion but have freely invited another. You have a kind and generous nature, Maggie, and I am most sincerely and humbly grateful."

Steele was overwhelmed by this outpouring and more than a little embarrassed by it. She gulped down what was left of her tea and stood up to leave, hoping she didn't look as anxious to get away as she felt.

"Goodbye, Anne," she said lightly. "Next time we get an epidemic alert, I'm going to try to get my shots from you instead of from Doctor Gordon."

"Be glad anytime you help," said Parker's metallic voice.

Back in her cabin, Steele took a good look at herself in the full-length mirror inside the wardrobe. She was pale: sickly pale. The natural color she'd had as a cadet at Annapolis was gone after three months in space. Her permanent duty station was on the bridge and her secondary specialty in engineering took her into the dark of the 'tween decks and the even darker environment of space itself when she took crews out onto the hull. Until she started to drill regularly at the gunner's position, she'd spend little time on the sunlit main deck where sailors could get some color in their faces.

And she'd been sweating. Despite a quick face wash, sweat still showed in her hair and in her uniform. Her resentment toward Gordon dissolved. If she looked this bad now, she probably looked like she was coming down with plague when she'd brought Ames on deck. She couldn't have blamed Gordon if he'd yanked her off duty in front of the whole crew. It must have gone strongly against his inclinations to wait until he could get her alone.

Steele sponged herself clean at the wash basin, brushed her hair, and put on a fresh uniform. She was anxious to get to her station on the bridge. She had not checked the ship's course or examined the navigational log since early morning. That log was her responsibility, and it was also her crutch.

Eventually, Steele knew, she would develop a sixth sense for *Lafayette*'s movements and learn to feel changes in course produced by gravity tides and energy fields and to distinguish them from deliberate helm movements, shifts of sail plates, or engine adjustments. But for now she needed to check the logged observations constantly to verify her impressions. There was no way she could hurry the development of the intuitive sense of a good navigator.

There was probably no way she could hurry the development of physiological controls either, she thought. If the morning's events had been a SOCRATES simulation, she would have been credited with a dry run, but she strongly doubted whether a telepathic assault by a fellow officer had been programmed into any Academy exercises. Accepting the assistance Doctor Parker had offered was really just as bad as it would have been to say yes to a drug from Doctor Gordon.

There was no use brooding about it. She'd do better next time. For now her duty was to bring herself current on the ship's movements since she'd had the watch.

The quartermaster on duty was Armadillo Finkelstein, known to his friends as Dilly, one of the few Colonials aboard who served on the bridge and the only one in any specialty to wear red stripes. His unfortunate name, typical of second-generation immigrants, did not suit his appearance or his personality. Had he been human, he would have been described as Chinese-American — a round Asian face, straight jet black hair, and Texas mannerisms, including the habit of sprawling his short round body cowboy style when at ease.

Finkelstein knew what Steele wanted as soon as she appeared at his station, and he handed over the Weather Observation Sheet. She accepted it with a nod. In her contacts with Finkelstein, Steele was usually as mute as he was. She studied the sheet silently and handed it back. Costello had already inspected and initialed it. Steele went to the navigation station and began to read the log. She noted that Captain Brook had checked the course when the watch changed and had made another alteration in course, probably to avoid the bank of dust clouds the lookout was still tracking to starboard.

Since the last war, interstellar dust banks were often seeded with organic virus mines. Although it was still tempting for any ship to net in a prize of concentrated matter, the danger now outweighed the potential benefit. Even passing near dust clouds was hazardous. The gravity of the ship would trap tiny particles between sail plates, carrying them like time bombs just waiting for a careless hullsweeper to carry them aboard. While it was not always possible to navigate around interstellar dust clouds, Brook did so whenever he could. Watch officers had orders to do so routinely without requesting permission.

Costello, making her rounds on the bridge, appeared at Steele's side. "Feeling better?" she asked.

"Yes, thanks."

"What did the doctors say was wrong with you?"

"I didn't get a diagnosis. Doctor Parker checked me out and said I'm fine."

"This wasn't some complication from SOCRATES then?"

"Oh, no. Nothing like that." Was this what the other officers thought had happened?

"If you're off the sick list, the first officer wants you to report."

"Am I in trouble?"

Costello hesitated. Strictly speaking, this was none of her business. But spacing out on the gundeck! She'd been worried sick that Maggie had involuntarily gone into a trance heralding a personality shift.

"If I were in command, you can bet you'd be in trouble. Big time trouble. Godamnit, Maggie, don't you understand how easy it is to get dependent on an artificial aid out here? No, you don't," she said bitterly, answering her own question. "And of course the med/life officers don't understand either. They know nothing about the stress line officers live with, nothing.

"It would be grand if we could hold off your baptism of fire until you've got your spacelegs, but that's not possible. We could be bloodying you any time now! There could be heavy action this afternoon! Officers are supposed to do their vomiting as they do their crying — out of sight of the crew. But I'd rather have had you fighting nausea unaided, even if you lost, than using an external device."

"Yes, ma'am." Steele reflexively snapped into a brace. Costello sighed. It hadn't been her intention to speak to Steele so sharply, especially since the captain apparently did not share her views.

"You asked me if you're in trouble. I should have given you a straight answer. It's Number One and not the captain who's calling for you. That means you're off the hook this time. If you were in for a reprimand, you'd be getting it straight from Brook. He doesn't delegate that sort of thing, and he doesn't delay it either. On the other hand, you've definitely got some explaining to do. You 'explain' to the first officer."

Steele was wide-eyed and grave. This was the first time she'd come so close to botching an assignment. She definitely would botch one eventually, Costello knew. Everyone did. You just had to hope the botch wouldn't be one that killed somebody.

In a way, it wasn't fair. Steele had done the best she could. Meritocrats always did. Unfortunately, if your best wasn't good enough, you were still held accountable. That was the way the Navy worked.

"Go find Rivera," Costello said taking a slate from Finkelstein. "Right now. You'll have to take your medicine."

The board at the signal station showed Rivera was out on the hull, inspecting the work of the sweepers on the external gun mounts. Steele set the channel for his space helmet, and contacted him through the powered communicator.

"Have you had your lunch?" he asked.

"No, sir," she said. She'd felt fortunate to have been able to hold on to her breakfast.

"Report to the wardroom then," Rivera said. "I'll meet you there as soon as I go through decontamination."

There was no boyish grin on Rivera's face when he entered the wardroom. Steele jumped to her feet.

"Clean your plate, Steele. You know better than to miss a meal." He poured himself a mug of mudd and sat nursing it, watching the junior lieutenant as she swallowed a bowl of vegetable soup and a chicken salad sandwich. When she finished, he went to the urn on the sideboard, hotted up his mudd and brought a mug of the steaming liquid to Steele. She drained it as quickly as she could.

It wasn't the most pleasant atmosphere for dining, but the food and even the mudd went down, and Steele was confident it would stay down.

Rivera called for a steward to remove the tray.

"Now we talk," he said. "First it is my duty to tell you that this is not a reprimand. This interview is in the nature of a debriefing and its purpose is instruction. Do you understand?"

"Yes, sir."

"Then to begin, I want you to explain to me exactly what was going on in your head before when you were supposed to be witnessing punishment."

Steele told him.

"The captain thought it must have been something like that. He was sure that if it was related to SOCRATES you would have obeyed orders and left the deck. But what you did was deliberate. You were on duty. You were the officer in charge during what is always a potentially explosive situation. But you were as unconscious of what was going on as if you'd been dead drunk."

"No excuse, sir," Steele said automatically.

"Very well. Still, excuses were made for you, Lieutenant. Though I suppose you missed that bit of byplay as you missed everything else that happened on the gundeck."

Whatever he was referring to, Steele had indeed missed it. Rivera read the question in her eyes.

"The med/life director left the formation before Ames was cut down and had what might be described as a quiet exchange of views with the captain." Steele had seen Gordon "exchange views" with the captain a few times. He usually wasn't quiet about it. But he usually didn't approach the captain in front of the crew.

In every other respect, Brook ran a tight ship. But he had given up on the med/life director. He listened to what Gordon had to say for its content and ignored its frequently disrespectful form.

"There's no one else alive the captain would take that kind of thing from except, maybe, the Queen," Rivera continued. "But he took it from Gordon standing in front of all our people. It seems that you were the subject of the conversation. Brook says that Gordon told him — and I quote — that he was shocked and outraged to find you assigned to direct punishment after such a short time in space and that he'd demand to have a formal protest entered in the log if you were given such duty again before he'd declared you fit for it." Steele bit her lip.

"That will, however, have no influence whatever on Brook's future orders to you. As far as he's concerned, it's the captain's business to determine the fitness of his officers, so he will record Gordon's protests and continue to make his own decisions on duty assignments. He doesn't believe in coddling young officers."

"Yes, sir." Steele was mortified. She didn't want coddling.

"On the other hand," Rivera continued, "Brook will not ignore Gordon's medical opinions. On the basis of his professional judgment, Doctor Gordon put you on the sick list. Apparently it had nothing to do with SOCRATES, but if some other physical condition beyond your control was responsible for your lapse on the gundeck, the captain will accept that as an extenuating circumstance. I want to hear it from you. Were you sick, Steele?"

"I don't think so, sir. Doctor Parker examined me and said there was nothing wrong."

"That was after you went below. Did you feel any physical symptoms before you withdrew your attention from you duty?"

"Yes, sir." That was an easy question to answer.

"Don't make me pump you, Steele. I'm trying to get you to describe your physical condition."

"I felt light-headed and nauseous. I tried doing deep breathing, but it didn't help. If I hadn't done what I did, I believe I might have fainted or vomited."

"Very well." Rivera rose and turned to look out the sun windows that lined the bulkhead on one side of the wardroom. This was the largest expanse of sunlight anywhere in officers' country, and the handsomely curtained windows gave the wardroom a homelike atmosphere unlike any other part of the ship. He turned to face Steele again.

"Even though you were mentally absent for most of it, you participated enough in the preliminaries for Charlie Ames's punishment to realize how much of it was psychological. The ceremonial aspects of a flogging are enormously important to Captain Brook. That lightening bolt he gave us, timed to coincide with the conclusion of punishment, cost the ship a pretty penny. Brook considered it worth the price to get the last inch of mileage possible out of the spectacle. We have very little flogging aboard *Lafayette.* Brook's attitude toward the procedure is the reason. The sailors are mortally terrified of the cat, and so our rate of serious offenses is probably lower than it is on any other ship in the fleet." Rivera returned to his seat.

"Given your options at the time, you made the correct decision. Had you lost control during Brook's carefully orchestrated climax, it would have struck exactly the wrong note. Nevertheless, the captain directed me to remind you that the traditionally approved method of dealing with the gruesome realities of our profession has always been to narrow your focus of attention and depersonalize the situation."

"Yes, sir." This might not count as a formal reprimand, but it certainly felt like one.

Rivera watched her for a moment, then leaned back in his chair, pushed back his hair and allowed a broad grin to spread over his face. "The captain also said that after I'd made you squirm enough to make sure you didn't take this too casually, I should tell you that he knows very well that the traditional method is difficult for meritocrats to use. It takes time to learn to control your natural empathy. More time than he gave you."

Steele's relief when he dropped his quarterdeck manner was so obvious that Rivera laughed. "You did get thrown into this assignment unusually early, Maggie. I knew neither Martha nor Liz would get it, since they've just had special assignments. And I was sure I wouldn't get it because I had the duty when Ames was caught. I expected Brook to give this assignment to Henry. I thought his name would come up ahead of mine anyway, and I'd have expected you to be at the end of the list.

"All told, I think you did remarkably well. If Brook had ever watched you facing your duty and downing a ration of mudd, I don't think he'd have put you on this." He sipped from his mug. Steele watched enviously. The first officer obviously enjoyed the nasty stuff. Rivera laughed again.

"Believe me, Maggie, it won't be long until you're as hooked on this stuff as the rest of us." He swallowed what was left in the mug and set it aside.

"All right, let's get back to business. First your problem. Are you aware that Ames's punishment has hurt you more than it hurt him?"

"I don't see how that's possible!" Steele remembered Ames's terrified face, the screaming on the gundeck, and the moans she heard in sickbay after he was brought below.

"He had a sharp five minutes — that's all. Unless there's a cut-deep cord or some unauthorized modification to the standard cat, the whip bruises more than it cuts. The swelling and the scratches look worse than they are. Oh, Ames hurts, all right, and he'll remember this. If he runs true to form, he'll also exaggerate it when he gets back to his mates because he won't want them to suspect he screamed more out of fear than out of pain. That's exactly what Brook wants. But you are still holding it like a cold lump in your gut. You still haven't depersonalized."

Rivera was right. When she thought about Ames, she felt pain. And she had to think about him; her work with him wasn't over.

"What I'm going to do," Rivera went on, "is to take you off sickbay visits and give you permanent duty at daily inspection."

Steele felt a flash of anger. Rivera knew she hated doing morning inspection and traded the duty for other assignments whenever she could. Hall didn't seem to mind it; he'd rather spend twenty minutes watching a few sailors take their licks than an hour trying to act cheerful among sick people. Now the first officer was going to force her to start each morning frightening sailors guilty of small offenses: faults in their rigging, tardiness at muster, or that horrendous charge "disorderliness during prayers," which generally meant giggling. These were punished on the order of the inspecting officer unless the sailor was foolish enough to want to argue about it or was a chronic offender, in which case the name went on the first lieutenant's report.

Steele found the whole business repellent — a fact Rivera knew as well as he knew she hated mudd. Despite this talk about "debriefing for the purpose of instruction," she was being sentenced to a punishment that would fit her crime.

"Is this a disciplinary action, sir?"

Rivera responded as if he had been slapped.

"Maggie! Do you think I'm playing games with you?"

His hurt eyes met her angry ones in a moment of silence. Two meritocrats at a standoff.

"Let's start over. This is an informal debriefing for the purpose of instruction. Sometimes instruction hurts, but that doesn't make it punishment. Are you with me this far?"

"I understand what you've said, sir."

"The authority to cause suffering as a means to an end that is not immediately and directly beneficial to the person who suffers — in other words, the authority to punish — rests solely with the captain. Captain Brook delegates very little of that authority and none at all when an officer is involved. He'd as soon let me fight the ship for him as he would allow me to punish an officer. And I'd be even less likely to usurp that power. I hope you don't think so badly of me as to believe I like that kind of work any better than you do."

Steele dropped her eyes. "Of course not, sir. I apologize, sir." She hadn't been thinking. It was obvious that the only way she would learn to deal with her reluctance to punish was to be involved in it.

Rivera grinned. "We're still friends then. I'll leave it to you to let me know when you've had enough; you're the best judge of how much time you need to feel reasonably comfortable in the role of disciplinarian."

Steele groaned inwardly. This wasn't punishment; it was something worse. Punishment had a limit to it. Now she was on her honor to keep herself at the assignment until her sensitivity to it was under control — until she had learned the lesson.

"Let's get back to Ames. You're responsible for preparing the report for the punishments book. I suppose you can do the section covering the time until you got Ames on deck. You looked like death warmed over when you joined the formation, but you seemed alert. How did it go?"

"Well enough. Ames behaved himself. We didn't have to use force, though Newcastle would have loved an excuse to get in a few licks of his own. I had to hold him back from excesses a couple of times. There were a few minutes in sickbay when it was touch and go whether Ames would keep control of himself. He started crying, but Gordon gave him a shake and told him to stop feeling sorry for himself. That snapped him out of it."

"How much further can you carry the report? Do you know how much punishment Ames took?"

Steele realized that she did not. Brook believed in keeping offenders in suspense. He'd tell them what form of punishment they'd get, but not announce how much until the last moment. She knew that Gordon had certified Ames fit for up to five dozen, but when Brook finished his sermon and Ames was being tied to the gratings, she was already fully occupied with her battle for control of her body.

"All right. I'll write that section. And we'll have to get Doctor Gordon to cover the time you were off duty and he had Ames in sickbay." Rivera's eyes twinkled. "I'll edit that part." Thank goodness, Steele thought. Otherwise the invitation to contribute to a punishment report would give Gordon a grand opportunity to spout off about corporal punishment in general and probably to repeat whatever he'd said to the captain about her unfitness for the assignment.

"You'll be releasing Ames from the brig later and can finish it up yourself."

Steele nodded.

Rivera leaned back in his chair. "You ought to know what happened. Brook gave him a dozen, and all things considered, he took it very well. I think it may have been just what he needed to straighten him out. I expect Charlie Ames will become a credit to the Navy yet."

* * *

Steele had expected Ames to be happier to see her when she came to release him from the brig than he had been when she'd come after him in the morning. But this, she thought, was ridiculous.

Ames was on his feet, ready for inspection, as soon as the cell door opened. He'd made up his bunk and placed the Bible precisely in the center of the table where it belonged. He had also made use of the washstand in the wardrobe; his hair was damp and combed flat and his face pink from scrubbing. But most unexpected, he was grinning. Steele could understand Ames being anxious to get out, but his exuberance was disconcerting.

"Do you feel well enough to join your squad or do you need to go to sickbay?"

"Oh, no, ma'am. I don't need to go to sickbay. I feel just fine. Really I do." Ames had received far more attention from the medical staff than he wanted. Steele could understand that, though she suspected that "just fine" was an exaggeration.

"Then where are you supposed to report?"

"The mess hall, ma'am. We get fed on the first shift." Ames had been counting off the half hours until his promised time of release, and the two bells that had just sounded meant both freedom and food.

So that was it! Steele looked at him in astonishment.

Ames wondered if he'd said something wrong. The food in the brig was terrible, and there'd been both Marines and medics hovering over him to make sure he finished every molecule.

Prisoners were fed what the medical/life support personnel called "UNS" — undifferentiated nutritional supplement. The Marines who dished it out in the brig called it "the disciplinary diet." Sailors called it "pig slop," which is what it literally was.

The chalk-white, tasteless substance had the consistency of a thick paste and was produced by recycling organic waste. The pigs got it in a trough mixed into their mash. Prisoners got it in a bowl without any addition to take the curse off it. It was nutritious and filling and two full meals of it had made Ames long for real food so badly he could hardly stand it.

"When Doctor Parker brought me up from sickbay, she said I'd find something extra on my plate tonight. Something I'd really like." Steele could think of no response. Ames's grin faded. He hoped the lieutenant didn't mean to keep him from his dinner for some reason. "I've been thinking about it all afternoon, ma'am." His eyes were pleading.

Steele rolled her eyes to the deckhead and then nodded toward the door. "Go on, Ames. Get out of here. Try not to do anything that gets you sent back in again."

"No, ma'am. I won't, ma'am. I clean my plate at meals and report on sick call if I'm hungry." He recited the rules. "And I don't steal food," he added realizing he'd forgotten something.

Steele watched him move, a little stiffly, toward the main hatch and shook her head. All of Ames's brains were still in his stomach. She didn't see how Rivera could believe a whipping was going to change that.

Steele realized that she would have to find out what the med/life officers had decided to add to Ames's ration that had made him spend the afternoon anticipating dinner rather than concentrating on his sore back and repenting his sins. From what Ames had said, it was Doctor Parker who would have the answer. Steele went looking for her.

Parker was eating a solitary supper from a tray at the lab bench in the isolation bay. Theoretically Doctor Parker had the right to dine in the wardroom. But since she was a Colonial, neither she nor the other officers ever considered the possibility that she might actually do such a thing. Steele was surprised to see that the physician had one of the large Admiralty charts unfolded on the bench and was studying it as she ate.

"Excuse me," Steele said. "I didn't mean to interrupt your dinner. I'll come back later."

"No. Please. That be all right." Parker sprang down from the stool. "Much glad have company. You stay. I make tea."

Steele hesitated, but Parker was clearly so pleased to have a visitor that she hadn't the heart to say no.

"That's an offer I can't refuse, Anne. You brew a wicked pot of tea."

Parker smiled and blushed at the compliment. "Sit by desk. Bad habit for me eat at bench." As the water heated, she searched among her collection of teas for something suitable for a guest. The herbs she used earlier had been chosen for their medicinal value. Now she wanted something more festive.

She located the elegant china tea set that was among the few personal possessions she had brought aboard the ship. Parker dearly loved her evening cup of tea. Until today, she had always enjoyed the special drink alone as a private treat. It was much nicer to share.

"Blackberry," she announced as she filled the delicate pot and sat. "Know this not be social visit, Maggie. Thank you for let me make that way. You bring question. I answer."

"Yes, I do have a question." Steele sipped her tea. A different flavor this time, more assertive and carrying the memory of warm Earth summers.

"When I let Ames out of the brig just now and sent him off to dinner, he was happy as a lark. He said you'd promised him something to eat."

"That true. Feed him soybean protein. With meals, between meals too. Tell him get pass. Come see me if be hungry. I give him any time."

"Soybean protein? That sounds awful."

Parker smiled. "Not tell him recipe." She went to a cabinet and brought a closed tin to the table. What was inside looked like potato chips.

"Not taste like real thing. Have some potato. Just little amount. Bake, not fry in lard. But Ames forget. Long time now he not eat chip. He like this. Eat a lot. Be good for him. He not be all time hungry, brain maybe work better. Not need whip again."

Steele nodded. This looked like exactly what Charlie Ames needed. "I certainly hope he won't need to be whipped again. Lieutenant Rivera thinks he won't."

Parker's eyes darkened. "Think Rivera talk sharp at you. Hope not too bad, Maggie. Line officer not understand. Gordon try tell captain. Not help."

"I'm a line officer, Anne," Steele said quietly.

"We not talk on that then." Parker refilled their cups. "Think med/life win today. You okay now. Think Ames be okay. We not talk why. Talk on that end up fight. Like sailor and Marine. Talk something else. Not fight."

The Colonial was as feisty as Gordon, Steele realized. She supposed a degree of combativeness was necessary for the job. The two of them apparently had agreed on her case, She wondered whether Parker ever used that hard metallic voice to argue with her superior.

"Well, let's talk about you then. Is Anne Parker your real name?" Steele had always wondered why first-generation

Colonial names were so similar to Earth names, often even reflecting what seemed like Earth cultural origins. Only in the second-generation did eccentric combinations — like Dilly Finkelstein's — appear.

"Not real name. Not can say real name in throat. Immigration clerk need voice name. Put down best he know. If be I know voice-talk then, I say . . ." She stopped and thought. "I say Gardener maybe. No, no Gardener. Say Horticulturist. My name be Anne Horticulturist." She nodded, pleased with the effect.

"What about the Anne part?"

"This more easy. Anne be how mama think on me. Be for saint day I be born. Be born in space. Mama get date for ship time. Look up saint for girl." Parker smiled. "More hard for mama. Clerk have much trouble. Call her Bertha. She not like name. I like Anne name fine. Like you call me Anne."

"And I like having you call me Maggie."

"You have extra name in middle. What that be?"

"You mean what does my middle initial stand for? Actually, I've never told that to many people. It was a nutty idea of my mother's. C stands for Clio. You know, the muse of history. Mom is an historian. When she was carrying me she was working on a book about Ferdinand Magellan, the fifteenth century navigator. I was supposed to be some kind of inspiration for her scholarly writing."

"You inspire mama?"

"To some things, maybe, but not to writing. She never finished her book, though she claims she's still working on it. After I was born, Mom decided she wanted to help make the universe a better place for me and my descendants, as she says. Not that I've decided about descendants. After my dad died, Mom resigned from her chair at Oxford and enlisted in the Navy. She claims she wanted space duty, but she was assigned to the Naval Academy. The Navy never sends commoners with young children into space, not even if they volunteer. They're too apt to get homesick, and then they get preoccupied and careless. Mom makes out as if it was the big disappointment of her life. But she'd have hated the regimentation on a warship."

"It be more easy at Academy?"

"Not for the cadets, it's not. But it's certainly the least regimented environment in the Navy for the commoners who teach there. They get away with murder. The theory is that scholars need lots of freedom, and do they ever take advantage of it. You should see my mother's office! No real sailor could stand that kind of clutter, and no one on shipboard would be allowed to keep a work area in such a jumble. And the fighting!"

"Tell to me." Anne couldn't remember how long it had been since anyone had shared a bit of gossip.

"Well, I'm sure you know that History is the largest department at Annapolis, and that means the commoners associated with it have plenty of opportunity to form factions. It's no secret that the academic politics in the History Department are more vicious than even Religion and Psychology — not that those people don't cut up pretty badly.

"The Superintendent usually just leaves them to battle it out among themselves, Still, at least once a term, they get themselves so embroiled in some idiot controversy or other that it interferes with their work. Then the admiral has to take them in hand.

"You wouldn't believe how stubborn they can be! A few years ago the squabbling got so bad between the age-of-sail faction — that's my mom's — and the bunch she calls the submariners, who are actually mainly concerned with airplanes, that the admiral threatened to flog the next scholar who held a meeting.

"Of course the commoners thought that was just dandy. The supe started getting anonymous reports that some group or other was holding secret meetings. The admiral finally quelled that one by putting the whole history faculty into confinement in their library cubicles. He only let them out of Nimitz long enough to teach their classes. They all had to eat by themselves, and he even made them sleep in the library. That cooled them off temporarily. But the next term they were off on something else.

"Admiral Thanatos often said that if it weren't for the steadying influence of the meritocratic students at the Academy, he believes the professors would be murdering each other. With poison, of course. As a group, commoner scholars haven't much physical courage. I don't know how they manage to control them at open admission schools like Oxford and Swarthmore."

Parker's eyes twinkled and her face was alive with soundless laughter. She had attended one of those open admission schools and shared the usual Navy view of academics.

"Tell me about your family, Anne."

"Not much tell. Father left on Colony. Think he die in Delphinian raids. Mama hold me not born when she go Earth. Now she work Venus mines. She say good job. Pay good."

Steele was embarrassed. Since the last war most work in the Venusian mines had been done by Colonials. The pay was good for relatively unskilled labor. The technology used to exploit the resources of the molten planet rewarded workers for simple patience and perseverence. Although the heat and humidity in the mines and the long commute to and from Earth made work on Venus unattractive to those who could find something better, employment opportunities for the mute immigrants were limited. That made her curious about something else.

"How did you manage to become a Navy doctor?"

"Hear call. Then work much hard. Decide try meritocrat exam. Colonial not much try that. Need get voice box first. Hurt plenty. Hard learn use too. I learn. Pass exam. Surprise everyone. Especially Mama. She cry. Say now she have no grandchildren."

Steele smiled. This was a common story. Parents always cried when a child was identified as a meritocrat. She remembered her mother wailing that if God wanted to single out her child, she'd rather He had struck her blind. Commoners never understood their meritocratic children. They thought being forced to sacrifice the ordinary pleasures of life in order to carry the leadership burdens of Earth was a kind of curse.

"I've never seen a Colonial voice box, Anne. How does it work?" It was an indelicate question, but Parker forgave the human's understandable curiosity. Usually she wrapped her neck, and the device was completely concealed by the collar of her officer's tunic. But in the lab she wore only a white coat over a scrub suit, leaving the box conspicuously visible. Parker tilted her head so Steele could have a clear view of the band supporting an oval silver disk set into a hole in her trachea.

"Need first this for talk," she explained. "Be vocal chords. In band be some controls. Volume most easy. I still not good do tone. Pitch hard too." She touched a small rectangular box pinned to her lab coat. "Here be power source. Voice box is must have for me," she added apologetically. "Ship allow battery charge when I need." Parker took a scarf from her desk drawer and wrapped her neck.

"When throat heal, next need train brain. All Colonial be pan-lingual for think-talk and hear-talk. All peoples think when talk. Be same if think-talk voice make sound. Read be more hard. No think in paper or black ink mark. I read five Earth language only. Talk for ear seven only." Parker knew that line officers normally spoke several dozen languages. But it was easy for them. Parker was proud of her accomplishment. "English be mine most perfectest sound voice language," she said.

"So you passed the exam and then trained for the Navy?"

"Yes. I be glad. Always want go space. Be doctor best Colonial can do."

"You mean you had another preference?" It didn't matter to the Admiralty what assignment a meritocrat preferred; officers were assigned where they were needed. But Steele was accustomed to think of Doctor Parker as a feature of sickbay. It was odd to think of her wanting to serve anywhere else.

"If all my wish could be, I navigate ship. I be born in space; think I be born for navigate space. But Admiralty say Colonial not can train for line. Not any job top deck. Say voice box not can give orders clear and fast. Guess that be true. Navy say learn medicine. Go study Johns Hopkins. Then go space. Voice box good enough for doctor orders."

The thought sometimes crossed Parker's mind that life would be so simple if humans did not find telepathic communication so painful. Steele's stoicism on the gundeck during Parker's intervention was truly extraordinary. Steele also had the fortitude to ask to take it a second time out of no other motive than pure kindness. And she barely flinched at the pain she must have experienced. Remarkable for a human.

Parker wondered at the mysterious ways of the Creator in forming two hominid species so similar and yet so fundamentally unable to communicate. She sensed that her efforts to bridge the gap were artificial and basically unnatural.

"I see you've kept up your interest in navigation anyway." Steele nodded toward the chart spread out on the lab bench. "That's why you suggested a navigational problem to me this morning. I didn't think about it at the time, but that was an unusual thing for a physician to come up with. I don't think Gordon would know the Point of Storms from the Sea of Sighs."

Parker nodded. "Doctor Gordon keep eyes on microscope. He happy leave telescope to line. Me would look stars if could."

Line officers could check out bridge observations any time they cared to, but the Colonial physician would have to have a good reason to go topside. It really was too bad, Steele thought, that Parker had to pursue her hobby with no reference but the published Admiralty charts.

"Would you like to hear what I did with your problem?" Steele asked. She'd spent so much time feeling guilty about having used the exercise as a crutch that she'd almost forgotten what a fascinating puzzle it was. No one was likely to take a ship from Mantu to Gibraltar by way of the Point of Storms, especially not in December. The high tide that Parker specified made the exercise marginally feasible, but only if you had very precise control at the helm. Her solution was, she was sure, highly unconventional. It depended on cutting out the engines and flipping sail plates twice to ride gravity currents more sensitively. She briefly outlined her ideas to Parker.

The Colonial was intrigued and went searching through her collection of navigational aids until she found a copy of the *Mantu Pilot* and an abacus. The two women bent their heads together over the three dimensional chart used to represent the five variables in the real equation and were soon deeply absorbed in their calculations.

When seven bells sounded two hours later, Steele realized that she was due on the bridge and had to get her dinner first.

Long after Steele's abrupt departure, Parker continued to think about her. She hardly dared hope that the ship's navigator would care to spend another evening in the isolation bay. Still, she couldn't help thinking how much more pleasant life aboard *Lafayette* would be if she had such visits from time to time.

CHAPTER EIGHT

The wardroom of HMS *Lafayette* was carefully designed and furnished to encourage emotional bonding between the officers, just as the crew's living spaces on the third deck were designed to promote healthy community relations. Meritocrats did not have the anti-social tendencies that living in crowded conditions normally brought out in the commoners, but for both officers and crew, devising means to keep hominids functioning in the confined, isolated environment of a twenty-first century warship was a triumph of applied psychology.

Because the meritocratic officers were indispensable to the well-being, indeed to the survival of the ship and those who lived aboard her, it was often said that the brain of the ship was on the bridge. The ship's heart, however, was in the wardroom.

As was customary, the wardroom was furnished to suit the tastes of the captain, although the commanding officer shared little of the camaraderie of officers' country. For different reasons, Captain Brook was almost as isolated aboard *Lafayette* as Doctor Parker was, though both would be shocked had anyone pointed out this similarity. Nevertheless, it was important to Brook to know that his subordinates were friends as well as colleagues, and he gave much attention to furnishing the space that was central to their social interaction.

In deference to the tradition of the ship, Brook favored an eighteenth century style. Because of their oath of poverty, meritocrats could accept no cash awards or gifts of any value. It was customary to reward a ship's officers by making gifts to the wardroom. In this way, *Lafayette* had acquired a pleasant collection of antiques mixed in with the standard issue provided by the Admiralty.

The wardroom was small. One luxury that could not be provided on even the largest of Earth's ships was space. The long table that was used for meals and meetings filled most of the deck, but it was designed so that it could be hoisted up and folded into the deckhead when it was not wanted. Similarly the screens, blackboards, and even the twenty-four hour clock on the bulkhead could be covered by damask drapes. The three artificial sun windows were curtained with the same fabric and an artificial fireplace was built into the narrow bulkhead facing the door.

A portrait of Lafayette painted by Charles Peale in 1780 had hung over the fireplace since the ship was commissioned, and an antique clock-barometer set stood on the mantelpiece. This ornament was a source of a considerable amusement since it was as useless an item for a space-going ship as could be imagined. It had been purchased for *Lafayette* by popular subscription during the first war, and the sincerity of the commoners who presented it to Captain Brook required that he accept it soberly with thanks and promise to give it a place in the wardroom.

The barometer was accurate — always absolutely steady at thirty inches of mercury. The clock enjoyed a more active life. It was an eight-day-key-wound model. For some reason, after its first bouts with above-light acceleration, it refused either to keep proper time or to run down. It had occasional fits of vigorous ticking followed by weeks of silence. At erratic intervals of months, or even years, the apparatus relieved itself of stately announcements of the passage of a watch, surely the longest watch in Naval history. It had sounded six bells, Costello had told Steele, the evening before Shankar died. He had joked about it saying whoever was standing the watch would expect to be relieved sometime during the next voyage.

On a morning in mid-October, Steele had breakfast late. Doctor Gordon made regular inspections of the watch bill, and if he thought someone wasn't getting enough rest issued a medical order to sleep in. Steele, Rivera and Captain Brook were current recipients of such orders. Steele was the only one required to obey it. The heavy weather the ship had been passing through for the better part of a week kept either Brook or Rivera constantly on the bridge and they would continue to relieve each other watch on watch until the ship was safe. After that, they'd obey the order to sleep.

Steele had no comparable responsibility, so after coming off the middle watch at dawn, she'd gone back to bed. It was mid-morning before she went to get her breakfast.

She found she would not be alone in the wardroom. Hall was there taking a mudd break. Steele was not happy to see him, which made her feel guilty. She didn't like being alone with him and recently he seemed always to be in a bad mood. But you were supposed to love your messmates, so she made an effort and greeted him cheerfully.

"Thanks for relieving me at morning inspection, Henry. I owe you one."

"No problem for me. I don't have a lubber's stomach." Hall frowned and swallowed half a mug of mudd.

Steele watched Hall as she stirred honey into her mug and sipped at it. She'd recently discovered the drink was much more tolerable when it was sweetened up a bit although Gordon's recent introduction of additional saltpeter increased the pungency of the mixture to such an extent that even some old salts complained about it.

"If you want, I'll do sickbay rounds for you this evening." Steele added honey and soy milk to her cereal.

"You don't owe me anything, Steele. All right?"

Steele put down her spoon. "Are you upset about something, Henry? If you are why don't you just spit it out?"

"All right, all right. I'll tell you what upsets me. It's you. You get treated around here like you're some goddamned invalid. Like this morning, Doc Gordon puts you on the sick list again. That's twice in less than a month."

"Henry, this was a sleep-in order. I'm not on the sick list."

"But you were last month when we whipped Ames. You must really have some special pull with the Old Man for him to have let you off with that kind of excuse. If it had been me, I'd have been in hack."

There was something strange about Hall, Steele thought. The captain didn't play favorites. No meritocrat did. The commoners didn't always believe that, but every meritocrat knew it was true. Fairness was instinctive for meritocrats.

"What are you trying to tell me, Henry?"

"That you're soft, Steele. That's what I'm telling you. You come aboard *Lafayette*, top of the class of 2080, and you think you're hot stuff. Well, you may be fast on those navigation calculations, but you don't have the guts it takes to be a combat leader. No one in your class does. If plebe year for the class of '80 had been the same as it was for mine, you'd have bilged the first summer."

Steele tried to understand what Hall was trying to convey. He had gone through his first three years at Annapolis under the command of Admiral Kalina. Admiral Thanatos came in the same year that her class began its training. But both admirals were qualified and experienced meritocrats. It hardly seemed appropriate for a young lieutenant to question the Admiralty.

On the other hand, it was entirely appropriate for him to criticize her. She was the junior officer aboard and so was expected to take criticism from everyone. Still, this seemed an odd way for him to do it.

"That doesn't seem to me to be a very helpful comment," she said. "Do you have some suggestion how I can improve?"

"You can't improve!" Hall seized the pot of mudd, refilled his mug, and filled Steele's to the brim. He picked up his mug and drained it without pausing for breath. "This is how a sailor drinks mudd. What about you?"

Steele looked at her mug. If she lifted it, liquid would slop over the brim. Surely he wasn't childish enough to be challenging her to a chugalug contest.

"See. You just don't have it, Maggie. When a sailor is whipped, you're always going to shut your eyes; and when the killing starts, you'll crack. You don't belong in the Navy. The examining board should have sent you into the Church."

For some reason Hall was trying to get her angry, Steele decided. Perhaps he believed that was a way to toughen her. That seemed to her a peculiar idea, but perhaps it had something to do with his Spartan curriculum at Annapolis. Admiral Thanatos believed anger was a source of weakness. She leaned over the table and brought her lips down to sip from the mug.

Rivera came through the door. After three hours of sleep, he would have an early lunch before going back to the bridge. He'd stopped to check the log entries before coming to the wardroom; the storm was abating.

"Good morning, sir." The two lieutenants greeted him simultaneously. Rivera smiled at them. It was good to see the young people together.

Steele took her breakfast dishes to the galley window where the steward ladled out a bowl of soup and prepared a sandwich for the first officer.

"I was on the bridge just now, Steele, and had a look at the punishments book. I happened to notice it hadn't been signed yet by the officer in charge at morning inspection. You'd better get to that before the end of the watch. You know how fussy Brook is about these things."

"Yes, sir. Thank's for reminding me, sir." Steele caught Hall's eye to be sure he'd picked up the hint.

Hall quickly got to his feet. "Well, I think I'll just go and have a look at the weather readings."

Both the captain and Lieutenant Lamashtu were on the bridge discussing the feasibility of sending out a team of hullsweepers to get the sails cleaned during the interval of calm. Of necessity, Brook had taken the ship directly through the asteroid belt that blocked all approaches to the Mantu system. Neither noticed Hall pull the punishments book and add his signature.

Hall had a history of sloppy paperwork-and had been reprimanded more than once for failing to put his signature into a report after a yeoman made the permanent record copy. Steele had saved him from another tongue lashing — or worse. And she had covered for him in front of the first officer right after he had been so nasty to her.

It was true that Steele was soft. It never much bothered him to see a sailor punished. But he didn't have to throw it in her face. She was part of the ship's team; and even if she had been an invalid, they were all supposed to work together to help each other out. What he'd done was to take out his bad mood on her because she was vulnerable.

The other officers never did things like that. He'd always thought that the other officers seemed so different because they were all so much older than he was. But Maggie was even younger. She could easily have told Rivera who really had the duty during morning inspection. But she hadn't. It would have been disloyal. It would not have been meritocratic behavior.

Why did Maggie seem always to do the meritocratic thing automatically while he seemed always to be putting his foot in it? It didn't make sense. He was a meritocrat. He'd passed the exam, after all.

Or maybe he hadn't.

Hall crossed the deck to get as far away from the conference between the captain and the engineer as he could before taking the ladder down to his cabin. A stormy sea began to roll outside the porthole as he entered.

Hall spent little time in his cabin unless he was sleeping — or when the captain had put him in hack for some infraction. But he needed some time to think. He pulled out his bunk and sat, his hands shaking.

Did the examiners ever make mistakes? Hall knew his brains were all right. He'd made decent grades at the Academy. And his immune system seemed all right, though he knew that all young people tended to have strong immune systems and the really startling differences between meritocrats and commoners did not appear until their late twenties. But he didn't have the rest of it. He didn't have the meritocratic character.

He should have realized this earlier! Now that he thought about it, it was all so perfectly clear. His father, his goddamn pushy ambitious father. He had the motive, the ability, and the opportunity. Everyone in the family knew that his father imagined himself to be a meritocrat. He'd gone in for the exam himself repeatedly and flunked seven times before he'd finally given up and accepted work as a commoner in the archival division of the Church.

But that wasn't the end of old Maxwell Hall's ambition. Oh, no. Then he started pushing his son. Henry never wanted to be a meritocrat. Ordinary kids seemed to have a lot more fun. But daddy pushed and pushed. Hall had been ready to give up after the first time he flunked; but daddy pestered and pestered until he tried again. Then, lo and behold, the notification came that he'd made a passing score!

Hall snorted. Maybe a passing score. Or maybe a smart Church archivist with a lot of brains and a lot of nerve and no integrity "fixing" things. What a totally foul thing to do to a little kid — not to mention the danger an unqualified person in a position of authority posed to society.

Hall knew exactly what he ought to do. He ought to stand up right now, get his butt back up to the bridge and tell Captain Brook that he believed he might not be fit to hold his commission. But Hall knew he wasn't going to do that. And that clinched it, since if he were a meritocrat, he would be courageous enough and selfless enough to do what was right even if it meant being busted and serving as a common sailor until he could be retested.

The certain knowledge sent the blood rushing to his head. He was an imposter. They'd find him out eventually. He was sure of it. It was a miracle he'd gotten away with it this long. His heart pounded as he squeezed his eyes tight and whispered a kind of prayer. He was innocent of intent to defile the meritocratic sacraments. If he could just make it back to Earth from this voyage, he'd resign his commission. Let his father go to blazes!

* * *

Steele would have left the wardroom when Hall did, but thanks to Hall's unasked-for refill of her mug, she still had mudd to drink. Once she'd worked the level down enough, she stirred in more honey.

She looked across the table at the first officer. He hadn't touched his food. He had his elbows on the table and his hands cupped over his eyes.

He really must be beat, she thought. It wasn't like the first officer to make a mistake about officer assignments even when they were switched over at the last minute. He not only memorized the watch bill and the work sheets for the officers but could usually tell you where any one of the five thousand crew members was at any given time.

Rivera sighed heavily and lowered his arms. As he reached for his spoon, he wiped some moisture from his eyes with the back of his hand. Then he noticed that Steele was watching him.

"Don't mind me," he said. "I get a little moody when the weather's like this."

That was not a good explanation. Whatever the conditions outside the hull, the environment inside the ship was constant and would stay that way — thanks to the many fail-safes of damage control — even if the hull was pierced.

"With all respect, sir, if you're not feeling well, you ought to report to sickbay."

Rivera smiled. All the officers monitored each other for signs of illness. Their standards were different from those of med/life. They understood that officers' duties might require them to push themselves further than the physicians would like, but they took care of each other. An infected officer could spread plague through the ship as effectively as anyone else. The junior lieutenant was shouldering this informal responsibility.

"It's nothing like that, Steele. It's just that weather like this reminds me of my brother. Gets me a little weepy, that's all."

Steele knew that Rivera was one of three children, all of whom had gone into space. People who lived together as intimately as officers on a warship didn't keep many secrets from each other. Rivera's younger sister, Rosa, had volunteered for the Navy toward the end of the First Galaxy War; she was now a yellow striper running the bakery aboard HMS *Peacock*. Rivera and Costello, whose husband served aboard the same vessel, shared a common interest in the flagship of the forward fleet. Rivera had never spoken about his brother much. She knew Rick was the oldest child in the family and had died during the war.

"I'm sorry, sir." Steele concentrated on her mudd. Rivera watched her quizzically and then laughed.

"Damn it, Maggie. I'm supposed to be the only one on the top deck who can do that."

"Do what, sir?"

"Do you expect me to believe you aren't conscious of it? You want to hear about my brother, right?"

Steele blushed. He'd read her mind. "I don't mean to intrude on your privacy, sir. I apologize."

"That's the trick, Steele! You didn't say anything; you just made me feel like talking. It's the talent of inviting confidences.

The sailors call it having a child's heart. Haven't you heard the saying, 'A captain with a child's heart always commands a happy ship?'"

"I guess so. But I never understood what it meant. Children don't command in space. I wouldn't feel real happy if Captain Brook was younger than I am. I'd feel scared."

"How would you feel about serving under me?"

"You're not a child either, sir," said Steele.

"Nor are you, Lieutenant. But both of us, it seems, have the child's heart. It's an aspect of meritocratic charisma that is most prominent in strongly empathetic personalities. It means you have a gift for using listening as an instrument of leadership. Think about it."

Rivera finished his soup and started on his sandwich. Steele realized her mug was empty, but she made no move to leave the wardroom. Whether it was just the insatiable curiosity that her mother had found so maddening while she was growing up or this thing Rivera called "a child's heart," she really did want to hear about Rivera's brother, to learn what made the first officer cry.

"All right, Lieutenant Steele. I can't resist you. Anyway, Doctor Parker told me over and over that I ought to share this with someone. It might as well be you."

Steele leaned toward him, her eyes bright and eager. Rivera shook his head and wondered to himself if he ever displayed such puppy-like enthusiasm. He pushed his hair back, poured himself some mudd, and began to tell his story.

"Ricardo — my big brother Rick — was born with something wrong with his brain. The way I heard it, our mother had been sick with one of those measles variants that started going around in the early 'forties. No one knew then that they were so dangerous. Rick was four before it was clear that he was brain damaged. Even then, my folks didn't want to admit it.

"It wasn't easy growing up with him. Our folks were both good church people — priests. They shared a parish in Guadalajara, and they were sure that lots of love could make everything all right. But Rick just wasn't a loveable kid. In fact, as early as I can remember him, he was downright mean. And when he got bigger he turned dangerous. My folks couldn't handle him, and neither could the reform school. He was just very slow mentally; there was no getting through to him with reason. Charlie Ames reminds me of him a little. But Rick was physically powerful: stubborn as a mule and strong as an ox. The Navy pressed him into service when I was eight and he was fourteen.

"My mother took us to see him off. Me and my kid sister, Rosa. My father wouldn't come. Rick had run from the press, and they'd had to take him to Fort McHenry in chains. That was as much as my dad wanted to see. My mother hoped they could calm him down while they had him in the barracks at the embarkation station so we could all wave goodbye. I can remember that trip; Mom kept telling us how wonderful the Navy was. She made a total convert of Rosa; she joined up as soon as she was old enough.

"Well, they calmed Rick down a lot. They put him under total sedation and carried him aboard the shuttle in a litter. That was how Rick joined the Navy." Rivera paused and stared into his mug. Steele said nothing, waiting for him to continue.

Suddenly, Rivera flashed her an amused look. "You're very good at this, you know. You've already gotten more out of me than Doctor Parker did in six months." He sipped his mudd, then noticed her empty mug. He picked up the pot. "May I? I hate to drink alone."

Steele pushed her mug forward. If another cup would get her more of Rivera's story, she'd pay the price.

"Rick was in space for three years his first time out, and when he got back to Earth, the press sent him right back to space. The Church authorities said he'd improved a little but not enough to let loose on Earth. This time he was out for five years.

"I went in for testing when I was ten and was at Annapolis when he got back from his second tour. Rick passed inspection and was given a choice of a long list of jobs he could have. He surprised everyone by saying he wanted to go back into space, and that's what he did. When I was commissioned and sent aboard *Constellation*, I found my brother serving in the crew.

"I never had much conversation with him. The rule against fraternization holds even for blood brothers. But I watched him, and it was hard to believe he was the same person. The meanness and the hot temper were completely gone. He was a willing worker, and he stayed out of trouble. He was assigned to the engineer's station as a hullsweeper. It's not a job that takes much intelligence, and it doesn't have much status. But it's a job that's essential to the safety of the ship. Rick understood that. He was proud of himself."

Rivera fell silent again.

"He died during a storm?"

Rivera nodded and looked out the wardroom window where a dark sky and tall grey-black waves simulated heavy weather in the North Atlantic.

"It was the same thing as we've been having since Wednesday. Asteroid turbulence. Rick went out with a crew to repair damage. Some rocks were still bumping around, but we couldn't wait. We had to get the patching done. The mate in command of the work crew got hit and went off in a spin. Rick tried to help and got his line snarled. By the time the medics got out there, it was too late to do anything for either of them. We couldn't get the bodies back through the airlock with all that rubble flying. The engineer went out to see what could be done, but finally we had to cut them loose. I was on the bridge when it happened. I saw the whole thing through the mirrors.

"I watched my brother die, Maggie. He died a hero, a genuine hero. What he did was unselfish and brave, and he did it by reflex. He did it just as a meritocrat would. He didn't have any other meritocratic qualities — none at all — but at that instant he had that one reflex that pushed him to help someone in trouble just as sharp and pure as any of Earth's elite. He was a credit to the Navy." Steele realized that was the same phrase he'd used a month earlier to express his hopes for Charlie Ames. Did he think Ames had hero potential? She asked him that.

"Yes, I do think so. Now, I know that most meritocrats say we have a responsibility toward the commoners because they need us. But I think there's more to it than that. The worst of them have some merit inside them. If we handle them right, that merit gets a chance to surface. They can't bring it up without help. But patience and firmness can bring up a lot. I would never have believed Rick could progress so much. It seemed hard to believe he could ever be controlled without massive doses of drugs or brain surgery that would have left him a vegetable. If the Navy could salvage Rick, it can salvage anyone. If officers expect to see merit surface, surprising things can happen. Yes, I think even Charlie Ames has potential."

"That's an interesting theory," Steele said, choosing her words carefully. Privately she thought it was rubbish, but a junior lieutenant didn't say that to the first officer. Rivera was talking like one of those liberal egalitarians who romanticized the lower orders. Of course some of them occasionally acted like meritocrats. But since they couldn't act that way consistently, they needed leadership from those who could and did.

"I know what you're thinking," Rivera said. "If you think my ideas are eccentric, you're in good company. That's how I ended up on Doctor Parker's couch. She finally convinced Captain Brook that the peculiarities of my political theories presented no danger to the ship and I got out of my weekly sessions. I was never so glad to have anything over with. Until you've had a Colonial shrink, you haven't known pain."

Here was another surprise. Steele would have expected anyone as liberal as Rivera in his views about the lower orders would have been tolerant of Colonials. But Rivera was clearly no eccentric on species. He was less comfortable with Doctor Parker than she was. But what was this about pain?

"Did Doctor Parker think-talk you when she you were in therapy with her?"

"Good God, no! I hope I didn't give you that impression. Doctor Parker is a decent woman." It surprised him that the young lieutenant, who seemed so naive, could entertain such an obscene idea. "It's just that awful voice of hers. Any time she thought I was holding something back, she'd prod me with questions. Ouch! Like a steel file scratching!" He grinned.

Something was wrong with Rivera's story. He was still holding back. His professed admiration of his brother's so-called heroic death was out of proportion.

"Sir, may I ask a question?"

"You are persistent, aren't you. As bad as Doctor Parker, without the ugly sound."

"May I?"

Rivera pushed back his hair and grinned. "Go ahead," he said. "I'm hooked."

"You said the Navy didn't use drugs or surgery on your brother. How was he tamed?"

Rivera sucked in his breath. How had she done this? Found the sore point and put her finger right on it. No one had ever gotten him to talk about this; he'd never even let himself think about it. Why was it so important to him that Rick had, indeed, died a hero's death? Why did he cry whenever he remembered it?

He considered avoiding the question, but a pair of clear blue eyes wouldn't let his go.

"Rick was stubborn and strong. Captain Morris was very patient and very persistent and unwilling to hang anyone when there was the smallest chance of salvage. Rick was tamed like an animal; he was broken with the lash."

* * *

Relaxing in the wardroom after dinner one evening late in November as *Lafayette* moved in an approach course toward Mantu system, Steele suddenly realized that she felt at home. The war seemed deceptively remote, perhaps even more remote than when she was on Earth training for combat. She felt warm, safe, and happy, although she knew that the ship was hurtling through cold, barren space and that danger was never far away.

Steele was among friends. No, it was more than that. She was part of a family. Except for her mother, no one she had ever known inspired the depth of affection she felt for the officers of *Lafayette*, even for those whom at first seemed least attractive.

She thought of Doctor Gordon, who tonight, as usual, brought all his worries with him to the dinner table. He expounded at great length on the causes of sexual dysfunction among honeybees before excusing himself saying he was going to make a surprise inspection of the apiary to see what those idiots down there were doing that had got the hives buzzing in the middle of the night.

Hall, who had the watch this evening, was also becoming easier to like now that she knew him better. It was odd, but even though he was senior to her, she felt a kind of protective fondness for him as she did for members of crew. Hall's belligerent manner hid a surprisingly sensitive character. She'd be tempted to describe him as insecure, except, of course, no meritocrat was deficient in self-confidence.

The captain and the first lieutenant were the officers she knew least well. Brook was always on duty. He took most of his meals in his day cabin, and practiced rigid self-control and self-discipline to maintain a professional distance from those under his command. Rivera's responsibilities were almost as heavy, and despite his more relaxed manner and their one revealing conversation, Steele still felt the distance of rank between them. Still, both of the senior officers had such powerfully charismatic personalities that it was impossible not to love them. Steele was as susceptible to their different types of charm as any member of the crew, and her admiration of their professional abilities grew every day.

Steele was aware of the novelty of her growing friendship with Anne Parker. The Colonial never came to the wardroom unless Captain Brook called a meeting that included med/life officers, and Steele had to seek her out if she wanted to visit with her. There was precious little time for visits in the schedule of a junior officer who was expected to cram training for every Navy line specialty into time left over after finishing her regular duties. Nevertheless, Steele usually managed to spend a few minutes with Parker almost every day and liked her more all the time.

And finally, there were Liz Costello and Martha Lamashtu, the two officers she knew best because they were most involved in her training. They were both with her now, in the wardroom, sharing a precious hour of free time. She could not have felt closer to them had they been her own mother and grandmother.

There were some comfortable places to sit in the wardroom, deeply upholstered pieces of furniture that made the room seem horribly cramped when the table was in use but which no one would willingly give up. Lamashtu had a favorite place: the corner of a rose velvet sofa. She sat this evening as she did every night she was off duty, her plump body curled into the cushions, and her lap covered with crocheting.

She was presently engaged in stitching together a pile of small blue squares embroidered with pink roses. It was to be a crib blanket, the last item of the third complete infant layette that the engineering officer had produced since the ship left the solar system. Costello sat next to her and fingered one of the intricately detailed pieces.

"This is a new design, isn't it, Martha? I don't seem to remember this little dewdrop thing on the petal being on the layette sets I dropped off on Earth for you."

"Yes, it's new. What I did was twist a little bit of silver thread into the yarn to make it shine that way. It takes longer to finish a square if I do dewdrops, and I had to slow down. If I run out of wool, I'll be stuck with whatever synthetic med/life can give me." She wrinkled her nose. Anyone who appreciated natural fibers found Navy synthetics a very poor substitute. "I want my wool to hold out as long as possible."

"I guess we all know what you'll be stuffing your duffel with when you come back from leave on the Colony." Costello continued to stroke the soft blue square.

"Every cubic centimeter I've got." Lamashtu chuckled. "And I'd get me a couple of little lambs, a boy and a girl, if I thought I could smuggle them past Doctor Parker."

"Parker says she'll be checking out cattle on the Colony," Steele broke in. "If she can find a good buy, we'll take on some frozen meat, and the crew will have roast beef for Christmas." Steele was sitting crosslegged on the rug in front of the artificial fire sipping a mug of mudd. She had finally come to enjoy the strong-flavored drink. Perhaps it was because Gordon had, for some reason known only to himself, cut back sharply on both saltpeter and licorice and added a hefty dose of cinnamon.

"Now, now, Maggie. Don't talk about little lambs as if they were just meat. Not that leg of lamb and lamb chops wouldn't be a nice change from pork." Lamashtu completed the fine stitching at the end of a square and carefully snipped off the yarn. She sat for a moment with her hands idle in her lap. "In fact, when I get a command, I believe I'll switch lamb for pork altogether. Maybe get us some goats too. Then my sailors would have milk and cheese, and I'd have a steady supply of angora for my baby blankets." It was unlikely at her age and relatively low place on the commissioning list that Lamashtu would ever get an independent command. But that didn't keep her from making plans, just in case.

"For such daring experimentation, you'll have to get a very special ship." Costello's eyes flashed mischievously. "Do you think the Navy is ready for, say, a heavy cruiser called the *Golden Fleece*? I can just see the press releases from the Office of War Information." She assumed the ponderous voice of a holograph news broadcaster. "HMS *Golden Fleece*, Captain Martha Lamashtu commanding, last month captured four Delphinian ships of the line in one twenty-four hour period. Captain Lamashtu credits the fighting spirit of her crew to a diet heavy in mutton chops and goat cheese and to the warm woolen mittens she issues to all hands assigned to hull damage control while the ship is under fire."

Lamashtu chuckled and began stitching another square into the blanket. "Someone else would have to crochet the mittens. I just crochet for babies."

"Don't you ever make anything for grownups?" Steele asked.

"Never have, Maggie. Doctor Parker got me started on this hobby while I was still with the crew. It's supposed to help me sublimate my maternal instincts."

"I thought there was something in the mudd to take care of that," Steele said innocently.

Both of the older women laughed. "No such luck, honey," Lamashtu said. "It keeps you from having babies, but it won't keep you from wanting them."

"Or from missing them," Costello added, her voice darkened for a moment, but she shook herself out of it. "Speaking of babies, Martha, I suppose you got the usual lecture from Doctor Gordon about keeping our people out of trouble ashore."

"Indeed I did. He came after me as soon as he found out I'd be the officer escort. Came right up into the 'tweendecks, he did, and bellowed at me over the noise while I was trying to show a new crew how to drain a hot line." Lamashtu looked up from her work. "Why don't you tell Maggie how it goes. I'm sure you've got it memorized."

Costello could mimic anyone, and she did a good Doctor Gordon. She sucked in her cheeks and opened her eyes wide in a serviceable imitation of the physician's gaunt hollow-eyed face and snapped out the instructions in an irritated tone: "Now listen here, Lieutenant. I don't want these healthy people brought back to me to crowd up sickbay. You see to it that they don't fill their stomachs with sugar candy and soda pop. Don't let them stay up all night carousing like a bunch of ninnies. They need their sleep as much on shore as they do in space. Keep them out of those goddamn barrooms. Between hangovers and fights those places are health hazards. And keep them out of the goddamn whore houses. I don't want anyone coming back pregnant."

"The proper reply when you get that speech, Maggie," said Lamashtu, "is to remind our med/life director that to sailors, liberty means sugar candy, late hours, boozing, and whoring. If we tried to enforce rules against that on shore, we'd have a mutiny on our hands. So the best we can do is make sure they all pack their toothbrushes and their morning-after pills and deal with the headaches and black eyes when they report back and go into quarantine.

"As far as that goes, the biggest problem in this quarantine is sure to be fleas and lice. Even if a sailor spent the full liberty time praying in a Colonial church, some of those little critters would get picked up. The Colony's a beautiful planet, Maggie, but it's not what you'd call a sanitary place."

"While you're checking the toothbrushes, Martha, make sure that there's a thorough search of the launch." Costello was suddenly serious. "You don't want to leave a dirty job for one of your messmates the way I did."

"Don't fret yourself over that, Liz. The commoners being what they are, someone's bound to spoil our record once in a while."

Steele's puzzled expression registered with both women simultaneously. She hadn't been told about the incident. It was old news now. Lamashtu explained. "We had a deserter, Maggie, just before you joined us. There was a stowaway aboard *Firefly* when Liz took the launch to Earth. It was a sailor named Lobbel who'd been pressed for a second tour and came though the quarantine Rivera did last spring. She was retaken very quickly

— never got out of the docking area. *Firefly* brought her right back to *Lafayette*, and Captain Brook had her hanged the next morning after prayers." Lamashtu picked up another square from the pile in her lap, her fingers worked the stitches automatically as she talked.

"I got the special duty. It was all very sad really; she wasn't quite twenty. It was hard for her to understand why she had to die for something that would be a minor offense on shore. I suppose it seemed to her equivalent to escape from confinement. I got through to her eventually, though it was touch and go for a time. I sat up with her most of the night. She accepted it finally and made a good death." Lamashtu laid her work aside and turned to face Costello.

"It wasn't your fault, Liz," she said patting her hand. "We all know that desertion is a premeditated crime, not a response to sudden temptation. If it hadn't been *Firefly*, it would have been something else. The folks who've made up their minds to run always find a way. That's why deep space is full of pirates."

Steele stared up at Lamashtu's placid brown face, which was surrounded by a mass of wooly white hair, as she bent again over her crocheting, and tried to imagine the officer who looked like everybody's grandmother presiding over the execution of a young sailor. It was a picture that would not come clear.

As Steele watched Lamashtu, Costello was watching her. Seeing the astonishment spread over the junior officer's face, Costello flinched and pressed her lips together. It was all too easy for Costello to visualize what must have occurred between Lamashtu and Jenny Lobbel the night before Lobbel's execution.

Lobbel was high-strung and desperate. When she was retaken at the dock in Bengal, she'd fought like a tiger. Costello herself had been so preoccupied with her coming visit to Shankar's family that she hadn't spotted the fleeing stowaway until after members of the launch crew began to give chase. It had taken a blow to the neck to bring her down and three strong blue stripers to force her back into the launch while dozens of shore sailors and civilians watched. Very bad for the *Lafayette*'s image. Very bad for the Navy's image. Scenes like that made it even harder than it already was to get voluntary enlistments.

Nothing would have been done to quiet Lobbel down on the trip back to *Lafayette*. It was forbidden to give any kind of drug to a criminal, because it might interfere with the development of emotions of guilt, fear, and repentance. So all the crew would have done was to bind her hands and feet, strap her down, and gag her. Most likely she'd been kept bound and gagged during her interview with the captain too, though Brook's presence often had a temporary calming effect even on violent individuals.

But poor Martha, charged to wrestle for Lobbel's immortal soul, would have gotten the full blast. Wild anger, shouting, cursing, until Lamashtu forced her to face her guilt. Then terror and hysterical tears. Finally resignation, repentance, prayers, and a drug that dimmed her consciousness in her last hours.

Costello also could visualize what it would have been like if Lamashtu had failed and it had been necessary to hang Lobbel still defiant, unrepentant, and fully conscious. It disturbed and annoyed Costello that Steele had obviously never taken the time to think seriously about exactly what happened when a sailor committed a capital crime. She was blinking her large blue eyes and staring at Lamashtu open-mouthed as though she had never seen her before.

"What's the matter, Fifth," Costello snapped. "Don't you think Lieutenant Lamashtu is up to the job?"

Whenever anyone called her "Fifth," emphasizing her status as the lowest-ranking lieutenant aboard, Steele knew she was in for a lecture. She braced herself for it.

"What surprises you? You know there are capital crimes in the Navy, just as there are in civilian law. If executions are less frequent, it's because sailors don't have much opportunity to commit serious offenses on a well-disciplined ship and because a ship's captain has more discretion in awarding punishment than is allowed to a civilian judge.

"When there's a hanging aboard this ship, one of us draws a special assignment. Lieutenant Lamashtu is as fit for the duty as anyone else. She does very well with the dying whether the death coming is natural or not — exceptionally well. Doctor Gordon often calls on her to help out in sickbay when they have a difficult terminal case.

"Helping a condemned criminal come to terms with death is a job that can be done well or badly. You can do it well only if you prepare yourself for it."

Steele had put down her mug and straightened her back. She was listening with grave attention. Again Costello found herself worrying about the gaps in Steele's Academy training. Annapolis students couldn't be given direct experience of combat, but they could certainly be required to witness an execution. Under Admiral Thanatos, the only exposure the cadets got to suffering and death, except for that experimental egg of his, was two weeks' service aboard a hospital ship. That wasn't the same, and it wasn't enough. Under the former superintendent, Admiral Kalina, the summer cruise included a month aboard the prison ship *Good Hope.*

The Admiralty's neat resolution of the ancient tension between those who favored the Athenian training ideal and those who favored the Spartan ideal probably had something to be said for it, Costello thought. Annapolis would get another Spartan superintendent pretty soon. And then, when *Lafayette* got another young officer, she'd find herself complaining about a junior lieutenant who had mastered none of the dead languages of Earth and had no knowledge at all of extraterrestrial literature beyond textbook summaries. Well, textbooks were better than nothing — if they were studied thoroughly.

"How well have you done your homework, Fifth? Stand up and describe the duties of the discipline officer when the punishment awarded is death."

Steele sprang to her feet. She had studied the relevant sections in *Naval Regulations* and was sure she could recite them perfectly if she hadn't been unexpectedly put under pressure this way. But that, she knew, was precisely the point Costello was trying to make. She might be given such an assignment at any time and would have to do what was required automatically. She would be under pressure, and she would not have time to look up the rules. Steele concentrated and called up the words.

"The responsibility of the disciplinary officer assigned in a capital case has spiritual, psychological and physical aspects, none of which may properly be neglected." Steele hesitated.

"Go on. If I asked you to recite the duties of a navigator when the ship is at anchor, you'd rattle it right off. You should have this down just as well."

"For the spiritual preparation of one condemned to death, the discipline officer exercises the powers and fulfills the functions of priest and confessor," Steele continued slowly, relieved to find that the words would come to her tongue if she concentrated. "Absolution may be given and last rites performed in the manner prescribed by the public mode of worship of the ship aboard which the offence was committed, provided that the offender makes full confession and is truly repentant, which last must be confirmed by polygraphic testing or the equivalent thereof. Those who receive absolution may be given non-lethal doses of sedative drugs. That may not be done for the unrepentant who are required to suffer the pangs of a hard death in hope that, in their final moments, physical agony may soften a stubborn heart and bring them yet to call on God's mercy."

"Enough of that," Costello interrupted. She could well understand Steele's reluctance to dwell on these lugubrious passages. "Skip to the end, and tell me, in your own words, how much of this may be modified at the captain's discretion."

"All of it," Steele replied promptly. In nine cases out of ten, that was the right answer.

"Sloppy, Steele! It's that kind of attitude that gets an officer court-martialed. *Naval Regulations* are pretty firm on a few points. The captain can't waive the death penalty in those cases — including desertion — where it's mandatory. The captain can't delay carrying out a death sentence more than forty-eight hours; that becomes cruel and unusual punishment. There's more. Study up on it, Fifth. You'll never fit yourself for command in space by sticking to subjects you like and ignoring what's unpleasant."

"Yes, ma'am."

Costello was finished. Steele had been properly chastised, and Costello indicated she could sit again. Silence descended over the wardroom, chilling the formerly cozy atmosphere like a cold fog. Lamashtu, who concentrated on her crocheting while Costello grilled the junior officer, finally broke the silence.

"Maggie, honey, I think it's time you were getting to bed. We're awfully close to the Mantu outer approach, so you're likely to get an early morning call to the bridge."

"Okay." Steele got to her feet. "Goodnight, Martha."

"Goodnight"

"Goodnight, Liz."

"Goodnight, Maggie."

After Steele left, the heavy silence reasserted itself until Lamashtu broke it again.

"Why are you so hard on that little gal, Liz? Maggie didn't need that pressure quiz on capital punishment."

"She did need it," Costello snapped. "And she needs more than that. Martha, I'm worried about her." Costello stood and began to pace the small area in front of the fireplace.

"I can't see why, Liz. It seems to me, she's doing just fine."

"She's not toughening up fast enough. You can see it in her face. When you mentioned you'd drawn the duty with Lobbel, she looked as if someone had told her that Santa Claus is a Delphinian agent. How's she going to manage when she has to hang someone? Or what's likely to happen a lot sooner, how's she going to manage when she takes a boarding party into action and her crew suffers casualties?"

"She'll do all right, Liz."

"Of course she'll do all right! That's not what I mean. She'll do all right, but she'll hurt inside. She'll hurt terribly."

"Now who isn't being tough enough? All meritocrats hurt. You can't protect Maggie from that."

"Henry hardened a lot faster than Maggie has."

Lamashtu pulled a fresh length of yarn from her work bag and slipped it into a tapestry needle. "Henry has some other problems, Liz. In fact, I sometimes think he may have hardened too much."

Lamashtu had ample opportunity to study the different styles of command of the two young officers; and from her perspective, as one who had come up from the third deck, she had no doubt which was more effective with ordinary sailors.

"The sailors like Maggie, Liz. They go the extra mile for her. Henry gets the bare minimum they can get away with." Lamashtu didn't reveal the nickname she'd heard some sailors apply to

Lieutenant Steele. They called her "Little Mama," which pleased Lamashtu enormously.

Costello halted her pacing and returned to her place on the sofa. "Martha, I've been dreaming about her. It started when we were still in quarantine, and now it's coming more often." Lamashtu put down her needle. Sailors paid attention to dreams.

"In the dream, Maggie comes in here. Into the wardroom. She's been run through with a long spear right under her heart. She isn't bleeding, and she can walk and move all right. But she's in pain. In agony. I'm over here, by the fireplace. And she looks at me, and I can see the pain flooding her eyes.

"I feel that she's calling to me, but I can't hear her. And I can't go to her. It's as if one of those heavy contamination control shields — like they have in the briefing launches — had come down and the signal link was cut. But I see her lips move, calling me, and then I wake up crying."

Lamashtu reached for Costello's hand and squeezed it. "Your first action was very bad, wasn't it, Liz?" Costello nodded. "And you were alone afterward?"

"I was sent out with the gunner. It was a small amphibious operation — pirates making a last stand on a hunk of rock called Flyspeck. It seemed routine, and I wouldn't even have been along except that it looked to the captain like a good training opportunity. It was a lot rougher than we'd expected. They'd built up a decent sized arsenal and were determined not to be taken alive. None were. But we tried. We lost over a third of our party, and we lost Lieutenant Nomura. I had to bag up the corpses and take the survivors back to the ship."

Lamashtu nodded. "That's all your dream means, Liz. You don't want Maggie to suffer the way you did. Probably Shiva's death, and Maggie coming aboard so soon after, got your old grieving and your feeling of responsibility toward a new officer all mixed up together. But there's no way in God's universe you can keep pain out of her life. Every meritocrat has to do her share of suffering. That's just the way it is. You can't help Maggie by taking it on yourself in advance."

"I've been doing that, haven't I." Costello shook her head. "Ever since I met that bright-eyed little kid in Annapolis, I've been hovering over her like a hen with one chick. Maybe I ought to turn myself into Doctor Parker and get a crochet hook."

"I don't think you need therapy, Liz. Besides, there's not enough wool on *Lafayette* for two of us."

Lamashtu snipped off a last tail of yarn and spread the now completed blanket out on her lap. "Babies draw a lot of comfort from these things. And they need a lot, poor dears, coming from a warm womb into a cold world." She folded the blanket carefully and put it into her work bag.

"Well, now, Liz, how would you like to help me plan my next project? When I get the liberty crew back from the Colony, it means ten days in quarantine with them and Doctor Parker. I'll need something really challenging to work on, or I'll die of boredom with no one to talk to."

"You never talk to Doctor Parker, do you, Martha?"

"Of course not. Unless it's ship's business."

"Maggie does, you know."

"I declare, Liz, are you worried about that too? If it doesn't bother the child to listen to that awful voice, I can't see how it does any harm. There are quite a number of inter-species friendships on the third deck. Everyone living so close and all, it tends to happen. Some humans even allow Colonials to speak to them telepathically."

"But those are commoners," Costello sniffed. "And I'll bet they're all blue stripers. You wouldn't find that kind of thing going on among the more sensitive sailors. I wouldn't think any chiefs would have Colonial friends."

"Wrong," Lamashtu grinned. "Not that I ever understood it myself, but Katie McDougall has had a steady affair with Mickey McCarthy almost since she came aboard."

"The galley chief and the captain's steward? Well! That's quite a surprise! Whatever could bring those two together?"

Lamashtu shrugged. "They're next to each other alphabetically on the roster." When you were a common sailor stuck on a ship for a long tour, you took your friends, and your lovers too, where you could find them. It wasn't that sailors wouldn't be fussier if they could. Life on the third deck of a warship just didn't give you much choice.

"I don't know what things are coming to in the Navy, Martha." Costello shook her head. "Training cadets in simulators, inter-species communication rampant below decks. Next thing you know, we'll have Colonials being admitted to the Naval Academy."

"Now that's one thing we can be sure will never happen. Neither the Queen nor the Admiralty would stand for that kind of social experimentation. It would damage the morale of the cadets beyond repair if they tried to integrate Annapolis. I'm as sure as I am of anything in the universe that no hominid with extraterrestrial origins will ever hold a line officer's commission in the Royal Navy. Why that would undercut the oldest traditions of the service!"

As if in response to the black woman's emphatic assertion of timeless Navy tradition, the antique clock on the mantel ticked twice and sounded seven bells.

CHAPTER NINE

When Steele studied the heavens for terrestrial navigation courses at Annapolis, the star of the Mantu planetary system appeared due north of Pegasus, roughly halfway between the star Enif of that constellation and Delphinus. What she saw through the telescope, of course, was light emitted many years or even centuries ago, and the two-dimensional illusions of "north," "south," and "halfway," were merely that: illusions. Mantu, however, was real enough. Most of it was delightfully real.

The Mantu system included five planets that could support hominid life and three that could not. All the former had thriving hominid populations; two of the latter were occupied by Earth's Royal Marines who defended and protected the entire system. None of the local populations were capable of defending themselves from Delphinian attack. Gibraltar, the outermost planet of the system, was just a big rock.

The Marines had their main base, Camp Shalom, on the largest planet. Mantu, which bore the same name as the system's star, was a planetary giant with seventeen moons, the outermost of which was Staten Satellite and the innermost, New South Bronx. The Mantu moons were first charted by a homesick New Yorker.

Once, astrophysicists said, there had been twenty-one moons, but four of these were destroyed in collisions when their complex paths passed too close together. The debris from this catastrophe now orbited the planet in a course of its own that was identified on the Admiralty charts as the Devil's Dustbin. It presented an enduring hazard to navigation.

Mantu was a strategic prize. All the moons were fortified. The dangers of taking a ship into orbit around a planet with such massive gravity and so many defenses meant that vessels must approach cautiously and could not enter the safe harbor ring without revealing their presence long before arrival.

Whoever held the garrison on Mantu controlled the Mantu system. Earth had held it since early in the First Galaxy War and intended to continue holding it, although the ground fighting against persistent Delphinian insurgency in this remote sector was a steady drain on Earth's resources.

Mantu was classified as uninhabitable chiefly because of its gravity. It had a breathable atmosphere if you could compensate for the pressure, and temperatures rose as high as ten degrees Celsius in the daytime. To protect personnel stationed there, gravity relievers were built into the structures erected on the planet and specially designed vehicles and clothing were issued to those Marines sent into the field.

Nevertheless, even with short periods on the moons or on a habitable planet for r and r, three years of duty on Mantu was thought to be all that hominid flesh could bear. Accordingly, Marines posted to Mantu were relieved triennially. The meritocratic officers, however, were not.

The skills needed to conduct tactical operations in Mantu's complex environment might be studied theoretically; and, indeed, all Annapolis cadets were taught as much as possible about this most valuable outpost. Mastery of the skills came only with experience—more than three years' experience. So while enlisted personnel rotated out every three years, some officers had served on Mantu since the first war. The long exile from their native planet did not leave them unscarred, but as meritocrats they accepted the burden because they understood the necessity.

For commoners, Mantu was rated as a hardship post. Fortunately for morale, Marines actually preferred that kind of assignment. It was part of their tradition, another one of those eccentricities that made sailors think all Marines were crazy.

Lafayette's sailors were skeptical when Marines insisted that there were some good things about garrison duty on Mantu. First off, Marines pointed out, the planet was solid ground and so, self-evidently from their point of view, a much better place to be than aboard any ship in existence. Then, there was more variety in the life there. (Sure, said the sailors: ice, mud . . .) There was a chance to stretch your legs. (If forced marches with a pack that literally weighed a ton was your choice of light exercise.)

The Marines didn't expect sailors to understand. Sailors always grumbled. That was their tradition. The Marines going to Mantu sympathized with fellow members of the Corps who would have to remain aboard *Lafayette* to help the Navy keep them in line. For their part, they were looking forward to settling into their barracks at Camp Shalom where a Marine general was in command and things were done the Marine way.

Lafayette's sailors did not grumble about making a stop in the Mantu system. They were looking forward to it for reasons of their own, reasons that seemed to them much more sensible. There were many ports in the Mantu system far more attractive than the Marine garrison, and *Lafayette* would be sure to call at one of them. A few sailors would certainly get a few days of liberty, and all could expect some interesting additions to their menu. A medical/life support officer would go ashore and bargain with planetary natives for fresh food, including delicacies that could not be produced aboard the ship but would be eaten in port to spare regular supplies.

As *Lafayette* approached Mantu, the topic debated with mounting enthusiasm on the third deck was which liberty port she would make. Wagering on the captain's probable decision was heavy. Of the five temperate planets, one did not qualify. Purgatory, the one-moon planet closest to the sun, was off limits. It had been uninhabited when Earth's Navy first entered the Mantu system and had been appropriated as a penal colony. Ships sent launches to Purgatory only to disembark convicts, who were then left to fend for themselves. No one ever left. Four possibilities remained: New Africa, Eden, Little Venus, and Purgatory's sister planet, the Colony.

Lafayette was still ten days away from the Mantu ring when word spread through the ship that Captain Brook had made his decision: the port of call would be the Colony. Wagering then turned to which of *Lafayette*'s sailors would be allowed shore leave. Those only recently boarded were disqualified, but all the rest— except those restricted because of bad behavior — could hope to be among the lucky one hundred who would ride the launch down to the surface and be free to amuse themselves and spend their money. They might have as much as a week on shore if the captain was not impatient to move them out again. However brief their stay, the sailors who got liberty would have to do ten days in the quarantine bubble before reentering *Lafayette.* No one doubted it would be worth the price.

Two officers would go down with the launch. Lamashtu and Hall drew straws for it, and Lamashtu won the line officer's slot. In med/life, Gordon disqualified himself. He told Parker, with a pretence of grumbling, that if there was one thing he hated more than quarantine, it was haggling with civilian merchants for coconuts and native beer. So, whether she liked it or not, she would have to do the chores for the med/life section.

Parker was as excited as a child. Gordon knew she had always wanted to visit the Colony, she told Steele. She didn't believe the med/life director had taken any shore leave himself since the war began. She made elaborate preparations for the trip, packing and repacking her duffel, making shopping lists, and trying to remember the names of relatives from the stories her mother had told. She asked Steele to help her cut her hair to a more practical length for travel and for quarantine. As *Lafayette* reached the outer approaches of the Mantu ring, the Colonials who came in on sick call signed to each other how young and pretty the doctor looked in her new hairdo.

Navigating a ship at above light speed and navigating at low speed inside a solar system ring were two related but distinctly different skills. Although the mathematical equations for the former were more complex, deep-space navigation was actually easier to master. Mistakes in deep space were usually easy to repair; all that would be lost was travel time. Close to shore, errors could be immediately fatal.

HMS *Lafayette*'s entry into the Mantu system marked the beginning of an intensive training period for the junior lieutenant. The captain kept Steele overtime on the bridge to give her as much hands on experience as possible in a secure sector of space. Once the ship began to operate inside hostile rings, navigational problems would be compounded by tactical ones.

Steele expected Hall to be assigned as her instructor, and he did work with her occasionally. But Captain Brook himself became her primary tutor. She now spent as many hours with him each day as she had formerly spent with Lamashtu. Steele was aware that the captain was giving her training top priority; he had delegated many of his routine duties to Rivera in order to concentrate on her instruction. Brook was a good teacher and Steele an eager pupil. Her pleasure as she mastered each new skill showed all over her face; and, as much as his dignity would allow, Brook was enjoying himself too.

The captain planned to spend several weeks inside the Mantu ring. The first stop after deceleration was the Colony, where *Lafayette* remained in orbit just long enough to send out the launch *Gnat* with the one hundred sailors and two officers bound for shore leave. Then the ship cruised at below light speed and anchored in orbit around each inhabited planet in turn, collecting intelligence and showing the flag. The flag itself, made of painted metal, was set in place above the bridge for these displays. It was dusted daily by teams of hullsweepers, who peered into the observation dome curiously as they worked, most of them never having seen the control center of their ship before.

The longest stop was at Purgatory, where *Lafayette* spent two days in crisscrossing orbits, searching for evidence of impermissible technological development or other dangerous activity among the convict population. The data collected was sent by laser blips to the Mantu garrison for evaluation.

After seven days, *Lafayette* returned to the Colony, *Gnat* docked at the quarantine bubble, and the ship set course away from the system's sun toward the planet Mantu, the last port of call before heading back out into deep space.

Brook stood behind Steele at the navigator's station and together they watched as Mantu came into view through the observation dome.

"This, as you no doubt know, is the most difficult approach in the system, indeed, it is one of the most difficult in the known universe." Brook, with his ship's power cells fully charged from weeks in the bright Mantu sun, powered up the chart screen to complement his lecture. "If I had any question as to whether the batteries on the satellites were friendly, I would never take *Lafayette* in here even though our armor is heavy enough to defend against them. Tell me why, Lieutenant."

"Sir, because coming out again we'd have the gravity at our back and be extremely vulnerable to any hostile craft, even a small one."

"Good. So if this were hostile territory, what would you do?"

"As navigator, sir?"

"No. As navigator you follow your captain's orders. What is the tactical solution if we wanted to secure a planet like this one?"

"Sir, a series of amphibious landings with our largest craft launched from wide orbit beyond Gibraltar and securing the satellites first."

"In the case of a planet of this size, with this complexity of satellite intervals, that would be an extremely costly operation. In fact, it would take a fleet to back it up. A single ship would never undertake such an operation alone. But you have given the correct answer. There is no other way it could be done. That is why Earth has held Mantu for so long; the Delphinians will not pay the price of a frontal assault.

"Fortunately, we are not dealing with my hypothetical situation. This is a friendly port, so we'll go all the way in and anchor in a planetary orbit. Explain to me why I choose not to hold a more remote orbit."

"The Marines, sir. They tend to be poor sailors. It's best to give them a short trip in the launches when that's possible. Especially when the ride is as bumpy as this one will be."

"Very good, Lieutenant. We will anchor as close in as we safely may. Plot the course, and then let me check it. I'll be in my day cabin." He left the chart screen running.

Steele was delighted to have use of the high-powered equipment. It was the same model she'd used in training at Annapolis, but Brook navigated without its aid in the other harbors. She called up the first chart, punched in the time variable, and watched the three-dimensional symbols move across the screen. When the first intersatellite channel came into view, she halted the movement. She began to copy coordinates onto a form and then stopped.

Brook would expect her to use the standard approach. He just intended to check it over to make sure her timing was right and that she didn't leave anything out in the sequence of orders or try to anchor the ship too close to the atmospheric reefs. But here was a tempting opportunity to get a master navigator's opinion on the unconventional course she had developed herself. It was one of the navigational puzzles she and Doctor Parker had posed for each other and spent hours discussing during the long months in space.

Steele started the chart moving again and plotted the course her way. If Brook disapproved when she submitted the form, he would just send her back to the chart table to do it over and no harm done.

Once she had actually completed the form and carried it down the ramp to the captain, she began to have some qualms. Captain Brook disapproved of taking unnecessary risks. "Boredom is the price paid by those who would enjoy safety in space," was a maxim he often quoted. He might feel her desire to innovate reflected an irresponsible desire for excitement and that plotting an unorthodox course the first time she had such an assignment showed a lack of seriousness. But it was done now; she handed over the form and watched Brook frown as he studied it.

"This isn't the book solution, Lieutenant."

"No, sir."

"You've never done a Mantu approach before."

"Only in the navigational simulator at the Academy, sir."

"It is usually unwise to depart from book solutions."

"Yes, sir."

Brook continued to study the form, stroking his beard and frowning. Then he began to nod his head. "Interesting, Lieutenant. You seem to have discovered a scenic route into Mantu harbor. Riding the currents between Brooklyn and Yonkers wouldn't work at the ebb, but . . ." He stood up and headed to the bridge. Steele followed him, near bursting with excitement.

Brook powered up the chart screen again, did some rapid calculations, and then called up all the charts Steele had used and several others she hadn't thought to consult. He nodded his head, leaned back, and drummed his fingers on the table. "This should work quite nicely. The tides will be near flood by the time we get there. This course will take us longer, but it will give us a measurable saving of energy." He switched off the screen and surrendered the navigator's position to Steele. "Go ahead,

Lieutenant. Take us in. The view of Little Venus as we approach Minimanhattan should be spectacular."

Steele began to transfer the course directions to the helm. Brook signaled his runners, and the orders went out to prepare to enter port. Hall bounded out of the main hatch and slid into his place at the helm, followed by Costello, who replaced the sailor who had been monitoring the signal traffic from the planet. Brook stood behind Steele's chair as she gave the orders that took *Lafayette* gently through the moons of Mantu.

The entry into the harbor proceeded without a hitch. As New South Bronx was left behind, and the ship settled into a low orbit, Brook gave Steele a few words of approval that made her cheeks glow and then turned his attention to the signal station.

Following standard procedures, *Lafayette* had sent several long messages to the Marine base beginning twenty-four hours before the ship decelerated to enter the Mantu ring and continuing as *Lafayette* followed her planned movements though the planetary system. The reply to each had been the same: the single word "acknowledged." So it was a surprise to Brook to have a top priority message from the commanding general of the Mantu garrison come in as soon as *Lafayette* cleared New South Bronx. General Dubois and her chief medical/life support officer, Doctor Mahamut, were already on their way to *Lafayette* aboard a briefing launch. The general wanted a face-to-face meeting with *Lafayette*'s captain and med/life director.

Brook had been in and out of the Mantu orbit countless times, but he had never met the garrison commander. The general's insistence on a meeting in a briefing launch puzzled him. He could not see that they had much to discuss. His mission was to set down one company of Marines and board another—a simple exchange of personnel.

If General DuBois wanted a meeting in orbit, Brook knew, she must have a very good reason. Sending a launch with the power to tear away from Mantu's massive gravity was an expensive operation. It must be some kind of medical problem, he decided, since DuBois wanted *Lafayette*'s med/life director involved in the meeting and had brought her Doctor Mahamut. Still, it was hard to conceive of a medical matter so sensitive that it could not be handled through discussions over the signal apparatus. Briefing launches were for top security use.

Brook shrugged. He'd learn what this was all about soon enough. Mantu was DuBois's command and it was her launch. He sent a runner to rouse Gordon from his laboratory.

In his quarters, deep in the bowels of the ship, Gordon buttoned himself into his Naval officer's dress uniform and cursed Marines. He wore the dark blue, stiff synthetic fabric tunic as little as possible. On his best day, he wasn't a good-looking man, but this getup made him look like a three-day-old corpse. The dark color emphasized his leanness, and the collar highlighted the deep scars in his bony face.

The thing was uncomfortable too. Idiot high neckband and eighteen idiot buttons, all to impress some idiot general. What was wrong with an honest white lab coat? He was sure the Marine general wouldn't make her physician get all dressed up for a briefing. He'd told Captain Brook as much. But would Brook listen to reason? Oh, no.

"Doctor Gordon," he says, "you will be representing my ship when you board the launch, and you will therefore dress appropriately." "No, Doctor," he says, "it is not at all the same thing as conferring through a holographic hookup. Stop arguing, Doctor," he says. "Just do as you are told."

Idiot Navy. Idiot buttons.

Gordon finally got the tunic adjusted and inspected himself in the wardrobe mirror. He looked just as bad as he expected. He didn't even look like a physician in this monkey suit. Gordon reached under the collar of the tunic and pulled out the heavy silver chain. He carefully removed the ring suspended from it. If Captain Brook wanted him to impress the Mantu officers, he'd wear his decoration.

As he slipped Galen's Ring onto his finger, he immediately felt better. He rarely wore the prized award, but whenever he did put it on his hand, it lifted his spirits almost as if it really had the magical powers the ancients attributed to it. He climbed the main hatch to the dock. It would be interesting to see the inside of a briefing launch. For all his years in space, Gordon had never been inside one.

The high-security vessels were expensive to maintain and were used only when it was necessary for people from separate biological environments to confer together face to face. The alternatives were time-consuming quarantine procedures, which were impractical unless the group intended to remain together for many months, or meetings inside a regular launch with all parties remaining sealed in space liners and helmets. Briefing launches were used by fleet admirals for strategy conferences with their senior officers or to convene courts-martial. Physicians were never involved in the former, and, unless they had enormous bad luck, were involved in the latter only as witnesses who could be questioned through a holographic hookup.

Captain Brook entered the launch first. When Gordon followed, he discovered that he had stepped into a separate compartment. The meeting area resembled the windowless conference rooms dug underground by the Admiralty on Earth for top security meetings, but the area around each chair was enclosed by a transparent box with its own contained air system and a single opening that would connect directly with an airlock. Captain Brook stood next to him beyond the contamination shield. They could have done without that, Gordon thought since he and Brook had entered from the same environment. He supposed it was cheaper just to build the launch to deal with the worst-case scenario.

The officers from Mantu stood opposite them. It wasn't hard to tell the doctor from the general. Doctor Mahamut was in mufti, wearing the same kind of long white smock that Gordon had left hanging in his surgery. Since he was representing the ship, Gordon decided not to give his captain a dirty look.

General DuBois might be indifferent to matters of uniform among her med/life officers, but she herself was all spit and polish and held herself even stiffer and straighter than Captain Brook. Gordon noted that DuBois was wearing both leg and arm braces and possibly a back brace as well, though with Marines it was hard to tell. When she raised her arm to salute, Gordon could see that the fingers of her hand were twisted into a claw.

Once the officers had exchanged traditional courtesies, the necessary communication lines were activated, and two separate conversations began. The two physicians diagnosed each other. Both looked tired and sick. Each told that to the other. Then they got on to their business.

"You're getting a healthy group." Gordon was proud of his record. "I lost a few Marine recruits during quarantine, but your veterans had nothing worse than space sickness. No one aboard *Lafayette* has had any serious illness since we left the Earth system. What are your problems?"

"We're clean." Doctor Mahamut pulled a piece of gauze from his pocket and twisted it around his finger. "The people I'm sending you have some muscle and bone disorders and the usual psychological complaints. But we've been free of active infection for a long time. There hasn't been any biological contact since we rotated out a group for r and r on New Africa three months ago." He sighed and stuffed the gauze back into his pocket. "I'm sure your people will be bringing in plenty of trouble. They're probably carriers of every new virus floating in space between here and the solar system."

Gordon shrugged. "So quarantine them. That's what I'm going to do with your people. They may have no active symptoms but still be carriers. Viruses mutate on the ground as well as in space dust, and I certainly won't be having any of your crowd breathing the air in my life support system until I've identified every antibody in everyone's blood."

Mahamut propped his head against his hand and sighed again.

"What's the matter? If you think we may be bringing in more than you can handle, I've stockpiled vaccine against everything we've run into that is highly virulent. If you want it, I'll send you some. But if it were me, I'd want to culture serums myself in quarantine and use that to protect the others. It's safer."

"I'm not worried about it, Doctor. It's just that quarantines and mass inoculations are the kind of thing that makes my days longer. And the days on Mantu last long enough anyway." That was certainly true. Gordon recalled that they lasted about seven months Earth time. So did the nights.

"I've been working on the company that's going out." Mahamut was playing with the strip of gauze again. "As soon as the bosses get the embarkation time worked out, I'll have to give them all shots to control spacesickness — the ride up from the surface always wipes them out. Then the quarantine for the relief company, immunizations for everyone else down here — just thinking about it is exhausting."

Gordon studied his opposite number carefully. Mahamut had tied a granny knot in the gauze strip and was picking at it to get it loose. Gordon reconsidered his snap diagnosis. Mahamut's fatigue was abnormal even for a Navy doctor. "How long have you been in service here," he demanded.

"Fifteen years come spring."

"You're due for relief. You're worn out."

Mahamut laughed dryly. "Aren't we all." He gave up on the knot and repocketed the gauze strip. "Thank you, Doctor Gordon, but we both know I'm not going to be relieved. The Navy has very few physicians with experience in high-gravity medicine. The Admiralty's not going to pull me out just because I'm tired. No, I expect I'll be here until I die, just as General DuBois will."

Gordon scowled. "How can you expect to do your work properly when your body is worn out?"

"The same way you do yours," Mahamut responded irritably. "If you really want to do something to help the Mantu infirmary, Doctor Gordon, I could use another officer. We used to have two Navy doctors here, but my senior died five years ago, and since then, I've been the only meritocratic physician on this station. We get casualties from the whole system in here. I've got more people hospitalized on any given day than you've got aboard your entire ship." Mahamut crossed his arms and leaned forward.

"So tell me, Doctor Gordon, do you have a backup on *Lafayette*? I had some time in space before they sent me here, and I know ships get replacements a lot more easily than the garrisons do. You'll probably contact a hospital ship within a few months and could pickup another meritocratic physician for *Lafayette*."

"I do have another officer serving with me, but you wouldn't want her. She's a Colonial."

"I see."

"I'll put in a word for you when we join the forward fleet. If a ship is scheduled to pass near here, it should be possible to get you a fresh med/life officer. Someone else should be getting some hands-on experience here, and you shouldn't be carrying this much responsibility alone. You'll get an ulcer."

"I have an ulcer, Doctor. And I suspect you do too." This physician from *Lafayette* looked as sick as anyone he'd ever seen outside a body bag.

"I don't, Doctor Mahamut. It's one thing I haven't got, although I've been told I may be a carrier."

"Have you passed one on to your captain?" Mahamut had glanced in Brook's direction several times as he spoke to Gordon. That man was not looking well either.

"No, thank God. He's suffering from hypertension, but otherwise he's healthy. What's wrong with your boss?"

"It's a form of arthritis. We get many cases like it on Mantu. When it appears in a commoner, I evacuate the patient. The condition usually clears up spontaneously after a little time in normal gravity. The general has had it for quite a few years. All I've been able to do is slow down its progress. The damage is probably irreversible now."

Gordon peered at DuBois through the transparent shield and glanced casually at Brook. Then he gasped and sprang to his feet, cursing the contamination barrier that kept him from his captain.

"Oh, Merciful Mother! Not now! Not here!" Brook's face was deep purple and his eyes bulged from his head. He was on the verge of apoplexy.

* * *

The rise in Brook's blood pressure began moments after the signal apparatus put him in voice contact with General DuBois. She wasted little time getting to the point of the interview.

"That's cover," she said nodding toward the physicians who had begun their conversation. "The story I put out is that your med/life man is having heartburn about the personnel transfers and that's why I had to bring mine up on the launch."

Med/life officers always had heartburn when personnel transferred, Brook thought. Line officers were used to it. It seemed a flimsy cover. Brook wondered why DuBois needed one.

The general didn't believe in honey-coating bad news, which was what she had for Brook. She gave it to him straight. "I let you bring *Lafayette* into a trap. Maybe I can give you a couple of hours warning before they hit you. Maybe not. Either way, you probably won't be able to save your ship. Sorry about that."

Brook felt as if he'd been hit in the stomach with a rifle butt. Before the shock subsided, he felt his rage mounting. He took a deep breath and began to count slowly to ten. When he was between eight and nine, DuBois began to elaborate. Brook abandoned his counting and tried to listen over the sound of his heart pounding in his ears.

"The Delphinians have your time table. They knew you were heading here and when you'd enter the port. And they've got a gunboat in heavy camouflage prowling through the planetary system. It's been watching you since you entered the ring. They've also got a task force of frigates and heavy cruisers somewhere just beyond Gibraltar. The plan is to come after *Lafayette* while you're working her out of the harbor. But they won't sit around if you change your schedule. If you don't move out with the tide, the gunboat has orders to risk the batteries on New South Bronx and come in after you. While you're backed up against the gravity, there won't be much you can do about it."

Brook started at one and began to count again. When he reached ten, he realized it was time he said something. The Thunderer held himself under control.

"I'm sure you had an excellent reason for allowing this to occur, General, and for making the decision to sacrifice my ship without consulting me," he said in his most courtly tone.

"Of course."

"May I inquire what the reason was?" Brook asked after a pause that seemed to him quite prolonged.

"That's what I called this briefing for." DuBois frowned. "Do you think I'd take this tub off the surface for the fun of riding in it? The thrust off hurts like hell." She grimaced as she shifted her stiff body in the leather chair. "Haven't you been listening to me? There's a swarm of Delphinians massed outside the ring. Delphinians, our enemy, right? A task force; you know what that is, right? Do you think that was sent out for your one lousy ship? I'm facing an invasion, a full scale invasion, and there's a fleet backing it up!"

"General DuBois, with all respect, I do not see how having my ship trapped in the harbor improves your defensive position. It would appear to me, ma'am, that *Lafayette* would have been more useful operating freely in open space."

"Do you think I'm an idiot, Captain Brook? Don't you think I know anything about Naval tactics? Of course it would be better to have *Lafayette* deployed somewhere outside the ring! If you can manage to get your mind off your damned ship for a few seconds and think in terms of the larger strategic considerations in this sector of space, I'll put you in the picture."

"Thank you, ma'am. That would be most helpful."

DuBois glared at Brook. Damn all ship captains. For them the whole universe was inside the hull of one vessel. They'd rather lose the war than lose that ship.

"Now listen. I told you the Delphinians have your timetable. How do you think I know that? I'll tell you how I know that. A good while back, maybe sixteen, eighteen months, we had a routine field exercise going on Gibraltar, giving the troops a taste of what it's like to operate in abnormally low gravity. So we had a corporal's guard out digging latrines. They uncovered a funny looking box that turned out to be a Delphinian communications relay. Pure luck. Shows that God is on our side.' She rubbed her gnarled hands together and nodded, expecting Brook to share her satisfaction. All she got was a standard Navy quarterdeck face.

"Well we put it back, just like it was, and since then, I've been listening in on all the blips passing between the Pegasus sector and Delphinus. Very interesting stuff."

"I'm sure it is, ma'am. How all this relates to *Lafayette*, however . . ."

"I just told you. There's a Delphinian gunboat ready to blow you to hell."

That sailors and Marines should have communication difficulties, Brook thought, was understandable. Perhaps it was unavoidable when the parties concerned were commoners. But he and DuBois were fellow officers. It shouldn't be so difficult for him to get a straight answer from the Marine. He braced himself for another try.

"If you will permit me an observation, General. Had I been in your position, I should have sent a blip to *Lafayette*. There was ample opportunity to contact us, in sequence or out, at any time since we have been inside the ring. You had our coordinates. All I needed was the merest hint that all was not as it should be, and I could have found a perfectly plausible reason for altering course or anchoring the ship in a shallow harbor instead of coming all the way into this deep gravity. Timetables change constantly. Your intelligence source would not have been compromised."

"You make it sound so easy. Just send out a blip." DuBois scowled. "I'm going to give you one more piece of information, Captain Brook, and if you still say you don't understand, so help me, I'm going to challenge your meritocratic fitness and demand your resignation."

Brook decided to give the General one last chance to make some sense. For several minutes he'd been contemplating challenging her fitness and ordering her to turn over her sword.

"The enemy has infiltrated Mantu. I don't know where and I don't know who, but there are at least two active Delphinian agents buried among the personnel on the base. I know for certain that someone with access to the blips is disloyal. My blips are not secure any more than those of the enemy are. The difference is, I know it. Now do you understand?"

The Marines did not warn the Navy because there was no secure channel. DuBois might have said so in the first place.

"I understand, General. If this is all you wished to discuss, I would like to return to my ship now and brief my officers. It is unfortunate for both of us that our firepower cannot be used to assist in your defense, but if *Lafayette* is attacked, she will go down fighting."

"Fine. Good luck. But there is something else. I want your signal officer temporarily reassigned to my command."

Brook felt his face reddening and heard a ringing in his ears. If he didn't get back aboard his ship very quickly, he feared he was going to be giving General DuBois a piece of his mind in a way that would set interservice cooperation back fifty years.

"General, Lieutenant Costello is my second officer," he said as calmly as he could. "You've just told me that *Lafayette* is in mortal danger, and I appreciate your reasons for having put her in this position. Nevertheless, if you take away the backup to my executive officer, you tie one hand behind my back in my efforts to keep us alive."

"Brook, it's in your interest as well as mine to get the pig spies smoked out of their cover. Until I've dug all the infiltrators out of the woodwork, I can't give you any help at all — no intelligence, no ground cover, no nothing. I have to do a very fast, very thorough investigation, and I've waited for your ship to get here so that I could get a meritocrat with a communications specialty to help in interrogation. Once I start this, the vermin are going to scatter, and I've got to squash all of them."

"General, surely you have personnel . . ."

Christ, this ship captain was slow! "Pay attention, Brook. I'll spell it out for you. Point one: there's close to half a million people to hunt through at Camp Shalom. Point two: I've got exactly nine meritocrats, and that's counting the quack over there, who's a non-combatant and won't touch the psychomonates. Which is point three: we'll have to use psychoactive drugs and maybe hurt some people, so I can't use commoners. Point four: my security officer has a communications specialty, but he can't do the job fast enough unless he has help. Point five: We have to finish this fast because, as I keep telling you, we're facing an invasion from a Delphinian fleet. Last point: You don't have to like it, but your ship is parked in my space. When I tell you to lend me an officer, you do it."

DuBois pulled an electronic notebook from her pocket and clutched it in her crippled hand. "So the name is Costello. Okay. I want her on the surface by 1600 hours. I'll send her back to you as soon as I've cleaned house. With two meritocrats on it, it won't take long."

The general pulled herself to her feet. Her leg braces locked with an audible click, and then the signal contact was broken. The interview was over.

Twenty minutes later *Lafayette*'s line officers were listening to their tight-lipped captain describe their vulnerable situation and lecture them on the traditions of the Royal Navy. As Brook reviewed the precedents for fighting one's ship until she sank, Gordon hunched over his desk in sickbay and drafted a forceful memo on the subject, "A Captain's Responsibility To His Ship Includes Staying Alive."

* * *

Annapolis instructors told their students that life in space would consist of long months of boredom interspersed with occasional hours of terror. In the Mantu harbor, Steele learned that even living with the prospect of danger could become monotonous.

Brook briefed his officers on the threat as soon as he knew about it himself, but he saw no reason to inform the crew. After a week during which all line officers had been in a state of full alert, Steele surrendered the watch to Rivera late one afternoon and headed straight for the wardroom. It was an enormous relief to get off the bridge, but she was still keyed up and hungry for someone to talk to. Happily, she found someone else was there taking a mudd break.

"Hi, Henry," she called out cheerfully. "I see you're reading trashy novels again."

Hall colored and pushed the battered paperbound volume into his pocket. Everyone knew he had a commoner's taste in escape reading and pulled sex-and-violence gothics set in the twentieth century from the crew's entertainment library. The ship had traded reading material with Camp Shalom, so there was some new stuff he hadn't read. He'd hesitated before bringing the novel into the wardroom, but then decided it would just arouse suspicion if he suddenly went high-brow in his choice of fiction.

Anyway, all the officers had some tastes in common with the third deck, so the novels wouldn't prove anything against him. The first officer drank beer, and even the captain was known to take an interest in Monday Night Football. Hall wondered what plebeian tastes Steele might have. He flushed. It must be the book he was reading that had made the thought flash through his mind that it might be fancy underwear.

"Want me to hot up your mudd?" She reached for his mug.

"Thanks." Only a meritocrat would be this nice to him after the way he'd behaved toward her during her first months aboard, Hall thought. Steele simply refused to hold a grudge, and Hall had been unable to resist warming to her. No commoner — and that was what he was — could resist meritocratic charm. As he grew friendlier, so did she. When Lamashtu was off on the Colony and then isolated in quarantine, Steele and Hall compensated for her absence by spending more of their free time together. And after Costello went off on loan to the Marines down on Mantu, he and Steele had gotten downright chummy.

Hall enjoyed this closer relationship, although it worried him. If Steele got to know him too well, she might easily tumble to the fact that he was an imposter. And as a meritocrat, she wouldn't hesitate a minute before challenging him.

Steele brought the two mugs back to the table and dropped into a chair. "I'll sure be glad when this is over, no matter what happens. Every watch the same: 'Anchored as before.' And then four hours hanging over the boxes wondering whether this is the watch it will happen, when something will come in at helm or signal and we go to general quarters. It's hard to believe you can get this tired and be so bored and feel this scared all at once."

"So it's finally getting to you too." Hall was relieved to hear Steele say she felt the same way he did. It had crossed his mind that his responses might be different from those of meritocrats.

"I've always been told it's waiting around expecting to get hit that's the worst part, and that you don't feel so scared once you're actually in action. Is that true?"

Hall was struck by Steele's unselfconscious confession of fear. He supposed it was safe to share his experience with her. Fear was so basic. It must be something a commoner felt the same way a meritocrat felt it, though maybe they reacted to the emotion differently. Steele hadn't asked him about that part of it. If she did, he could change the subject.

"I'd say waiting is the worst part. I think it's because you're all set to do something, stress hormones pumping and that stuff, and you can't let it out. Once there's something to do, it's different. It's a different kind of being afraid. I don't think its nearly so bad."

"Do you ever envy the crew?" Steele's bright eyes held his as she lifted her mug to drink.

This question was hitting too close to home. Hall was about to make some excuse to leave the wardroom when Steele went on to answer it herself. "Down on the third deck, they have no idea what a dangerous spot we're in and everything possible is being done to keep them from getting bored. I bet they're enjoying this time in orbit more than any time since we left Earth. Routine maintenance work is way down. With the officers all on alert, drills are way down. They got a whole pile of new books from trading with the Marine garrison and can even run the holographs because we've got a solar source for power. And Gordon's given them absolutely beautiful weather. Have you been down on the gundeck in the evenings? Not a trace of a cloud, and the moon just coming full this week."

"I've been spending my evenings reading the Bible." This was true. Besides the worry everyone else shared about the Delphinians, Hall was tormented by his sin of deception. Still, now that he'd said it, Hall realized the statement made him sound like an awful prig.

"The sailors will all be on deck tonight. The moon is full. Why don't you come down with me and watch them?"

Hall glanced at Steele sharply. Was this some kind of test? Maybe Brook had guessed that he had a commoner in the wardroom and Steele was supposed to take him below to see how he'd react to mingling with his true peers.

"There's a rule against fraternization, Steele."

"I don't mean to fraternize. The sailors wouldn't allow it anyway. I just mean to watch. Don't you ever watch our people playing? I go down with Martha all the time."

Steele wasn't trying to entrap him, Hall decided. Meritocrats didn't do that kind of thing. If Brook wanted him tested, he'd just call him in and put him on a lie detector.

"I'd really like your company, Henry. I feel conspicuous going down there all alone. I'd ask Martha, but she's still worn out from quarantine."

It had never occurred to Hall to observe the crew in a recreation area; it smacked of voyeurism. But, since Steele had suggested it, it must be all right. At least it would be better than being alone in his cabin with his conscience. He really missed Costello; she was the only officer who enjoyed playing cards.

"Okay. Why not?"

The rule on the gundeck was normally silence—no unnecessary talking for work crews, respectful attention at muster and prayers, and absolute quiet at general quarters. When the area was opened for recreation, the crew could make all the noise they wanted, and that was quite a bit. The contrast was striking.

"Christ!" Hall came through the hatch behind the sentry box. "The Marines could be in here screaming on bayonet drill and you'd never notice it."

"It's not that bad. You can hear signals easily enough. It's noisier than this at Annapolis any time they let the battalion sound off. Or have you forgotten your old school days already?"

"The memories fade." Hall had not been happy at Annapolis, and he didn't think about it much. He glanced around the deck. He recognized all the red and yellow stripers and most of the sailors who had been aboard during *Lafayette*'s previous voyage. He knew only a few of the new sailors: those who had come through his quarantine and a dozen or so who had made themselves conspicuous in some way, mostly by getting into trouble. He knew Charlie Ames.

Ames was a center of attention. The awkward boy had the unexpected talent of walking on his hands, which he was doing for an admiring audience that encouraged him to greater speed with cries of "Go, Chips, go!"

"How come they decided to call him Chips, Maggie? He's not a carpenter. Is Ames a poker player?"

Steele laughed and explained what she was sure was the origin of the nickname. The idea of Ames as a poker player was funny. On *Lafayette*, poker was played only by the gunner's mates and their special friends; and they played for hard coin, not for chips.

Between watching the sailors in their leisure hours and listening to Lamashtu reminisce about her days on the third deck, Steele had become something of an expert on the sociology of the ship's lower orders. It did not altogether conform to the theoretical hierarchy described by the textbooks.

On *Lafayette*, the gunner's mates were at the top of the heap. Steele thought that the six men and three women who commanded weapon banks might well have established their dominance simply by their size and animal strength. The inseparable team of Newcastle and Dover, known to their mates as Coal and Chalkie, were the acknowledged leaders of the group.

There was a section of the gundeck that was tacitly reserved for the gunner's mates, a choice position on the side of the mast farthest from the main hatch and the sentry post. There they played poker constantly for high stakes. There was no rule against gambling provided it did not lead to fights, and other sailors gambled; but only the gunner's mates played poker. Occasionally favored sailors — usually chiefs from other stations — might be invited to join the nine for an evening. It was a treasured form of recognition, worth losing a month's pay for, which was the usual price for an outsider who sat in on a poker session with the experts.

Next in the hierarchy, and habitually seated right next to them, was the group of thirteen Colonials, twelve women and one man, that the sailors called "the coven." All were blue stripers and most of them worked in the bilges in the dirtiest jobs on the lowest level of the ship.

The coven's leaders were a tiny black woman who wore her steel grey hair in dreadlocks, tucked up while she was on duty but pulled out wild and free for evenings on deck, and a short, slightly built white man whose salt-and-pepper hair was habitually cropped short so that he always looked as if he were fresh out of quarantine. Steele knew his name was Billy Katz and that he was a mortician's apprentice. Presumably because he operated the crematorium, sailors called him Ash. His companion, whose name was on the ship's roster as something unpronounceable beginning with an S, did something unspeakable in organic waste recycling under the barnyard slaughterhouse. The sailors called her Shadow.

Like the gunner's mates, the coven spent most of their time playing cards; but theirs was a fortune-telling deck that they read for each other and occasionally for other sailors, both Colonial and human, who could pay the price. The charge was higher for humans, who also needed to pay a translator willing to accept telepathic communication. Becky Petrie was among those waiting for a reading.

Below the card-playing elites, groups formed that seemed to Steele to have no clear relation to rank or specialty. Messmates stuck together more than a purely random distribution would dictate. Some of the younger sailors were gundeck groupies, who sought out the old salts who worked at the weapon banks to hear them tell stories. Others, especially the volunteers looking forward to Navy careers, joined study groups; Steele noticed Kathy Clark sitting by herself working an abacus, doing homework for Lamashtu's mathematics club.

There were many groups of dancers, singers, and musicians. These were the noisiest people on deck. They stayed as far away from each other as they could get since their musical tastes were wildly dissimilar—ranging from close-harmony madrigal singers to foot-stomping voodoo dancers. Steele recognized Waldo Bunyan among those practicing a complicated gymnastic routine; he was providing the base for an acrobatic tower. Some groups played ball games and competed with dancers for the open spaces between the weapon banks. If the competition grew too vigorous, Marines, who stood guard at all the hatches, would move in and break it up.

The off-duty Marines all stuck together in groups of their own. Even when the company headed for Mantu had been aboard, Marines were a minority set apart, whether they liked it or not, because of their uniforms and because of the Corps' identification with enforcement of the press and ship police functions. Generally, from everything Steele could see, this suited the Marines just fine. The sailors hated the Marines, and the feeling was reciprocated. In that, at least, *Lafayette* conformed to textbook patterns.

There were no Colonials among the Marines. The Corps did not accept them. And there were no Colonials among groups restricted to chiefs. But Colonials were spotted through most of the other groups. There were also a few groups besides the coven that were restricted to Colonials, one of which, Steele suspected, was composed of telepathic singers.

Some groups were very small. Lovers in assorted combinations of gender and species, carried blankets up to the catwalks for the greatest privacy and best view of the moon. Other groups of two or three friends were in the habit of going regularly to the same place on the gundeck just to talk or simply watch the activity around them.

As she and Hall were doing now, Steele thought. Except that the two of them were slumming, and every soul on the gundeck knew it.

The meritocratic visit to the gundeck didn't last long. A Colonial runner bounded out of the main hatch, looked around for the officers and then sprinted over, knuckling his forehead. Before he could reach them, Steele was on her way back toward the main hatch with Hall close behind. There must be action on the bridge.

Finally!

CHAPTER TEN

Once the officers were gone, there were subtle shifts in the activity on the gundeck. Some sailors had more than innocent amusement on their minds. Now they could get down to serious business.

"Would you look at that, Angel! The little Hellcat is going after Kathy Clark again!" Otto Schmidt was people-watching with Michael Gabriel from a favored spot on an upper catwalk. Gabriel turned to watch Petrie. She had left the group waiting for readings with the coven and was squatting next to the older girl, who was backed up against the gratings at the engine room ramp. Petrie was smiling unpleasantly and reaching for the abacus. Clark was losing her temper.

"In a minute, she'll have Kathy mad enough to throw a punch. That will bring the sentries around and get Kathy on report. Spoil Kathy's good record, that's what she wants."

"What does she have against Kathy, anyway, Butcher?"

"Beats me. Maybe nothing. The grommet has a lot of grudges. If hate could kill, there'd be a lot of us dead." From their position high above the deck, the two yellow stripers watched Petrie pull some coins from her pants pocket and drop them on the deck one at a time.

"Butcher! Is that gold she's got? Where'd a new-pressed blue striper get gold?"

Schmidt stirred uneasily. Angel was among the few people he'd told about his aborted arrangement with the Colonial coven and its discovery by the gunner's mates and the grommet.

"Butcher, you didn't!"

"Well, yes I did. What else could I have done?"

Gabriel shook his head and rolled his eyes up toward the bright December moon.

"Hey! There she goes!" Schmidt grabbed the rope and leaned forward over the catwalk to get a better look. Kathy Clark was on her feet, kicking and stamping on the coins, her fists knotted. Petrie remained crouched on the ground, still smiling. Petrie never fought. She was always the innocent victim.

The sailors nearby carefully moved away. It wasn't good to get too close to a fight. Then, before the Marines picked up the vibrations, another element entered the picture.

"Oh, my! Look, Butcher! The gunners must have decided Kathy deserves some protection. Here comes Tattoo."

Alya Petrov, a solidly built brunette well over six feet tall, had casually detached herself from the group of poker players and moved deliberately toward the ramp. Petrie was too intent on her victim to notice the woman approaching. Suddenly, Petrov was behind her. She seized Petrie by the wrist, pulled her to her feet and clapped an arm around her shoulders in what looked from a distance — say the distance of the closest sentry post — like a friendly hug. Petrov said something to Clark who shook her head. Then Petrov scooped up the coins and walked off into the shadow behind the hatchway with Petrie still in her embrace.

The two med/life mates stood up and hung over the edge of the catwalk, watching until the pair were out of sight. "That's the second time one of the gunner's mates has rescued someone that Petrie girl was teasing. What do you think, Butcher? They don't usually believe in second chances. Is Petrie going to have an accident this time?"

"We'll know soon enough. I sure wouldn't mind seeing it happen. Let her spend a week in sickbay. I wish I could figure out some way to get her out of the barnyard permanently."

"You still think she killed Beth on purpose, don't you."

"Of course she did it on purpose! I was her squad leader in quarantine and got right up on top of her hate list her first day aboard. She knew how I felt about that old sow. Hell, everyone in life support knew. Killing Beth was a way she figured she could hurt me real bad without me being able to do a damned thing about it."

Gabriel smiled sympathetically. Schmidt's affection for the black and white porker was notorious. The piglet he called Beth had been the runt of the litter, and he'd fed her from a bottle when she was tiny. She grew up big and fat, the queen of the barnyard. And even when she was too old to breed, Schmidt kept finding excuses to keep her at the trough.

"How come you got stuck with Petrie in the barnyard in the first place?"

"It was the goddamed aptitude tests," said Schmidt morosely. "In case you couldn't guess, it seems little Becky is a natural killer. People call me Butcher, but it's kind of a joke, because they know I don't like the slaughterhouse. I know we've got the animals here because we have to eat them, and butchering is part of my job, but I'd just as soon have someone else cut their throats. So they give me Petrie to train. There's typical meritocratic efficiency. Makes everybody happy. Hah!"

"I suppose you couldn't say anything to Doctor Gordon," Gabriel suggested tentatively.

"Not likely. What would I say? 'Doctor Gordon, sir, I've got a sailor assigned to me, and she killed my pet pig. So I'd like her sent somewhere else, if it's not too much bother, sir.' Would you have the guts to go to the director with something like that?"

Gabriel tittered. "I guess I wouldn't."

The pair sat in silence listening to the cacophony below. Because they were expecting it, they heard Petrie's scream when it came. A few moments later, Petrov reappeared around the hatchway, carrying the girl. When she passed the gun station near which Schmidt and Gabriel were sitting, she looked up and caught their attention.

"My little friend here found something that belongs to you, Butcher," she called. "Come on down. She wants to give it back."

"Looks like the gunners are watching out for you too," said Gabriel as both swung down the ladders.

Petrov drew them into a tight huddle around the white faced girl in her arms. "She says you gave her five coins, Butcher. Is that right?"

"It was seven, actually," said Schmidt.

"Fish them out of my pocket, Butcher. I found the other two in her pants." Petrov scowled into Petrie's face. "I don't like liars, Hellcat, and I don't like troublemakers. But you know what I really hate? I really bad don't like snitches. Sometimes people I don't like get awfully clumsy, trip over their own fat feet, maybe fall down the recycling chute and get turned into pig slop." She shifted Petrie roughly in her arms and carried her across the deck to the sentry station at the main mast. Schmidt and Gabriel watched from a distance.

"There's an accident here to report," said Petrov to the short black Marine standing rigid at the hatch. "This kid thinks she can dance with the grownups, but she can't. Someone stomped on her foot. Her name's Becky Petrie."

"Who did it?"

Petrov shrugged. "It's dark over there. I couldn't see exactly what happened. The kid couldn't either. Could you, sweetheart." She glared at Petrie.

"No," Becky muttered.

"All right, I'll report it. How bad is it? Does she need to go to sickbay?"

"How should I know? I'm a gunner, not a medic. You're the one on duty here. You tell me. If you say she should go to sickbay, I'll carry her down."

Damn sailors, the Marine thought. They never made things easy for you if they could help it.

"Does that foot hurt you much, sailor?"

"No!" Petrie spat out the word defiantly.

"Okay, kid. I'll just leave you here then." Petrov dropped Petrie on the deck and returned to her card game. Petrie clutched her leg and howled.

Gabriel and Schmidt exchanged a look, and then Gabriel sighed and moved over to the sentry box. Gabriel didn't like Petrie, and he didn't like Marines, and none of this was really any of his business. But he was a graduate of the Johns Hopkins Medical School, and when he accepted his diploma, he had taken an oath.

"I'm a medic. Want me to take a look?" The sentry stepped aside. Gabriel bent down and examined Petrie's foot as well as he could. It was obvious even in the moonlight that there were fractures, bad ones. Bone protruded through the skin. She probably had a broken arch.

"I'll take her down to sickbay," he said to the sentry. "You can report this as multiple fractures to the right foot — accidental injury, not due to her own misconduct."

"Thanks," the Marine said, grateful to be relieved of this complication on his watch.

Gabriel hoisted Petrie over his shoulder and carried her down the main hatch. For once, the grommet didn't make any trouble; she had fainted.

* * *

Captain Brook remained bent over the chart table where he was using the screen, flashing through a series of moving diagrams of the Mantu moons, seeming to pause barely long enough to glance at one before calling up the next. He continued to study the charts as he spoke to his officers. All of them had been called to the bridge as soon as he had the news from Camp Shalom: DuBois had her spies; Costello was coming home; and *Lafayette* was getting full intelligence on the Delphinian gunboat, now identified as the *Snapping Turtle.*

Brook had the history of the gunboat's movements through the system since the small but heavily armed ship had entered the Mantu ring shortly before *Lafayette*'s arrival. He knew something of *Snapping Turtle.* She was a nicely built little craft originally constructed as a scout, but now carrying heavy armament in a fore and aft concentration; her commander, at last report, was said to favor her vertical axis when on a lee shore. *Lafayette* was still in grave danger, but now that Brook knew what he was fighting, he was in his element.

"Our enemy is anchored in camouflage around Harlem," Brook reported. "She has maintained the same orbit since we arrived in the harbor, so it is safe to assume she will continue to do so until she anticipates movement from us. I feel all the more confident in this prediction because *Snapping Turtle*'s orbit, relative to ours, has been drifting. Any attempt on their part to compensate for the drift would create ripples and break their camouflage. Since they have no reason to suppose we suspect their presence, they will not want to risk that."

Brook switched off the screen, and turned to face the ring of officers. The worried frown that had been etched on the captain's face since his session with General DuBois melted away and was replaced by the warm smile which those who served under his command rarely saw. "We have a window of opportunity," he announced.

"For brief periods of time, approximately fifty minutes, our enemy's orbit takes her behind Harlem so that she cannot directly observe either the gate of Camp Shalom or our docking orbit. This is the circumstance I intend to exploit.

"I have instructed Lieutenant Costello to load the Marines onto *Firefly* as fast as they can move as soon as the gunboat drops behind Harlem. She'll bring them up at maximum speed; and as soon as we secure the launch, I'm taking us out."

Steele was bursting to ask how, but Brook was issuing orders. "Lieutenant Rivera, we need to have the gundeck cleared for action, but I would prefer not to alarm the crew prematurely. Go below and find some pretext for getting the waisters out of the way. A readiness drill for your mates should do, and you may brief them on our actual situation as soon as you deem it appropriate." Rivera acknowledged the order and left the bridge.

"Lieutenant Lamashtu, yours is the usual drill. Start hoarding. Our batteries are full charged, but I'm going to be demanding a great deal from them all at once. As soon as our people are safely aboard, we'll go to general quarters." Lamashtu stood up and patted Steele and Hall on the shoulder as she left.

"Lieutenant Hall, you have three assignments. Listen carefully, please. One, you are to set up the launch dock on the third deck to receive *Firefly*. That's the third deck dock, not the quarantine port. Two, you will assist in engineering's energy conservation activity by draining the life support system of the quarantine bubble. Three, when *Firefly* is secure, send Costello to the bridge on the double and you take charge of the Marines.

"The Marines will undoubtedly be in bad shape. You are to do everything you can to make them comfortable. The ride off the planet will have shaken them, and when we do a jump start out of orbit, they'll feel even worse. Doctor Gordon is not to make it harder for them by poking them with needles. He is not to begin drawing blood or initiating any other invasive procedures until after we secure from general quarters. Repeat your orders back to me so I'm sure you understand them."

Hall rattled them off without hesitation. There was nothing wrong with his memory.

"Very good. You will encounter one small problem, Lieutenant. These orders will displease Doctor Gordon. He will raise objections, but I do not have the time to argue with him. Neither do you. You must not permit him to interfere with your duties. You may tell the medical/life support director that I will record his objections in the log. If he is inconveniently persistent, you are to put him under arrest."

"Aye, aye, Captain."

Something in Hall's tone bothered Brook. "Inform the doctor that I have given you this authority before you exercise it. The threat should be sufficient, and I would prefer Doctor Gordon remain at his battle station in sickbay rather than be confined in the brig. We will be navigating a hazardous course, and we may well have casualties even if we avoid combat."

"Aye, aye, Captain." This time Brook let him go.

"You will take the helm, Lieutenant Steele. I'm going to navigate. We will draw power for the full range of instruments, but be prepared to override them at my order. I believe you will find this an interesting variation on the standard solution for leaving the Mantu harbor late in December." Steele caught the flicker of humor in Brook's expression.

"On occasion one must, of necessity, depart from book solutions, Lieutenant. When that is the case, I have always believed, there is no reason why one should not be allowed to enjoy it." Steele moved into the helm position next to Brook and watched as he punched up the charts.

"Let us review what I have in mind. In ship's time, *Snapping Turtle* will be blind beginning at 21:06:14." He froze the harbor pilot at that position. "I've allowed Costello seven minutes to board her people and twenty-one to get them parked in the airlock." He moved the chart to 21:34:14. "We'll add a small margin for error." The chart moved to an even 21:35:00.

"Now, what do you make of this, Lieutenant?"

The word that sprang to Steele's mind was "disaster": tides running out, solar winds in the middle of hurricane season, satellites in their worst possible configuration, and the Devil's

Dustbin just settling in for a four hour stay — not to mention being backed up against a lee shore with the enemy holding the gravity advantage.

"I thought we might try something the enemy would not anticipate." Brook put a symbol representing *Lafayette* onto the screen. "A full power liftoff can get us into the Hudson channel before the tide is fully drained. We will then shift course sharply to avoid Bensonhurst." Steele flinched as the screen reflected Brook's proposed maneuver. Even in the image, the course shift brought the ship and the satellite much too close for comfort. "Before our Delphinian friends notice we are not where they left us, Soho will be fully blocking the channel, and it will not be possible to follow us out that way for . . ." Brook pushed the chart forward through time, leaned back and smiled. "I make it seven months plus a few days," he said waving a hand at the display. "That should be an ample head start for us, don't you agree, Lieutenant?"

Steele was speechless. The enemy certainly would not be expecting *Lafayette* to try a channel run at this season, especially at the high speed Brook proposed to maintain. The course change to avoid Bensonhurst that Brook spoke of so casually meant changing bearings by angles of over seventy degrees three times within a period of under two minutes. It would take meticulous piloting to avoid a collision, and it would put enormous strain on the engines. If it worked, *Lafayette* was home free, although *Snapping Turtle* was not likely to wait for the channel to clear before leaving the system. There were easier routes.

"A pity this activity will consume so much of our power reserve." Brook punched up another chart, this one looking back toward the planet from the Staten Satellite orbit and revealing a clear passage to Harlem. "We might have taken a prize."

Steele was infected by Brook's mood. She'd never watched him in action during a crisis before and felt a surge of happiness as she realized that he'd chosen her to work beside him now. Hall was the regular helm officer and might have expected to be kept at that post. Of rights, Steele, as junior officer, should have been the one sent below to battle with Doctor Gordon and babysit spacesick Marines. Instead she would be at Brook's side.

And Brook was going to pull it off. Of that she had not the slightest doubt. The meritocratic charisma, the self-confidence, the easy assurance of the captain surrounded him like an aura. This was what it meant to command a Queen's ship.

* * *

The ship secured from general quarters shortly after midnight. After making their final reports to the captain, all the officers except Lieutenant Lamashtu went to the wardroom. Lamashtu would be nursing her overworked engines for the rest of the night. Rivera gulped a mug of mudd and went up to the bridge. After spending anxious hours on the gundeck with weapons ready to deal with the Delphinian fleet at maximum distance and the *Snapping Turtle* at intermediate range while short range lasers at all banks battled the debris in the Devil's Dustbin, the first officer hoped for a quiet middle watch. Costello, Hall and Steele, all too keyed up to sleep, drank mudd and let the tension drain.

"If anyone ever offers one of you kids a free trip to Mantu, see if you can trade it in for a tour aboard the *Good Hope.*" Costello rubbed the back of her neck and winced. Steele smiled, rose to stand behind her and massaged her shoulders. "I'm glad you're back, Liz. I've missed you."

Costello reached back to pat Steele's hand. "Got to get over that, Maggie. Separations are part of our business. You know that. Ask Henry. He's learned to take them in stride."

Hall shrugged. "The duty on Mantu was that bad, then." Hall had spent a month on the prison ship while in training at Annapolis. It wasn't a fun place for a vacation.

"Yup."

"But everything's all straightened out at Camp Shalom now?"

"Seems so."

"Well, that's great!"

"I suppose."

"You sound real down, Liz. Are you just tired, or did something go wrong?"

"Nothing went wrong, Henry. It was all routine. We caught the general's spies for her. She had two of them shot this morning."

Steele gave Costello's shoulders a final squeeze. Costello turned to look at her. "Witnessing a formal execution is a rotten way to start the day, Maggie, especially the way the Marines do it." Steele dropped her eyes and returned to her mudd.

Hall refilled his mug. "Gee! How can they do that on Mantu? Can horse guards even stand up in that gravity?" Hall would be the one wanting all the gory details, Costello thought, although it was Steele who really needed it.

"They make some modifications, Henry. They put the horses in antigravity armor. But DuBois's such a stickler for tradition, she makes Captain Brook look downright casual.

"Everyone had to parade out under the open sky — which on Mantu is a major undertaking in itself — and they did this with a full band, a color guard, and yes, even those incredible Mantu horse guards. Then when everyone had formed up three sides of a square, the poor devils who were the stars of the show had to drag out their own coffins. The boxes were on wheels, but the pair pulling them had been given only partial armor — nothing but skeletal braces above the waist — so it wasn't easy for them. The horse guard trotted along behind them, gave them a shove when they needed it, and closed up the fourth side of the square."

Costello paused and glanced at Steele. The junior officer stirred her mudd, her head bent. As the silence grew longer, Steele looked up and met Costello's eyes. Costello ignored Hall and spoke directly to her.

"The coffins were set up just so, and then the condemned had to sit on them, looking sicker every second, while the chaplain delivered a long-winded sermon and the firing squad somehow managed to hold their weapons at the ready position. Then, just when they were going to get on with it, one of our victims fainted. We all had to wait while the medic they had to sign the death certificates went back to get a bottle of ammonia salts, gave him the stimulent and got him paying proper attention again."

Steele sipped her mudd and tried to appear unaffected by the gruesome description. Costello sighed.

"Okay, Maggie. I don't suppose *Lafayette* will be sending you to witness a Marine Corps execution any time soon. It certainly was a long morning for me. The Navy could have executed the entire crew of a pirate ship in the time it took the Marines to finish off that miserable pair."

"I wouldn't waste any sympathy on them," Hall said. "There's something to be said for a lingering death in some cases. I think traitors deserve everything they get."

"It's not really a matter of what they deserve," Costello responded irritably. "If you'd ever worked on this kind of investigation, you'd know that traitors usually turn out to be more pathetic than wicked. They start out doing something small for money, thinking it won't really do much harm, and then they find themselves caught up in blackmail. Sometimes it seems they're almost glad to be caught. They're revolted by what they're doing, but they don't have the courage to stop and take the consequences. When the Marines execute traitors, it's not because they 'deserve it,' but because for this kind of premeditated crime, it's the most effective deterrent."

Steele pushed aside her mug and folded her hands. "I have a question, Liz." Finally, Costello thought.

"If there ever was a just war in the history of the universe, it's the one we're fighting now. The issue is whether hominids can live peacefully in this galaxy or are going to be eaten by our enemy. No one should need any fancy propaganda to be convinced that aiding Delphinus is a bad idea. So just what went wrong on Mantu? How could Delphinian agents penetrate a Marine garrison?"

"It isn't all that complicated, Maggie. Commoners are notoriously self-centered. They wouldn't collaborate if they thought of themselves or someone in their family being served up with sauce on some Delphinian's dinner plate. But they never think of it happening to them, and, of course, the enemy doesn't mention the possibility when they go out recruiting.

"We got the whole sad story during interrogation. Three Marines were approached by agents — hominid agents — while they were on leave on New Africa. It is sad but true that any member of the lower orders can be bought for the right price, and the Delphinians were willing to spend a lot to infiltrate Mantu. So three of Earth's finest commoners, three Royal Marines, took the bait and went to work for the enemy."

"But how could the officers have let that happen?" When commoners misbehaved, it was because the meritocrats responsible for them hadn't done their work properly. That was what they taught at Annapolis.

"An Admiralty board will have to answer that one, Maggie. What you have to realize is that the Marine Corps has some problems that we don't have. It's much easier to control sailors. Our people are securely confined inside the ship. Also, only a minority of sailors are volunteers. The Marines get a better class of people. They accept the hardships of military service out of pure patriotism, or at least the closest to it that exists among the commoners. And so the Marines have to allow their people more freedom. They can't shield them from all temptation without taking away all their liberty."

"But surely they could have done routine inspections and picked up those with abnormal guilt readings before this thing got so far out of hand."

"That's what I'd have done if I had General DuBois's job, Maggie, but she felt such inspections would damage morale. Maybe it's just a sailor's prejudice, but personally I think all those meritocrats on Mantu take that 'semper fidelis' nonsense too seriously. Their security officer — Lieutenant Abuto — he was so shook when we found out the bad apples were Marines, that I was the one who had to go in and break it to the general. And when I told her that three of her Marines had sold out to the enemy, she nearly choked on it. She'd been certain we'd find the spies among the Colonial civilians they have working on the base. Marines may all be volunteers, they may be the best Earth has below the meritocratic level as far as character goes, but they are still not meritocrats, and that means they are corruptible. I think the Mantu officers forgot that."

"There's something else I'm curious about, Liz. You were only down there a few days, and that base is huge. Captain Brook told us there were half a million people. How did you pick out the infiltrators so fast? And how can you be sure you got them all?"

"Don't you know how this is done, Maggie? Didn't you cover security and intelligence operations as part of your communications training?"

"No. I had a choice of doing any six out of the eight communications specialties because it wasn't my major. I didn't do security. I was told I'd get it on the job."

"More curriculum reform. I suppose it would violate one of our precious Navy traditions if they left the requirements at the Academy the same long enough for officers in service beyond their first tour to know what they could expect of new graduates. Well, learning on the job's not a bad method. After all, that's all Martha ever had, and she's as versatile an officer as any I've ever served with.

"All right, I'll remember to have Brook assign you to work with me next time something like this comes up. The procedure is pretty straight forward. You start by slamming the exits. Since the Mantu garrison is dug in underground, we did that much as it would be done on a ship, securing all the signal apparatus and the launches. Then we went through with the ball lie detectors as a rough divider and used them on everyone, officers too, because on rare occasions even meritocrats may go bad.

"At the start, I was the only person completely above suspicion because I was an outsider. I examined the officer cadre and the general. Only I couldn't use the ball on her because her hands are arthritic and won't grip, so Lieutenant Abuto and I had to hook her up to the full body function detector. It took longer to clear the general than it did to clear anyone else in the first phase.

"After that we ran everyone through with the balls very fast and narrowed things down quite a bit. The balls aren't absolutely reliable, and we got a good many false positive readings. After all, those folks were understandably feeling pretty nervous. But from our perspective, the balls are quite safe because you don't get false negatives.

"Then we went to work on the people with positive readings using drugs. If you know what you're doing, it's usually not necessary to use anything stronger than the old fashioned standbys scopolamine or sodium amytal. If all you want to do is identify a guilty party, that's enough. There are more powerful substances known as psychomonates that sharpen unconscious perceptions and memories. These will let you identify what we call the dupes — people who in total innocence have been used to commit harmful acts. The ball will identify them, but they honestly don't know exactly what they've done.

"The trouble with the psychomonates is that it takes a long time to prepare a subject for questioning because you have to make sure you use a form compatible with body chemistry and be absolutely accurate about dosage. If you miscalculate, the stuff can have lethal side effects. You'll get your information, but your subject will be dead soon afterward. And if you happen to be working for a Marine general who is planning a formal execution, that will get you in very bad trouble."

"But *Lafayette*'s own Lieutenant Costello stayed out of trouble," Hall grinned.

"I did. But Lieutenant Abuto may still have some. I told you DuBois shot two of the three this morning, but the third case we smoked out is a touchy one. Abuto will have to use psychomonates. They can't afford to shoot the third Marine until they do a depth interrogation." Costello laced her hands behind her neck, stretched out her legs, and leaned back.

"It seems this fellow came back from New Africa with some kind of back injury, not enough to put him out of commission, but bad enough to have him in and out of sickbay a lot getting treatment and pain pills. No one thought anything of it; back pain is normal on Mantu. But Doctor Mahamut's station would be a prime target for a saboteur.

"If this Marine contaminated something, he may have been exposed to it. That would explain why, on the conscious level, he doesn't appear to know what he did. He knows he took money; he knows he's guilty of something, but he couldn't tell us what. Maybe he hasn't done anything yet. Maybe he was supposed to take some action timed to coincide with an attack by the Delphinian fleet. Anyway, if he did contaminate something and it isn't found, they could face some nasty problems. But that's all General DuBois's worry now. The Marines figured they could handle it alone and let this tired-out Navy lieutenant go home." Costello stretched and yawned broadly.

"No sense my going to bed. I don't expect to be left in peace very long. Gordon's mad as a hornet about us coming out of *Firefly* into his nice disease-free environment. As soon as he's done looking for athlete's foot among the Marines, he'll be after me to see what malevolent microbes I've carried aboard."

"How about a few hands of gin rummy, Liz," Hall suggested. "I've got a deck in my cabin, and I've got to be up soon anyway to take the morning watch."

"What a splendid idea. You're on, Henry." Hall got up to leave, then paused. "It wasn't just Maggie who missed you, Liz. I missed you too," he said awkwardly and darted from the room.

Costello raised her eyebrows. "What have you done to Henry? I expected him to be teaching you to toughen up. Now it appears you've been teaching him something." Costello thought for a moment. "It's an improvement."

* * *

In a private room in the isolation bay, the pretty Japanese Marine was relaxed. She smiled at Doctor Gordon as he removed her lunch tray and sat next to her. It was an unusual experience for the physician. Since the Pox had blasted his face and chemotherapy had taken his hair, pretty women did not smile at him. The expressions he usually found on the faces of his patients of either sex were disgust or terror, frequently both. Had Corporal Toyo Yokomoto not been more than a little drunk, she'd no doubt be looking at him the same way.

Gordon smiled back. Yokomoto was enjoying her treatment so far; he had ordered a special meal for her including a good measure of hot sake. Her experience with medical/life support officers since she'd joined the Marine Corps certainly could never have been this pleasant. It was not the regular practice of Navy physicians to prescribe overdoses of alcohol, certainly not so early in the day.

Of course, Yokomoto did not yet know she was ill. It was going to be Gordon's job to tell her, just as it had been his job to tell Captain Brook about it an hour earlier. Yokomoto had Pearson's Plague. She would be dead within two days, and she had already infected everyone aboard.

The captain would have explained this to the crew when he put the ship on epidemic alert. Yokomoto was now the only person aboard who did not know. Gordon poured her another tablespoon of sake and spoke to her with more gentleness than those who knew him would have thought him capable of.

Gordon had not been gentle when he spoke to the captain. Indeed, had the med/life director not been keenly aware that he was speaking to a man with dangerously high blood pressure, the Thunderer might have discovered that there was at least one officer in the Royal Navy who could thunder more terribly than he. Between his knowledge that Brook was already under more strain than was good for him and some slight constraints imposed by traditions of Naval courtesy, Gordon managed to deliver his bad news in restrained language with his fury apparent only in his tone of voice.

Pearson's Plague was one of the foul souvenirs left behind in the wake of the First Galaxy War. Strategic thinkers on both sides viewed their enemies in that struggle as pathological agents. To Delphinians, Earth humans were a hominid mutation spreading infection among their food stock, an infection that made the food resist being eaten. Earth viewed Delphinians as a consuming cancer. Each side then turned to biological warfare with the avowed purpose of eradicating the other. It hadn't worked, but it had left the galaxy awash with mutating microbes. Pearson's Plague was among the most loathsome.

Doctor Parker identified the Plague virus as soon as she had blood samples. Yokomoto had a fully incubated case. Since none of the other Marines who had boarded with her showed any evidence of it in their blood, the physicians concluded that Yokomoto had been infected by inoculation, probably through a deliberately contaminated needle when the company was given injections for spacesickness.

Pearson's Plague, like bubonic plague, the dreaded Black Death of Earth, spread even more rapidly by contagion through the lungs; and Yokomoto had been in a highly infectious stage of the disease when she came aboard, though she had, as yet, no visible symptoms. As soon as she took her first breath from Lafayette's central life support system, one of the deadliest viruses known had gone out to attack the lungs of every person — and pig — on the ship. Only the chickens were immune.

"What action do you propose, Doctor?" With his customary calm, Brook tried to convey to Gordon his full confidence in the capacity of the medical/life support section to deal with any situation in its areas of responsibility.

"Yokomoto is going to die. There is nothing at all I can do for her except to try to control the pain, and there's a limit to what I can do there. Plague is one thing I haven't had myself, but I have watched victims die. It doesn't take them easily. The only way Yokomoto will get out of this without hours of agony is if someone not bound by a physician's oath commits murder."

Brook waited patiently for Gordon to continue. He knew his med/life director would welcome an opportunity to deliver a harangue on the subject of quarantine and Brook had no intention of providing it.

Finally Gordon broke the silence as Brook knew he would. "There is a prophylactic treatment available," he said grudgingly. "If I can get the serum into the veins of everyone else on the ship within the next forty-eight hours, they'll be able to fight off the virus before it turns deadly."

Brook nodded. "How do you wish to proceed?"

"I'll have to start with the new Marines — I don't know exactly how long any of them may have been sharing air with Yokomoto — but they are most at risk. And I'll put the vets to work on the pigs. Pigs are always easier than sailors." Gordon glared at the captain, who refused to be shaken from his air of benign kindliness.

"I suppose they are, Doctor, but I trust you will do something for our sailors as well."

"The sailors are what you've got to worry about. The Plague serum provides only temporary protection. It will be effective for a few days at most, and it can't be repeated. If we get another active case of Plague aboard, the serum won't do any good."

"Exactly what are you trying to tell me, Doctor."

"I'm trying to tell you that it's essential that everyone, everyone without exception, takes the treatment. All you need is one moron who decides he'd rather not get stuck with a needle hiding out in the head or somewhere and this whole exercise will be useless. We'll have another live source of infection breathing our air, the immune responses will wear off, and by Christmas there'll be nothing left alive on *Lafayette* except chickens."

"That does not appear to me to constitute an insurmountable problem, Doctor. I believe I have some small influence with the crew. You just tell me what you need, and I'll see to it that everyone obeys your orders."

"You'd better. I'm going to have enough to do without trying to round up reluctant patients. But I should warn you that this is a very nasty procedure. The shot is painful and the side effects hit fast and hard. Everyone who takes it is going to be plenty uncomfortable for a good half hour afterward, and some will feel it a lot longer. When the crew get to discussing this among themselves, I guarantee that some of them will be stupid enough to try to avoid it."

"Thank you for giving me that information, Doctor, but I believe the discipline that holds the crew at their battle stations will hold up through an epidemic alert. I will promise you that. Now, is there any other way I can be of assistance."

"Yes. I need more personnel. I'll get everyone on the medical crew including the vets working on this, but that won't be enough. There are too many people to treat and not enough time. So I want as many line officers as you can spare. They've all had the basics of med/life training, and I can brief them on everything else they'll need to know fast enough."

"Very well, Doctor. I'll keep Hall and Costello. They'll stand alternate watches. You can have Rivera, Lamashtu and Steele."

"Good enough. I'll be ready to start on the crew in about three hours. Parker is already working on the serum. We'll have to get the medical team taken care of first, so send the officers to her right away. And leave a free half hour in your schedule sometime this afternoon. I'll be up with your dose as soon as I've got the operation moving in the wards."

Sometimes Brook envied sailors. If Gordon said the treatment was going to be painful, it would be; but only a few of the commoners would have to take it from the med/life director as he would. Brook sighed. Another one of the burdens of command.

And so, fewer than eight hours after securing from general quarters, *Lafayette* went on epidemic alert. To save time, Brook spoke to the crew from the bridge. He preferred to deliver his orations before a live audience rather than as a three-dimensional talking head declaiming at a signal monitor like some nautical Wizard of Oz; but the nature of the emergency, as Gordon had described it, did not permit the delay necessary to muster the crew on the gundeck. The emergency also justified drawing power for the remote monitors despite the depleted stores. Hall, who had the watch, and the bridge crew would provide a live audience.

"Now hear this. This is the captain speaking. Epidemic alert. Repeat, epidemic alert. This is not a drill."

Having, he supposed, gained the attention of the sailors in various locations who would be watching his holographic image, Brook lapsed into his usual style of discourse.

"By the treachery of our perfidious enemy, one of our brave Marines from the garrison at Camp Shalom was infected with the loathsome disease known as Pearson's Plague. Not realizing that she was a carrier, she unwittingly brought it aboard *Lafayette.* Our physicians say she will suffer intensely for many hours and then die. The Plague is inevitably fatal and highly contagious. It is my sad duty to inform you that all of us have been exposed.

"Fortunately, our dedicated health care personnel have a treatment by which we may all be saved. The treatment they can give us does not promise permanent or absolute protection. Nevertheless, it will keep us safe provided that no one else gets sick. And no one else will get sick provided everyone on board is treated." Brook paused for dramatic effect. "If even one person fails to take the treatment, he or she will certainly fall victim to the Plague, die a horrible death, and at the same time infect all the rest of us." Brook paused again.

"Sometime within the next thirty-six hours each of you will receive an order telling you where to report to take an injection. When you get that order, you are to drop whatever you may be doing and go where you are told immediately. Anyone who fails to give full cooperation to med/life personnel at this time is endangering the lives of everyone aboard." Brook paused again, took a full breath and launched into his conclusion.

"Be mindful that your self-interest in these difficult hours coincides with your duty. Failure to obey a medical order during this alert will be punished with all the severity that such a betrayal of our community would demand. Captain out."

He glanced around the bridge at the faces lit by the red emergency lights. None of them seemed particularly upset. After all, epidemic alerts were not infrequent although there was usually less urgency about them. Then the captain noticed that the watch officer's face was working with emotion.

"Is something wrong, Lieutenant? What is troubling you?" Hall usually had no difficulty concealing his feelings.

"It's that Marine," Hall blurted out. "She was infected by one of her people, wasn't she, sir. Another Marine, just like she is. He put that poison in her on purpose. Shooting is too good for that godamned piece of scum! I hope he roasts in hell!"

"How dare you!" Brook hissed darting a sharp look at the sailors who had their eyes locked on their observation panels and gave no indication of having heard Hall's outburst. "How dare you stand on the bridge of one of Her Majesty's ships and use such language! For a Queen's officer to blaspheme God's justice, above all when our lives are in mortal danger, is inexcusable. The criminal responsible for spreading Plague is awaiting execution on Mantu. The form of his death is for General DuBois to decide. What God in His mercy may see fit to do when the case has been transferred to His jurisdiction is not for us to recommend. In time of war we are all murderers. 'Judge not, that ye be not judged.' I relieve you, Lieutenant Hall. Go to your quarters, remember your own sins, and pray that God may forgive you."

There was just too much to remember, Hall thought as he stumbled desperately down the ramp toward his cabin. No matter how hard he tried, he couldn't seem to avoid making mistakes. If only he wasn't so tired, he'd never have let himself go that way. He knew perfectly well that Brook felt strongly about using theological terms profanely. That was Brook's personal quirk, not a universal meritocratic characteristic. But a Naval officer who didn't respect his captain's quirks was a bloody idiot! And no meritocrat was that. So here he was in hack again; and if Brook got to thinking about what had just occurred, he might soon be in the brig.

Hall pulled down his bunk and curled up on it. He wished he could sleep. The insomnia that had begun to trouble him over the past few weeks added another dimension to the problem of concealing his commoner identity. It was a symptom he should report. By failing to report it he was not only violating a Navy regulation but giving further proof of his lack of meritocratic virtue.

If once Doctor Parker got hold of him, it would all be over. There'd be no hiding the truth from her. It was now too late to confess to the captain. Hall had known for two months now that he was no meritocrat, and yet he had continued to exercise meritocratic authority. That was a capital offense. The captain would surely hang him. The only way out was to kill himself before he was caught; but if he had the courage for that, he'd have the courage to face the captain.

If only he could sleep! The more he worried, the less he slept, and the more likely he was to make a fatal mistake. And the less he slept, the more likely it became that Doctor Gordon or an officer would suspect something was wrong and order him to sickbay for examination.

Hall swung himself out of his bunk. The captain had ordered him to pray for forgiveness. He couldn't sleep anyway, so he might as well try it. He dropped to his knees and began to recite the prayers of the Holy Rosary.

CHAPTER ELEVEN

In the bulging belly of the ship, supporting life rather than inflicting death was the primary mission. Medical personnel drilled for epidemic alerts as intensely as weapon crews drilled for battle stations on the gundeck. When the three line officers arrived at the sickbay laundry, now designated as a temporary treatment ward, the area swarmed with blue stripers moving with the precision of Marines in perfect silence as they set up cots in rows of five and tucked in the sheets. Every yellow striper in the medical section was gathered at the end of the ward, huddled around Gordon and Parker, when the three line officers reported.

"Here we are, Doctor," Rivera announced. "Ready for your orders, and I must say this does inspire confidence. It's as quiet as the gundeck before an action."

Gordon curtly acknowledged their presence and muttered something to Parker, who nodded and made a dumb sailor's sign to four of the yellow stripers. None of them were Colonial, but they obeyed the order, stripping off their uniforms and taking their places in the first row of cots. Gordon checked their pulse rates, then took his place in the fifth cot, sitting upright covered by a sheet. Galen's Ring on its silver chain gleamed dully against the scarred skin of his hairless chest.

The sound of rapidly padding bare feet and the rattle of rolling carts, broke the silence. Parker took charge of one cart, rapidly checking the trays and hypodermic needles.

"Medical team ready," she said. "You need talk line officers. They not train on this."

"You brief them. The line got us into this. I don't want to talk to them."

"You brief, we start. Make me do, all afternoon be here."

Gordon looked around the ward, saw everything ready to go on his signal, and stopped wasting time.

"The three of you will take this end of the ward. Patients come though treatment best if they can relax. The sailors trust you, and they'll obey you; but you can't just order someone to stop being afraid. Whatever it is you do when you've got a nervous sailor at an airlock or a gun station is what I want from you down here. You are going to get most of the hard cases, the ones who need cozying along. But I expect you to calm them down fast. We need to keep a steady flow of patients in and out of the ward.

"You work with five at a time. Start with whoever seems most tense. They only get worse if they have to wait. The procedure is a standard intramuscular injection; you won't have any trouble with it. Just be sure you hold your patient still and use the needle fast. For God's sake, don't try to be gentle. If you hesitate, you'll only hurt them more, and it's bad enough as it is."

Parker had finished her set ups and now stood at Gordon's side. "You say enough. Now you be first. You most tense this group." Gordon gave an irritated snort and turned onto his stomach. Parker administered the injection. If Gordon found it painful, he gave no sign. Parker picked up the lecture.

"Main danger this treatment be fever. Too high fever be killer. Here be cold cloths. Have other ways if cloth not enough. Call special team. Use this signal. Team come fast."

Parker pulled the sheet up to Gordon's shoulders and tucked it in.

"Patients have delirium. Some move too much. Could fall from cot. Use straps if sheet not hold. Most not need."

Parker moved from cot to cot as she spoke; and when she'd reached the last, Steele could see that Gordon was already feverish. His eyes had glazed over; and while he'd listened attentively to the first part of Parker's briefing, he now no longer seemed to hear her. Parker was soon back at his cot where she wrung out a cold compress and pressed it on his forehead.

"Simple nursing all can do now. Watch careful."

Within a few minutes, all five of Parker's patients were delirious, moaning and tossing in their cots. Parker moved from one to another applying the cold compresses. Steele was sure she also would have soothed her patients with soft words except that her mechanical voice could never be anything but ugly and harsh.

In about twenty minutes the fevers began to break. One patient after another emerged from delirium. Parker had all of them out of the cots and dressed within a total elapsed time of thirty minutes and pronounced them fit for duty. The four medics scattered to their positions in other emergency wards, each followed by their support staff who would be the first to be inoculated there.

Doctor Gordon took the longest to come around. He was the oldest member of the group and in poor physical condition to begin with. "Most be okay half hour," Parker said as she worked over the doctor. "If not be, use signal. Get emergency team. We put in sickbay for watch."

"Don't try it with me, Parker. I'm declaring myself fit." As if to prove the point, Gordon began to issue instructions while he was still dressing. The cots were made up with fresh linen. Doctor Parker, the three officers, and another one of Gordon's mates were set up for the second round.

Steele took the cot next to Parker. Gordon began with Lamashtu, who was the oldest officer and who responded to the injection with a resentful "ouch!"

"Stop that, Martha," Gordon scolded. "You're setting a bad example for the others."

"Wish I could get this from you, Anne," Steele sighed.

"Make no difference. Gordon or me, both be same. Both work fast. Close eyes. Soon be over."

There was a standard procedure for dealing with anticipated pain — a deep breath, hold it, and exhale through your nose. Steele decided that on a scale of one to ten, it wasn't the worst pain she'd ever dealt with, but it was in the running. Pain radiated down her leg, and the injection site throbbed even after Gordon withdrew the needle and went after Parker. She took a few more deep breaths, and heard Rivera grunt as Gordon reached his last patient. Parker moved restlessly in the cot at her side. Lamashtu called out something she couldn't understand.

And then the engine room was on fire. She struggled to bring down the damage control shield before the flames spread to the reserve tanks, but the panel was stuck. Straining to see through thickening smoke, she watched as the Admiralty's highest test synthetic melted in the heat. Drops of molten metal fell on her face and body, burning through the space liner. The hot line burst. Scalding steam filled the compartment. On every side, sailors screamed and groaned as flames enveloped them. The siren wailed; the signal for all hands to abandon ship rang in her ears.

And then silence. She was naked and soaking wet. She was inside the egg after a bad trip. She had failed the exercise. It was too late to get another chance. She wouldn't graduate with her class; she wouldn't get her commission.

But that couldn't be. She was certified on SOCRATES. She'd finished the training. All of it. She didn't have to be in the egg ever again. She was an officer aboard HMS *Lafayette.*

She smelled something sharp — ammonia. Her head pounded and every joint in her body ached. Slowly, she opened her eyes.

It wasn't SOCRATES. A soft, cool hand stroked her forehead. Dark eyes hovered over her, deep, liquid, compassionate eyes.

"It's all right, Maggie. Wake up now. Everything's all right. Wake up."

She blinked, shook her head to clear it and smiled wanly. Instantly, the eyes and the voice hardened.

"Hit the deck, Steele. We need this cot. This row will be your station." Steele sat up and shook her head to clear it. Gordon was working over Parker. "Come on, Anne. You're all right now. Open your eyes for me. That's right. Everything's fine now."

Fifteen cots at the far end of the ward were assigned to the officers. As the hours passed, Steele, working the middle row, knew she wasn't as effective as the others. She scarcely recognized most of the sailors assigned to her, while Lamashtu and Rivera knew them all, had some personal greeting for each, and seemed to know exactly what to say to put every one at ease.

"Now here's a sailor who won't mind being stuck with a needle," Rivera said cheerfully as Alya Petrov reported to him.

"I don't mind the needle, sir; but I could do without the fever."

"It's better to do your sweating on the gundeck, right, Tattoo? I feel the same way myself."

Steele looked up from the tray of hypodermics to see who Rivera was talking to. This was the first sailor to claim to be indifferent to the needle. When she stripped herself, Steele understood why. Petrov was covered with tattoos from neck to ankles. *Naval Regulations* prohibited tattooing on any part of the body not covered by the uniform. Petrov had pushed the rule to the limit. Only her face, feet, and hands were a natural color. Standing naked, she appeared to be fully dressed.

And she didn't mind the needle. She lay totally relaxed as Rivera gave her the injection. Steele wondered why she had been assigned to their section at all. It looked like a routine case. The reason became clear when the fever hit her. Rivera had been expecting it, and an team rolled in an ice bath almost at once. Rivera continued to glance in her direction, his eyes clouded with worry, as he worked with his other patients. When her fever broke, he was at her side, griping her hands and murmuring words of encouragement as the emergency crew worked over her. Finally he called for a litter to remove her to sickbay.

"Someday we're going to lose Petrov on one of these alerts," Rivera said. The cots were empty for a few minutes as orderlies worked to change the linen and ready them for the next set of patients. "The reaction to some of these short term serums is cumulative. It gets worse for her every time. She doesn't want to leave the service, but this may be her last tour if med/life can't find some way to counteract it."

And speaking of the devil. The med/life director took that moment to appear in the ward, moving rapidly and scowling as he inspected each line of cots. The sailors changing the linens worked even faster. As he approached the officers, Gordon gave each a sharp look and then pointed to Steele.

"You. Go to bed. I'll take over here. You'll go back on duty in four hours. Someone will call you."

Steele obediently went to her quarters. Only when she was inside her cabin did she realize how tired she was. It was well past midnight, and she had been working with the med/life team since shortly after noon.

* * *

His face red with fury and his hands trembling, Richard Gordon cursed as he poured water into a glass, slapped a tablet into his mouth and swallowed it. He paced impatiently back and forth across the deck waiting for the tranquilizer to take hold. Taking the pill made him feel even angrier. He disapproved of these fast-acting chemicals on principle, used them sparingly on others, and avoided them completely himself. Still he knew that if anyone else aboard *Lafayette* had been brought to him with the symptoms he was now displaying, he'd have prescribed double the dose and put him to bed in a straitjacket.

Come on, come on, damnit! He couldn't wait all day. The pacing helped. He could finally feel the chemical working. He went back to the pile of computer printout that had triggered his rage and rechecked it carefully. He was still furious, but the edge was off it. That was all he needed. He had to take this to the captain, and he had to explain the problem without cursing. For the rest, he just hoped the captain's blood pressure was up to the strain. He took two deep breaths and checked his pulse. All right. It was good enough. He left his office carrying the printout, slammed the door behind him, and took the main ladder to the top deck.

The Marine on guard at the hatchway was surprised to see the med/life director on the bridge but stepped aside to let him pass. Officers went where they pleased. Gordon squinted into the darkness and then crossed the bridge to the ramp leading to the captain's quarters.

"Halt right where you are, Doctor." The sentry might not want to interfere with a meritocrat. The watch officer was not so inhibited. "The last I heard, we were still on epidemic alert," Costello said. "Your station is in sickbay. Have you been given permission to leave it?"

"I've got an emergency, Costello. I have to see Brook."

"Has he asked you to report?"

"No, goddamnit! Why should he ask me to report? He won't know there's an emergency until I tell him."

Costello crossed her arms and shook her head. "I don't know where you get your ideas of protocol, Doctor, but while I have the watch no one calls on the captain without permission."

"All right! All right! I'm requesting permission!"

"I'll find out whether he'll see you." Costello unfolded her arms. "Take some advice, Doctor. Calm down before you go in.

The captain, you may recall, has had some emergencies of his own recently, and he's not in the mood to tolerate emotional outbursts. Hall's got himself in hack for running off at the mouth. Having a medical specialty doesn't exempt you from the basic rules of courtesy."

Gordon waited by the hatch stamping impatiently and muttering curses until Costello returned and told him he had permission to see the captain. "This had better be important, Gordon. I had to wake him."

"It's important, Costello," Gordon snapped and pounded down the ramp.

If he were to be damned for a deadly sin, Brook often thought, it would certainly be for the sin of anger. When the med/life director reported and saluted stiffly, Brook recognized the signs of a man heading for hell along the same highway and sympathized. Nothing was so difficult as to hold back a rage.

"A soft answer turneth away wrath," Brook thought. Using the benevolent tones he usually reserved for reading aloud from *The Book of Common Prayer*, he invited the physician to state his concerns. Gordon recognized what he thought of as the captain's God the Father voice and realized he was trying to help. Between the pill he had swallowed and the cordial reception, he made his report. He avoided profanity. That was all he could manage.

"This is exactly what I was afraid of." He slammed the computer printout on the captain's desk. "We've got the last of the crew who obey orders taking treatment now, but there is still one insubordinate fool loose on the ship who hasn't reported."

"Do you know who it is, Doctor," Brook rumbled benignly.

"Of course I know who it is! Do you think I don't keep records? It's the sailor whose name isn't on the sheet, that's who it is!"

Brook looked at the stack of paper lying beside him on which the names of several thousand sailors and a few hundred Marines were printed with the coded log entries describing their medical histories for their entire period of Naval service.

"Perhaps you could give me the missing name, Doctor."

"The name isn't important!" Gordon pounded his fist on the desk. "The point is the idiot is harboring Plague. In less than two hours that vicious virus will be ripe and exhaled into our life support system again, and . . ."

"My dear Doctor Gordon," Brook interrupted. "No one gets lost on this ship. Tell me for whom I'm searching, and the patient will be delivered to you."

"There isn't much time!"

"Precisely."

Gordon stared at Brook for a moment, snatched up the computer sheets and rifled through them. Then he threw them back on the desk with a snort and began searching through the pockets of his lab coat. Finally he came up with a balled up wad of paper. He smoothed it out and began to read. "Last name Bunyan. First name Waldo. Blood type A positive. Height . . ."

"The name is all I will require, Doctor. Return to your duty station. I promise you that Waldo Bunyan will be along shortly. And if you will permit me to offer you some medical advice that it seems I hear constantly from my personal physician, namely yourself, 'Don't push yourself so hard.'"

"I've got a Marine dying of Plague in the isolation bay. And if I don't have a needle in this Bunyan person very soon, I'm going to have a whole ship full of people needing help to get through their death agonies. I don't have time to pamper myself." Brook was aware of the effort it must have cost Gordon not to slam the door.

Brook smiled and shook his head. It was always so much easier to get some perspective on another person's problems than it was to get it on your own. There would be no difficulty locating "this Bunyan person." He sent a runner for the first officer.

"Do you know a sailor named Waldo Bunyan?"

"Sure do, Captain. He's a big guy, hard to miss. He goes to quarters in section 3/6 of the auxiliary engine bay, trains with Petrov on weapons drills. Generally good tempered, a little timid. Costello told me she had him in Schmidt's squad during quarantine because he tends to fight when he's scared."

Brook stroked his beard. "You continue to amaze me, Roderigo. It is never necessary to boot the computer to obtain information on personnel when I have you. You will, no doubt, have the life histories of all the Mantu Marines within the week."

"I try to learn what I can, sir."

"Well, Waldo Bunyan is acting in character. He failed to show up for the Plague treatment, and Doctor Gordon is in a lather about it. He'll have a stroke before I do if we don't help him out. So take a few Marines and dig Bunyan out from wherever he's hiding."

Finding Bunyan wasn't difficult. Sailors rarely had much imagination. Rivera found Bunyan hiding in the head in his berthing area. Getting him into the treatment ward was a bit harder. They had to carry him down the three ramps strapped to a litter.

The emergency ward was empty except for a single cot, and Steele was the only officer left on duty . She had been told to wait for Bunyan. Both Gordon and Parker were in isolation with the Plague victim.

"Sorry about this, Steele," Rivera said as the screaming, struggling patient was brought in. "I think I could have calmed him down for you if I'd had more time, but this was the best I could manage."

If Rivera couldn't do it, Steele thought, there was no chance she could. Bunyan would just have to take it the way he was. Through the combined efforts of four Marines and a pair of bluestripers, Bunyan was stripped and strapped down on the cot. Steele winced as she drove the needle deep into the tight muscle. It was ironic that those who feared it most suffered most. The Marines watched, breathing heavily, until the fever hit and Bunyan finally relaxed. Rivera then dismissed them and went to report to the captain that he had got his man.

Bunyan was still delirious when the signal securing from epidemic alert sounded. Before his fever broke, a runner brought Steele a message from the captain. Bunyan would have one hour to recover; then he'd be called in for captain's mast. Since Steele was already with him, she was to act as his legal counsel.

Just great, Steele thought, wishing the Navy wasn't always so keen to exploit meritocratic versatility. First she was Waldo Bunyan's nurse, and now she was his lawyer.

He was as hard to deal with as a client as he had been as a patient. Steele conferred with him right in the ward, where a party of sailors was replacing the laundry equipment that had been stowed away during the alert. Bunyan was suspicious and sullen.

"Lieutenant Costello gave a lecture on Navy law the first day of quarantine. Do you remember it?"

"No."

"No, what? Or have you forgotten the first day's lecture on military courtesies too?"

"No, ma'am."

"Have you ever been up before a civilian police court?"

"Yes, ma'am."

"Well, it's pretty much the same. You'll be put on the ball to make sure you're not tempted to lie. The charges will be explained to you, and you'll be questioned to make sure you understand. The main difference is in the ceremony. The sergeant major will take charge of you once you reach the top deck and tell you exactly what to do. Just follow directions. As far as responding to Captain Brook is concerned, the less you say the better. My advice is to confine yourself to four responses: 'Yes, sir,' 'No, sir,' 'No excuse, sir,' and 'Amen' when the captain reads from Scripture. That's the quickest way for you to get through it."

"Yes, ma'am." Bunyan twisted the hem of his shirt. "What happens to me then."

"That's up to the captain."

Bunyan tightened his jaw. "He's going to flog me, isn't he?"

"Try not to think about that. You're upsetting yourself."

"I'm not letting anyone flog me," Bunyan rose to his feet.

"Sit down," Steele said quietly, remaining absolutely still. "You're in deep trouble now, but not so bad that you can't make it worse."

Bunyan hesitated a moment and then sat. The captain read the sections of *Naval Regulations* dealing with mutiny every Sunday after prayers. To threaten an officer, physically or verbally, was a hanging offense.

"What about my rights? In the police court I have rights. I can argue my side."

"What do you have to argue about? You had an order and you disobeyed it. Do you deny that? And if Lieutenant Rivera hadn't found you, your disobedience would have killed all your shipmates. Or are you going to try to persuade Captain Brook that Doctor Gordon had it all wrong."

"I don't want a flogging."

"You didn't want to join the Navy either. And you didn't want the shot I gave you just now. When you're called to the Queen's service, what you want doesn't count. If you fight against authority, you only make it harder on yourself."

"I think I should have a chance to say how I feel."

"Bunyan, if you tell the captain you don't want a flogging, it will sound to him like a lack of penitence. I strongly advise you not to do it."

"I can do it then if I want?"

"You can ask the captain for permission to speak. If he grants it, you can ask him to impose alternative punishment. He doesn't have to grant either request. As far as that goes, if he thought alternative punishment would be in your best interest, he'd impose it whether you asked for it or not."

"What is alternative punishment?"

"Something — anything — the captain thinks fits the crime. Frankly, it's risky to ask for it. You're putting yourself entirely at the mercy of the captain's personal sense of justice. Although you can trust his fairness — he is, after all, a meritocrat — most sailors would rather take a standard punishment."

"That's a flogging."

"Right. And alternative punishment is something designed to hurt you just as much, probably more because it's personalized. That's why most sailors won't ask for it and why most captains won't order it except in extreme cases."

"If I ask for alternative punishment, can I change my mind when I know what it is?"

Bunyan had the makings of a regular space lawyer, Steele thought, and there was no more useless talent in the meritocratically governed Navy.

"No, you may not. If the captain grants your request for alternative punishment, you must accept it." Bunyan frowned. "And make no mistake, if he denies it and orders a flogging, you'll accept that too." Bunyan's frown deepened.

Bunyan was going to be a big problem. Steele was resigned to it. A problem for her as his counsel, a problem for the Marines, a problem for the captain, and one hell of a problem for the discipline officer who, if her impression of the captain's special assignment roster was correct, was going to be Henry Hall.

Hall certainly seemed overdue for a dirty job. It would be up to him to convince this big stubborn man to submit to punishment, whatever it was, with meekness and contrition. She was glad it wasn't going to be her responsibility.

"I can see you don't like what I've told you, but have I made it clear? Have I answered all your questions?" Steele had unconsciously softened her tone; and, for a moment, she dropped her quarterdeck face. This big sailor's fear was his greatest enemy. It had made him suffer more than necessary from the Plague treatment, and it would make him suffer more than necessary now. She wished she could do more to help him.

Bunyan sensed Steele's compassion. It confused him, but he responded to her charisma despite himself and dropped his sulky frown. Unexpectedly, he found himself apologizing for fighting her when she had been trying to save his life and thanking her for the gentle nursing he remembered receiving as he came out of the fever. He was rewarded with a bright smile.

"I'm very glad to hear you speak that way, Bunyan. Try to remember that when the captain punishes you, it's also for your benefit in the long run." She stood up. "If you have no more questions, I'll leave you now. I've arranged for you to get your lunch in the sickbay mess. Your escort will pick you up there and bring you to the captain when he's ready to take up your case. Put on a fresh uniform, and be sure you don't forget the cap. You'll have it off more than you have it on, but it's required when you're called to the top deck."

* * *

When Bunyan came out of the shower in sickbay and went to a basin to shave, Becky Petrie was waiting for him. No privacy, Bunyan thought, tightening the towel around his waist. Navy life was like having an oversized family in an undersized house.

That wasn't all bad, of course. He'd made some close friends on this ship, people he loved like his own flesh and blood. But a few of his shipmates he hated like his own flesh and blood. Petrie in particular was a royal pain. No one had gotten under his skin the way she did since his creepy kid sister had taken it as her mission in life to torment him twenty-five years ago.

Rhonda had grown up to be a good looking woman. Bunyan wondered whether Petrie might turn out pretty. He looked her over briefly. It didn't seem likely. Petrie was leaning on her crutches. Her small, skinny body was wrapped in the bright red robe that was standard issue in sickbay. Her hair had grown in slowly and unevenly after being shaved off for quarantine and stood out from her head in wispy clumps. She had sharp cheek bones, a long narrow nose, and green snake eyes set close together. She chewed on a thumbnail and spat out the pieces as she watched him lather his face.

Bunyan had already shaved once this morning, but doing it again couldn't hurt. Since he had to go up to the top deck, it might help his case to look sharp. He wished he'd been able to bring his solar shaver into space; it was a lot easier on his skin.

"Boy, you sure are stupid," Petrie said as he picked up the Navy issue razor.

Just ignore the twerp, Bunyan thought. That was the way to handle her.

"You gonna scream as loud as Chips did when they whip you?"

Bunyan's hand jerked, and he nicked his face. He tried to dab at the cut unobtrusively so Petrie wouldn't see it. It was no use. She knew she'd hit a nerve. Now there'd be no stopping her. He just mustn't get mad, mustn't give her any encouragement.

"Bet you do. Bet you scream a lot more. I was watching when Lieutenant Rivera brought you in on the stretcher. You sure did yell." She shifted her weight and started to chew on her other thumb. "We've had pigs in the slaughterhouse that made less noise while they were having their throats cut." She spoke with such relish that Bunyan could not resist a horrified sideways glance. She had removed her thumb from her mouth, and her fingers were moving as if fondling the handle of a knife. Her eyes gleamed as she wet her lips.

Bunyan's hand trembled, and he nicked his neck. There was no use even trying to hide this cut. He cursed as he wiped off the blood. What a spiteful ghoul this kid was. Compared to her, Rhonda had been a little angel.

Petrie watched Bunyan's attempts to staunch his cuts with interest. When he'd gotten the bleeding under control and picked up the razor, she spoke again.

"I sure don't want to miss seeing you whipped. When are they going to give it to you?"

Just don't say anything, Bunyan told himself. Just keep quiet, and she'll get bored and lay off.

"Drat! I'm going to be laid up down here at least to the end of the week. I don't suppose they'll keep you waiting for it that long." She looked at Bunyan hopefully. When he didn't answer, she continued her monologue.

"Probably they'll give it to you tomorrow morning. Sometimes they have punishment right after prayers. If you get it then, I can probably get to watch." Petrie was now talking as much to herself as to Bunyan. "If I told Doctor Parker, I wanted to go to hear prayers, I bet she'd get someone to carry me up."

"Don't make too many plans," Bunyan burst out. "Maybe I won't get whipped at all." He'd made up his mind. He was going to ask the captain for alternative punishment despite what Lieutenant Steele had said.

Petrie threw back her head and laughed. She had an unpleasant laugh, a high pitched nasal cackle. "If you believe that, you're even dumber than I thought." Petrie narrowed her eyes and examined Bunyan keenly.

"Hey!" She propped her crutches against the bulkhead and hopped over to Bunyan's side, getting as close to him as she could, leaning on the sink. "Hey! You really believe that, don't you! You don't think what you did was all that bad. How about a bet? Huh? You wanna put some money on it? A gold coin says you're gonna get the cat."

Bunyan's patience snapped. He threw down his razor, seized Petrie's crutches, and jammed them into the space between the deckhead and the shower stall where she could see but not reach them. Then he pulled on his uniform and left her. Petrie's stream of juvenile cursing was extremely satisfying, and he went to his lunch with a good appetite.

There were facilities for feeding several hundred ambulatory patients in sickbay, but only one dining table was in use when Bunyan picked up his tray. There had been very little illness aboard *Lafayette*, and most of the people eating there were sickbay staff. Of the patients, fully half were in only for overnight observation because of reactions to the Plague serum. Bunyan recognized one of these: Alya Petrov.

Petrov was someone special to Bunyan, although she had never paid much attention to him. Bunyan, like every other sailor aboard, was sent to drill periodically on the gundeck. Brook wanted all hands to have enough combat training to assure that the ship would never be at the mercy of an enemy because casualties on the gundeck left her with no one alive except overspecialized cooks and swineherds.

When Bunyan drilled with the gunners, he worked at Petrov's section. He worked himself into a fine sweat under her urging and never grudged a second of it. There was excitement and a sense of urgency during weapons drills that he never felt in the engine room, where Big Mama liked things serene.

Even more than that, he loved to watch Petrov move. A big woman, nearly as tall as he was, she had the grace of a leopard; and when she stretched or bent too far, a glimpse of exotic tattoo was visible at the ankle or wrist under the edge of her uniform. The loose robe she now wore revealed several inches of tattoo along her lower arm. Bunyan set his tray down next to hers.

Without speaking, Petrov got up and carried her tray to the other end of the table. Conversation had stopped when Bunyan appeared, and a freezing silence hovered in the room. Bunyan realized that a decision had been reached somewhere to send him to Coventry. He'd been branded as a violator of the code of the third deck, as someone who was disloyal to his shipmates. Now he would be ostracized until the powers on the lower deck decided he had been taught a lesson. Hell. It was bad enough the officers were on his neck.

Petrie's noisy arrival shattered the silence. She had somehow retrieved her crutches but now had another complaint. "Somebody's gotta help me get my lunch," she whined. "I can't carry a tray myself."

Gabriel got up from his place. "Sit down. I'll get it for you."

Petrie pulled out the chair opposite Bunyan's and sat letting her crutches fall to the deck with a clatter. Either Petrie didn't know or didn't care that Bunyan was a social outcast. She picked up the conversation he had broken off in the head.

"I'll give you odds. Two to one. How about it? Two gold coins to your one says your gonna get whipped."

"Stifle yourself, Hellcat," growled a voice from the other end of the table. Petrie leaned over to find out who had spoken, discovered it was Petrov, and stifled herself.

The meal was eaten in silence. Everyone ignored Bunyan except Petrie, who kept quiet but never took her eyes off him. Bunyan tried not to squirm. The food stuck in his throat; and although he badly wanted a second cup of mudd, he couldn't bring himself to ask anyone to pass the pot. He was almost relieved when four Marines carrying rifles showed up looking for him.

Some sailors said that Marines were not really human; they were robots that worked off batteries. The behavior of the team that came to take Bunyan to the top deck was the sort of thing that gave credence to the idea. The quartet had a standard assignment — take into custody and escort — and they ran through it like a set of clockwork figures, doing it by the numbers.

Everything Marines did, they did by the numbers. They were trained that way deliberately to ensure that these commoner volunteers who were agents of meritocratic police authority stuck to the regulations and did not drift either into slackness or abuses of power. When Marines had an assignment, the officers knew precisely how it would be executed, for the Marines would follow the drill no matter how awkward the result. Let the sailors sneer; the Marines were proud of it. If the sneering got out of hand, well, there was a drill for that too.

"Attention on deck!"

First on his feet was the sole Marine at the table whose reflexes reacted to jerk his body into a stiff brace although he had been given a heavy dose of muscle relaxant. The sickbay staff were up next. The remaining patients did the best they could, several of them leaning against chairs for support. Petrie made a big show of hopping on one foot until she caught a warning look from the Marine corporal.

"Waldo Bunyan, identify yourself!"

Everyone else at the table was wearing either a red patient's robe or a medic's smock. Bunyan was the only one in the regular uniform. And Bunyan knew the Marines must have been shown his picture. You'd think they could just come round and tap him on the shoulder. But oh, no. They had to make a production out of it. He identified himself. Two of the Marines moved behind him, rifles at the ready, and a third snapped on a set of handcuffs.

"As you were!"

Everyone except Bunyan sat again while the Marine sergeant went through the rest of the routine, reciting the formal phrases in a sing-song chant. Bunyan wasn't listening. He was watching Petrie, who still had her eyes on him and was delicately waving her fork in tempo with the Marine's words. She held his gaze as the Marine finished speaking. Then, smiling slightly, she pulled a pair of coins from her pocket and held them between thumb and forefinger while tracing a question mark in the air.

It was bad luck to refuse to bet on yourself. Bunyan frowned and then abruptly nodded his head as the Marines lead him off. The girl put the coins back in her pocket and hugged herself, her mouth open in silent laughter.

* * *

"I suppose you were surprised to be told that you are the one getting this special assignment." Captain Brook studied the view outside the day cabin windows. It was already getting dark on this shortest day of the year, which had been cloudy to begin with. The season was appropriate for the cutbacks in energy consumption ordered in every department after the ship's hasty departure from Mantu. He hoped to find a star suitable for recharging the ship's batteries before the end of the year.

"Well, yes, sir. I am a bit surprised. I was the one who found him in the head, and I rather thought it was Lieutenant Hall's turn." Rivera, just coming off the afternoon watch, had been hoping for a little time for himself. Perhaps that was selfish, but it had been a long week; and meritocrats, just like the ship, couldn't run indefinitely without recharging their batteries.

"You have been involved in this matter more than I'd like. Unfortunately, this is an unusually difficult case. I am not sure anyone can do much with Waldo Bunyan at this stage, but if anyone can, it's you."

"Thank you, sir. I'll do my best."

"Lieutenant Steele has also had more than her fair share of involvement in this case, for similar reasons. Number Five is a very promising officer — a lot like you in many ways."

Rivera grinned. "I take that as a compliment, sir. I hope that means you're going to send Steele to the gundeck for training soon. I'm looking forward to working with her."

"Yes, I imagine you are." Although Brook did not socialize with his officers, he kept a finger on the emotional pulse of the wardroom. It was astonishing how quickly Steele had become one of the family. It was barely half a year since she had come aboard, and there had been no heavy action during that time, nothing either to hasten bonding or to seriously test her mettle. Yet the captain was aware that all his officers trusted her as fully as they did each other. Concern about SOCRATES had faded. When the time came, they were confident they could help Steele through it.

Even Lieutenant Hall had bonded with Steele. That was doubtless good for him, and, given enough time, she might be able to shape him up yet where the others — including himself — had failed. But for the moment, Brook held to his earlier resolution to keep Hall away from any sensitive assignment.

Rivera was the only officer who had not yet had an opportunity to work closely with the junior lieutenant, but Brook had no doubt at all that the two of them would be compatible. Indeed, he fully expected to see more than that. Brook had lived long enough to have confidence in his judgments about people; and if ever he had seen a natural team, it was Rivera and Steele. It would be good for the ship; he hoped it would be good for them.

"It is my intention to start Lieutenant Steele drilling on the gundeck after the first of the year. The engineering department will require her assistance until we have recovered from our recent energy drains." Brook stroked his beard as he observed his first officer's response to this information. "Right now, however, I'm giving you a dirty job to do."

"Yes, sir." The grin spread over Rivera's face had nothing to do with the current order.

"Very well. Let's get on with it. I suppose you can guess how Bunyan came to be pressed into service."

"I'd say he was an addict, Captain. Right?"

"Correct. He turned himself in for treatment some years ago after he found he was hooked on some chemical — I can't recall what; it's in the med/life records — and he was detoxified at public expense. Then he went back to the habit, and when he was no longer able to work or take care of himself, he ended up as a public charge again. This time, after he was clean, the authorities decided he ought to give the Navy some time and, perhaps, learn a measure of self control."

"I figured at his age, coming in for a first tour, it would have been something like that, sir. It also explains why he's so skittish about needles."

"Skittish!" Brook snorted. "That's not the report I got! The man was frightened out of his wits — what wits he has, which don't appear to be anything to brag about. I'm sure it's unnecessary for me to explain to you how important it is for us to cure him of that. Anyone who would disobey an order during an epidemic alert is the sort who would leave his post during any dangerous situation. He's a menace to all of us who are shut up in this vessel with him until he learns to manage his fear."

"Yes, I understand that, sir."

"Unfortunately, he doesn't." Brook shook his head and sighed. "The mast went very badly, Roderigo. With my best efforts, I could not bring up any trace of contrition in Bunyan. He was totally preoccupied with himself. His attitude toward punishment was abominable. He even asked me to give him an alternative in place of flogging."

Rivera raised his eyebrows.

"I know what you're thinking. He really left himself open for a total immersion therapy. Extra duty in the isolation ward would be an obvious choice. Given his sensitivities, the booster shots he'd have to take would alone almost balance the books, and he could have begun his punishment hours cleaning up after the Plague victim tonight. That would have fit the crime all right. It would, however, have been cruel and unusual in the case of Waldo Bunyan; and I doubt that, in the long run, it would be any more effective than flogging."

"The crew expect to see him flogged, sir. You virtually promised that when you put the ship on epidemic alert."

"Yes, I am aware of that aspect. Bunyan's offense was one that touched on the personal welfare of the sailors. If they believe he has been punished too leniently, we are apt to see some nasty vigilante incident in which they try to make up the difference. Nevertheless, punishment is primarily for the benefit of the offender, and its impact on others is secondary. I will not be intimidated by vigilantes; I am prepared to deal with them too, if I must. I would have given Bunyan the alternative if I thought it would benefit him; but by requesting it, he confirmed my impression that he has excellent potential as a subject for corporal punishment. Because of his disproportionate reactions to the mere threat of physical pain, he should respond well to the lash once he has focused his attention properly. He has not thought through the gravity of his act of disobedience. That is the root of his problem. He will not improve his attitude without assistance."

"I understand, sir. That's to be my job."

"You can be wonderfully persuasive, Roderigo. I've seen you tame sailors I was ready to give up on. You know what lies ahead if Bunyan takes his punishment without accepting his guilt. He'll get the whipping anyway, and the next time his cowardice gets the best of him, he'll get the same. With enough repetitions, even a fool will learn how to avoid a negative stimulus."

That was how it had been done to Rick, Rivera thought, and the memory of his brother, as it always did, jerked at something buried deep inside his heart. No one should have to suffer what Rick had.

"I know you find that prospect distasteful. For sailors to obey because they fear us and the punishments we may inflict more than they fear facing death in the line of duty is a poor mode of governance. For some, unfortunately, there is no other way. I earnestly hope that it will not be necessary for Waldo Bunyan to endure such training. That is why I am putting you in charge. Go to him now, and stick with him all night if that's what it takes."

"Aye, aye, sir." Rivera rose to leave.

"Roderigo."

"Sir?"

"I am sincerely sorry that I found it necessary to burden you with this task. I am aware that I have worked you hard, in many ways, over the past few days. You haven't had much sleep since we left Mantu, and no time to devote to your volunteer projects."

The captain remained skeptical of Rivera's ambitious aspirations for members of the lower orders, but once he had been reassured that these posed no danger to the ship, he had encouraged his first officer's activities.

"That's all right, sir, though I admit I have missed meeting with my Bible study group There hasn't been a class this week, and I'd promised I'd hold one tonight when I got off duty. Some of them are very keen on reading Jeremiah in Aramaic. I'd hate to see them lose interest."

"Luke 15:4."

"Of course, sir." That did sum it up very neatly: "What man of you, having an hundred sheep, if he lose one of them, doth not leave the ninety and nine in the wilderness, and go after that which is lost, until he find it?" Rivera went to see what he could do for the straying lamb.

* * *

Bunyan was just beginning to adjust to the unfamiliar silence. There was no place else he'd been in the whole ship that was as quiet as this cell. Even in the berthing area after lights out, when anyone who so much as coughed loudly would be grabbed by a Marine and hauled off to sickbay, you could at least hear other people breathing. Here there was no sound at all.

"Attention on deck!"

Bunyan, startled, leaped to his feet. Jesus Christ! Even in the brig! What in hell could the Marines want with him now? The door of his cell swung open and the first officer stepped inside.

"As you were, Waldo."

Bunyan sat on the bunk, his hands on his knees, and watched the lieutenant suspiciously. He'd had more than enough of officers for one day. Didn't the meritocrats have anything else to do except hound one poor sailor? He'd been put in confinement, and he was going to be whipped. Wasn't that enough?

"You still sore at me for forcing you to take the shot?"

Bunyan squirmed in embarrassment. He'd almost forgotten about that. It seemed like a long time ago.

"No, sir. I'm not sore."

"Then I'd like to know why you're glaring at me that way? I'm not your enemy."

A cloud of distrust dropped over Bunyan's face.

"You don't believe that, do you. Well, it's true. You don't have a better friend on this ship. I saved your life for you."

"Yes, sir," Bunyan said flatly.

"You don't sound very grateful."

Bunyan sat silent and sullen, staring at the deck. Rivera prayed for an inspiration. He did not want this man to go up for punishment the way he had gone into sickbay. Somehow an inspiration came.

"There is someone I think you should meet, Waldo. Get up. I'm taking you to the isolation ward."

Bunyan clenched his teeth. He was terrified of the isolation ward, and he was sure the first officer knew it.

"I'm not going. You can't give me extra punishment — sir."

"There you go again. Who said anything about punishment? There's a very brave woman dying on our ship tonight, dying the way you would be dying if it hadn't been for me. There's a religious duty to visit the sick. I'm giving you an opportunity to perform it."

"I don't want to."

"Waldo," Rivera said gently. "Look at me. You've been avoiding my eye."

Bunyan raised his head.

"Sailors often have to do things they don't want to do. You can be sure this won't be the most unpleasant thing I'll ever ask of you. The woman in the isolation ward is a Marine. Her name is Toyo Yokomoto. She is twenty-four years old, and for the last three years she has been serving voluntarily in the Mantu system. I don't know if you ever followed the holograph news reports while you were on Earth, but there has been heavy action around Mantu for a long time, and life for Marines hasn't exactly been full of fun. She's been cold; she's been crushed in heavy gravity; she's lived for months in muddy trenches; and she was wounded twice badly enough to need time in the hospital. Then just as her company was being rotated out, her number came up. She's dying now because a Delphinian agent deliberately infected her with a disease that will cause her body to swell until it literally explodes." Rivera's eyes were locked to Bunyan's.

Bunyan did not understand why this story made him feel sad. Tragedies involving people he didn't know normally didn't affect him much, especially when he had troubles of his own.

"She deserves a visit, Waldo. Because our med/life people worked so efficiently — and because I dragged you out of the head in time — she's the only one who is going to die. Someone should tell her that the rest of us are safe and that we appreciate her sacrifice. As the last sailor to take the serum, you're the logical one to do it. You're immune to what she's got. There is nothing in the isolation ward that can hurt you now. So get on your feet. You're coming with me."

He was going to do it, Bunyan realized with some surprise. He was going to stand up and follow the first officer tame as a lamb. His messmates had told him this kind of thing could happen. The gunner would talk quietly and smile and the next thing you knew you were doing something crazy — going out on the hull while the ship was under fire or boarding a launch to attack a heavily defended enemy. All the officers could do that to you, they said, but Lieutenant Rivera was the worst. He could charm you right out of your skin. It was like being hypnotized.

Rivera saw he had him. His brown eyes sparkled and his smile broadened into a grin as Bunyan stood up.

"Released in my custody," he said to the guard as he strode briskly from the cell without bothering to cuff the prisoner, call for an escort, or even to check whether Bunyan was actually behind him. Bunyan followed.

Gordon came out of Yokomoto's room in response to Rivera's knock and closed the door behind him.

"We'd like to visit the patient, if we may."

"I cut off visits quite a while ago, Lieutenant," Gordon said, his eyes resting on Bunyan. He remembered the big sailor for some reason. Ah, yes — a minor accident in engineering. He came in with a cut hand and made a big fuss over taking a tetanus shot.

"I've been assigned as discipline officer, Doctor. This sailor is Waldo Bunyan."

"I see." Gordon looked at Bunyan again. Stupidity. Definitely more trouble than a pig. Thank God he was now the line's problem. "All right. A short visit. I want both of you to understand one thing. Yokomoto is still in uniform. She wants to die in it, and I'm going to honor her request. But she is not to try to stand or salute, Lieutenant. As for you, sailor, remember that this Marine outranks you and mind your manners."

Corporal Yokomoto wasn't pretty anymore. Her body had begun to bloat, and soon her eyes would be swollen shut. Already they had closed to mere slits. She was sitting up, still wearing her uniform. But she wouldn't die with her boots on. Her puffy feet were bare. Several seams of the uniform had been opened to relieve the pressure on her body, and one sleeve of her tunic was slit so medication could be injected directly into a vein. As Rivera and Bunyan entered, Yokomoto squinted at them.

"Who is there?" she asked, straining to see.

"You have visitors, Toyo," Gordon said. "This is our first officer, Lieutenant Rivera, and the sailor with him is named Waldo Bunyan."

"I beg your pardon, Lieutenant. I have orders not to stand, sir."

"It's quite all right, Corporal. I am here only to pay my respects and to accompany one of our sailors who has a special reason for wanting to speak to you."

"A sailor?" Yokomoto spoke slowly as though she had some difficulty concentrating. "I don't know any sailors, never had any friends who were sailors. All my friends are Marines. Except this ship's officers, sir. They've been very good to me. Especially this one, this doctor officer." She lifted her free arm and reached blindly toward Gordon.

Gordon grasped her hand. "It's all right, Toyo. I won't leave you. Talk to your visitor."

Bunyan stared at Yokomoto without speaking. She was hideous, but he couldn't take his eyes off her. Yokomoto peered at him and made an effort to focus her attention.

"Well, sailor," she said finally. "Since you're here, what do you want to talk about?"

"I'm supposed to tell you," Bunyan began nervously, "that is, I want to tell you that everyone aboard *Lafayette* has taken the Plague serum and no one is going to die."

"Except me," Yokomoto said.

Bunyan gasped. Yokomoto couldn't see his reaction very well, but she sensed it. It pleased her, and she drew strength from it. Commoners who were trained for combat usually faced death very bravely. The Marines, in particular, were proud of that. Corporal Yokomoto meant to make a good death.

"I'm sorry," Bunyan gulped. "I know they told me no one could do anything to save you. They said it would hurt a lot. I didn't mean . . ."

"It's okay, sailor," Yokomoto interrupted. "If you're looking for a long life and an easy death, you don't join the Marines. I'm just sorry the pigs got me this way. I know they hoped to kill all of you too, and I'm glad to know we've cheated them out of that. One casualty isn't too bad. I don't know much about war in space; I've done all my fighting on the ground. But I'd think a big ship like this one could do plenty of damage. So you and your mates will pay them back for me. Is that so, sailor?"

Bunyan was silent. His face was working with emotion, but Yokomoto couldn't see it. She made an effort to open her eyes, and the pain made her wince.

"Are you still there, sailor?" she said sharply as a few tears slid from under her reddened eyelids. "Godamnit, the war is over for me, but I want to be avenged! Is there any fight in you sailors, or is it true that you gobs wouldn't even go to your battle stations if Marines didn't drive you there with bayonets?"

Yokomoto's sudden anger alarmed Bunyan, and he was not sure what to say. No one had yet forced him to his battle station; but, then, he'd never yet seen a battle. Then he thought of an answer, something he had heard Alya Petrov say and that he sincerely believed must be true. "Sailors fight," he said. "We follow our officers. When they're with us, sailors are just as good as Marines."

"Is that so? Then I guess we're going to win the war." Yokomoto slowly shifted her awkward body. Her outburst had increased her torment, but she was determined not to let a swabby see her writhe.

"It was nice meeting you, sailor." Her voice was tight. "If you ever make it to heaven, you can tell me how it goes. They say you'll find me on guard duty."

Gordon had been watching Yokomoto intently. He knew this brave show was important to her, but it had gone far enough.

"Out!" he barked. "Go! Now! Both of you!"

When the door shut behind them, Yokomoto gave in to her agony and screamed. Gordon was already increasing the level of the drug running into her vein. It was very close to a lethal dose; he would not be able to hold off the death throes much longer.

But for a short while, it was still enough. As her pain eased, Yokomoto gradually relaxed. Gordon sat next to her and took her swollen hand between both of his. In a few minutes the drug took hold, and Yokomoto smiled at him.

* * *

Corporal Toyo Yokomoto died shortly before dawn. Captain Brook read the funeral service after morning prayers. For his sermon, he chose his text from the book of Revelation: "Be thou faithful unto death, and I will give thee a crown of life."

There were no dry eyes on the gundeck; even officers were permitted to cry at funerals. Although only the Marines from Mantu had known Yokomoto when she was well, the Lafayettes were moved by the eulogies delivered by her friends and by the knowledge that the death that she had suffered was one that all of them had nearly shared.

The service concluded with the singing of "Eternal Father" by the ship's choir and the playing of taps by a Marine bugler. An honor guard carried Yokomoto's ashes, purged of virus by fire, down the ramp to the 'tween decks where they were expelled though an airlock to float forever in space, mixed with the cosmic dust of the universe.

Four hours later, all hands were mustered on deck again for another ceremony: the punishment of Waldo Bunyan. Captain Brook gave him thirty-nine — the Biblical maximum. He took it much better than anyone expected.

CHAPTER TWELVE

Chief Katie McDougall, who ran the galley of HMS *Lafayette*, sat alone, perched on a high stool with a pad on her knees, talking to herself. At least that was how it appeared to the crew of cook's apprentices working around her, scrubbing the deck and sterilizing counter surfaces in expectation of an inspection by Doctor Gordon.

McDougall was actually in conversation with Mickey McCarthy, the Colonial who served as Captain Brook's steward. After several years of practice, McDougall had learned how to project her thoughts to Mickey telepathically. She was now quite fluent, but she still had to speak aloud to concentrate her thoughts. McCarthy was in the wardroom pantry two decks above, polishing silver. He and McDougall were planning the menu for Christmas Eve when the captain would host a formal dinner for his officers.

"It doesn't seem right, somehow." McDougall tapped her pencil on her pad and then doodled something that might have been either a fish standing on its tail or a Christmas tree. "Feeding the crew caviar and serving oysters in the wardroom seems backwards."

"Can't be anything but oysters, Katie, my love. I've gone and looked it up. Oysters are the only seafood brought from the Colony with a low enough sodium count to fit in the captain's diet; and we can't be serving one thing to him and something else to the others." The Colonial's telepathic voice carried a distinct brogue that had quite startled McDougall the first time she had permitted McCarthy to think-talk her. His peculiar Noah's Ark story that he claimed explained how his family could trace its origins to what he called the Emerald Island on a planet suspiciously like Earth seemed pretty fanciful to her. Nevertheless, the longer she knew him, the harder it was for her to remember that Mickey McDougall was an Alien and not a cousin from County Mayo.

"It's perfectly dreadful trying to plan a party around someone on a diet." McDougall added some round balls to her doodle, transforming it unambiguously into a Christmas tree. "Well, oysters it is then." She wrote "Oysters" on the top line of the pad and scribbled out the doodle. "But I'll do them fancy. I'll have to think about how. Now, roast beef will still be all right for the entree, won't it? I just can't see giving the officers chicken for Christmas when we have all that lovely meat in the freezer."

"Roast beef is no problem at all. I'll just be sure to trim all the fat from the captain's portion when I carve and serve it *au jus.*"

"You mean I can't even make a sauce?"

"Oh, make a sauce, Katie. By all means, make a sauce. How can we have a grand dinner without a sauce for the entree? We'll just put the sauce in the silver boat, and I'll simply fail to present it at the captain's place."

"Won't he notice that, Mickey?"

"Ah, Katie, my captain scarcely notices my existence." There was a note of sadness in McCarthy's projected voice. The Colonial had served the captain ever since he had taken command of *Lafayette* and was closer to him and probably knew him better than anyone on the ship. It was McCarthy who watched the captain's diet and carried a tray to him when it was time for him to eat; and it was McCarthy who made sure the captain's blood pressure medication was in front of his nose when it was time for him to swallow the tablets. When the captain's long hours pushed him to the edge of exhaustion, it was McCarthy who would pull out his bunk and lay out his nightshirt, all so unobtrusively that the captain thought it was his own idea to go to bed. The steward was devoted to the captain, but Brook took all his efforts for granted. In all the years he had been in the captain's service, McCarthy had never had a word of thanks.

"When I wait on my good captain on Christmas Eve," McCarthy continued, rubbing a bowl, "I shall be, as always, invisible as a summer breeze and silent as a floating cloud."

McDougall giggled. "If the captain knew you had so much blarney in you!"

"So much there is about me my captain does not know! But who would be telling him, Katie, my love? Not a child of Earth in all space, save thee, has heard my poetic soul pour forth its beauteous melodies."

McDougall's giggles intensified. The blue stripers, both human and Colonial, who were scrubbing the counter behind her, rolled their eyes at each other. Although they were all new to the Navy, it seemed to them a bad sign when the chief sat and giggled to herself when they were about to be inspected.

The chief appeared to agree that giggles were inappropriate. "Stop that," she said loudly. "I'm on duty."

"Aye, aye, ma'am," McCarthy replied. The incongruity of the telepathic voice and the formal sailor's response did McDougall in completely. She dissolved into helpless laughter.

McCarthy examined the gleaming display of wardroom silver with satisfaction. He'd finished the larger pieces including the candlesticks, silver sauce boat, and punch bowl. All that remained was the flatware. "All work and no play is bad for the lower orders, Katie. Let's take a break. I'll mix up some bogs and bring them to the galley. Then we can plan the dessert."

A bog was what you got when you added Irish whiskey to hot mudd. It was the way both McDougall and McCarthy took their grog ration. To the relief of her crew, McDougall was quiet for a few minutes. Then the middle-aged Colonial with thinning red hair and a face full of freckles, whom they recognized as the senior steward, appeared in the galley carrying two mugs on a tray. He sat silently on a stool beside McDougall as the chief began to talk to herself again.

* * *

While McCarthy and McDougall were drinking bogs and discussing Christmas puddings, the line officers were in the wardroom working on the Santa Claus list. All were present except Lamashtu, who had the watch, and the captain, who was at the chart table working out a course to a planetless star where the ship could draw power with minimal chance of detection or interruption by a hostile vessel.

It was Costello's turn to play Santa Claus this year, selecting the gifts and filling the stockings, so she was in charge of making up the Christmas list and presided at the meeting. The officers worked with two computer-generated lists that ostensibly distinguished those sailors and Marines who were naughty from those who were nice. The nice ones would get cash bonuses and some small gifts from the ship's stores in their stockings. The naughty ones would get chicken feathers.

Unfortunately the computer had limitations. All it could do was to separate those whose names appeared in the punishments book sometime during the past year from those who had clean records. The meritocrats knew that the conduct of some people who were never on report fell short of a standard deserving reward, and that there were others, who had done something that merited punishment but afterward improved their behavior, who deserved positive reinforcement from Santa. Consequently, the officers considered each case individually. It was a big job, but as they generally agreed, they worked their way through the alphabet with reasonable speed.

"All right, John Petibon gets a gift." She checked the name on her clipboard. "What about Becky Petrie?"

"Cross her off." Costello looked at Rivera quizzically.

"You surprise me, Rod. She seems to me to be doing remarkably well, and I'd have thought you, of all people, would be more encouraging." The grommet had been a hellion during quarantine, but since then she'd never once been on report.

"Sorry, Liz. My vote is firm. Petrie's not nice. I fully expect to see her hang before this voyage is over."

"You surprise me, too," Hall said. "I'm the one who's supposed to be so hard boiled. Isn't Petrie that little kid on crutches they've been carrying up for prayers the last couple of days? That impressed me. She could have gotten a medical excuse, but she's been up for services twice a day even with that cast on her foot. I'm with Liz. I think Petrie must have reformed."

"Well! We have a division. Henry and I think she's nice, and Rod thinks she's naughty. What about you, Maggie?"

"I really don't know much about her, Liz. I haven't worked with her since quarantine."

"Just go with your intuition, Maggie." Rivera was curious what the junior officer might have picked up. She seemed to have unusually sensitive antennae. "Meritocratic intuition is reliable, and that's what we're trying to tap."

"Then I'd have to say she's naughty. When I've been around sickbay recently, I've overheard some sailors call her 'Hellcat'. Those names they give each other usually mean something."

Costello looked at Steele, then at Rivera, and drummed her fingers on the table. "I'm changing my vote. No sailor with a nickname like Hellcat is up to any good." Costello took up her pen and crossed off the name. "I'm afraid you're right, Rod. If Petrie's set a course for hell on this ship, she'll get there with a noose around her neck."

Costello picked up the list. "Next is Alya Petrov. What about it, Rod? She's one of your mates. Any reason to scratch her?"

"This is the same thing that was brought up with some others." Rivera stretched out his legs and pushed back his cowlick. "I'm fairly certain that Petrov has been involved in vigilante activity. Still, there has never been a formal complaint, and she's never been caught doing anything punishable. We seem to go over this every year. If the sailors suspected that we know about their informal police system and tolerate it, it would undercut our own moral authority. But what's the alternative? We'd have to undertake a full-scale investigation, which is always hell on morale; and then, when we've identified the vigilantes, the charge is 'usurping meritocratic functions.' That's a capital offense. So the end result would be a mass execution, hanging the sailors with the most highly developed moral sense ever found among the lower orders. I want no part of anything like that; I'm sure none of us do. So unless one of you sees another way out of this bind, I think we have to go on as we have; mere suspicion of vigilante activity doesn't put chicken feathers in anyone's stocking."

"Any discussion?" Costello glanced around the table and then put a check by the name. "All right, Petrov stays on the list with the nice ones. How about Peter Petrucci?"

"I hope no one has anything bad to say about him," Steele said. "He's a real pet of Martha's, and he seems to me as nice as anyone who works in engineering."

And so it went, down to Bettina Zyvoloskovitch who, having overcome an early tendency to tardiness at musters, was added to Santa Claus's list.

* * *

Santa Claus and stockings were indulgences for the commoners. The meritocrats observed Christmas as a holy night and a time to honor traditional customs. One such custom for the officers of H.M.S. *Lafayette* was the captain's Christmas dinner, a full dress affair which Brook hosted on Christmas eve and which was, without doubt, the social highlight of the year for those on the top deck. Even the formal dinners that the captain gave for his officers after a victory in space were not so splendid. The Christmas dinner, after all, could be planned in advance while victory dinners must be arranged on the spur of the moment.

Steele had known for months that she could expect an invitation to dinner to be hand-carried to her quarters by a runner on the morning of the party. She was actually waiting for it when there was a knock at her door and the fresh-faced young Colonial knuckled her forehead and handed over a large stiff envelope. Inside was a hand-lettered card, prepared by the captain's yeoman using his finest calligraphy, by which the pleasure of her company was requested at dinner in the wardroom at 1900 hours.

The captain's request for one's company was an order. The RSVP lettered in the lower left hand corner of the card was a traditional formality. All of *Lafayette*'s officers accepted with pleasure, except Doctor Parker, who understood perfectly well that the rules were different for her, and declined with regret.

Parker, however, was determined that someone else would be absent from the captain's Christmas dinner. Doctor Gordon should be in bed. She told him so and argued with him. But her voice box was no match for Gordon's quick tongue; and, besides, he outranked her. So Parker took an extraordinary action. She hung her lab coat behind the door in the isolation bay, buttoned on her officer's dress tunic, and took the main ladder to the bridge. She would take her case to Captain Brook.

Steele was startled to see the Colonial on the top deck. Parker's serious expression made it plain she was there on business, and she struggled with the phrases required to request permission to speak to the captain.

"You'll have to explain your business to me first." Steele met the Colonial's formality with her own. "We don't usually interrupt Captain Brook during the forenoon watch."

"This be very important. Doctor Gordon very sick. Must go off duty. Must go right now. Very serious. Could die. He be stubborn. I say him 'Go to bed.' He say I not can order. He be right. Captain must order. Now. Not can wait."

"Can you tell me what you think is wrong with him? You're going outside your chain of command. It may be better if I speak to the captain for you."

"Yes. I thank you to do that. My voice not good. Captain not like hear."

Steele colored. She had avoided putting it so bluntly. Brook did find Parker's voice repellent and had said so more than once.

"You talk captain." Parker's face reflected her sense of urgency. "You say Doctor Gordon long time not good sleep. Three days not sleep any. Think he bad react to Plague serum. Not eat good. Think also fever. He not let me measure." She stopped, her face drawn with frustration.

"This not like always for him. More bad. Not can explain good. Too much medical. Even think-talk, you not understand. Doctor Gordon bad sick. You see him morning prayers. If be you look, you know. He very bad sick."

Gordon had seemed unlike his usual self at the morning muster, Steele recalled. Not that she'd minded, but he hadn't given her his usual close inspection as they lined up. He'd been quiet and subdued; and, come to think of it, he'd been breathing hard as if climbing up the gravity-free ladder from the lower deck had been an effort.

"Go quick. Tell captain. Say he just look Doctor Gordon, he see I be right. Must put doctor off duty. No wait."

Steele nodded and headed for the captain's quarters.

Brook was surprised by Steele's report as much because of the source she cited for her information as by the information itself. Brook was aware of the friendship between the junior lieutenant and the Colonial physician, but he couldn't say he understood it. Brook was a species bigot and freely acknowledged that fact. He couldn't imagine how Steele could bear to spend time in close contact with a Colonial. He knew that many human members of the crew didn't like to have Parker touch them. But they had no choice; they had to do as they were told.

Nevertheless, bigot though he was, Brook approved of the relationship Steele had with Parker. Meritocrats were so few and the need for officers with the fleet was so urgent, that even Colonial meritocrats might have to be put in the line if the war went on much longer. Brook hoped that he would not live to see it. But it was a promising trait in the young lieutenant that she could tolerate close contact with those repulsive mutes. She might find herself serving with one on the top deck some day.

According to Steele, the Colonial physician was at this moment standing on the bridge waiting for his decision on her petition. He wondered how it would feel to speak with her as Steele did without getting the creeps. He'd probably never know. Nevertheless, Doctor Parker was a meritocrat and by all accounts an excellent physician. If Doctor Gordon should go on the sick list she'd be the one to know. There was no help for it; he'd have to take her report. Brook sent a runner to fetch Doctor Gordon and told Steele to send both doctors to him when he arrived.

Gordon put on his dress tunic before reporting to the top deck. He lacked the energy even to curse at the buttons, which seemed unusually hard to fasten. Finally, he gave it up, left half of them undone, and doggedly mounted the main ladder.

His Colonial second reached out to steady him as he exited at the bridge and supported him as they walked together down the ramp to the captain's day cabin. Gordon made no effort to shake her off. When Brook got a look at him, he wondered how a man with a medical degree could be so insensitive to his own condition. It didn't take a physician to know the med/life director had reached his physical limits.

"Doctor Parker, please give me your professional opinion. How would you describe Doctor Gordon's condition and what treatment do you recommend?"

Parker decided to make it as painless for Brook as she could and answered briefly. "Exhaustion. Sleep."

"Do you have any argument with that diagnosis and prescription, Doctor Gordon?"

Gordon, who had found the climb from the third deck almost more than he could manage turned dull eyes on Parker and then answered the captain as briefly as she had.

"No, sir."

To Brook this lack of back talk from the med/life director was the most alarming symptom of all. Gordon was like a dragon whose fire had gone out.

"Very well. Doctor Parker, take Doctor Gordon to his quarters and give him whatever treatment you believe appropriate. You will command med/life until you certify him fit to return to duty."

"Captain," said Gordon in a strangely weak voice, "I don't think I've ever heard you give an order I've welcomed more."

"Merry Christmas, Doctor," Brook said soberly.

Parker made Gordon wait for a litter to carry him back down the main ladder; and once they reached his cabin in the sickbay complex, she undressed him and put him to bed as if he were a child. His spirits improved enough to let him snap at her.

"Parker, I'm only letting you get away with this because I' m too sick to fight you."

"That be point. You not be sick, you not be patient." She fluffed up a pillow behind his back so he could sit up and then went to stir a concoction she had brought into his cabin on a tray.

"Before you knock me out, Parker, I want you to listen to a few things. If I don't come out of this, remember that Brook has to donate a pint for the blood bank next week. Also, Hall's been looking run down. If he doesn't bring himself down here in the next day or two with some specific complaint, call him in and do a complete physical. Lamashtu's got to . . ."

"You say this many time. You write for me night orders. I keep. Have big pile. You not worry. If be you die, not need haunt ship. I do same you want. Keep healthy officers."

Gordon laughed. His Colonial colleague had a sense of humor. It always surprised him.

"You not die now. I give orders. You be okay. You sleep. Then wake up. Be like new. Holler at mates. Give officers hell. All signs be normal."

"Next you'll be telling me you'll also have my Pox scars cleared up and my head full of curly hair."

"Not promise you that. I not be Galen Ring doctor. You want hair, must do for self." She poured the foaming mixture into a mug and handed it to him. "I prescribe for help to sleep."

"What is it?" Gordon examined the contents of the mug suspiciously. It wasn't what he would have prescribed.

"Egg. Fresh cream I bring from Colony. Honey. Nutmeg. Good dose brandy."

"Eggnog? At this time of day? The sun's not over the yardarm yet, Parker."

"No difference to you." She switched off his porthole leaving only the red emergency light. "Not argue. Drink. Be medicine. Not need enjoy you not want."

Gordon took a sip and decided to enjoy it. Parker smiled at him approvingly; and Gordon had a fleeting memory of a time when, as a small boy, he'd been given hot milk at bedtime to help him sleep on Christmas Eve.

Parker took the empty mug, rearranged the pillows, and tucked him in under the blanket.

"Will you promise you'll wake me up if you hear reindeer on the gundeck?"

"Promise." Parker sat on the single chair in the cabin and watched Gordon until he fell asleep. He went out almost instantly. That was all she could do, she thought. His body would have to heal itself. But before she left, she telepathically recited the prayer for the sick. Gordon was unconscious; it would cause him no discomfort. And he needed the prayer. Parker had never seen him so ill.

* * *

Steele spent the afternoon with Lamashtu in engineering. Several work crews were out on the hull replacing damaged sail plates. Lamashtu had persuaded Brook to let the ship drift with the tides for another day before taking the ship into above-light acceleration toward a star for refueling. Damage done when *Lafayette* hurled through the Devil's Dustbin had to be repaired before the sails could absorb energy with full efficiency. There was no sense draining reserves further until the repair work was done. Besides, she said, it was Christmas Eve. She wanted to let her crew knock off early.

The final argument was the one that carried the most weight with the captain, who appreciated the importance of Christmas festivities in the usually monotonous life of the third deck. Steele was also a beneficiary of the shortened work day, since Lamashtu sent her off at the same time she released her sailors at the end of the afternoon watch.

Steele went directly to her cabin. It was much too early to dress for the captain's party, but she couldn't wait. This would be her first opportunity to wear her full dress uniform. Very few ceremonies requiring full dress were held on Earth these days. The Admiralty considered them unnecessary and wasteful in wartime. In space, they were permitted at the captain's discretion. Knowing, as everyone did, of Captain George Brook's devotion to tradition and ceremony, Steele knew she would have some use for the uniform when she made up her space bag.

The full dress uniform of the Royal Earth Navy was quite different from the service dress or work uniforms. The function of the former was to identify those entitled to exercise meritocratic authority. The design was appropriately simple and modest. Functionally, the full dress uniform more closely resembled the vestments of a priest. The few tailors on Earth who sewed them believed they had a power in themselves to protect and reenforce meritocratic virtue in the wearer. This might be mere lower orders superstition, Steele thought, but she knew the tailor who had made her uniform had called in a parish priest to bless it. Even if it couldn't be proved scientifically, she was sure the good thoughts made a difference.

She removed the white wool garments from the wardrobe and spread them on the bunk. The tailor had said white wool symbolized the sacrifice of the Lamb of God and the eighteen-carat gold trim on the sleeves and epaulets signified Divine immutability. As with all other officers' uniforms, two pins were worn on the collar: her personal commissioning number and the sextant denoting current assignment as *Lafayette* navigator.

Every detail of the full dress uniform was prescribed. Except for authorized decorations, nothing could be added except a chronograph, the Naval Academy class ring, and a wedding band. On *Lafayette* only two officers, Costello and Brook, wore wedding bands. Brook continued to wear his even though his wife had been killed early in the First Galaxy War.

Steele had no decorations and no wedding band; but as she examined the pieces of the uniform spread out on the bunk, she realized that there was one small area of free choice open to her when she dressed for dinner. What didn't show, didn't count. She could decide for herself about underwear. Ordinarily she wore the standard Navy issue; but there was another set tucked into the bottom of her wardrobe that she had brought into space to humor her mother.

Letitia Steele was one of those women who believed it important always to wear nice underwear in case one should unexpectedly find oneself taken to a hospital. She had a collection of nice things herself and had begun buying frilly undergarments for her daughter as soon as little Maggie was toilet trained.

When she was honest with herself, Steele had to admit that she loved the silly bits of satin and lace; although, if her mother had not been so serious in pressing on her this set of sky blue underwear as a parting gift, she would not have packed anything so frivolous in her duffel. In fact it made her smile to think of Doctor Gordon or one of his mates discovering that a line officer wore lacy underwear under her uniform.

She certainly was not dressing this evening with the idea of ending up in sickbay, but the blue satin lingerie seemed appropriate for the first time. The captain's dinner was a social event; and for Steele, parties and fancy underwear had always gone together. She took the set from the wardrobe and set the pieces out down next to the uniform.

There was one final item to examine — the ceremonial sword. Steele had been trained to fight with a sword and with other primitive weapons. One never knew, Annapolis instructors said, so it was best to be prepared. But the dress sword was not intended to be used in combat. Actually, there was nothing wrong with the basic design. It had a good heft and was made of high quality steel with a blood channel cut to the hilt. Nevertheless, the artisan who crafted it had obviously been more concerned with the fine detailing of the gold ornamentation on the hilt and the scrollwork on the blade than with finishing the edge.

Steel rubbed her finger down its length. The sword was as dull as a butter knife. Such reversed priorities were only to be expected from a civilian. The sword would never pass inspection. Not that anyone was likely to check, but a sword, after all, was a weapon and should be kept serviceable even if it never came out of the scabbard. She picked it up and took it down to engineering to see what Lamashtu had available in the way of sharpening stones. One didn't wear a sword with a dull edge to a formal event.

* * *

The wardroom was transformed for the captain's Christmas dinner. An embroidered linen tablecloth and napkins, antique porcelain plates, crystal goblets, and heavy sterling flatware replaced the trays, white pottery dinnerware and stainless steel utensils that were the Navy's standard issue. For formal dinners, the wardroom's treasures were brought out.

After extended consultation with a Colonial sailor who worked in the hothouse, the captain's steward selected an arrangement of red blossoms of salvia and bee balm for the large silver flower bowl. It was fortunate so many medicinal plants had aesthetic qualities as well.

Because place cards were traditional, McCarthy arranged for these to be made by the captain's yeoman, although traditional etiquette dictated the seating arrangements. The captain sat at the head of the table, his back toward the door. Costello, as the ranking woman, sat at its foot by the fireplace. Steele, as the lowest ranking woman, was to the captain's left; and Rivera, as the second ranked male, was to Costello's right. The result when this was sorted out was that Steele and Rivera sat side by side. Across from them, Martha Lamashtu sat alone on the captain's right.

A memo from sickbay in Doctor Parker's hand conveyed Doctor Gordon's regrets, and his place was empty. Henry Hall might have been seated there, but he was the unlucky officer assigned to stand watch this evening. Steele felt a bit sorry for him, but someone had to do it; and it did seem that Hall was overdue for an assignment to disagreeable duty. This watch would be an easy one. *Lafayette*, her engines disengaged, was drifting with the tides, setting her own course in response to the competing gravitational forces of distant celestial objects. Hall would not miss the whole party. It was Brook's practice to excuse himself when dessert was served and go to relieve the watch officer who would miss the ceremony at the start of the meal but could still enjoy the food.

Steele was surprised by Brook's choice for the blessing. His theme was death and he resurrected the memories of those members of the ship's company who had died since the previous Christmas. There were more than Steele had realized. The months prior to Steele's boarding had seen many losses, some in hostile action, and many more from accident and illness. Lieutenant Shankar's death was particularly remembered; the captain quoted Julius Caesar's saying that "a sudden death is best" and the blessing he requested was "that we may at all times be prepared for death, for ourselves and for those we love, for in life we are in death. Amen."

After this sober beginning, however, conversation took a predictable turn, as Lamashtu began to tell stories of Christmas in the Old Navy, the peacetime Navy before the First Galaxy War when Lamashtu was still in her teens.

"Now my first tour was on *Falcon*, you have to remember; and Captain Bakshi was — well, she wasn't the religious type. Christmas Eve was like crossing the line. The crew got to live it up. There was cheating on the grog ration that we thought she didn't know about, noise, dancing. It went on until all hours. The Marines played it cool so long as no one really got hurt. And, see, no one had told us new sailors about the Christmas bonus. The older folks were keeping it a secret, like. So round about midnight this real old sailor . . ." Lamashtu grinned at the memory. "Yeah, he was real old. He must have been over thirty. Anyway he comes over to where some of us young ones are skylarking and he says all serious, 'Children, it's getting on toward midnight. I'm going to hang up my stocking for Santa Claus now, and you better hang yours.

"So we all laugh like he's making some joke, but he's serious. And he calls some of his mates over and they all start clucking: 'These little kids say they don't believe in Santa! What's the younger generation coming to!' and all like that. Then they go get stockings from their space liners and hook them up outside their lockers. Well we young ones watch this, and then we think, why not? We'll go along with the gag. So we go get our stockings and hang them up too." Lamashtu took a deep swallow from her wine glass.

"Then the next morning when we go to get ready for muster, we see those space liner stockings full of coins and cookies. And that was no joke! No sailor had that kind of loot to give away, and no sailor who had it would give it away anyhow. So we were all wide-eyed true believers for a few hours until the older folks couldn't keep a straight face anymore and set us wise. It never entered our heads that the officers had filled the stockings."

"I don't believe you," Costello laughed. "You could never have been that gullible."

"Well, I was. And I bet that old trick would still work today if the sailors wanted to try it. Even before the wars, the first few months in space were pretty rough for new sailors. It seemed to us that all officers ever did was make you do things you didn't want to do."

"The stockings are just another way of getting the sailors to do what we want," Rivera said.

"I know that now. I didn't then. There's a whole lot about motivating sailors I never even suspected until after I was part of the wardroom."

"Christmas stockings are very useful, but they are no substitute for prize money, and there's been none of that distributed on this voyage." It was the captain's first contribution to the general conversation. "We do not always want to encourage sailors to be nice. There are times when we need the mindless aggressive instincts and blood lust that are so characteristic of the class of commoners the Admiralty sends us. Unfortunately, that also must be reenforced. When Christ's kingdom comes, war will cease. Until then, there is no substitute for regular distributions of prize money to keep up fighting spirit."

"It was bad luck at Mantu, sir. If we could have met those cruisers in open space . . ." The gunner also regretted the missed opportunity.

"Yes, yes, First. If. The fact remains that *Lafayette* has been in deep space for half a year, and we have nothing to show for it."

The captain was edgy this evening, Steele thought. Perhaps the strange sensation of the ship drifting disturbed him. She could sense the unfamiliar motion herself, though it was not spoiling her mood. But, of course, she did not carry the responsibility.

Brook seemingly read her thoughts. "Forgive me. A host should not dampen the spirits of his guests by introducing serious topics of conversation. I have fallen into an unfortunate habit of spending my dinner hour reviewing the cares of my command. Please forgive my lapse of manners." He turned to face Lamashtu, determined to make up for having marred the festive atmosphere by playing the role of gracious host.

"In particular, I have been neglecting you, dear lady, a grievous discourtesy since the gentleman who ought now to be seated to your right has not been able to give us the pleasure of his company and conversation on this occasion."

Lamashtu laughed. She had served under Captain Brook for almost two decades, most of that time as a common sailor. His courtly manner was something new for her. Certainly no one had ever referred to her as a lady before — that was what they called the women who dressed up in teeter-totter high heels and big billowy skirts in the historical romances she used to devour when she was a girl. There was also something terribly funny about his reference to the pleasure of Doctor Gordon's conversation. When Gordon came to the wardroom the other officers did their best to keep him quiet while they were eating. His contributions to the general table talk tended to drift predictably onto unappetizing subjects.

Lamashtu rose to the occasion, became courtly herself, and addressing the captain alternately as 'kind sir' and 'my lord,' she soon had the entire company drawn into the gently ribald teasing that was a staple of wardroom conversation.

The joke revolved around who was and who was not bound by the meritocratic oath of chastity. Steele was too young to take it, so she was fair game. Costello was bound by a marriage vow, so although she had not taken the oath, she was off limits. Hall, having observed Costello suffering from the separation from her husband and children, had sworn the oath before Captain Brook on his twenty-first birthday, as soon as he was eligible. Rivera practiced chastity, but because his mother was so opposed to his refusing her even the hope of grandchildren, he had promised her he would not take the vow. Captain Brook was faithful to the memory of his deceased wife and believed that taking an oath of chastity after her death would dishonor his marriage vows.

Among the med/life officers, Gordon was sworn to chastity; even if he were able, he would not risk even the smallest chance of fathering a child with the genetic defects that gripped his body. Parker, like Rivera, had refused the oath because of her mother's opposition. But since she as well as her mother disapproved of interspecies intercourse and there were virtually no possibilities of her finding a Colonial lover in the Navy, it came to the same thing. Furthermore, no one in the wardroom would think of mentioning her name in the game; that would be an obscenity.

When the wardroom got into teasing about chastity, only Gordon, Costello and Hall were absolutely excluded. Lamashtu, who became a meritocrat after she was old enough to be a grandmother, declined to take the oath, saying she'd spent too many years having a new boy in every port to want to give up that freedom. As a meritocrat, her choice of lovers was now restricted by her rank as well as by her age. The 'boys' she met in port these days were usually old shipmates confined to nursing homes. Still, Lamashtu insisted that knowing she had the right "to mess around" if she chose made an old girl feel young. Before Steele came aboard to add a titillating complexity to wardroom teasing, the usual joke was to match Lamashtu and the captain, with the occasional variation of matching the captain and Rivera.

"Prithee tell me, kind sir," Lamashtu said to Brook, leaning her chin on her hand and batting her eyelashes. "Hast thou taken thy ration of mudd this day or might I yet hope to conceive a sweet babe this holy night?"

The remark bordered on sacrilege, but Captain Brook, in the spirit of the occasion, emptied his wine glass, brushed his moustache and politely leered at the engineer. After a few more exchanges, both Brook and Lamashtu wearied of the game and began to talk about the captain's grandchildren and the engineer's flock of young relatives back on Earth, a conversation into which Costello entered with enthusiasm.

Steele and Rivera, who had no special interest in babies, were thus left to entertain each other, which turned out to be no trouble at all. They had a surprisingly large number of things in common. Both agreed that the greatest hardship of service in space was the absence of chocolate ice cream; that if one had a choice of vacation spots on Earth the ocean had it all over the mountains — except in the winter, and the absence of snow for skiing was the second greatest hardship of service in space. They discovered that as children both had sung soprano in a church choir (Steele was now an alto and Rivera a bass); and that both of their mothers believed in astrology (Steele was a Virgo and Rivera a Leo but neither could remember whether that was good or not). When they had gotten this far, they also found that dinner was over, dessert was on the table, and the captain was about to leave. He had been trying for some moments to get their attention and finally resorted to tapping his fork against his glass.

"Before I go, permit me to offer a final toast, although I am sure our good Doctor Gordon would say all of us have had far too much to drink already." He raised his glass. "To Margaret and Roderigo and the first green shoots of young love. It's been a long time since I've read the marriage service on this ship," he added as he set down his glass. "Perhaps at Easter."

Steele felt herself blush crimson. She and Rivera had certainly set themselves up for this one! Costello and Lamashtu were grinning, but she didn't dare look to see what the expression on Rivera's face might be. The first officer was twice her age; surely he would be laughing at the joke. Feeling very awkward and very naive, Steele rose from the table as soon as the captain was gone.

"If you'll excuse me," she said in a voice she hoped sounded casual, "I think I'll take some of this cake down to sickbay for Doctor Parker."

"Maggie." Steele turned toward Rivera. His face was as red as she was sure hers must be. "Maggie." He too seemed to have some difficulty speaking. "That's really very kind of you. Very kind to think of the Colonial. Tell her . . . tell her 'Merry Christmas' from me."

"That's very kind of you, Rod. I'll do that."

* * *

As Brook went onto the bridge, he automatically glanced first at the observation dome. The stars appeared to move in a slow steady path across the window. Brook watched thoughtfully, then sucked his breath in sharply. Their position was not shifting at ten second intervals. *Lafayette* was not rotating in the random pattern required by his standing orders as well as by *Naval Regulations* when a vessel drifted with the tides. That was why he had had the gnawing sense all evening that something was wrong with the ship's movements.

He swept his eyes around the circle of observation ports. No sailors sat at the stations. The watch observations were on automatic, an outrageous waste of energy while the ship was tapping its reserves. Allowing the bridgehands to go below early on Christmas Eve was a usual practice, but not under these circumstances. Hall should have known better.

There was something very wrong about an officer who could not even stand a watch on a drifting ship without making serious mistakes. There was something very wrong with Henry Hall. Brook abruptly realized with a surge of remorse that he had neglected his clear duty, violated his own meritocratic oath. He should have challenged Hall's fitness and relieved him of meritocratic responsibilities months ago.

He strode across the bridge. Unless Henry Hall was dead, there was no acceptable excuse for an officer neglecting random rotation or squandering energy on automated observation.

Hall was not dead. He was stretched out in the helm chair sleeping peacefully in the glow of the red emergency lights. Brook picked up the bridge log that lay at his side. The last entry was initialed by Lamashtu and was almost two hours old.

Brook swiftly made the rounds of the bridge. The screens displayed current data. He slapped open a control panel. The energy-sparing default settings were in place — the automatic save was offline. The station records wiped clean every quarter hour. Current sightings were useless now, totally useless. Even at sub-light drift, the observations were meaningless out of context. Brook coldly calculated the consequences.

First, they were lost. It might take days to fix the position of a ship allowed to drift for even half an hour with no record of its movement. Second, they were blind. The long range observation instruments were valueless at sublight speed unless they were set to scan at a rate and in a direction that would compensate for the differential between the ship and its potential objects of observation — craft traveling faster than light. Third, *Lafayette* was as conspicuous as a floating lighthouse beacon, her mass and trace energy emissions fully exposed.

Since the engines were deprived of power, *Lafayette* could not run from an enemy. Since she was blind, she could not fire her weapons at one. Brook felt a rage rising in him that he knew he would be unable to control. Choking down his fury, he ordered the sentry at the hatchway to go below. When the bridge was clear, he paused only long enough to slap off the now useless automated observation devices and did his duty as a meritocrat. Henry Hall was awakened by the voice of the Thunderer — uncontrolled, ear-splitting, and blasphemous.

CHAPTER THIRTEEN

There was only one way to get to sickbay from the wardroom, and that was to go up two levels to the bridge and then down the main ladder. Steele, feeling unaccountably lighthearted and energetic, swung herself onto the closest auxiliary ladder and climbed straight up, while the captain, as befitted his dignity, was making more leisurely progress up the connecting ramps. Steele reached the bridge, gave the Marine a bright smile as she acknowledged his salute, and dropped into the main ladder before Brook arrived on the scene.

Within the weightlessness of the wide cylinder, Steele slowed her progress. Flipping automatically so that her "descent" to the lower deck became a climb instead, she pulled herself hand over hand toward her destination but then reconsidered. She really was in no hurry to reach sickbay. What she really wanted was a little time to herself, to savor her good feelings and to think about some personal matters she usually had no time to ponder.

She let her body drift to the inner wall of the mast at the point where the damage-control seal that closed off the top deck from the gundeck folded into the side of the cylinder. She hovered there in weightlessness, conscious of being in a symbolically significant part of the ship. There were two other damage-control shields in the main mast: one above and one below the 'tween decks. These protected personnel from potential accidents involving stored munitions or the engines and from radiation and toxic wastes associated with the use of emergency power sources.

The top deck shield, where Steele now rested, had a more somber function: it protected the officers from the crew. From above the bridge shield, meritocrats in a last extremity would take their stand against mutiny. Within the mast, located just above the shield, were devices that could cut off, generally or selectively, all life support functions in the areas below — just another way in which the ship's captain might exercise the power of life and death. There were times when it had to be done.

It was a fitting spot to think about the responsibility of command in space — and about love. Meritocrats could not be corrupted by power. That had been proven repeatedly in Earth's recent history under the most extreme circumstances, and Steele was quite certain about that. What worried her was the possibility of corruption by love.

The Navy had a lot riding on the bonding between officers and crew; through it, eight meritocrats énforced obedience on thousands of commoners in situations in which they might require them to give their lives. If an officer had a relationship, especially a vowed relationship, with another individual, could the primary loyalty to the people you commanded hold up? It wouldn't matter so much for junior officers, but no one stayed junior forever. Either you died, or you moved into more responsibility. Command in space was a job that demanded a full measure of devotion. It demanded sacrifice.

The Church said the vow of chastity was voluntary for meritocrats. Steele had come to believe that for meritocrats who served in space, in wartime, at any rate, it was a moral imperative. She did not know what it might be like in peacetime; both Brook and Costello had married in times of peace. But Earth had been at war as long as she could remember and no one could see any end to it.

When Steele and her classmates talked about the oath of chastity at Annapolis most had agreed that simply facing up to realities and making a clean decision before you met someone special and got emotionally involved was the easiest way. Brook's remark about marriage, even if he hadn't meant it seriously, had opened up an issue she thought she had already settled. It wasn't such an easy subject to set aside, especially for teenagers — that was why they wouldn't let you take the oath until you had a few years to let your hormones settle and to think through all the implications.

So much for that. She had three more years to "mess around," as Lamashtu put it, if that was what she decided she wanted to do. And chastity didn't mean you couldn't have friends. Steele grinned as she pushed herself back to the ropes and continued her progress toward the third deck.

Steele decided not to take the main ladder all the way to the lowest level of the ship as she usually did. Instead she exited at the top level of the third deck, which was home for the crew. She'd been intrigued by Lamashtu's story about Christmas Eve partying among the sailors and wanted to see how much of that still went on.

On all levels of all decks, ship designers worked with a series of concentric circles beginning at the main mast, with the diameters within the bell-shaped vessel increasing as one descended. There was a lot more room in the crew's living area than there was on the gundeck. The main hatch opened directly into the mess hall, gaudily decorated for the holiday dinner. Sailors and Marines were still congregated at the tables, where McDougall's crew had served up a meal to remember.

Steele walked through the mess hall on her way to the ramp to the second level, and the diners pretended not to notice her although she was well aware of being watched.

The ramp was located in the second ring, which housed the crew's recreation area. There, in spaces liberally provided with holographic windows, the crew had access to as much entertainment and opportunity for innocent fun as the ingenuity of the ship's designers and the limitations of space travel permitted. There was a swimming pool iced over for skating during the winter months, squash courts, and a variety of conversation areas, all far more spacious than the officers's wardroom although very crowded since they served so many people. Here, too, was the ship's store, doing a brisk business this holiday night as sailors bought gifts for friends and took advantage of their supplemental grog rations to hold private parties. Like the mess hall, the recreation area was loaded with garish decorations.

She spotted the Colonial coven hovering over a thick red candle circled with mistletoe. For some reason they were very keen on candles though before they could light one they had to pay for the oxygen it consumed. The gunner's mates were playing their usual game of poker, but had dressed up — or, in one case, undressed — for the occasion. Tattoo's tattoos were her party outfit; it saved expense on upkeep and left her space in her duffel for other things when she went on liberty.

The crew's berthing area was located in the outermost ring. Here, outside the lockers, sailors and Marines would hang the stockings of their space liners before lights out. Steele glanced in that direction before taking the ramp to the second level.

Here the barnyard occupied the entire outer ring except for the docking areas. Bays for the ship's launches were built into the hull at intervals on every level of the ship except the bridge. The barnyard's occupants, appropriately enough, were having a silent night, their deckhead bright with stars and a waning moon, with only a few Colonial swineherd apprentices keeping watch. Whatever they were doing to entertain themselves wasn't making any noise.

Heading back toward the center of the ship and the next ramp, Steele passed through the circle housing the hydroponic bay, which everyone called the farm. Only one sailor was on watch here: Lillian Shaper, the Colonial everyone called Hothouse because she so loved the hot steamy climate of her work station. Shaper considered spending Christmas Eve surrounded by her flowers a great treat, and everyone else working in the farm was glad to have her volunteer to take the watch so they could join in the carousing in the recreation area. Shaper knuckled her forehead when she saw Steele, and then flashed her fingers in a "Merry Christmas" greeting and signaled her to wait. Disappearing into her jungle of plants, she came out with a sprig of mistletoe attached to a hand-painted Christmas card. Steele accepted the gift with a smile.

Before continuing her trek downward, she paused for a moment to watch the huge perpetually-moving waterfall behind a transparent seal, that surrounded the main mast on this level. Sailors assigned to this station were responsible for purifying and reconstituting the water supply on which the entire ship relied.

Steele didn't linger in the third level. Here, the laundry and clothing production and maintenance units clustered around the main mast next to inorganic waste reprocessing and general manufacturing. On the outermost ring, beneath the barnyard, the slaughterhouse and food storage bays filled the space.

Marines patrolled all parts of the ship on a regular schedule, but Steele encountered none of them. She continued down to the fourth and lowest level, the bilges, where the ring below the slaughterhouse processed organic waste. The center ring contained the mortuary, sickbay laundry, and storage for controlled substances. By the main mast, the sickbay galley, isolation ward, and offices and cabins for the two medical/life support officers filled the space not occupied by patient beds. Here, as usual, Anne Parker was alone in the isolation ward.

The Colonial did not have the Admiralty charts spread out tonight; she had a rosary in her lap and was praying. When she saw Steele, she slipped the beads into the pocket of her lab coat and held out her arms to greet her friend with a hug. The young lieutenant in her white uniform, smiling radiantly and carrying a sprig of mistletoe, looked like a Christmas fairy. When she untied a napkin and held out a plate of elaborately frosted cake, the illusion was complete.

"So glad you come. Hope you would. You sit. I have here much special." Parker unlocked a cabinet a brought out a round tin box. "Here something you not have long time. Be good with Christmas cake. Smell."

Steele sniffed at the contents. "Coffee! Is that allowed?"

"I head doctor tonight. I prescribe. Roast fresh. For me too. No worse drink brandy."

There had been a lot of wine served in the wardroom, well over the limit for a daily ration. But toasting in wine at formal dinners was a Navy tradition. So was serving brandy after dessert. Brook had used his authority to waive med/life's standing rules, noting Parker's routine objection in the log.

Parker spilled the beans into a ceramic bowl and began to crush them with a pestle.

"How is Dr. Gordon?"

"Not know yet. He still sleep. I pray for him." Parker reached into her pocket and lifted out the beads. "Rosary of Our Lady."

"I didn't realize you were Catholic, Anne."

"Not Catholic. This be prayer of Colonial peoples. Very old. From before come to Colony. From . . ." she groped for the word, "from Home." Hesitating just an instant, Anne lifted the beads in two hands and held them out to Maggie. "You can hold," she said.

Steele accepted the beads respectfully, knowing that to Anne this was a holy object. The rosary was made of crystal beads. Some of them appeared to be gems from Earth — clear and rose quartz, amethyst, and deep red garnet. The rosary beads were identical in size except for one larger sphere of cloudy black obsidian. Other beads Steele could not identify.

"Here how we say," Parker said pointing at the black ball. "Start here. Prayer of begin and end. Then here, each bead be name for Holy Mother. Then pink bead. Prayer say you love her. Tell your prayer. Then red bead. Listen for answer and thank. Then all repeat. Come back to begin and end."

Steele gently fingered the beads. Maybe there was a power in them even if it was only the power projected into them by Parker's faith. She smiled as she returned them to the physician. Parker kissed them, slipped them into her pocket and picked up the bowl of coffee beans again.

Steele watched her. Parker had tears in her eyes.

"You think a lot of your boss, don't you?"

Parker nodded, wiped her eyes, and returned to her grinding.

"He can't be the easiest person in the world to work for. I know I've never heard you say a word against him, but I assumed that was just loyalty to your superior. It's a lot more than that, isn't it?"

Parker put down the bowl. "Doctor Gordon very great man. You not can know. Not just great doctor. More." Parker held out her hands in her effort to make herself understood, and then folded them in her lap. She had a voice box; she would not gesticulate like a Colonial commoner.

"Chief doctor say who come to ship. I join Navy, not sure anyone want. Think I work hospital ship. Maybe prison ship, maybe Marine embarkation station. Not think get near space command. Then Galen Ring doctor pick. Not think great doctor take Colonial. He not care I not Earthborn. He all time hurt, so maybe he not notice. Think it little detail. He say Anne Parker be good doctor. Do his way. That all he care. This be third tour I be with him. Be he die, be my command. But he be for me like father. Like Captain Brook be for you. If be this great man die, I mourn like daughter. Be then orphan alone."

Steele put an arm around her friend's shoulder. "He won't die, Anne. Not tonight. God won't send death on Christmas."

It was a kindly-meant thought but naive. Parker smiled and patted Steele's hand. The physician had been practicing medicine in space long enough to know that those forces in the universe that ruled death had a special fondness for night hours and no particular regard for Christmas.

"That be my prayer. He live be my Christmas gift. Now here be yours by me." Parker wiped her eyes again and put on a resolutely cheerful face. Mourning Doctor Gordon in advance would not do him any good. And, after all, this was Christmas Eve and the closest thing to a Christmas party she'd had since joining the Navy.

Steele fetched plates and forks from the sickbay galley as Parker carried the crushed beans to the lab bench. The rich odor of perking coffee soon filled the air. The two women fussed over the doctor's desk, setting the mistletoe in a test tube as a centerpiece, dividing the cake, and setting out mugs to receive the usually forbidden treat. Parker brought the retort to the table and began to pour.

Abruptly her body went rigid. The glass retort crashed to the deck, and as Steele watched with alarm, an expression of horror spread over the physician's face. Tears spilled from huge hazel eyes as her mouth opened wide. Parker didn't make a sound, but Steele felt a freezing chill race up her spine. Then, inside her head, she heard for the first time the indescribable sensation of a Colonial screaming.

"Anne! Anne! What is it?" Steele sprang to her feet and threw her arms around her friend. "What's wrong with you?"

Parker stared at Steele, horror darkening her staring eyes, opening and closing her mouth but unable to make her artificial larynx function.

"Just think-talk me, Anne, if you can't speak. It's all right! Just tell me what's wrong."

Parker made a visible effort to control herself, horrified that she'd let Steele hear her scream. She knew what was decent. She knew what was proper professionally. She forced herself to use the voice box. "They're dead. All officer on top deck dead. Only one *Lafayette* person alive there. He be Colonial. Be captain's steward, Mickey McCarthy."

Parker picked up the piercing immediacy of McCarthy's telepathic communication, his wail of lamentation and instantaneous transmission of his perspective on an ultimate horror. In his natural voice, it all came at once.

The steward remembered weeks of planning and careful preparation designed to create an event to please and relax the officers — especially his captain, whose care was his special responsibility. He remembered selecting the china and the wine glasses, choosing the wine, and hovering over McDougall as she prepared the oyster appetiser until she chased him from the galley playfully threatening him with her sauce spoon. He remembered helping the captain dress, trimming his beard, sharpening his sword, polishing his boots; and he remembered how the sight of the officers gathered in the wardroom, resplendent in their dress uniforms, made his heart swell with pride in the leaders he served.

He remembered the details of his unobtrusive service at the table, the perfection of each dish, the officers' palpable enjoyment of their food and of each other's company. He recalled watching the lines of care soften even in his captain's face, as he relaxed with the others just as McCarthy planned they should. They looked younger, happy, at peace, the way these good people deserved to on Christmas night.

Then the captain left, and Lieutenant Steele left, and they were expecting Lieutenant Hall to join them. McCarthy had a plate in a slow oven with slices of the rarest cut of roast beef, which he knew Hall preferred, and a double portion of Yorkshire pudding. While they waited, Lieutenant Costello pulled out a deck of trick cards and with much laughing, she rehearsed with Rivera and Lamashtu a joke she planned to play on Hall after dinner.

Then the door had opened, but it was not Lieutenant Hall who entered. Death came in. With the speed only a heat pistol could deliver, three meritocrats died before McCarthy's eyes.

Parker kept control of her larynx, but tears rolled down her face as the mechanical phrases came from her lips. "Mickey McCarthy be in wardroom. The killers not care he live. They kill Costello, Lamashtu, Rivera. He right there. He see all die. He not see Lieutenant Hall, not see captain. He hear killers talk. They say they kill two officer on bridge. Two now wear officer tunics."

Intellectualize and depersonalize. Steele swallowed hard and took a deep breath. She was glad this news came to her filtered through Parker. She would not let herself visualize what Parker described. She'd keep it abstract. She'd stay distanced. When she spoke her voice was steady. After six months in space, Steele knew the conventional parts of her Annapolis training would hold. Someday SOCRATES might surface; but she was no longer counting on it. Here and now, before she ever expected it, she had the responsibility to take command.

"Mickey told you this from the wardroom? Can you people think-talk each other from that distance?" Parker stiffened. She didn't like the phrase "you people," and she was self-conscious about telepathy anyway. As a Navy officer she obeyed the rules against using it aboard ship. But this was no time for species sensitivity. Steele clearly had a need to know, and Parker knew the young officer well enough by now to understand that when she made insensitive comments she did so out of ignorance. Someday Parker might try to explain — but not now. She nodded in response to the question.

"Then we have a line of communication to the top deck." There were details about that communication system Steele wished she understood better. Could Parker be sure about who was speaking to her? And was what she heard the truth? She knew the captain's steward as well as she knew any Colonial except Parker. He was constantly on the top deck and had been in and out of the officer's galley and wardroom throughout this evening's dinner. He certainly didn't seem the type to play a vicious practical joke on the ship's physician.

"Doctor Parker, I know you're upset, but you have to work with me now." Their little Christmas party was over; Steele was now the ranking line officer and Parker the only other functioning meritocrat on the ship. Intellectualize and depersonalize. "There must be something you med/life officers learn that works the way our combat desensitization training does. I've been down here enough to know your work can get plenty grim and gory. I have to question Mickey, and I have to do it through you. I didn't hear him describe what happened the way you did, but if the steward just watched three people die, he'll have to have his backbone stiffened if he is to be of any use to us. Can you steady yourself? Can you steady him? Tell Mickey you've got his report and passed it on to me and that everything is under control."

Parker nodded. Whether everything actually was under control was not the issue. This was the message the commoner needed. "Give me minute." She turned away from Steele and went to the lab bench where she moistened a cloth and wiped her face. When she turned again, her eyes were cold. Intellectualize and depersonalize. That's how she'd gotten through the last hours with Toyo Yokomoto.

"I talk Chief McCarthy now."

Steele realized she'd fallen into the wardroom's habit of referring to the captain's steward by his first name though he wore yellow stripes and ranked among the senior enlisted personnel on the ship.

"He say glad you be by me. He hope that. Afraid think-talk you direct. Afraid talk me too. Know it against rule. Say he need tell someone. He not tell friends in crew. Think they be no help. Only be panic they know."

"Very good. Can you get him to give you an orderly account of what happened? Can he name the people who did this?"

Parker listened and then frowned. "This be very strange. Chief McCarthy say killers not be Lafayettes. He very sure that. Not wear clothes like normal. Some have tattoo on faces; not could be Navy, not Marines. He say they come from other ship. Say they be pirates."

Parker continued to listen as Steele wondered how in the universe pirates could have gotten onto the bridge of the Navy's largest warship. Mickey — that is, Chief McCarthy — actually had a good deal of information. He said that the pirates, had taken over the wardroom and piled the corpses of their victims at one end. They'd ordered the steward to bring them food and liquor, speaking quite openly in front of him, as humans were in the habit of doing with Colonials.

The pirates arrived on a launch belonging to a vessel they called the *Pagan Queen*, commanded by a personage they called 'Granny.' This ship, from what McCarthy said, was run in the slipshod manner characteristic of pirates. Pirates typically operated close to a planetary base and were known for slack shipboard discipline and disregard of rules of hygiene and economy that were traditional aboard Navy ships. If pirates ran short of food or fuel, they counted on stealing what they needed. If their ship fell apart, they'd steal a replacement.

Pirates all knew that once they took up the life they had a price on their heads. They didn't expect to live long; and in their crude way, they lived to enjoy what life they had. They'd been enjoying Christmas eve with a shipwide binge that had gone on for several days because their clocks and calendars tended to operate only approximately. The upshot was they were thoroughly lost and until Granny, who was the only one among them who could navigate in deep space, sobered up, they were likely to stay lost.

Pagan Queen kept regular watches, such as they were, and during what they called their morning watch, sometime late in the afternoon, someone had spotted *Lafayette*. The captain sent all hands to battle stations and did her best to move her ship as far away as possible as fast as she could. Then she thought it over, and turned *Pagan Queen* back toward the dreadnought. If her drunken watch officer had seen the Navy ship, then, surely, the Navy ship had spotted hers. So how come they weren't being chased? After a few experimental peek-a-boo passes, Granny concluded that *Lafayette* must be a dead ship.

The huge vessel was drifting and making no sail adjustments to rotate course. That convinced the pirate captain that they had run across a hulk ripe for salvage. Everyone aboard must have died of disease or life-support failure. If it was the former, the members of her prize crew might all die too unless the epidemic was one of those they'd already experienced. It didn't matter to her; she wasn't planning to board. And there were ways to sell infected meat. If it was ground and frozen, no one would know where she'd found it.

So Granny poured some strong coffee down the throats of the most sober members of her crew, and set them out in a launch to board the pride of Earth's Navy and claim her as salvage. The pirate's boarding craft docked at the airlock reserved for the captain's gig. The sail plates in that area were dammaged during the escape from Mantu. Work crews had stripped the hull to replace them, but had not completed the work. The pirates did not even have to pick open the airlock; they just walked in.

As they climbed the ramp to the bridge, they were startled to hear voices — shouting, McCarthy reported, although he couldn't imagine anyone shouting on the bridge of *Lafayette*. The pirates laughed that someone had been cussing up a storm so that their whole party made it to the bridge without being noticed. They found two officers there, McCarthy reported, and killed them on the spot. One of them was the captain.

Parker tried to soothe McCarthy as she conveyed this information to Steele. It was hard to do both at once, but she warned the steward that he must be careful not to draw attention to himself. He could do his grieving later.

"Pirates kill Brook, kill Hall. Then think. If be two officers alive, may be more. Go look. Hear voices in wardroom. Have heat pistols ready. Come fast. Officers not expect. All die."

"What's the size of the invading force? Does McCarthy have any idea?"

"Twelve."

"That's not possible! Is McCarthy sure they don't have at least a couple of hundred people spread out across the bridge and on the gundeck?"

"McCarthy very sure. All be in wardroom. Talk prize shares. Need give half their captain. Split rest twelve ways. Think much live meat here. They not expect. Make them happy."

Steele digested this information. If it was true that twelve pirates had seized the ship, the boarding of *Lafayette* would go down in history as the greatest humiliation ever suffered by the Royal Navy. Still, Steele hoped it might be true; it would make it that much easier to retake the ship. Steele still had many questions, but she couldn't expect the steward to have the answers. If she just had a better sense of what was going on, where the enemy was and what they were doing, she could make plans. The other questions could wait.

Parker spoke again. The pirates were making plans too. "McCarthy say pirates now talk what they do. Say someone need watch main hatch. Think maybe they not kill all officers. That be big worry. See there be six chairs at table. See six glasses for brandy. Know they kill two officers on bridge. Kill three in wardroom. Argue where sixth officer be. Argue who go stand watch. While argue, drink brandy."

"Tell McCarthy to be generous with it."

"They check uniforms. Say captain on bridge. Helm officer on bridge. See no med/life officer. Say all Navy ship have doctor. All say 'Look for med/life officer.' Draw lots see who go look, who stand watch." Parker paused. Both she and Steele knew what would happen now. The pirates would look for a medical/life support officer in sickbay.

"Then this is where we start. How much help can you give me, Parker. Can you defend yourself?"

"Can, but won't."

"I don't understand."

"'First do no harm.'"

Steele understood. Parker had learned to defend herself as all Colonial children growing up on Earth had to do. But when she became a physician she took an oath that, being a meritocrat, she would never violate. Meritocratic physicians, even those serving on warships, were strict pacifists. Parker would allow herself to be killed before she would deliberately injure anyone.

"Have you any objection to deceiving a murderer so that someone else can do harm?"

Parker hesitated.

"If you're not sure, then you're going to do it," Steele said flatly. Of all the people she could have had at her side when she first went into combat, it was her luck to be standing beside a conscientious objector. "When the pirates send someone down, you're going to help set the trap. I'm sure Doctor Hippocrates won't be upset by a few minutes of play acting in a good cause."

Steele had spent enough time in sickbay to know where she wanted to make her stand. The pirate would come straight down the main ladder; there would be no reason to take the scenic route. Steele wanted to be as close to the hatch as possible so that the pirate would have no need to do any exploring, possibly finding Doctor Gordon asleep in his cabin.

Gordon's office and surgery opened directly opposite the main hatch. That would be the stage. Now for the costumes. "You have the easy role, Parker. Just play yourself. Get into your tunic so that our friend will have no trouble identifying you as an officer. I'm going to be a blue striper, an orderly or something. Meet me in Gordon's treatment room."

As Parker hung up her lab coat and went after her uniform jacket, Steele ran to the sickbay laundry and looked among the stacks of freshly pressed uniforms for something that might fit. They all looked too large, but she grabbed the smallest she could find and crossed over to Gordon's office where Parker was buttoning up her tunic.

"They pick man name Bad Air. He come now. Have heat pistol. Say he kill doctor. Then all meritocrat be dead. Pirates be safe."

Steele nodded and stripped to her underwear. Parker's eyebrows flickered when she saw the unexpected layer of blue lace and satin, but she handed over the pieces of the sailor's uniform without comment. The cuffs of the white pants were far too long. Steele rolled them up. The shirt was a better fit.

"Where can I hide my stuff?"

Parker picked up the ceremonial uniform and the dress sword and dumped them into a laundry bin.

"Where's the sentry? Why don't we have a Marine posted by the hatch?"

"Not think we need tonight. Not think anyone use main ladder. Give Marine time off. Always do for Christmas. Some sailor eat too much can come down ramp for medicine."

"Bad luck for us. What about the patrol?"

Parker checked her chronograph. "Now be by farm. Then do barnyard. Pass by here, twenty minutes."

"All right. You and I have to do this alone then as a sister act. Curtain going up. Make some noise, Parker. Chew me out about something. We don't want our friend Bad Air to lose his way."

Steele pushed the door to Gordon's office and to the treatment room wide open, pulled the linen from the table and began to make it up again. Parker watched the short figure in the baggy pants and criticized the fit of her uniform. Presently, they heard the sound of booted feet and had their first sight of the enemy.

Bad Air presented a bizarre appearance. Deserters from Earth's warships who turned to piracy dressed deliberately to defy the hated Navy's regulations. Bad Air wore his hair in a long braid that looked none too clean and had a full bristling beard and moustache. A tattoo that realistically portrayed a third eye glared malevolently from the middle of his forehead and seemed to wink when he raised his eyebrows.

He wore massive amounts of clothing and jewelry, piled together with no reason or order, a mixture of styles that looked as if they had been collected at random from whatever was currently selling as high fashion on the most decadent planets in the galaxy. The top layer was a new acquisition — a white Navy officer's full dress tunic, worn unbuttoned over a fur undershirt. The stylized battery that adorned the collar identified it as that which had belonged to Lieutenant Martha Lamashtu.

"Well, well, what have we here? That's one thing you can say for Her Majesty's Navy; it's always predictable. Any ship in the fleet, any hour of the day or night, there'll always be an officer ragging a sailor — though I never heard one with a voice this ugly when I did my time."

Parker turned to confront the intruder and heard Steele giggle behind her as some silly ward attendant might. She was inspired to some dramatic flights of her own. She ran her eye over the intruder sternly.

"Give name, sailor. This area off limits without pass. Also you be out of uniform. Seem be drunk too. You have much trouble."

"You want my name, ma'am?" The pirate put sarcastic emphasis on the last word. "Well, I don't have a name anymore. I just forgot whatever it is people like you used to call me, forgot it the same time I burned the Navy serial number off my back. My friends, now, well they call me Fart. But I'm not in any trouble at all; you're the one in trouble."

"You be on report to first officer. Drunk, disorderly, insolent. Much violations."

"Sorry to disappoint you, ma'am, but the first officer's not taking any reports. Neither is the captain. They're dead, you see.

So are all this ship's officers. Except you, and I'm here to take care of that."

Parker had no difficulty producing the reaction of shock and horror that the pirate expected.

He smiled and turned to Steele. "That news doesn't bother you, does it kid? You a grommet? You look to be about the right age. Maybe you'd like a berth on another ship. This one's about to close down."

"Gee, ya mean it? Does everybody on your ship get to dress like you? You sure look sharp!"

Bad Air — or, rather, Fart as the name translated out of the telepathic mode — brushed his moustache and preened himself.

"We all dress any way we want to. Some of us have better taste than others." He put his arm around Steele and pulled her behind him out of his line of fire. "Just let me take care of a little business here, and you and I will go upstairs and meet your new shipmates. We're having a party. You like parties, don't you kid?"

"Yeah! Sure! This mean doctor wouldn't let me go to a party tonight. She made me work extra duty."

"Well, you won't have to worry about her any more."

As Fart pulled the heat pistol from his belt, Steele struck her first blow — to the back of his knees. Her second blow brought his head to the deck, and the third knocked him unconscious. She'd never used the third blow on a live target before; it was always pulled in practice.

The heat pistol dropped from Fart's hand. As it fell, its control was knocked to high and it skittered beneath a cabinet. Steele flattened on the deck, stretching her arm to reach it as she watched the penetrating rays burn into the bulkhead. At the maximum setting the charge wouldn't last long. Steele dashed to Gordon's desk, grabbed a pencil, and sprawled on the deck again. Before she could recover the weapon, it had melted a hole through the panel. She tested it. It fizzled and went dead.

"Damn!" Steele examined the pistol. Unlike the personal weapons issued to officers, this one had no fingerprint safety mechanism. Anyone could use it. If it was charged. But Fart was not wearing a recharger belt, and the Navy did not leave rechargers lying about. The only ones on the ship were either in the 'tween decks or in officers's quarters. She threw the weapon back under the cabinet. "Double damn!"

Parker was on her knees by the pirate feeling the pulse in his neck. "Man wake soon. What you want do?"

"We've got to keep him quiet and out of the way." Steele looked around Gordon's surgery for a place to park a pirate. "What have you got down here? Can we strap him to the treatment table?"

"That not what sickbay be for."

Steele wheeled on Parker. "Sickbay isn't meant for murdering physicians either. For God's sake, Parker, let's not have a line against med/life battle. If I get us through this, you can log all your objections to everything I do, but cooperate with me now. I'd dump the prisoner in the brig if I could, but I can't."

"Yes, ma'am." Captain Brook was dead and the mantle of authority had passed. Steele's requests were now orders.

Parker was used to lifting dead weight. She gripped the pirate under his shoulders, and with Steele taking his feet got him onto the treatment table and fastened the straps.

"I need a gag for him. I won't make you do it, Parker. Just get me a rag or some gauze or something and adhesive tape." Steele felt the unconscious man's pulse for herself while Parker went after the supplies. She was relieved to find it strong and regular; she'd judged the force of the blow to his neck accurately. It was a blow that could kill, and she wanted this pirate alive. There would be no other prisoners.

"Who's on duty down here tonight?" Steele worked on the gag and watched the wall clock. She had to get her attack team organized and moving before the enemy upstairs started looking for Fart. "I need some people to stand guard. Not you; you're my link to what's going on in the wardroom."

"I have four on ward. I bring two." Parker returned with Paul Gabriel and a nurse named Allison Jones. The pair stared at the prisoner wide-eyed, gulped and swallowed hard when told about the massacre on the top deck, and then settled in to watch the unconscious man until Marines arrived to relieve them. Steele and Parker went out through the sickbay laundry to intercept the patrol on the third deck.

When Fart came around, he found himself trussed up like a turkey staring at the deckhead. He could tell he wasn't alone. Two people were talking to each other from some place outside his line of vision. What he heard made him nervous. The man, in particular, was describing what he'd like to do with a scalpel if he wasn't under orders to keep "that inhuman monster" safe and secure. The man had a vivid imagination. Fart listened unwillingly to the lurid fantasies until they were unexpectedly interrupted.

"What are you doing here, Angel?" A girl on crutches thumped into the room and stood where Fart could see her. She bent over and stared at his face. "Are you and Jonesy building a Frankenstein?" The girl poked at his tattooed eye with a nail-bitten finger. It seemed to fascinate her that the tattooed eye did not blink, but the other two did. It had been a painful poke.

"What's Hellcat doing wandering around at this hour?" said the man's voice. That was Angel? "Didn't Doctor Parker order a sleeping pill for her?"

"I had a pill, but I didn't swallow it," said the girl, not taking her eyes from Fart's face. "Wow! Just wait till Doctor Gordon sees this monster stretched out on his table. He'll lay an egg." She took hold of his beard and gave it a strong tug. It stayed attached, but his eyes closed again.

"Get your hands off him, Hellcat!" the woman ordered sharply.

"Why should I? You don't have any business messing around here. If you want me to keep quiet, you'd better let me in on what you're up to."

Outside Fart's line of vision, Jones and Gabriel exchanged a glance. Gabriel nodded, strode to Petrie's side and scooped her up under one arm while taking her crutches under the other.

"Hey!" she yelled as he carried her out into the corridor. "What are you doing?"

"Putting you back to sleep. Santa Claus doesn't like little kids snooping around on Christmas Eve."

"The hell with that! You let me go or I'm going to scream for Doctor Parker."

"And tell her what? That you couldn't sleep because you faked taking your pill? You want the officers to know you disobeyed a medical order?"

Petrie decided she didn't. She let Gabriel carry her back to the nearly empty ward where the other patients were sleeping soundly. He identified her bunk by the rumpled sheets and dumped her on it.

"Now hand over that pill." Petrie reluctantly pulled out the handkerchief she had hidden under the mattress. Gabriel snatched it from her. There were a good many tablets in it, several of which Gabriel was sure had never been prescribed for Petrie. He picked out two of her sleeping pills, and emptied the others into his pocket.

"Hey! Those are mine!"

"Sure, they are. And you're planning to turn them into cash as soon as you're running free on the gundeck again, aren't you. Well your little nest egg has just gone missing. Maybe you'd like to report it to the Marines when you wake up. Seems as if you're going to oversleep tomorrow, though." Gabriel pushed Petrie's head back, forced open her jaws, and shoved the two tablets down her throat as if he were dosing a pig. She swallowed.

"That's a good girl. In a moment you'll be off in dreamland."

"Rats!" Petrie muttered crossly as Gabriel waited for her to pass out. "It's not fair. Why should I have to miss all the fun?"

* * *

Steele kept Gordon's office as her headquarters. She didn't know how long it would be before the pirates missed Fart. If he didn't return in a reasonable time, they might assume he had simply found some way to amuse himself on the third deck, perhaps doing some looting before they shut down life support and flash-froze their cargo. Or they might assume he had run into trouble and cut life support with Fart still trapped below. Or they might send someone out looking for him.

Steele now had the Marines on alert; anyone entering the main hatch from the top deck would be unable to exit anywhere but sickbay. If she could trap another pirate alone, that would be one fewer to deal with in the wardroom. The reports she had from McCarthy were that the pirates were still partying, finishing off the leftovers from dinner and getting into the bottles of fine wines stored in the galley. Picturing this desecration of the part of the ship that held so many warm memories left Steele tense with cold fury as she put together her team of killers.

Whom she could use was determined by the weapons available. Everything really worthwhile was either locked up in the 'tween decks or in the officers' cabins. The rifles carried by Marines were unloaded. Furthermore, Marines were trained to use only authorized armament; and when they killed, they did it by the numbers. Steele needed people who would kill with whatever she could provide without fussing about whether they were doing it right. She knew whom to ask first.

"I want the names of fifteen people who know how to kill with a knife and can be trusted to obey orders."

Newcastle and Dover exchanged a nervous glance as they stood with Steele in Gordon's office where a Marine corporal had told them to report. Anyone who killed with a knife, hadn't done it while obeying orders. Sailors were not taught to use knives; heat pistols or laser rifles were the only real weapons ever issued to commoners on warships. Marines drilled with bayonets, which had no practical use in modern warfare but were retained for the sake of tradition. The Marines kept these secure. No sailor ever got his hands on one unless he stole it.

"Come on, you two. Don't get shy with me. The only weapons we've got to take back our ship are what I can get out of life support stations, and that's knives. If you don't want to end up inside some Delphinian's belly, you've got to get me some sailors who can cut throats. I'm not going to use the information against anyone. Give me some names!"

Newcastle and Dover looked at Steele and then at each other. Dover shuffled his feet and wet his lips. "I've killed with a knife, ma'am. Newcastle hasn't."

"All right. Dover, you're on the team. You stand by, Newcastle; I'll have other work for you later. Now who else can use a knife?"

The men looked at each other again, and then dropped their eyes to the deck. Steele suddenly understood the problem. They wouldn't snitch. She should have remembered that.

"Never mind giving names then. Just go and bring me some volunteers. Don't let anyone volunteer who can't be trusted or won't know what to do to keep from getting hurt. And remember, this is all on a 'need to know' basis. Except for the Marines, you are the only people outside sickbay who know what has happened. I don't want your talent search triggering a panic." The big men raised their heads and grinned at each other, then pounded up the ramp toward the crew's living quarters.

"Excuse me, Lieutenant — I mean, Captain Steele." Gabriel had overheard the conversation. "You might want to ask Otto Schmidt to volunteer. He's had plenty of experience killing with a knife."

"Thank you for trying to help, Gabriel. But killing people is a little different from slaughtering hogs."

"I don't think so, ma'am," Gabriel said seriously. "Everything's laid out pretty much the same inside. I'd volunteer to go help too, ma'am, if it weren't for my oath. But Butcher would do better anyway. When I cut people, they're not struggling."

"Do you really think Schmidt would want to do this? He's life support just like you, and this work is going to be dangerous."

"Just because we're wearing yellow stripes doesn't mean we're cowards, ma'am," Gabriel said indignantly.

"Very well." Steele was surprised to find the otherworldly medic so intense. "You go after Schmidt; tell him if he wants to volunteer, he's on the team." Gabriel smiled seraphically and trotted up the ramp.

Parker sat at Gordon's desk, her hands covering her face. Steele spoke to her gently. "You have to come with us, you know. There's no other way." Parker lowered her hands and nodded.

"You order, I follow. Not carry weapon."

"All right. Has McCarthy reported any change?"

Parker shook her head. "Pirates same. But McCarthy much bad. Say please hurry."

"Tell him very soon." Parker's face reflected the content of the silent communication as she reassured the steward. "Tell him you will let him know exactly when we'll be barging in on him. If he can do something — anything — to distract whoever is sitting directly opposite the door, the place where Lieutenant Costello was, it will help us. Tell him he can make it seem like an accident; I don't want him hurt." Parker nodded again and smiled.

"He say . . ." She blushed. "He say if be he have poison, all now be finish. Use bad language. Say if be thirty year younger, not need poison."

"One other thing, and this is an order. When we go to the top deck, you think-talk me. I know it's against regulations; I'll take the responsibility."

Five minutes later Steele had sixteen experienced killers squatting on the deck in Gordon's office. Schmidt, looking as ferocious as he had when he took command of a squad in quarantine, reported carrying a case of butcher's knives. She wasn't surprised to see that three more gunner's mates had joined Dover. One of these was Joan Barcelona, the woman the others called Astral. She claimed to have had experience killing with a knife in a former incarnation; and seeing her fierce expression, Steele decided not to argue about her credentials. The other two were Wolf Wendovski and Abraham Bitterschoen, who tested several knives and debated the merits of each before making their choices. There were several Colonials in the group as well, including the small black woman from the coven who was known as Shadow.

Steele stood barefoot in the ill-fitting sailor's uniform, her dress sword belted around her hips, and addressed her troops. "They have heat pistols. The weapons have not been recharged since they boarded, and they have been fired, but they still have plenty of power for a few killing shots so watch out for them. There is one pirate on watch on the bridge. She has to be taken out quietly; I'll do it. You just worry about where you put your feet. It's dark there and easy to trip, so move slowly and be careful. Hold on to the rail. We can't afford any noise. There's more light once we get near the wardroom.

"Our problem there is the layout of the space. The cabin is narrow and not very long. The pirates in there, especially the ones at the table, will find it hard to stand up quickly. The steward will create a diversion, then on my signal, you'll go in screaming. If we move fast and stay out of each other's way, we'll be finished before any of them can pull a weapon. Don't try anything fancy.

I don't need prisoners, and I don't want casualties. We've taken enough from them already."

The sailors were eager to move out. They had their knives concealed in various ways — up sleeves, in space liner stockings, or pushed into the waistbands of their pants. All wore the weapons easily, confident that they had the sharp edges stowed safely where they could retrieve them quickly.

"All right. Let's go. God bless us."

With mutters of "amen" from the humans and the appropriate gesture of devotion from the Colonials, the armed band entered the main ladder and prepared to assault the bridge. The Colonial physician, still wearing her officer's tunic, followed.

Steele had always assumed that when she killed for the first time, her victim would be a Delphinian, and that she'd go into combat wearing the uniform and carrying the weapons she'd been trained to use. Instead, she could see, as she pressed herself against the wall of the mast cylinder, that the pirate guarding the hatch was a human who except for her exotic clothing and hairstyle looked for all the world like one of the sailors she was trained to care for and protect.

The woman was not standing guard as a Royal Marine would have done. She stood leaning against a rail, smoking a pipe of something that would have to be cleaned out of the ship's life support system, and watching the stars moving slowly across the observation dome. Steele drew her ornate sword from its scabbard, and as soon as her eyes were sufficiently adjusted to the darkness, crept soundlessly onto the bridge.

There were ways to kill with a blade that were fast and nearly painless. And there were ways to fight with a sword that were honorable and approved by tradition. All that counted now was silence. Steele used her weapon in a way that would have shocked her fencing masters at Annapolis: she struck the pirate from behind. The woman made no sound except to draw in one hard sucking breath. Steele knew immediately that the wound was mortal, but death would not come so quickly or painlessly as it might. She twisted the blade and withdrew it, aware that she had not killed clean; she had missed the heart. As the sailors crossed the bridge, one of them gave the dying pirate a vicious kick.

From the moment she left the main mast, Steele could hear the sounds of revelry in the wardroom. She took her crew down the ladder by her cabin, then waited only long enough for a final check with McCarthy. A crash of glassware and cutlery as he pulled the tablecloth from the table was the signal to attack.

Steele was the first one in. Leaving the pirate who had her back to the door for Dover to deal with, she leapt onto the table and threw herself on the man seated at its foot who was battling to free himself from the tangle of cloth and dinnerware. She ran him through unchivalrously while his arms were pinned. Then, leaving him to bleed out his life on the linen, she crouched and whirled to see who might need her help.

No one did.

Of the ten pirates, all were dead or dying. Several had been attacked by more than one of her sailors, none of whom had any interest in giving their victims an easy death or leaving the corpse free of mutilation. Schmidt, out of habit, slit open the belly of his victim and disemboweled him after slicing through the major artery in his throat. Near the door, one pirate was still screaming as Shadow and another Colonial toyed with her. Shadow had sliced off her ears, and the other had run his knife into her arms and shoulders while avoiding vital organs.

"For God's sake, finish it!" Steele bellowed. Shadow shrugged, drove her blade into her victim's heart and spat on her. The pirate's screaming stopped, but the silence lasted only an instant. Relishing their victory, the sailors whooped and hollered and clapped each other over the back with bloody hands. Again, Steele pitched her voice to cut through the din. "Quiet!" The noise subsided. Her sailors looked up at her grinning, wiping their blades off against their shirts, and waiting for her praise.

Parker appeared in the doorway, and Steele now noticed McCarthy for the first time. He was hunched trembling against the corpse of Lieutenant Rivera in a corner near the fireplace. The remains of the man who had killed the first officer lay tangled in the table linen and bleeding at his feet. As Parker pushed her way through the carnage to reach him, McCarthy vomited.

Steele realized the sailors wanted a speech. She was no George Brook and knew it; she kept it brief. "You've done well. You've all done very well. You're entitled to blood money, and I'll see that you get it. Dismissed."

She jumped from the table as the sailors filed out of the room. McCarthy wept soundlessly in Parker's arms, as she gently helped him to his feet.

"Lieutenant Parker."

"I know, Captain." Parker spoke telepathically. "You still need me for work on the line. I won't retreat into sickbay. Just let me get McCarthy below and send up crews from the mortuary and organic waste to clean up. Then I will be at your disposal again."

Steele stood alone facing the slaughter. Bodies of the attackers sprawled on the rug, against the upholstered furniture and over the table where they had fallen, their blood, pouring from gaping wounds, staining the white wool dress tunics and trousers they had taken from the officers of *Lafayette.* The remains of her colleagues, stripped and bloodless, were heaped together near the fireplace. It was ironic that the pirates had given their victims a clean death with pistol rays whereas she, an officer and a meritocrat, had resorted to butchery. Steele automatically examined her sword, wiped it clean against the trouser leg of the corpse closest to the door and returned it to its scabbard.

In the quiet, she could feel her body systems returning to normal. She had come this far on reflexes built up through repetitive training, fueled by anger and adrenalin. But Parker was right; her work was just beginning.

She looked toward the fireplace where the head of Liz Costello's corpse faced the door, eyes staring blindly. In the silence, the antique clock on the mantel began to tick and then sounded eight bells — the end of a watch.

"Oh, Liz," Steele found herself saying aloud. "Oh, Liz, I hurt!" She slumped into the captain's chair at the head of the table and covered her face with her hands.

CHAPTER FOURTEEN

Her eyes closed, Steele's body began to tremble and her stomach to heave. She felt overwhelmed by grief and horror; a sob tore at her throat and tears threatened to spill down her face. She mustn't break down now; the work wasn't finished yet.

There was something else. The stench. The odor that permeated the wardroom: a mixture of fresh blood, spilled intestines, and vomit. The stench of a slaughterhouse. Or of a battlefield. The odor tugged at her consciousness like the wisp of memory from a dream that instantaneously pulls a vivid vision from oblivion into piercing clarity. The reek of blood, guts, and vomit was familiar. Steele had inhaled this foul perfume before. Inhaled it often. Breathed it in deeply. Breathe deep and slow. Deep and slow. Keep the rhythm. Deep and slow.

The voice Steele heard was her own, the one she used when speaking to herself. Breathe in and out. It's just a bad smell. There's nothing caustic, nothing toxic. The danger is past. Breathe deep and slow.

The Helmet. That's what Steele had called it when it came to her in SOCRATES. She remembered now. She continued to breathe rhythmically, sensing the Helmet ease into place. It felt so familiar, so welcome. The ache in her heart faded and she had a sense of being wrapped in cotton wool as though she had lost one of her primary senses. It was like the temporary loss of hearing in a pressure suit, or of smell due to a bad cold.

Under ordinary circumstances the Helmet would be uncomfortable, but circumstances were not ordinary. Steele gladly surrendered sensitivity. She had worn the Helmet before. It would slip on and off like a garment. She remembered. She would wear it now with gratitude.

Lowering her hands, Steele surveyed the carnage around her. When the teams from the bilges arrived, she watched them begin their grisly work with cold eyes and a quarterdeck face that held naturally. She was as unmoved as if they had been stewards clearing up after an ordinary dinner.

* * *

When Gordon opened his eyes, he saw two women in Navy service uniforms looking down at him. The faces were familiar, but the uniforms were wrong. Steele was wearing the captain's insignia on her collar. Even more grotesque, his second in command had pinned the gold line lieutenant's pin next to the silver caduceus on her collar.

"Can't you tell Christmas from Halloween, Parker? You're out of uniform."

Parker smiled. "He be alert now, Captain. You talk him." She adjusted his pillow and helped him sit up. He listened as Steele described how the world of the *Lafayette* had turned upside down in the few hours since he had gone to sleep.

"This is a hell of a thing to wake up to!"

"I'm sure it must be, Doctor." Steele looked strange, older somehow. From the story she'd just told, Gordon decided she had a right to.

"Parker tells me your condition has stabilized, that you're back to what's normal for you. I need your help. Can you work?"

"I think so." Gordon shifted his body. Nothing hurt any more than it usually did. "Yes, of course I can work. What do you want me to do?"

"The ship that attacked us, the *Pagan Queen*, is still lurking around somewhere. I have to go after her; but there is something wrong on the bridge, and I can't get a reading."

"I'm no bridge officer, Steele. You want to hunt a ship, you get Parker to help. She likes that kind of thing."

"I intend to have Parker work on the bridge. I want something else from you." Steele hesitated. She knew Gordon wasn't going to like this. "I've taken a prisoner. He uses the name Fart. Parker says he's in good physical condition; I didn't injure him when I took him. He can give me the information I need if his brain is stimulated. I want you to use psychomonates on him."

Gordon scowled. "That's a dangerous procedure, Steele."

"I know that, Doctor."

"This Fart, whoever he is, is a stranger. I won't have a medical history to work from. I'll have to estimate dosage and that won't be much better than blind guessing. If I get it wrong, I'll kill him."

"I know that too, Doctor Gordon. But if the drug doesn't kill him, I will have to hang him. It's bad enough that we have to have a funeral on Christmas morning without following it up with an execution."

"And just what makes you think God would be more offended by a hanging on Christmas morning than by a physician committing murder on Christmas night?"

"Doctor, please. I must get coordinates on *Pagan Queen*. We are blind until I can sight on a known target and synchronize the instruments. And if the pirate isn't boarded within the next few hours, we will lose the advantage of surprise and may take casualties. I have to do a depth interrogation. There just isn't any other way. If it will make it easier for you, work through a mate. You know what needs to be done. Just give the orders. You need not touch the prisoner at all."

"That's a quibble."

"Yes."

If it had been Brook, Gordon thought, he would have fought harder. But as he looked at the pale young woman suddenly forced to shoulder a crushing responsibility, he knew he would not add to her burdens. He had taken an oath, but so had she.

"All right. But I won't work with a surgeon's mate. The commoner physicians may not be tender about their oath, but I am. I'll get a vet to help."

Steele sighed in relief. She'd feared she might have to give Gordon a direct order. "Send a runner to the bridge when you've got him ready. I'm taking Parker with me."

"Prisoner in your surgery," Parker said, and both women left.

In his surgery! Gordon pulled on his clothes and went to his station. A full Marine guard was posted at the entrance to sickbay, crowding up the corridor by the main mast. Gordon glared at them, but Marines never responded to dirty looks. They saluted him by presenting arms and stepped aside to let him pass. When he entered the treatment room and saw the pirate with his dirty hair and piles of non-regulation clothing bound to the examining table, he took out his fury on his mates.

Sometimes Gordon wondered whether he might find himself with considerable explaining to do at the Last Judgement because of his habit of relieving his emotions by bellowing at others. He remembered how Captain Brook kept his rages all tightly corked. Gordon doubted whether that had been healthy, but as it turned out it had made no difference. The captain hadn't died of it.

As for himself, he didn't have Brooks's iron character, and he assumed sickbay staff were used to his ways. Whether they were or not, they were going to get a blast. In his surgery!

"What the hell do you think I'm running here, a New Australian drunk tank? This is a Navy medical facility. Unstrap that man and take out that gag! This isn't the brig! I've seen the pair of you handle a patient twice the size of this one without using straps. Let him scream if he wants to. It won't bother anyone. Get him out of those filthy rags, and clean him up so I can see what he looks like. I'll be in my office." He stomped out and slammed the door.

Gabriel and Jones grinned at each other. Whatever else had changed aboard *Lafayette*, the med/life director was back to normal. They got to work cleaning up the pirate.

Once they started on him, Fart realized, to his sorrow, that this was something he had been through before. When Navy medics said clean, they meant clean. He knew better than to struggle or put up an argument. That was how you got a mouth full of soap.

They gave him a bath that was rather more than a bath. Starting at his feet, Gabriel clipped his toenails and cleaned between his toes. Jones swabbed out his ears, flossed his teeth, and put drops in his eyes. They shaved his face, removing both beard and eyebrows, and then shaved his head and body. They followed this up with a thorough scrub during which Jones gave up on removing the tattoo from his forehead only after giving it her best effort with carbolic soap and a stiff brush. They were getting ready to pump out his stomach when Gordon came back into the room to find out what was taking so long.

"Godalmighty! What do you think you're doing? I said to clean him up, not to prep him for admission to quarantine. Give him some clothes. Not a uniform for God's sake. Put him in a scrub suit. Then one of you go tell Schmidt I want him." The door slammed again.

"I'll go, Angel," Jones said. "Is Butcher still bunking in the barnyard, do you know?"

"No, he went back to his regular berth after we secured from epidemic alert."

"What do you think the director wants with him anyhow? Butcher's getting a lot of overtime tonight."

Gabriel shrugged. "It's none of our business, is it. Butcher won't mind so long as he gets paid."

Who's the butcher, Fart wondered. The angel who had fantasized about vivisection was bad enough; what did they want a butcher for?

Jones went off to wake Schmidt, and Gabriel sorted through a cabinet, selected a scrub suit, and watched the pirate dress. Fart kept a wary eye on his attendant. The expression on this Angel's face was very unsettling. He was smiling. Very sweetly smiling.

"Do you ever think about hell, pirate? I do. They say they have a staff of fallen angels on duty to torture the damned. It goes on and on forever." Gabriel nodded beatifically. "You'll be there soon, I expect. Yes, I expect you'll be there very soon."

Abruptly, the cadaverous officer with the violent temper entered the room accompanied by a hulking sailor with a lantern jaw. "You're dismissed, Gabriel. Get out of here. I've sent Jones back to bed too. This is no work for a medic." Gabriel, still smiling, drifted off.

Gordon stared at Fart for a moment, then went to a cabinet, fetched an adhesive bandage and firmly covered the non-regulation tattoo.

"What are you going to do to me?"

"Test your blood. Schmidt, take a sample and bring me a full-spectrum analysis."

This, it seemed to Fart, was work for a medic. At least it had been when he was in the Navy, and the mean-looking sailor drew blood as though he knew what he was doing.

"What else? What is going on here? I want to know what is going to happen to me?"

Gordon, who had been leaning against the bulkhead with his arms crossed and head lowered, looked up. He did not want to talk to this man — his patient, or should he say his victim. But he didn't treat people without explaining the procedure or answering their questions.

"You're being prepared for depth interrogation. I will use your blood chemistry analysis to formulate a psychomonate suitable for intravenous injection. The drug will sharpen your memory and perceptions and force you to make full and truthful responses when you're questioned."

This sounded complicated. Fart asked something simpler. "Will it hurt?"

"A little." Gordon frowned at the pirate. Fart had a lot of gall to complain about pain with all the blood he had on his hands. "If you're lucky, it will kill you. Fast."

"What's that supposed to mean?"

"You figure it out," Gordon snapped. "You've been in the Navy. I've got a pile of death certificates on my desk, five meritocrats, and they don't refer to natural causes. What happens to murderers on a warship?"

Fart thought about it, and decided it might not be a bad thing to die of some side effect from a drug. Especially if it was fast.

Gordon waited for Schmidt to complete the blood analysis, worked out the psychomonate formula as accurately as he could, and then left. He didn't want to watch.

Thirty minutes later, he returned and questioned the pirate briefly. When asked how he felt, Fart accurately gave his blood pressure, pulse rate, neural index, and red cell count before Gordon could shut him up.

"He's ready. I'm leaving you in full charge now, Schmidt. I'll call the captain, and then I'm going to my quarters."

* * *

The pirate sat in the visitor's chair in Gordon's office, his arm bound to the armrest and the bottle of clear fluid suspended from a stand behind him, slowly releasing its contents through a tube into his bloodstream. Schmidt hovered over him, monitoring the indicators, while Steele faced him across the desk with a pad in front of her. Steele was not surprised to see the pirate full of smiles. Psychomonates worked by producing euphoria. Her expression was grim.

"We'll start with your name." She did not intend to conduct a formal interrogation with someone called Fart. "What is your full given name?"

"James Lawrence Francis Hillyard, the third. The Lawrence is after my mother's side and . . ."

"That's sufficient. I would like to keep this interview brief, Mr. Hillyard." Steele was aware of the need to frame her questions precisely. Under the influence of psychomonates, a subject could drown an interrogator in a flood of irrelevant detail. Historians might value that kind of thing; she didn't have the time. What she wanted was information on *Pagan Queen*, just enough to let her locate and board the ship.

"What is the mass of the vessel you came from?" From mass, Steele could set calibrations for weapons and estimate the enemy's potential speed and maneuverability.

"Well, let me see. *Pagan Queen*'s registry papers showed a burden of two hundred seventeen tons, but that's empty. We've got cargo in the hold . . ."

"That's enough. What's the size of her establishment? How many are aboard?"

"You mean right now, right? Well, eleven came over with me, so I don't count them." Hillyard began to tick off names in his mind and calculated totals on his fingers. "We got the Old Woman plus three mates and without me and my buddies, we got forty-seven sailors, so that makes fifty-two we got aboard all together if you count the goat."

Steele decided not to count the goat.

"Any prisoners? Any live hominids in the cargo bay?"

"Oh, sure. I thought you said not to talk about the cargo. We got six on the hoof. Four human and two Colonial. There's another six in cold storage."

"What is your armament."

"Fourteen cannon, twelve of them short range and the other two intermediate, except they don't work very good. The Old Woman said they need . . ."

"Limit yourself to the numbers, please."

"Okay. Besides the cannon we got two gross of laser rifles and a gross of heat pistols minus one dozen that we brought with us, plus we got seventeen Marine bayonets that Halfass picked up one time, only they don't fit on our rifles, and we got a peashooter Slut swiped from a fair booth on Murphy's Mountain."

Steele decided not to count the peashooter. *Pagan Queen* was in no way a formidable enemy. There would be no difficulty taking her once she was located.

"Where is your vessel?"

"In orbit," Hillyard answered cheerfully and with uncharacteristic brevity.

"In orbit around what?"

"Why, around this ship, of course. There's nothing else this massive within a hundred light years. In fact that made sort of a problem for us cause we're kind of low on fuel, but then . . ."

"That will do." When this story got out *Lafayette* would be the laughing stock of the fleet. A pirate ship using the pride of the Royal Navy for a docking orbit and drawing power from her gravitational mass. At least *Pagan Queen* would be easy to find.

Steele picked up her pad and stood. Schmidt grinned at her, taking credit for how well the drug had worked. Steele's face remained expressionless. "Thank you, Chief Schmidt. Your work again was very satisfactory, and you've earned another bonus. I won't be needing the prisoner any more. After you've stabilized him, you can take him to the brig."

* * *

Gordon sat heavily at the table in his cabin. It was heaped with pediatric texts that he studied for personal pleasure when he had any time for himself, which wasn't often. He was still ill, he thought. Steele had got to him at a weak moment. He had just done something he was afraid he was going to regret for the rest of his life.

There was a tap on the door, and Parker entered the cabin carrying a tray. She cleared a space on the table and set it down.

"Eat."

"Not now, Parker."

"Yes, now. Eat or you take tube feeding."

"Make up your mind, Parker. Are you a med/life officer or in the line?" He waved a finger to indicate the insignia on her collar.

"Steele order me be both. Many thing for top deck must have meritocrat do. Steele need me be both till ship safe." Gordon scowled at her. Parker stamped her foot. "This not for me easy. Not my choice have pirate come, make me do two job. You not fight me. You eat. Please."

"Please! Oh, foul blow, Doctor Parker!"

But he did have to eat. Parker was right. She stood over him as he cleaned his plate. The food helped. He sipped his mudd and began to feel a little better. There was another tap at the door. It was Otto Schmidt.

"The man you had me working on, Doctor Gordon. He's dead, sir. I guess I must of left the needle in too long."

"Well write it up in the medical log. The sickbay forms are the same as those in your section. You already did a blood analysis, and he didn't die of anything contagious."

"Yes, sir." Schmidt was unaccustomed to having the med/life director delegating so much responsibility. "What do I do with the body, sir?"

Gordon lurched to his feet, knocking the tray to the deck. "Why the hell are you asking me questions? You know goddamn well what the routine is! That piece of slime isn't going to get a burial in space with a flag draped over him! Why do I have to spell it out for you? The body goes into organic waste recycling the same as a diseased pig. What the hell else would I want you to do with the corpse? Stuff it as a trophy so I can display it in my surgery?"

Parker put a hand on Gordon's shoulder and gently guided him back toward his chair. "Sit," she said. "You, Schmidt, do work. Not bother Doctor Gordon. You have problem, you ask to me."

Schmidt eyed both physicians nervously and backed out of the cabin. When he was gone, Gordon was aware of being the subject of Parker's cool appraisal. "Now don't you try ordering me back to bed. I'm all right now, physically anyway. And how long is it since you've had any sleep? If you're planning on filling two slots for *Lafayette*, you'd better start taking double good care of your health."

* * *

As Steele confirmed the presence of an object of just over two hundred tons mass orbiting the *Lafayette*, she realized that the last place she would have thought to look for *Pagan Queen* was inside *Lafayette*'s own local gravity field. A few hours, at most, of random rotation would put the vessel smack over the bridge dome. Right under her nose — and such a puny target. An object that size could be pulverized by a single burst from one of *Lafayette*'s smallest caliber anti-asteroid guns.

Of course, blowing up salvageable craft was not the Navy way. Nor did the Navy allow captains their accustomed wide discretionary powers when pirates were the prey. The regulations governing piracy had a whole volume to themselves in *Naval Regulations*. Because apprehension of pirates was haphazard and their crimes so appalling, the punishment prescribed was more severe by far than for any other crime perpetrated in space. The blood-thirsty attitudes of *Lafayette*'s sailors confirmed that the commoners' sense of justice would be satisfied only by draconian punishment. Also, the Admiralty insisted that potential pirates who calculated the odds would risk less horrendous punishments and so be undeterred by them.

To what extent the Navy's implacable policy deterred pirates was uncertain. There had been plenty of them swarming through space on both sides of the Pegasus station ever since the wars opened a tempting market for hominid flesh. Perhaps without the Navy there would be more. Steele didn't know. But she did know her duty as an officer in command of a Navy ship. She had to apprehend the pirates and enforce the law. The first would not be difficult. As for the second . . .

The Helmet knew it had done such things before. It had memories, memories from the training sessions in SOCRATES that Steele did not share and that she had been warned never to try to retrieve on her own. Every one of them had the potential to trigger a psychotic episode. She would now share only those memories that the Helmet drew on, and the Helmet would cushion them.

Steele wished she had some memories of her own involving *Lafayette* boarding parties. She must take command although she had never participated in boarding operations even in exercises. She was supposed to rotate into training on the gundeck after the first of the year, but a fat lot of good that did her now. The plain fact was, she had tactical know-how but no personal experience whatever and no one to advise her.

She stretched her intuition and searched *Naval Regulations* for alternatives to what appeared to be her only choice. Finding none, she made the decision to do something that was repugnant to the very foundations of the meritocratic system: she'd have to ask advice and depend on the support of a commoner. She sent a runner for Chief Newcastle.

The black gunner's mate was waiting for a call. Chalkie and the other gunners had come back to the berthing area in their blood-stained uniforms with whispered confidences to their friends about derring-do on the top deck and promised blood money. Newcastle wanted his chance to go for gold and glory, and Steele had promised she'd have a job for him.

"We'll go out on *Wasp*." Steele checked the launches; this was the one up on the rotation list. Her systems had been inspected within the past week, and she was fully fueled. "The vessel we're attacking is two hundred seventeen tons with fourteen guns and a crew of about fifty."

"With all respect, Captain, shouldn't we go after the big ship first? Take out the *Pagan Queen* and then pick up her launches?"

Steele shook her head. "I know this is going to be hard to believe, Newcastle. It's going to give *Lafayette* a place in Naval history that none of us would want for her. This two hundred and seventeen tonner is the *Pagan Queen*."

Newcastle scowled. He was proud of the reputation of his ship. Now the veteran of scores of legendary victories had been grievously wounded by the equivalent of a space-going rowboat.

"Something went very wrong here on the bridge for a few hours last evening, Chief. A flea wounded an elephant. That's over; we can't change it. But we can swat the flea."

Bloody damn right they'd swat it, Newcastle thought. But if he had anything to say about it, the flea would get its little legs pulled off slowly one at a time before it got squashed.

"I want this operation to go the way our honored dead would want it to go. I've never taken out a *Lafayette* boarding party. You've been part of many. So I want you to tell me exactly how you believe Lieutenant Rivera would have set it up, what gear we need, and who would be on the team."

Newcastle considered. "Are you planning on putting a prize crew aboard, ma'am?"

Steele shook her head. There could be no prize crew without an officer in charge. She wouldn't say it to Newcastle, but he knew it as well as she did. A prize crew in its own ship without a meritocratic officer would inevitably be taken over by the most depraved members of the group and itself turn pirate.

"Then we don't need much gear, ma'am. A craft that small. *Wasp* can just grapple her and tow her back here. Then you can take anything you want aboard her through an airlock. We just go with the launch's twenty-four guns and a rifle apiece for the boarding party. Add a medic and a first aid kit for luck, and we're set for any resistance that runt could put up."

"Good. Now who would Lieutenant Rivera have assigned to the team?"

Newcastle's face fell. "Not me, ma'am. It's not my turn."

"That's all right. I'm picking you out of turn. Now who else."

"Well, Marines, ma'am. At least half the party Marines; the rest sailors."

"Which Marines? Which sailors?" She shouldn't have to ask questions like these; Rivera would have put together a boarding party and be out the airlock within five minutes of a call to general quarters.

"I don't know about Marines, ma'am. They're all the same, aren't they? I mean, I think Lieutenant Rivera would just tell Sergeant Major Pipp how many he wanted and they'd be at the dock when we suited up."

"All right. I'll do the same. Now what about sailors? Who would Lieutenant Rivera have taken?"

"If I was going, he'd take the people at my weapon station, keep the team together like. And then some of Dover's crew and Barcelona's would take over our guns."

"Is that it?"

"No, ma'am." Newcastle knew for sure Rivera would have put two more sailors in the launch, and he didn't like the idea of going into combat with either of them. "Lieutenant Rivera would have taken Charlie Ames and Waldo Bunyan."

"I see." Yes, she thought, that is exactly what Rivera would have done: given the two sailors who had disgraced themselves a chance to make it up. This was going to be a very easy action; all the sailors would have to do was obey orders, and no one would get hurt. Thinking it over, she decided being in on the boarding would certainly do Ames some good, and she was confident Newcastle could keep him in line.

She had serious misgivings about Waldo Bunyan. Rivera might have been able to handle him, but she wasn't sure she could. She needed to give her full attention to the boarding operation; unlike Rivera, she couldn't do it with one hand while coaxing along a coward with the other.

"Very well. We'll take your gun crew and Charlie Ames. Bunyan will go out some other time." Newcastle breathed a sigh of relief. One loser he could manage.

One bell into the middle watch, *Wasp* pulled away from her third-deck dock, the sailors driving the vessel and the Marines clutching their weapons and trying not to get spacesick. Steele kept an eye on them. You couldn't help but admire Marines. They might puke, but they would never complain.

As the launch drew close to *Pagan Queen's* orbit, the sailors working the helm and standing ready at the guns began to curse the bits of debris they had to dodge or blast away. The pirate ship had the filthy habit of jettisoning her garbage.

Meanwhile, aboard *Pagan Queen*, the sailor on watch dropped his pipe on the deck and went to wake the captain rousing everyone else aboard as he went. "Fart's coming back! They must of found some great stuff. Hope they remembered to grab some food. They brought a new ship for us, too. Looks to be in great shape, and real clean. Come look at it!"

Pagan Queen's old woman lumbered up to the bridge, rubbed a place clean on the smoke-fogged observation dome and peered through it at the approaching craft using a hand-held telescope. It was a real nice looking vessel. Fast. Big too. It must be packed with booty.

Only there was something wrong. Fart couldn't drive that well; no one in the crew could. Any of her sailors would be rolling a vessel that big all over its axis. She dropped the glass.

"You stupid shit! Fart's not driving that launch. That's Navy at the helm! Jesus H. Christ!" The captain heaved herself into the hatch. "Dump the cargo! Hide the bullion! Everyone for theirself." She was the first to reach the lowest deck and begin dragging the cadavers in cold storage to the airlock.

Steele saw the airlock open and twelve bodies drift into space. Half emerged stiff as rails, moving gracefully in the *Pagan Queen*'s wake. The others went out at erratic intervals, limbs flailing wildly.

"Can we speed up, Newcastle? Damn! I'd hoped we could be on her before they got the wind up."

"I can give us a little more speed, ma'am, but it's not going to do those folks any good." Steele could see that the bodies that went out alive imploded even faster than those that had been frozen. There was no need to hurry to retrieve those remains; a cleanup crew could go out after them in the morning.

Relentlessly she shifted her attention to the mechanics of boarding *Pagan Queen*, sadly aware that in one important respect she had already failed her mission; the pirate's prisoners had not been liberated.

The *Pagan Queen* gave no sign of intention to resist boarding. Nothing shifted on her hull. Even when *Wasp* ran out her guns, the smaller ship did not respond. Typical.

Wasp grappled the smaller craft below her belly and a dozen Marines, relieved to have come to the end of the ride, gave their space armor a final check and went out the airlock to take up their positions on the captive vessel's hull. Using laser rifles at full power, they sealed the gunports and all but one airlock, the one leading directly to the bridge. By the numbers, the Marines then stormed the bridge and secured it without difficulty.

Not a single pirate could be found on the top deck. Standing and fighting against overwhelming odds was not the pirate way. Steele knew where she would find them. Forty-seven people were crammed into the hold on the lower deck, a few in chains and the rest bound with rope. Every one of them swore to being a prisoner, unwillingly forced aboard the pirate ship.

One elderly woman, the most heavily chained, held up her hands and began to shout something about liberation and the day of jubilee. Steele examined her wrists. No abrasions; she hadn't been cuffed long enough even to redden the skin.

The boarding party liberated a goat discovered in the captain's quarters and then, leaving Marines on guard, returned to the *Wasp* and towed *Pagan Queen* back to HMS *Lafayette*.

* * *

Ordinarily, *Naval Regulations* approved of speedy justice. But not for pirates. The preferred procedure was to send a captured pirate ship with its crew to a planetary prize court where the pirates would be kept confined in uncomfortable quarters, which were described in detail, and kept alive on a disciplinary diet while legal action took its leisurely course. After a few months of this, during which time their only exercise would be trips to and from court by a route passing the gallows, a date for execution would be set and after, perhaps, half a year, the authorities would finally finish with the business.

Lafayette was far from any planetary base, drifting in a byway of space, and needing to get to a star for refueling. Steele was already feeling a sense of urgency about getting the ship underway. Taking *Pagan Queen* in tow and detouring to a prize court was out of the question.

Naval Regulations did set out alternatives when preferred procedures were "inconvenient." Any Navy captain was authorized to execute pirates in space — in a manner specified with grisly exactitude. But in marked contrast to the Navy's usual brisk attitude toward executions, where forty-eight hours was the maximum time anyone could be kept waiting for it, pirates had to wait at least ten days. Again, Steele felt that her ship's unusual situation made that impossible. She checked to make sure and confirmed that the-ten day requirement could be waived at the captain's discretion.

And so shortly after two o'clock on Christmas morning, Steele returned to *Pagan Queen* to enforce Navy justice. Court was set up on the bridge, the cleanest and largest clear area on the ship. *Lafayette* sailors brought over two tables (one for Steele and one for the yeoman who kept the record), two chairs (the accused would stand), a Navy lie detector and a guillotine (one each).

Steele knew her use of the last went against the spirit of the law and that her crew would grumble about it. Pirates were always beheaded, but they were supposed to be hanged first. Of all forms of execution, beheading — assuming the executioner was reasonably skillful — was the swiftest and least painful, quite the opposite of what the law prescribed for pirates. Sailors might well resent pirates being allowed an easier death than deserters or ordinary murderers.

But hanging took time, and Steele had none to spare. She wanted the crew to wake on Christmas morning aboard a ship back on course with the nightmare of *Pagan Queen* behind them. She'd rather deal with grumbling than waste half a day hanging pirates when there was vital work to be done for the ship.

The summary hearings progressed swiftly, and after the first few, Steele found she could scarcely distinguish one defendant from another.

"State your name." The yeoman wrote down whatever the defendant chose to give as a name, always an alias, usually an outlandish nickname.

"Do you swear to tell the truth, so help you God?"

"I do."

"Have you committed any act or acts of piracy or collaborated or assisted in the commission of such acts at any time during war or peace in any part of space?"

"Oh, no, ma'am! Oh, I would never, ma'am! Pirates are such awfully wicked people, ma'am. They should all fry in hell for eternity, ma'am!"

"Take the ball." A Marine would hand over the lie detector and make sure the accused held it properly. "I repeat the question: Have you committed any act or acts of piracy or collaborated or assisted in the commission of such acts at any time during war or peace in any part of space?"

"Oh no, ma'am! Oh, I would never, ma'am . . ." Meanwhile the indicators on the ball would flash like Christmas tree lights.

"Guilty of the crime of piracy. The sentence is death. Bring up the next prisoner."

The executioner worked with equal speed and lack of ceremony at the other end of the bridge. Billy Katz, the Colonial mortician's apprentice, came with the guillotine. He usually used the apparatus, which was a portable model resembling a large paper cutter, only on cadavers; but since there were Marines around to hold his subjects still, he was perfectly willing to do the work of an executioner. He was pretty sure he'd get a bonus for it. Usually only humans got such opportunities.

Katz began by shaving off hair to the level of the bottom of the ear and storing the clippings in a basket for recycling. Then he removed clothing down to the waist, setting that aside to be cleaned and sold for the sailors' fund at the ship's store. The guillotine was designed with recycling in mind, so he had little to do here. The severed heads fell into a holding tank; blood drained into a tub, and the corpses were stacked together for transport to organic waste recycling. By the time Katz had everything neatly stowed, Marines would be marching briskly across the deck with another customer.

Before the end of the middle watch, *Pagan Queen* was a lifeless hulk, her crew reduced to cadavers swallowed up in *Lafayette*'s bilges, her main life-support apparatus slashed and her hull pierced through on every deck. In the morning, work crews would salvage everything aboard that might be of use to the warship and then take her apart piece by piece for recycling. Another crew would take out a launch and salvage the organic and inorganic matter spilled into space.

Steele sat at the chart table on *Lafayette*'s bridge and considered the irony of it all. The energy reserve of *Pagan Queen* was so low that in another two days even sending out a launch like the one that had attacked *Lafayette* would have been impossible. Through their carelessness, they had travelled so far into deep space that even without the Navy's intervention, all aboard her would have been dead within a month.

The pirates had large reserves of air, water, and rum; but food and fuel were running low. Pirates liked their comforts, and starvation was a hard way to go. Being what they were, they would probably have resorted to cannibalism, prolonging their agony and giving themselves grisly deaths without any assistance from the Royal Navy.

At eight bells, Parker came straight from morning rounds onto the bridge, peering through the red light and picking her way cautiously through the unfamiliar territory toward the chart table. Steele absently nodded a greeting while watching with more attention the fresh bridge crew relieving the sailors at the observation ports.

"I can last another hour or so, Parker, if you need time to get up to speed."

Steele's voice was steady and relaxed. Parker wished she could see her better, preferably under the bright lights of an examination room. She didn't believe Steele could possibly have another hour in her — especially not after seeing this morning what the captain had sent into the mortuary overnight.

The new watch was in place. Steele saw nothing out of the ordinary in the way the sailors relieved each other. No unnecessary conversation, which was good. Dilly Finklestein relieved the quartermaster, his hands flashing the Colonial sign, and got a grunt in return.

"I take watch, now, captain. Doctor Gordon say you go sleep."

Steele smiled. "Well, that's good news. I thought he'd be wanting to count my white corpuscles to see if SOCRATES has side effects."

That was, in fact, exactly what Gordon wanted. Parker too. But they'd decided sleep was more essential. Odd, Steele didn't seem nearly as tired as Parker would have expected. In theory one subpersonality could work while the other slept. Could Steele have been sleep-walking her way through the last eight hours? She sounded normal enough.

"Don't stare at me that way, Anne!" Steele's laugh was the one Parker knew. "SOCRATES kicked in just as Admiral Thanatos said it would. You and Gordon have the famous *Proceedings* article, and I know you've been waiting for this to happen ever since I came aboard. Well, SOCRATES kicked in, and I didn't explode. It worked very well. The subpersonality is a perfect fit and not obtrusive at all. Look around. Morning after a massacre. An orderly bridge, ship secure, crew quiet."

Steele was right, but that was part of what was so disturbing. Sailors didn't know any better, but it was eerie to have Maggie Steele accept mass carnage as routine. Parker accepted it; all the old officers would have accepted it. But in Maggie it seemed somehow all wrong.

"Oh, all right." Steele stood up and stretched. "I'm resigned to having you and Gordon all over me as soon as I can work out a way to reorganize a ship that's supposed to have five bridge officers so it can function with one. One and a half, counting you, but I know med/life needs a full staff no matter what happens up here. Just help us get through these first hours, and I'll give you back to the third deck."

Parker slid into Steele's position at the chart table. Steele pulled over the log. "This should be an easy watch. If any hell was going to break loose below decks it would have happened by now. So the first entry is 'drifting as before.' Just keep up the random rotation — the sailors know what to do — and call me immediately if anything unusual happens. Don't try to work it out yourself. In any event call me at seven bells. I'll take the forenoon watch."

"Where call you if need. You be in captain quarters?"

"No! No, not tonight." Turning over the con had done something to the Helmet. Steele became aware of its weight. Although she knew she ought to move immediately into the cabin that was the communication center on the top deck, she couldn't face taking over Captain Brook's quarters right now. "I'm going down to my quarters on the third level. Call me there."

Steele reentered the cabin she'd left in such a different mood what seemed a very long time ago. She looked around with dull eyes, very conscious now of the weight of the Helmet. She began to prepare for bed. The blue satin underwear was all that was left of her party clothes. She held the lacy pieces for a moment and then threw them into the recycling unit. She knew she could never wear them again. She pulled down her bunk, and something tumbled out onto the deck.

It was a package wrapped in a square of red synthetic cloth tied with a length of white wool yarn. It took Steele a moment to realize what it was — a Christmas present. There was a note pinned to it. Steele recognized Lamashtu's heavy block script. "Christmas isn't Christmas without a child to give a present to. So here's a little something for the wardroom's youngest on her first Christmas in space. Never lose your child's heart, Maggie, and may the joy of Christmas be with you always."

Steele pulled off the wrapping and stared at the gift. It was an oversized crib blanket, deep blue squares adorned with pink roses and tiny green leaves lit with sparkling dew drops. The Helmet pressed heavy over her senses. It had served its purpose. She took a deep breath and exhaled slowly; the Helmet dissolved.

At once, a flood of tears spilled from her eyes and anguished wailing racked her body. Waves of pain welled up from under her heart. It was worse than anything she had ever felt; worse than anything she could have imagined. She thought her heart would burst from it. She threw herself down on the bunk, wrapped herself in the soft blanket, and with heaving sobs confronted her grief, horror, fear and loneliness.

Finally, near dawn, she fell asleep.

CHAPTER FIFTEEN

Anne Parker knew enough about navigating deep space to know she had no business standing a watch. An amateur's book knowledge of coastal charts and experience in command of waisters on the third deck wouldn't cut it. She also knew that the few hours of sleep she'd had wasn't enough to qualify her as "fully rested and alert." Even worse, despite rushing through the early rounds on the third deck to a degree that left her decidedly uncomfortable, she'd arrived on the bridge just as the watch was changing. It would take a good half hour for her eyes to adjust.

Parker gripped the copy of *Watch Officers Guide* she'd pulled from the tactical library hoping to snatch a few minutes to read it but knowing in her heart that this was no time for a crash course. The night orders were on the chart table; these were brief, and Steele had already summarized them for her, but she would be unable to read them until she had her night vision. She felt as unprepared to take the con as she had felt about anything since she was caught once by a pop quiz in grade school. Parker was not in the habit of muddling through in her work, and she didn't like the feeling.

Someone came up behind her. Parker whirled in her seat. It was Finkelstein. Why had the Colonial left his post? Where was it, anyway? The quartermaster's job was to collect the readings from the sailors at observation stations and have them ready for entry in the log at — what was it — quarter-hour intervals. Finkelstein thrust a slate at her. Parker looked at it, then looked at him and wondered what she was to do with it. Blind as she was, how could she even read, much less approve.

Finkelstein was close enough so she could see his round face wore a broad smile — too broad to be quite respectful. Parker felt the blood rising to her face, hoping it would not be obvious in the red dimness. Finkelstein certainly had good reason to laugh at her. What was a physician doing taking the con? What was anyone doing wearing a double insignia, presuming to serve both med/life and the line? And, most of all, what was a Colonial doing at the command center of a warship.

She hadn't much choice but to approve Finkelstein's data unexamined. Worse than a slap-dash rush through morning rounds, this necessity rankled. She had to assume that the quartermaster knew his job and had done it properly, yet she had no way of knowing for sure. Unless he did something outrageous, like wiring an explosive charge to the helm, she wouldn't have a clue as to whether he was following regulations. Damn! How much difference could it make! She snatched the slate, initialed it, and thrust it back at Finkelstein. If the ship was headed into a black hole, so be it. At least *Lafayette* would go down as tradition demanded with a meritocrat at the helm.

Finkelstein, still grinning, took the slate, and tugged his forelock before returning the slate to the chart table, where it was immediately seized by a yeoman and replaced with a blank one. So that was what she had been supposed to do. As Finkelstein retrieved the clean slate, Parker felt a hesitant tingle at the base of her skull.

Parker sprang to her feet. She might not know the details of bridge procedure, but she knew one rule that held for Colonials anywhere in the Navy. "Not you dare, sailor!" Her metallic voice rang out in the silence of the bridge. "You think-talk me, it be one word, you be in brig."

Finkelstein grew rigid, tugged his forelock repeatedly, and returned to his post. Everyone on the bridge turned and stared. "Eyes to front!" Her voice cracked as she fought to control her larynx. The sailors obeyed. Parker sank into her chair and found she was trembling.

Why did it have to be Finkelstein on this watch? There were all sorts of special rules for Colonials. Refraining from think-talk was only the most obvious. As a physician, Parker wasn't much concerned with them. Except for checking out Finkelstein's fitness and his rigging she couldn't be sure of anything about him. Were sailors supposed to communicate at all before they were addressed? Would it have been proper for him to try to sign to her if he wanted to say something? Not that she'd be able to make out much of hand signals right now in this light.

She gripped the *Watch Officers Guide* firmly to keep her hands steady. Around her sailors made their readings and scratched on their slates. Otherwise the bridge was again perfectly silent. Gradually, Parker calmed herself. In the final analysis, none of this was her responsibility. It was Steele's. The captain knew perfectly well that a physician could not effectively stand watch. Parker was here because Steele had confidence in Finkelstein. The regulations said a meritocrat must always be in control of the helm, but Parker's presence was a formality. She could now see Finkelstein as he moved from station to station, transferring data from each to his slate. It was like watching an orchestra play under the direction of the first violin with a vacant podium. Good enough for the morning watch with the ship drifting. Good enough unless the crew got used to it and it gave them ideas.

Parker sighed. A Colonial on the bridge. An historic first. A token. She hoped this double duty would end soon. For tonight, if she saw anyone saunter up to the helm carrying an armload of dynamite, she'd know enough to rouse the captain. Gradually, her breathing slowed and she began to relax.

One bell sounded — 0430. Finkelstein returned to her side. This time she initialed the slate and handed him the fresh one without looking at it or him. Reaching into her pocket she found her rosary was still there. For the rest of the watch, Parker silently told her beads and watched the stars streak across the heavens.

* * *

The orders were to wake the captain at seven bells. Steward Alice Little placed the breakfast tray on the cabin table and turned on the sun porthole. The thin grey light of a clear December dawn seeped into the cabin. The captain did not stir.

Little had joined the Navy at the beginning of the Second Galaxy War because she wanted to make the universe safe for hominids. On the aptitude tests, she'd scored high on selflessness and empathy, almost as high as a meritocrat. But she tested low on strength and very low on physical courage. On the third deck, they still called her Chicken. For that reason, the Marine Corps, which was the service most human volunteers joined, wouldn't take her. But the recruiters told her that the Navy could use anyone, so she decided to take them up on it.

At first glance, the results of Little's aptitude tests suggested her greatest talents had little military application: the top three were infant care, domestic arts, and elementary education. But the Navy was very adaptable. Her first assignment was as an orderly in the isolation ward. Unfortunately, being around sick people made her feel sick. Her next assignment was in the barnyard, caring for piglets. She lasted there only a week; she couldn't stand thinking about the cute little things growing up to be killed for food. She cried all the time, which upset the sows. Finally she was transferred to Katie McDougall's section in food services and trained as a steward.

At first she hadn't liked that. Almost all the other sailors in that specialty were Colonials, but Chief McDougall, who was human, had persuaded her it was a good opportunity. Little did like feeding people; and once you got to know them, it wasn't bad working with Colonials. Besides, McDougall had said, as a human she could get promoted fast if she did a good job. Now she had a shot at yellow stripes if she pleased Captain Steele.

The middle-aged steward had never been this close to Steele before except during inspections; and then it was the officer, not the sailor, who did the inspecting. Nevertheless, Little had always privately thought that the ship's newest officer was the most adorable thing she had ever seen — a small rounded figure, prematurely greying blonde curls, and large intensely blue eyes. When she dropped her quarterdeck face, as she did more frequently than most officers, she had a smile that was pure joy, a smile so brilliant it seemed it could light the universe.

A night of bloodshed and a few hours of restless sleep had not helped Steele's looks. The curls were matted on a sodden pillow. The captain had cried herself to sleep. When the blue eyes opened, they would be red and swollen; and Little felt sure that there would be no smile this morning. Little sighed, aware that her own eyes and nose were red. This was not a happy morning for *Lafayette*.

The captain was sleeping the sleep of exhaustion. Little wished she could let her sleep until noon and then bring her camomile tea in bed and treat the sore eyes with cotton balls soaked in cornflower water, but those were not the orders. She called the captain's name, several times, and then shook her shoulder until she came awake.

As she returned to consciousness, Steele was first aware of pain: physical pain in her throbbing head and an excruciating mixture of grief, horror, disgust and other sensations she could not put a name to that burned under her heart. Vivid memories of heaped corpses and the metallic odor of fresh blood imposed themselves between her and her surroundings with a finality that said they would be with her forever.

Then she noticed the steward.

"Mickey — Chief McCarthy — is he all right?"

"He's being kept in sickbay, ma'am. The doctors think he needs a few days of bed rest." As do you, Captain Steele, Little thought, but the ship can't spare you for that.

"And you're his stand-in?" Steele did smile, after all. She recalled that this steward was widely known as Chicken, and the plump little woman was peering at her through intense black eyes exactly like a mother hen inspecting a chick. Delighted by the smile, Little smiled back.

"If you sign off on the paperwork, ma'am, I'm his replacement. Chief McCarthy has requested a transfer to the main galley, and Doctor Gordon already approved it."

"I see. Well, I'm awake now, Little. You can go."

"With respect, ma'am, Doctor Gordon said I was to stay with you until you'd finished your breakfast."

Steele glanced at the tray with distaste.

"You'll like it, ma'am, really you will. It's special this morning because of it being Christmas. There's even real coffee for you. The prescription is under the pot." The "prescription" turned out to be a formal memo:

To: Captain
From: Med/Life Director
Subject: You

The Navy doesn't have a form for this kind of memo; but this satisfied Captain Brook, so it should satisfy you.
1. Eat your breakfast. That is an order.
2. Take the medication on your tray. It includes one cup of coffee and two tablets of acetylsalicylic acid. That is also an order.
3. Mudd is optional this morning, so long as you drink it when Little brings it to you later in the day.
4. I've told Little I'll hold her personally responsible if you fail to obey orders 1. and 2. She'd like to keep this job. If she doesn't, it will be your fault.
5. From now on you're going to get a lot more attention from me than you're used to. You won't like it; neither did Brook. If you want to make it easy on yourself, let Little carry out my orders the way McCarthy did. You'll see less of me that way.

Steele sipped her coffee as she read. Little sighed with relief.

* * *

Chief Yeoman Timothy Tinling found his niche in the Navy early in life. A small, now elderly man with a taste for detail and excellent penmanship, Tinling suffered from an unusual physical impairment: myopia. One of the unequivocal successes of twenty-first century medicine was correction of faulty vision; but the surgical techniques did not work on Tinling. By all objective standards, his eyes were normal; but he was psychologically predisposed habitually to focus them no farther than a few feet from the end of his nose. He was the only person on the ship who owned a pair of eyeglasses. He wore them to watch Monday night football; he didn't need them for his work.

Tinling enjoyed a benefit of defective vision during the summary hearings aboard *Pagan Queen.* He heard screams and sounds of chopping from across the deck but saw only his neat record of trials and convictions. The yeoman continued working through the night. Catastrophes always generated paperwork. He rounded it up and sorted it out for the new captain, arranging it exactly as he always did for Captain Brook, in four baskets precisely aligned on one side of the large desk that dominated the day cabin. Two additional baskets — one for recycling and one for Tinling's further attention — were set out on the other side.

The baskets were arranged in the order Brook liked to attack his work. Basket one was Routine — all the masses of department reports and logs that Brook would speed-read and sign off on. This morning it contained the paperwork normally directed to every department head as well as that for the captain. Tinling pulled out duplicates and non-essentials and got it all into the single basket.

Basket two was Important and Urgent. Nothing *really* important and urgent ever went into that basket because the captain was always called immediately to deal with a genuine crisis. The second basket held any crisis that could be confined to paper. Five death certificates were there; the mortuary needed the captain's approval of a cremation order and wanted instruction on funeral arrangements.

Basket three, Important but not Urgent, included the priorities Brook had set for the upcoming day's work; his primary concern was the engines. To this, Tinling had added a memo in Steele's own hand suggesting possible short-cuts for calculating the ship's position based on observations she had recorded during the middle watch.

The fourth basket was for matters that were Trivial but Urgent, requiring a command decision within a few hours. Steele perversely decided to start with that one. Tinling made note of that for future reference and left her alone to get on with it.

Sergeant Major Pipp wanted instruction on morning inspection. Regulations required the presence of an officer if Marines were to administer punishment. Would the captain continue to perform this duty? Yes, she would. There was no one to whom she could delegate it. But not this morning. She decided to cancel the inspection and allow all defaulters an amnesty for petty offenses in honor of Christmas.

Next, the mortuary wanted permission to display the trophy string from *Pagan Queen* on the gundeck. Gordon had scribbled an endorsement stating that Brook customarily allowed the Naval

Justice Marker to be hung from the Lafayette figurehead on the main mast until he could deposit it in a permanent location.

The NJM was the thing Liz Costello used to call "the Kali necklace." The term was Shankar's invention, a reference to the necklace of human skulls worn by the Indian goddess Kali-Ma. The name had caught on in the *Lafayette* wardroom. The marker was, in fact, a chain of skulls. But unlike the goddess's necklace these were not wide-eyed and bloody. After all, this was a ceremonial artifact of Her Majesty's Navy, not some pagan trinket. The NJM skulls were carefully cleaned of hair and flesh, strung together through the eye sockets with space-tempered wire, and finished off with a large metallic seal. The seal bore the insignia of Earth and a ritual warning concerning the fate of pirates who fell into the hands of the Royal Navy, which, it was implied, patrolled everywhere.

Originally, the Navy had planted these markers in space at the spot a pirate ship was taken; but these soon became so numerous as to pose a hazard to navigation. Current policy required that they be placed either at the pirate's home port, or, if that was "impossible or inconvenient" on any planet or asteroid potentially useful as a pirate base. That meant it could be dumped just about anywhere except inside a black hole.

When pirates were executed on their own ship and that ship was sent into a prize port, the marker stayed on display at the main mast of the pirate vessel for whatever impact it might have on the sailors who had boarded her and served as prize crew. Since *Pagan Queen* had been dismantled and recycled, display aboard *Lafayette* was in order.

This whole business of organic trophies seemed to Steele downright ghoulish, but it was part of the Navy policy of terrorizing pirates. She didn't much relish the idea of reading prayers twice a day with a chain of skulls hanging over her head, but she couldn't think of any reason other than her personal prejudice for breaking with Brook's tradition. She approved the request from the mortuary.

The last matter in the trivial but urgent category concerned the pirates' goat. Steele stared at the amount of paperwork and series of endorsements up the chain of command that this one small animal had engendered since being transferred to *Lafayette* from *Pagan Queen.*

The paper trail began with a petition from mortician's apprentice Billy Ash. It was a rather awkwardly worded plea for the life of the goat, obviously prepared by a yeoman not especially skilled in Colonial sign. The petition was made on behalf of what the yeoman had translated as the Colonial Prayer Fellowship. They, he said, considered the appearance of a goat on Christmas Eve as a message from God, and they would happily pay for what food, water, and oxygen the goat consumed and begged that they might be allowed to visit the animal when it might be convenient for the barnyard crew.

Otto Schmidt's evaluation of the goat was next in the pile. He had examined the animal and pronounced it healthy. He also volunteered that adding a goat to the barnyard would be no special bother. Goats had no special dietary requirements, and it could bunk with the pigs.

Gordon's contribution set out some pros and cons. The ship could spare life support for an additional animal. Earlier requests from Colonials wishing to communicate with either the chickens or the pigs had been denied because the food animals were upset by it. Parker's opinion, set out in an appended memo dated several years earlier, was that being addressed as channels for the Supreme Deity put strange ideas about life and death into the heads of meat animals and spoiled their appetites. Gordon concluded by stating that this precedent was irrelevant since goat meat was not in any of his menu plans.

The whole wad of paper was bucked up to the captain with no recommendation one way or the other from med/life. The animal could live or die; it was up to her.

As she finished reading the goat file, Steele realized tears were rolling down her cheeks. She impatiently wiped them away. Crying about a goat!

She put aside the basket of Trivia and reached for another. There were the death certificates. Abruptly, her professional detachment cracked and the well of emotions that had overwhelmed her the night before flowed over again. She put her head down on crossed arms and sobbed.

The Helmet hovered at the edge of consciousness.

No! Steele jerked herself upright. She wouldn't go back in that iron mask again, not while she had will to carry on without it. Memories of the previous night swam around her: the battle to retake the ship sharp and painful and those of the execution rituals wrapped in cotton wool. Were these her memories or those of the Helmet? Or were they, for the first time, memories belonging to both of them?

The goat. That creature was one part of the *Pagan Queen* crew she could think of without flinching. Trotting out of the captain's cabin, the animal seemed happy to follow Charlie Ames, who collared it with a length of rope. It glanced around the bloody deck as though it had seen it all before, then turned full attention to Ames, butting him from behind in a friendly fashion to get his attention and nuzzling his pockets. Ames and the goat had stumbled together across the planks into the *Lafayette.*

Since it was her decision, there was no way Steele was going to pass a death sentence on the goat. She scribbled out authorization for food and lodging for one ruminant mammal, piled it on top of the other papers in the goat's dossier and tossed the whole thing into the Tinling basket. Let the yeoman decide how much he needed to file.

Tinling later observed that after "Trivial but Urgent," the captain worked on "Important and Urgent" next on "Routine" and had finished off, with "Important but not Urgent." She left the day cabin carrying the navigation notes and spent the rest of the forenoon watch on the bridge.

Reorientation of the ship in the five dimensions of space could be accomplished in two ways: through tedious calculations or by blind luck. After hours of labor on the former, Steele impulsively keyed in coordinates for the last logged entry in Lamashtu's last watch and hit pay dirt.

The last noted random course adjustment coincided with a sharp one, probably intended to be of short duration and to be followed by an equal and opposite compensatory shift. This was the standard pattern for navigating to avoid dust clouds. Whatever happened to Hall must have happened before he returned the course to its original drift. Consequently, *Lafayette* moved during the night in a great circle that had taken them to almost exactly the position they had been in the evening before. It wasn't exact, but it was close enough for Steele to identify one clear starmark and a charted time anomaly. A patient scan of associated space streams brought up a second identifiable star — enough to fix position.

Steele leaned back in her chair and stretched. She felt stiff. Two bells sounded. It was past noon. The watch had changed an hour ago; she hadn't even noticed the bells. Steele rubbed her eyes and then the back of her neck. Looking over toward the quartermaster's station, she saw that the same sailor who had the duty in the forenoon watch was still working. No one had dared disturb her when she was so deeply absorbed or to leave their posts without permission. The whole bridge crew had worked for an hour past their lunch break.

Speaking of lunch, she noticed that someone had put a tray next to her at the chart table. That someone was Alice Little, who was huddled by the rail, trying to stay out of the way of the bridge crew, but clearly intent on getting the food into the captain at the earliest possible opportunity. As soon as she saw Steele come alert, she dashed to her side with a pot of mudd, nearly colliding with the quartermaster who descended on her with the watch log.

Steele dealt with both of their demands simultaneously, even as her attention wandered again. Something had to be done to allow her to concentrate fully when she needed to without paralyzing the whole ship. She cleaned her plate without noticing what was on it and drank a cup of mudd as she watched the two quartermasters now on the bridge arranging to exchange the con while both familiarized themselves with the fresh position entries Steele had just put into the log. Navigation was no longer in crisis. This afternoon, she could worry about personnel.

She set down her mug. With a satisfied cluck, Little picked up the tray and carried it off. Steele put on a pair of dark glasses to protect her night vision and left the bridge.

For eighty percent of the crew, the death of five line officers would scarcely be noticed. Once Parker went back to her regular duties and Gordon was restored to his usual state of poor health, the waisters would work as they always did under the command of familiar med/life officers. The ten percent of the crew that worked either in engineering or on the bridge would easily adjust to the changes Steele had to make. She'd worked closely with the sailors in both sections and knew all the chiefs.

Trouble, if it came, would come on the gundeck. Although they made up a fraction of the crew, the work of the gunners was the reason all the rest of them were in space. If you went strictly by *Naval Regulations*, the ship's junior lieutenant was the one who ought to have been assigned to supervise daily routine on the gundeck. That officer, the book said, had the duty of exercising sailors at the weapons banks and supervising deck maintenance and safety drills at damage control shields and other rigging. Captain Brook had run her training out of sequence by starting her in engineering. All she knew about the gundeck, except booklearning and buried memories from SOCRATES, was what she had picked up in casual conversation with Lieutenant Rivera.

Rivera liked to joke that there was nothing in space more dangerous than idle gunners. These were people who held their jobs because they had an aptitude for killing and a taste for violence. Their training deliberately reenforced these qualities under the euphemism "fighting spirit." Since fighting was the mission of the ship, the minority of sailors who actually worked with weapons enjoyed a superior social status. Yet very little time in space was spent in combat. Life on a warship, as the cliché went, was ninety percent tedium and ten percent terror with nothing in between.

During the tedious times, everyone aboard the ship had useful work except the gunners, who did nothing but maintain their work area and equipment and train to keep their skills up. Rivera liked to refer to his gundeck exercises as "fighting the devil," because he competed with the Lord of Mischief to find work for idle hands. It was a challenge that absorbed him fully. He spent several hours every day with the crews exercising on the gundeck and additional hours working on what he called his "lesson plans." When he went to the wardroom for a mudd break, he usually had a big pigskin binder with him, his personal log, over which he would labor with pen and colored pencils, diagramming drills and recording the results of methods he tested. He might sit for half an hour staring at the pages, running a hand through his cowlick, ignoring the conversation around him and letting his mudd grow cold, and then take off in a fury of scribbling.

Rivera's drills were designed to push his crews to their limit, and then to stretch that limit a little more and then a little more so that excellence was not merely maintained but challenges were increased. The best gunners in the Navy were constantly getting better. That, he insisted, was not merely good for the ship; it was also the best way to keep drill from becoming boring.

The construction of drills depended upon Rivera's intimate knowledge of his sailors. He knew them as a gundeck team, as members of a gun station, as members of a weapon crew, and as individual hominids. He was famous for working out a hypothetical situation in which, as it was played out, the survival of the ship came to depend on the activity at one gun, or even on the action of a single sailor.

Each of the nine gunner's mates could recall an occasion when just as they were about to put a sailor on report for slacking off, an exercise would be called that left that individual the focus of several hundred pairs of eyes as he or she failed to do what the situation called for. Rivera told a story about a sailor they called Birdie, whom he was determined to salvage even though the mate at his station thought should be sent down to work solid waste. Rivera had drawn power to holograph a drill. When it was over, and everyone was staring at Birdie, Rivera started up the replay the way they reran fumbles in Monday night football, and Birdie got to watch himself single-handedly losing the ship. Birdie never lost his concentration during drills again after that.

Many of Rivera's exercises postulated catastrophic damage to the ship. Long-range weapons might have to be aimed without computer support or short-range cannon need to be dragged through an air-lock and remounted on the hull. In his scenarios, it was common to have the helm lose power, putting the ship in stays or to have a whole bank of weapon ports jam. When drilling small teams, he often hypothesized extensive damage to the gundeck itself so that damage-control partitions had to be dropped and two or three weapon banks had to reload fast enough to do the work of nine. He even, on occasion, postulated his own death, giving the mates experience in putting one of their own in overall command and dividing up responsibility for the abandoned station.

But never had Rivera postulated a situation in which gunner's mates would be left alone for an extended period. They might do twenty minutes of hot action, taking orders direct from the bridge, but that was their limit for initiative. To expect self-direction — or even self-control — beyond that, was absurd. Even Rivera, with his enthusiasm for the potential in commoners, would not expect gunner's mates to keep the devil at bay for long in the absence of supervision.

Steele went in search of Rivera's log. Perhaps something in there would help her decide what to do. It would be better to send all the gunners below to work in life support where Gordon and Parker could keep an eye on them than to leave them as loose cannon around the weapon banks.

Rivera's log was easy to find. It lay open on the table in his cabin with his pen resting next to it. He'd been working on it just before going to the wardroom for Christmas dinner. Like her own, the first officer's cabin was sparsely furnished and contained few personal items. Steele noticed one family photograph — two little boys and a girl dressed in Scout uniforms and grinning at the camera. The younger boy had a cowlick falling over one eye.

Steele's guilty sense of intruding on the dead man's privacy was heightened when she looked at the log and discovered he had been writing about her. Rivera was designing a round of training exercises — it seemed to be a three month plan — all for the benefit of Lieutenant Steele. First she was just to observe and read selections from a long list of books; each assignment had a set of study questions. The next stage hypothesized damage control situations, with the gundeck divided, putting Steele in command of two weapon banks as Rivera worked the others. Then Rivera began repeatedly plotting his death from a variety of causes giving the mates about ten minutes on their own before Steele took over. In the margins by the last series of drills, Rivera had posed some questions for himself, mostly relating to SOCRATES. He was hoping to find some way gently to trigger it in the course of an exercise in which the premises would be horrific enough even though the death and destruction were only hypothetical.

Underneath all the dramatic scenarios, Steele could recognize the fundamental lessons that were run over and over again in different combinations: safety rules, concentration, speed, automatic performance of by-the-numbers drills for operating specific weapons systems and boarding launches, doing more than one thing at a time and doing both right, staying cool even under circumstances designed to produce burn-out. It was almost as if Rivera had been writing formula holograph scripts for a thriller series. Looking at the coming attractions, Steele had no idea how most of them could be resolved.

Steele leafed through the older entries, where Rivera recorded how well the crews performed on each exercise and what he and they had learned from it. This looked more promising. If the gunners drilled on reruns, they might miss the excitement of Rivera's cliff-hangers, but it would certainly keep them busy, and she'd have the help of Rivera's notes to determine whether they'd got it right.

Steele flipped to the beginning of the volume and skimmed through, flagging exercises in which Rivera had killed himself off fairly early in the drill. She could rework these well enough to keep them busy for a while. Then, if necessary, she'd just make them do reruns indefinitely.

That decided, there was only one further problem. She could set the assignments, but she couldn't spend all her time watching them. If the sailors weren't watched, they'd all be gold-bricking. That was the nature of sailors. Now that no meritocrats were available to supervise gundeck drills, the only thing to do was to call in the Marines.

The Marines wouldn't like this duty. Standing motionless at positions on the gundeck as sailors scurried through drills that were entirely meaningless to Marines would be a crashing bore. Besides, it was extra work for the Corps, and the leathernecks were no fonder of extra duty than any other commoners. So she'd have to find some way to motivate the Marines to accept the unusual assignment.

Steele carried Rivera's log to the day cabin and sent a runner for the sergeant major. It was time to try out the theory she'd learned in Psychology 169: Marine Motivation.

* * *

Sergeant Major Philip Pipp had been trying for hours to think of an excuse for calling on the captain. He was uncomfortable cut loose from his familiar chain of command. Marine officers did not accompany the forces assigned to ships. The soldiers were an adjunct to the command of the gunner. Although the Marines were proud to be trusted to deploy without meritocratic officers and to manage their own affairs through the hierarchy of non-commissioned officers, Pipp, being at the top of that hierarchy, understood the vulnerability of his position.

You made rank in the Marine Corps by doing exactly what you were told, and, as far as possible, anticipating what you might be told so you could do it quickly enough to impress your immediate superior. Pipp's forte was anticipating orders, which he did by carefully studying those who gave them. He had both Rivera and Brook nicely figured out and had also studied Costello, Hall, and Lamashtu just in case. But Steele had never been assigned where he could watch her closely.

In the hours since the change of command, Pipp had tried to get information from his subordinates, so far as he felt he could do so without loss of dignity, but he hadn't learned much. They said Steele was squeamish about corporal punishment, even more than most of the officers. Pipp hoped that didn't mean she was going to clog up the brig.

Before responding to the call from the captain, Pipp took a few moments to retire to his quarters and check out his rigging. He hadn't become Sergeant Major by underestimating the importance of appearances. He inspected his small, slim form and approved: straight, strac, and suitably hairy. Self-conscious about the baldness that made him, he felt, too much resemble some newly pressed swabby, he cultivated a large bristling moustache that seemed a larger version of his remarkably bushy eyebrows. His image was perfect, he was ready to meet the new captain.

Steele was ready for the meeting too. The dark glasses she wore were functional — if she was needed on the bridge, she wanted no delay in regaining her night vision — but they also helped hide any emotion that might otherwise penetrate a quarterdeck face.

Pipp reported with a formal flourish. Rather than match his military manner, Steele stepped from behind her desk, greeted him warmly with a handshake, and ushered him to a chair. Then she returned to her seat and swiveled her chair to face him. She was aware of the large holograph windows behind her. Gordon had given them a bright Christmas day. Behind the windows, brilliant sunlight glinted from the whitecaps as the ship appeared to roll and pitch in a fresh wind. It made Pipp squint. Steele leaned back, steepled her fingers, and smiled. Pipp sat rigid in his chair as she expected him to. Nothing made Marines so tense as being invited to relax.

"I would like your advice, Sergeant Major. You command a fighting force yourself, so I feel that I can speak to you freely about my present dilemma. The gundeck crew is currently without leadership."

She paused. Pipp's moustache twitched. Because of its size, the bushy adornment revealed more than he imagined. It gave a whole new meaning to keeping a stiff upper lip. Pipp did not like being asked for advice. He might be held responsible for the results if it was followed. Besides, he couldn't tell what the captain was driving at so he couldn't be sure what she wanted to hear. Yes, Rivera was dead, but Steele wasn't. Therefore the gundeck had leadership. There was a lengthening silence. Pipp responded in the only way he could think of.

"Yes, Captain, ma'am," he barked.

Steele appeared not to notice his hesitation. "So of course," she resumed smoothly, "some major changes must be made." She reached across the desk and pulled the model of *Lafayette* closer, fingering the bright regularly pitted ring that represented the gundeck with its armored weapon banks at the ready. "It would be a mistake to spike the cannon, don't you agree?"

Pipp coughed and rubbed his nose vigorously. He didn't know beans about Naval weaponry, but spiking the armament of a ship deployed in a war zone certainly appeared to be unwise. And since the captain had already indicated what her opinion was, he risked saying so.

"I'm so glad you see it that way. While I am sure your force is quite capable of dealing effectively with any disruption that might result should gunners be assigned to work in unskilled assignments on the third deck, it really would be a great pity to draw our teeth, so to speak."

Pipp thought furiously. Steele was speaking to him as one military leader to another, which was enormously flattering. He was not about to confess he hadn't a clue what she was talking about, if he could possibly figure it out well enough to fake it. What in Hades did he know about the gun crews? Well, they fought the ship. Without them, you might as well spike the cannon. Also, they tended to make more trouble than the rest of the crew combined. When there were fights to break up or some controlled substance turned up missing, odds were that the culprit would be someone with the guncrew. Not always, but often enough to put the lot of them on the short list of usual suspects. The humans were as bad as the Colonials. Definitely not the sort of people he would want to go into battle with, not the Marine sort at all. But suppose he was stuck with them as Captain Steele was. Well, he jolly well wouldn't want them roaming loose near anything dangerous unless he kept a good eye on them.

So that was what she was driving at. Rivera not only provided leadership on the gundeck, he also policed it. The Marines were always on call, of course, but the first officer's presence kept the sailors at their work and orderly. The captain couldn't spend all her time supervising the deck; she had to drive the ship and that sort of thing. She couldn't let the gunners just run wild. Someone would have to look after them.

"Your Marines will always stand ready to do their duty, ma'am, and to see that the sailors do theirs."

"Splendid." She pushed the ship model back to its place. "Gunners need constant employment to keep them physically fit, usefully occupied, and sufficiently tired at the end of the watch to keep them from getting into trouble during their free time." She steepled her fingers again and slowly swiveled her chair so she faced away from Pipp. "I've been considering having the gunners participate in the Marine Corps training exercises. How does that strike you?"

Steele knew perfectly well how it would strike the sergeant major. She didn't have to watch him to know he was about to swallow his whiskers. The marching and drills that the Marines practiced were far more than exercise for them. Their band music and close order routines symbolized the pride of the Corps. It would be sacrilege to have sailors stepping out to the beat of a Sousa march. If sailors could do it, it wouldn't mean anything to be a Marine.

Pipp made a sound between choking and coughing. "Training sailors in Marine exercises would be — ah, uhm. It would be unusual, ma'am."

"Ah, well, perhaps I am asking too much. It would, indeed, be difficult to train sailors in rifle maneuvers. You couldn't be expected to do it."

Pipp and his moustache bristled. "We could do it, ma'am. It might take a while to get them looking strac, but they'd be trainable." Pipp had a terrible picture in his head of sailors — including Colonials — sharing the sacred experience of mustering for a drill sergeant. "I would only observe that . . . Training sailors with rifles and bayonets . . . Well, it might not be . . . it might not be prudent, ma'am."

"Oh? Why not? Are your safety precautions inadequate? Would sailors be apt to injure themselves in training? If so, the drills themselves might be . . ."

"No, ma'am!" Pipp interrupted. Cripes! If she ordered the Marine drills halted as overly dangerous, he'd have trouble keeping his people out of mischief! "The drills are perfectly safe. It's only that teaching sailors how to use such weapons . . . ."

"Well, surely such knowledge would pose no danger so long as they never have unauthorized access to them. Is there any question of security in the arsenal?"

Steele watched Pipp from behind her dark glasses. He was certainly a textbook Marine. He was on the defensive — hit from three directions at once. He was terrified that sailors might be forced on his drill teams but couldn't say so. At the same time, he was challenged to guarantee the safety of bayonet drills and to give assurances that the Marine guards were not slacking off on the job in the most sensitive area of the ship. He was ripe for her to surface her real agenda.

"Of course, there is another possibility." Steele stifled a smile by frowning. Pipp's eyebrows were twitching as he leaned forward expectantly. "I hesitate even to suggest it because it would mean considerably more work for your force."

"The Marines are not afraid of hard work, ma'am," Pipp replied eagerly. Nothing could be worse than putting sailors into a Marine dress parade.

When *Lafayette*'s Marines mustered for evening inspection, Sergeant Major Pipp made them a little speech and explained the alternatives. There was considerable enthusiasm for the order to double guards everywhere in the ship and patrol the gundeck watch on watch.

CHAPTER SIXTEEN

Above the gundeck, the constellations of Earth's winter sky twinkled dimly, outshone by the brightness of a full moon. On a night such as this, sailors by tradition had the right to go on deck. Tonight, the air was cold and the aereographer's mates pumped it across the deck in sharp gusts. Only those with serious business to attend to took advantage of the opportunity to sit under the starry sky.

The gunner's mates and the Colonial coven, all wrapped in their warmest clothing, squatted in separate circles as practiced hands shuffled cards and slapped them on the deck. The humans kept up a murmured conversation.

"Sergeant Major's got the wind up. Double guards." Wendovski studied his hand, rearranged the cards and raised the bid by two coins.

"Sergeant Major doesn't double guards without orders. It's the captain that's got the wind up." Newcastle saw the bid and raised it another two coins.

"I'd hope she would. I wouldn't trust us sitting up here tonight, would you?" Petrov folded.

"Hell no, but I'm no meritocrat." Newcastle scooped in the pot. Dover dealt another round. Bids were seen and raised. Barcelona threw in her hand.

"I got a bad feeling about this. One officer for a ship full of scum." Bitterschoen chewed his lip, glanced at Petrov whose face was a studied blank, and threw down his cards. "In her place, know what I'd do? I'd shut down the gundeck and send us all below, down to the bilges to muck out after the pigs, that's what I'd do."

"Yeah, I been thinking the same thing."

"No fighting, no prize money." Wendowski counted his coins and decided to fold.

"So don't rub it in! What can we do about it?" Raven Bigfoot looked at the two pairs in her hand, looked at Petrov, and added another coin to the pot.

"There must be something. Shit! I'm counting on a potful of money out of this voyage." Petrov saw the bid and raised. "I've probably got to swallow the anchor after this one. The medics don't think I'd get certified fit for another. I got only sixteen years toward a pension. I need enough for a down payment on a burial plot on Earth."

"I been on ships with just one meritocrat — a captain and a sailor medic. We did okay. Fought just as well." The others might not need the cash as badly as Petrov, but they all had plans for prize money.

"Sure! Some sloop or frigate with a few hundred, maybe a thousand sailors. We got five times that many. Five times as much trouble. Five officers plus a captain like we had was what we needed to keep a taut ship."

Petrov and Dover split the pot.

"Maybe we could, kind of like 'help,'" Newcastle suggested.

"That's a laugh," Barcelona studied her cards and smiled smugly. It was a shitty hand.

"What's so funny?"

"How you going to help, Coal? You got yourself some 'meritocratic instincts?'"

"I don't need no 'instincts' to know how meritocrats like things done on the ship. I don't do them all, but I know what they are. You know: Iron your underwear. Wash behind your ears. When you haven't got anything else to do, paint something or polish the brightwork. Hey, it doesn't make any sense, but when everyone's jumping to do things the way officers want, that's when you've got a taut ship. So, I'm just saying that maybe if everybody acts like every day was a major inspection or something, the captain would decide she's still got good discipline and leave us alone."

The gunners looked at each other. It wasn't a bad idea. "Yeah. We could just kind of let the word get around that we're expanding our interests," said Petrov. "Tuck in your shirt or get your nose busted."

The rules aboard a warship were legion. Even a full complement of officers and Marines never managed to get everyone to obey all of them all the time. But the gunners had an advantage. Sailors knew exactly how much they could get away with under lawful authority and pushed it to the limit. The justice of their messmates, however, was unpredictable and usually disproportionate; it didn't pay to challenge it.

"How long have we got? How long you figure it'll be before she tells us we're getting transfers?" Bitterschoen was dealing.

"How long before one of your dumb sailors blows up a cannon?" Bigfoot tossed her thick black pigtail over her shoulder and bid one coin.

"What do you mean by that, Pittypat? I got fewer apes working my station than you have."

"Well it wasn't no Colonial in my bank taking over a laser and jamming a door on the last drill. The apes in my section know their place."

"Cool it!" The rising volume of voices had brought a Marine pacing around the circle, leather boots striking the wooden deck. Wendovski turned and snarled; the Marine backed off.

"We gotta deal them in, you know. Won't work if we don't deal them in."

"Is that you talking, Coal? You become some kind of ape-lover all of a sudden?"

"Don't have to love them to know we need them. If the gundeck doesn't shape up, we go down below; maybe lose our stripes too. How many 'accidents' can you arrange without med/life starting to poke around?"

The next hand was played in silence as the gunners considered this limitation on their enforcement powers. Occasionally one or another turned to look speculatively at the circle of Colonials tossing cards on the deck by the main mast.

* * *

"Botulism," Shadow suggested. Death crossed the Page of Cups. The thirteen Colonials squatted around the cards and considered the implications of the layout.

"Too easy to trace."

"Is there anyone in the galley we could set up, Millie?"

"No one I'd want to see hang." Millicent Tang washed dishes for the starboard mess. The humans in the galley were very decent for squawkers.

Shadow shuffled and spread the cards again. This time the Devil crossed the Page of Cups. "Salmonella, then. You've got that around anywhere there's dead meat. Hellcat always has her fingers in her mouth."

"That won't kill her unless we're awfully lucky." Wilhelmina Martinez scooped sand in the barnyard and knew whereof she spoke. The next spread featured the nine of cups reversed.

"I've never heard you ladies so bloody-minded." Billy Katz broke into the conversation. "She's just a child, probably didn't realize what she was doing."

The twelve women thought at him all at once, then deferred to Martinez. "Even if it hadn't been our lovely goat she was teasing, it's high time someone put a stop to this dreadful behavior. It's not the first time she's tormented some helpless animal. Chief Schmidt won't do anything about it. I've reported her, and other people have too. Not just Colonials either. The blabbermouths are just as upset. But the mate keeps making excuses for her. I can't imagine why. He's just like you, saying she's only a child, and it's not worth taking to the officers."

"Men are so sappy about children. Especially girl children," said Shadow. She reshuffled the cards and laid out a full spread around the Page of Cups. Death and the Devil both came up again. The spread was a powerful one with four other major arcana cards. The only light-colored cards to appear were reversed. The reading was self-explanatory.

"Becky Petrie is not an ordinary child," Shadow commented unecessarily. "She's only going to get worse as she gets older." She pointed to where the Tower and Moon cards were juxtaposed near the top of the spread. "Eliminating her now is a service to the Navy. As Colonials we have a special obligation to support the war effort."

The appeal to patriotism satisfied Katz. Shadow spread the cards again. "A soup, perhaps," Tang suggested. "Rummage around a bit in the bilges. There must be forty or fifty things that could plausibly be traced to the barnyard. If one doesn't work, another may do the job."

* * *

When the engine repair was complete, Steele put *Lafayette* on course for a star the Admiralty charts identified as Twinkle. The star owed its name to a three-year-old boy, who, early in the twenty-first century had won the right to name a star because his grandfather contributed $5000 to NASA. Twinkle had seemed to him a good name at the time, and there had never been reason to change it.

Twinkle was by no means a major star. Barely visible from Earth, it wasn't any great shakes close up either. It had no planets, no physical anomalies, and comparatively little energy. Twinkle was just a run-of-the-mill fueling station, far off the main space routes, that would do for recharging if a ship happened to be in the neighborhood. *Lafayette* moved into a close docking orbit at the end of January and began the tedious business of topping off the batteries.

Black sails spread, *Lafayette* circled Twinkle. Then circled again. And again. With velocity constant with respect to the rest of the galaxy, the monotony of weather and tactical observations exhausted the bridge crews and left virtually nothing to be done in engineering.

Steele found her paperwork took less time every morning. Even the Routine basket now had little in it. The sick book entries were few; most of the sailors who turned out for sick call had only minor complaints and were treated and released the same day. Becky Petrie was the only long-term occupant of sickbay. The punishments book showed a sharply increased number of entries after the Marines began their crackdown. Then the number fell to the usual level, and then it suddenly plummeted. All over the ship, sailors were reporting for duty promptly, avoiding citations for tardiness or shirking, and even passing unannounced inspections with clean fingernails and neatly folded handkerchiefs. Steele couldn't understand how the Marines had managed that, but this deviation from normal behavior certainly did not constitute a problem.

Even on the bridge, where sailors were accustomed to work directly under the demanding eyes of meritocrats, hands pushed themselves to an even higher level of readiness. Although it was always too dark to see, Steele was aware of sailors paying unusual attention to the brightwork; she could smell the metal polish.

As a Lieutenant, Steele had followed the watch bill. Now every watch was hers. Except for the routines of morning prayers and evening reports, the passing hours did not dictate any particular activity. Her elevation to command made social calls on Doctor Parker inappropriate; there was no one to chat with in the wardroom. As weeks passed, *Lafayette* circled Twinkle, and her captain spent the days hunched over the chart table, plotting the course that would take them to the Pegasus station.

Steele immediately scrapped Captain Brook's plan, the one she had studied ever since she came aboard. Brook had deliberately chosen an indirect route to the fleet rendezvous. Steele knew that those of her Naval Academy classmates assigned to the forward fleet would have arrived there by transport months ago. *Lafayette* was going the long way around and would approach Pegasus through the Delphinian ring with its plentiful star clusters, deliberately provoking an attack from enemy vessels on patrol or docked at port planets.

The big battleships represented Earth's greatest tactical advantage in the war: superior firepower. The Delphinian Navy, operating closer to home, had an advantage in numbers, speed and maneuverability. A fleet of frigates could do in a dreadnought that couldn't turn and run when it needed to. But *Lafayette*, with her newly installed modifications, was something new. She was big, but she was also maneuverable — the retreat from Mantu proved that. The gun crews had been drilling constantly on tactical refinements that took advantage of the ship's special abilities. Brook indended to arrive at the rendezvous at Pegasus with an armada of prizes in convoy and an army of prisoners for exchange.

Steele recalled intense discussions in the wardroom, anticipation of a few months of glory for *Lafayette* before the dreadnought passed under the command of the Admiral of the Forward Fleet and had her wings clipped. The big ship would skip in and out of enemy solar systems with the impudence of a frigate. In their enthusiasm, Steele remembered, they spoke as if *Lafayette* might turn the tide of the war singlehanded.

And so she might have. But not now. Not with an untried officer in command. Forced to make her own decision on her own fitness, Steele agreed with Captain Brook. She wouldn't trust the ship to what she knew of the Helmet. She couldn't fault the Helmet's ability to act or its competence on the one occasion it had taken control, but supervising a mass execution was no proof that the Helmet had sufficient skill or appropriate experience to assume full tactical command of *Lafayette.* Steele sure didn't have it; and with her old messmates gone, there would be no one to help set the Helmet straight if it went off course.

Although it went against all her training and instincts, Steele couldn't justify adhering to Brook's plan. So she studied alternatives, routes to minimize rather than maximize the chance of contact with the enemy, routes that would bring *Lafayette* under the protection of the fleet sooner rather than later.

Searching the charts, Steele returned repeatedly to a set which, to an unpracticed eye, would appear perfectly blank, the set covering what was known as The Great Void. Of all sectors of known space, it was among the least frequently travelled, for the obvious reason that there was virtually nothing there. Rarely, a ship off course and in distress found a passage through the Void the only feasible way to get from one port to another. These voyages provided the data for the Admiralty charts and proved that the crossing was possible.

Steele powered the computer to get the complete records of these crossings. Logs of ships much smaller and slower than *Lafayette*, ships without such modern luxuries as weather control and holographic sun ports, told how hominids had survived the long passage across the barren strip of space. The crossings were harrowing experiences, months in a vast well of space so empty of stars that it had once been thought to be a black hole. The Void wasn't that, although charts showed a few holes buried still deeper in the blackness.

Steele looked at these carefully. Black holes could be milked for power, but the procedure was dangerous, and going anywhere near them meant storms for certain and possibly other unpleasant surprises. Best avoid the holes and stick to what was the most clearly marked route. From Twinkle to Last Chance. Then to the almost dead red giant discouragingly named Dead Red. It would take aeons to draw a charge from such a star. A ship would expend more on survival needs while trying to load a battery than the starshine could ever make up. Still, Dead Red was worth a flyby to pick up what little there was. For the ships that had made it across the Great Void, Dead Red was a beacon, even its dim glow a relief after months of unrelieved blackness. From Dead Red there was no choice. Only one small yellow star in the Void before a final push to the region where the galaxy thickened to normal density within striking distance of Enif, the outpost of the Pegasus Station.

Lafayette lingered in orbit around Twinkle until the main batteries and backups were charged full. Then, with silver sails gleaming, the ship headed for Last Chance and the Great Void.

* * *

While the captain plotted a course, life aboard *Lafayette* went on as usual. The sailors complained about the food and the weather and the godawfulness of life in the Navy. They gossiped about their messmates, plotted revenge against Marines and planned how they'd spend their pay if they ever got leave. Meanwhile, the Marines, suspicious of unprecedented excesses of good order and discipline and not to be outdone, saw to their drills and duties with fierce intensity. The chickens and pigs ate and scratched, procreated and fussed over their offspring in their usual fashion. The goat pondered the meaning of life.

The pirate goat was neither more nor less intelligent than other members of its species. If left to itself, it would not have indulged in philosophical speculation. But it was not left to itself. The Colonials who paid its food bills visited during the dog watches, bringing special treats and filling its brain with odd thoughts. These it chewed and digested mindlessly along with the goodies.

For a month, the goat let the thoughts dance through its grey matter. Then, one afternoon, it dawned on the animal that the creatures resembling its old *Pagan Queen* shipmates were attempting to communicate. It was a momentous occasion for all parties. The Colonials explained their role in Goat's life. They provided the fodder in the manger and the delicious morsels from the galley garbage bins. They had caused the disappearance of the small two-legged animal that the goat, now that it realized it was gone, was glad to hear was not expected to come back. In return, all the Colonials asked was for Goat to tell them the meaning of life. It seemed churlish to refuse.

Between farts and belches, the goat shared some of its most cherished memories.

"Maaa," said the goat.

"Something's coming! Oh, Ash! This is so exciting! The goat is having a thought!"

"Well, shut down your own, damnit! Let the rest of us hear!"

Minds as blank as they could make them, the Colonials stared at the goat, which shook itself, pranced around its pen, defecated, and had another thought.

"'Goat wants nurse,'" Hotchkins translated slowly. "What do you imagine that means? Oh, I do hope the goat isn't sick? Should we get a vet?"

"Will you be quiet?" Shadow hissed the thought and to emphasize it flashed the sign for "shut up." The Colonials waited as the goat settled down to chew its cud and review its thought.

"It's a special nurse it wants. Ash, did you see a nurse aboard *Pagan Queen*?"

"From what I saw on that garbage scow, I don't think they had any medical/life support specialists. The goat was their one-animal recycling crew."

Goat filtered these foreign ideas through its own brain and surfaced another memory.

"That's it! Oh, the poor dear! Of course! They used to have two goats."

"And something happened to the other one. Nurse. No, Nanny." The Colonials joined in sympathy, and the goat washed up another wave of memory.

"Oh, how awful! Ash, didn't you tell us, the pirates were low on food? Do you think our goat knows . . ."

"Well, it will if you keep spewing your thoughts out while it's in the loop with us."

Goat hadn't the faintest idea what they were thinking about. It blinked and chewed and remembered Nanny.

Hotchkins sighed. "That is so beautiful. The goat knows what heaven is."

The goat recalled its mate and its mother, then noticed a bit of synthetic wood from the fence that had fallen into the hay. Goat snapped it up and munched. The image of heaven faded.

* * *

Having set the course for the ship, Steele had completed the last of her urgent duties. Inspections of the gundeck and engineering crews could only be made so often; her presence made the sailors nervous and interfered with their work. During the long, dull passages before the massacre, the officers — especially the junior lieutenant — always had something to do. The captain saw to that. She realized now that developing training plans for his officers gave the captain useful occupation. Steele had no one she could appropriately instruct.

Steele wished she had someone she could tutor in deep space navigation. It would have been interesting to teach this science to some of the bridge crew. A few certainly appeared to have an aptitude. But navigation was forbidden knowledge. Members of the lower orders in the Navy could never have a legitimate use for it. Even if the knowledge did not corrupt, tempting its possessor to desert and sell the skill to pirates, a navigator was a valuable commodity and so a target for kidnappers. Better not to lead the lower orders into temptation; keep navigation to meritocrats.

Steele considered suggesting to Doctor Parker that she study deep space navigation. Lessons would allow them to spend time together. But Steele knew this was a selfish thought and would not be fair to the physician. Suggestions from the captain were orders. Work might be slow on the top deck, but it continued at its usual brisk pace on the third.

After Steele permitted Parker to resign her temporary field commission, neither had an excuse to exchange more than a few words with the other until *Lafayette* approached Last Chance. Normally, communications from med/life were directed through the senior officer, but Parker would lead any team that went down to one of this star's planets. She got to present med/life's requests. The two women faced each other over the captain's desk in the day cabin, both aware of the friendship they had briefly shared as peers that was now forbidden by *Naval Regulations* and the ancient customs of the service.

"Yes, Green Pasture is listed as an open port. The other two are just bare rock. Green Pasture has potential to support hominid life, but otherwise there isn't much known about it."

"Not need other ship report, ma'am. Med/life not trust other ship. We do study, we know it be right."

Parker was firmly in the med/life camp again. It was a pity, Steele thought, that when they finally got a chance to talk after all these months, it would only be to do battle.

"Doctor, there is some urgency for us to reach our destination. I'm afraid this is not a good time to pause for scientific studies."

"Never good time for science. Need do this, captain. Not do now, then when?"

After the wars were over, Steele thought. If they ever were. Maybe she could cut some slack for med/life. "Well, how much studying are we talking about? How long do you need?"

"Ideal would be six year, eight month. Earth measure. Season cycle for planet be three year, four month. Do twice, have no error." Parker clamped on her quarterdeck face. She'd promised Gordon she'd push hard on this, otherwise he would have insisted on taking the med/life demands to the captain himself.

Steele stared at her, and then burst out laughing. Parker lost her mask and covered her mouth with her hand.

"All right, Doctor. What have you two quacks decided you're willing to settle for?"

"Half day. Be long enough see what live, what grow. Do exchange. Make port call like be decent."

Parker was in earnest now. Traditions of space travel built on solid self-interest demanded ships call at every open port. These isolated habitable planets were the life-buoys of space. All spacefarers had a healthy fear of crippling storms and shipwreck that could leave sailors stranded for life at an oasis in a remote sector of the universe. To pass by one in a sound ship, was a reminder of what was owed to fortune. The custom of exchange — "Take what you need; leave what you can spare" — was an offering to the fates. Sailors whose situation was not desperate left supplies from ship stores for anyone unfortunate enough to need them. Anything on the planet useful to the wayfarer could be taken in return.

"Good, grief, Parker! Is that all you wanted? Why couldn't you just say so right out? Is there some rule in the Navy that medical officers can't talk to a captain without it being like negotiating with some Delphinian?"

"No, ma'am. Not rule."

"Well, that's a relief."

"Be tradition, ma'am."

"Of course. Very well, your request for half a day on Green Pasture is granted. Will one launch be enough?"

"That be enough for first look, ma'am. We say if be we need more." Parker stood ready to leave. "Thank you, captain." Steele dismissed her and sighed as she watched her go.

* * *

The sailors and Marines who went down to Green Pasture disembarked in a lagoon on what felt like a May morning. Although they were under orders to keep their space liners sealed, rowing to land over the quiet water felt very much like a picnic outing back on Earth. Most of the sailors on this mission were from the farm or the barnyard. Martinez had a place. She suspected it was to placate the Colonials for the loss of the goat, for the animal was also going ashore. She tried to say goodbye as they rowed to the beach, but the goat wasn't listening.

The goat was busy breathing. Out under a genuine planetary atmosphere, there was something different in the air. For most of its recent life, the air Goat breathed had been flavored first with pirate and then with pig. Both aromas were noticeably absent in this new environment. On the beach, goat and hominids disembarked and, after their different fashions, explored the world known as Green Pasture.

This part of the planet, at least at this season, was lush and green. Parker made a list, and the sailors collected stores useful to the ship — some necessities and some luxuries. Casks of natural water and tanks of natural air would refresh the synthesized equivalents in *Lafayette*'s life support system. That and the silicon beach sand were useful staples.

Behind the beach, wooded land gave evidence of visits from earlier spacefarers. The lagoon was a conspicuous landmark. Any sailor would be likely to favor it to land a small craft. Caches of hardware and manufactured articles from several cultures were clearly marked just above the high-water line, and an odd mix of vegetation from distinct planetary systems had worked out an ecological balance.

The animal life was less conspicuous, though a chorus of snorts, whistles and grunts revealed its presence. Even members of species originally domesticated for food ran wild in the open ports and reverted to early instincts for self-preservation. Since *Lafayette* had no acute needs, none of them were touched. But Parker did find a few things under rocks that would be fresh scratch for the ship's chickens.

Goat, wandering into the woods, was recognized as a herbivore and saw more than the sailors. There were plenty of pigs, Goat noted without enthusiasm. Monkeys swinging overhead chattered and threw fruit at him. He curled his lip at them, bleated something rude, and then tasted what landed at his feet. Most of it was an improvement over Navy food. He was sampling an overripe banana, so similar in texture to the universal nutritional supplement, when the indigenous goats found him.

Back on the beach, Parker supervised the last of the packing, giving special attention to the live organics, then confirmed that *Lafayette*'s contributions to the planet were properly identified and that Kali's necklace was conspicuously displayed. It would be a relief to have that relic off the ship. As the planetary sun began to sink, she ordered the sailors back to the launch, watching impatiently as the Marines urged them on.

No one wanted this pleasant afternoon to end, but the launch had to catch the solar tide or waste valuable fuel reserves. The last of the sailors were aboard the boats and the Marines were getting ready to follow when Parker heard a shout and a rattle of rifles. Abruptly, a red-coated figure knocked her to the ground, sprawling over her and pushing her face into the sand.

"Permission to fire, ma'am!"

Parker struggled to free her head.

"What be it? What you want shoot?"

"It's a Delphinian, ma'am. Mean looking one too."

The creature stumbling toward the water was between five and six feet tall, about average height for its species. But it could not have weighed much over three hundred pounds, decidedly lean for the porcine people. Wearing the tattered remnants of a Delphinian Navy uniform, its thick arms were raised in Earth's sign of surrender. It held a shred of white cloth. Parker wished with all her heart she could for a moment be free of her oath and order the Marines to blow it to hell.

"Not kill. Law be rescue castaway. Take for *Lafayette*."

"If you say so, ma'am." The Marines reluctantly lowered their weapons, went through their by-the-numbers drill for securing a prisoner, and stowed it aboard the launch with the cargo.

"Hey, soldier," a sailor shouted. "Who you going to kill to feed that thing?"

"Is that swine going to sleep in the barnyard or with you lobsters in the 'tweendecks?"

"Stick it in quarantine so the sight of it don't make none of us throw up."

"No, I say stick it on the gundeck so the lobsters can use it for bayonet practice."

Parker ignored the sailors' chatter. She listened warily to the Delphinian. Like her own species, Delphinians relied on telepathic communication. This one wasn't saying much — giving just a serial number and ship name, claiming POW status. It could sense her hostility, and Parker made no attempt to conceal her disgust. The very sight of the beady eyes and bristled face turned her stomach, bringing back a tide of childhood nightmares. The Delphinian closed its eyes and turned its head away.

They kept the Delphinian in quarantine for ten days and then transferred it to the brig. Steele inspected its cell. It met Navy requirements — it was clean, heated to 70 degrees Fahrenheit, and lit by one fluorescent bulb. The prisoner could drew a full ration of air and water. The Navy had no clothing that would fit the broad bodies and thick limbs of Delphinians, but the bunk was furnished with extra blankets. The prisoner covered itself with one of these when the captain entered its cell. Steele avoided looking at it directly. Avoiding thinking about it was harder.

Of all the barbarities of the wars with Delphinus, treatment of POWs was, perhaps, the most grotesque. Despite repeated attempts by both sides, there was no convention between the parties regulating treatment of prisoners. Nevertheless, each side, after its fashion, gave preferential treatment to captured combatants if only to encourage similar indulgence by the enemy.

For hominids taken by Delphinians, that meant being kept in a segregated stockyard, apart from common food herds, no forced breeding (although breeding would be strongly encouraged since offspring did not share combatant status), and a rather foggy guarantee that combatants would not be used as food unless it became "absolutely necessary" in the absence of other meat supplies.

What was known of conditions in the Delphinian stockyards came from the testimony of the small number of prisoners successfully exchanged. Almost all of them were sickly, too diseased for the Delphinians to want. Even when they lived, they could rarely describe what stockyard conditions were like for healthy prisoners.

Earth insisted that the Delphinian stockyards themselves constituted an atrocity. Unfortunately, a similar charge could plausibly be leveled against the conditions under which the Navy confined its captives. The death rate among Delphinians captured by Earth was substantially higher than the death rate among hominids captured by the enemy.

The problem was feeding them. Delphinian dietary needs were once a high priority for Navy research and development. Indeed, in the early years following contact and the immediate outbreak of war with the hominid-eating species, the Navy made heavy investment in attempts to find an alternative food source for Delphinian prisoners. The research had a long-range goal of finding something that the entire species would accept in lieu of its traditional diet.

The Navy first tried feeding prisoners the same foods provided to their own sailors. Force feeding them, actually, because Delphinians viewed pigs, the Navy staple meat, as only slightly less evolved members of their own species and were nauseated by the smell of their cooked flesh. They found the flesh of some larger species of Earth anthropoids palatable, but this diet also proved unsatisfactory. The large apes were endangered species on Earth, and their flesh was difficult for Delphinians to metabolize. Sooner or later they developed a fatal form of kwashiorkor. The Navy reluctantly concluded that Delphinians could digest only one form of animal protein.

Short of allowing prisoners to eat hominid flesh, which would be intolerable, the only food Earth could supply and Delphinians could keep down was synthetic protein, the Navy's "undifferentiated nutritional staple." Although pigs, chickens and hominid sailors could survive on it indefinitely, it was nutritionally incomplete for Delphinians. However much they were fed, they eventually starved.

Lafayette's prisoner would die faster than most. Although the landing party confirmed that a variety of anthropoids lived on Green Pasture, the Delphinian was emaciated when it was brought aboard.

In late August, as *Lafayette* prepared to make her flyby of Dead Red, the Sergeant Major brought a petition from the brig up the chain of command. The Delphinian was not expected to live out the week, and it wanted to speak to the captain.

Pipp brought it to the captain himself, bristling at the presumption of the prisoner. "You don't have to do it, ma'am," he said, watching Steele's jaw go rigid as she read it. "It's a dying request, but it's not like it was one of ours."

"Thank you, Pipp." She waved a dismissal, her eyes still on the brief message. Steele had hoped that by some miracle she might get this prisoner alive to the Pegasus station. She expected to be the agent of death for many Delphinians before she was much older. That was the mission of a warrior. But slow starvation was an ugly way to kill.

During the long empty hours on the top deck, Steele found herself wrestling with philosophical questions that had been thoroughly examined in Philosophy 185: The Just War. The textbook answers were unsatisfying. She should be able to leave her prisoner to die with a clear conscience. Somehow, she continued to feel guilt and a nagging conviction that the death she was bringing to the first Delphinian she had ever seen was mean and dishonorable.

It wanted to be heard before it died. She'd give it that. When the watch changed, Steele went to the 'tweendecks and amazed the sentries by going into the prisoner's cell and facing the Delphinian alone.

The Delphinian was weak, but alert. Steele made eye contact and realized she could read nothing in its unfamiliar physiognomy. The black eyes held life and intelligence but no personality. No soul.

"You have my permission to speak." She flinched at the telepathic contact. The chill along her spine was different from what she felt when Anne Parker communicated, but was unmistakable. It took a few moments for transmission to adjust. The Delphinian was not fluent in inter-species communication. It's "voice" cracked and wavered before settling into an unexpectedly pleasant, clearly feminine alto.

"Call me Little Yellow Flower," the Delphinian began awkwardly. Steele's brain strained to adjust the signal and then took it in.

"My name is Buttercup. My last service was aboard the Delphinian corvette *Boadacious.*"

The Delphinian peered at Steele. Did the human understand? That strange small nose, tiny ears that barely moved. It was impossible to tell.

"Very well, Buttercup. I am here at your request, but I have duties elsewhere, so please be brief."

Buttercup sighed. She could not read the human's features but it understood. And the sounds it made as it thought were quite pleasant, even musical.

"I had a dream, Captain. It was very fine and beautiful and it is too good to die with me. I tried to explain it to my officers on *Boadacious*, but they didn't like it at all. I was punished for it." Buttercup attempted to arrange her blanket so it covered her large body more modestly. "Your *veterinarians/medics* saw all my scars and kept talking about them; it was very embarrassing."

"Tell me about your dream." Steele was already regretting she had come. Buttercup was not in any hurry to get to the point.

"I am not an educated *sow/woman*, just a simple sailor. I always thought that if wise *animals/people* would only listen to me and try to understand, they could improve my idea so it would work."

"And what is your idea," Steele asked impatiently.

"My idea is very simple. You see, if Delphinians did not eat *hominids/people*, we could have universal peace."

Yes, Steele thought. Very nice. But Delphinians did eat people. The prisoner's own condition proved that Delphinians had to eat people. So much for peace.

"I joined the Navy during the first war," Buttercup said. "It seemed to me it was the only way to protect my home and family. Your Navy came into our planetary systems and spread some awful disease among our flocks. Many Delphinians were starving. Our warships were the only way to drive you off."

This revisionist account of the First Galactic War was what could be expected from the enemy, Steele thought. Buttercup neglected to mention that the Navy went into their planetary system only after the Delphinians had attacked the Colony and massacred millions of its inhabitants.

"I stayed in the Navy after the war. Our leaders said we had to stay prepared, that we couldn't trust you to keep your word, that you might try to stop our hunting again even though we had to hunt now to replace our herds. We kept our patrols watching you the best we could."

"Please get to the point. I am aware that your Navy had warships observing in Solar space. Your attempt to establish a permanent base in our asteroid belt is what forced Earth to go to war again."

"Well, I don't know about that kind of thing. I'm just a simple sailor. But I was very sorry to have war come again, especially when it went on so long, even longer now than the first time. I grew old in these wars. It's almost twenty years of my life that I spent in space, and I never had any *piglets/children*, which is a great disappointment to me, and I wonder why it has to be this way."

This had gone on long enough. The prisoner was babbling. "Yes, well, I'm sure we all regret the necessity of war. Perhaps in the life to come . . ." Steele hesitated. Did Delphinians believe in an afterlife? Most cultures did.

"Yes, yes!" the Delphinian interrupted. "You understand, then. If there is peace in heaven, then all we have to do is live as they do in heaven and we can have peace in our galaxy."

"And how do they live in heaven," Steele asked cautiously. She suspected the Delphinian system did not envision a land where the inhabitants dined on milk and honey.

"Like it says in your Bible. That's what gave me the idea." The Delphinian quoted verses that, although they were filtered through an alien mind, Steele immediately identified and translated back into the original King James phrases: "The wolf also shall dwell with the lamb, and the leopard shall lie down with the kid; and the calf and the young lion and the fatling together . . . and the lion shall eat straw like the ox."

"How did you become familiar with our Bible?"

"We had lots of your Bibles on *Boadacious*. Every time we took a ship we picked up dozens. Most of them were recycled. But not having much to do in space, some of us learned to read them. When I read this part, I thought it was so beautiful. And I thought I would try it."

"Try what?"

"Just what it says. Well, not exactly what it says. I couldn't really live eating just straw."

Steele began to understand. This Delphinian sailor had what it believed to be a Divine revelation after reading literature sacred to a wartime enemy, and while under its influence began to follow a diet excluding hominid meat. No wonder its officers had punished it.

Steele could just imagine how a similar episode would have played out on *Lafayette* under Captain Brook. Brook would tolerate peculiar religious ideas provided they did not interfere with the operations of the ship. But if a sailor refused to clean her plate, Doctor Gordon would have her up on charges of endangering her health. If she persisted in refusing to eat, the prescription was flogging. No wonder this Delphinian had scars on her hide. If she tried to persuade others to "work for peace by fasting," the charge would be sedition. Brook would have hanged her.

"It is such a beautiful dream. I don't understand why the officers were so angry. They said I was upsetting my messmates, that dietary rules as extreme as those I wanted to follow would make Delphinians too weak to fight. I said, I didn't want to have any more fighting. I wanted to have peace in my time. They said I was crazy. Is it crazy to want peace?"

Steele refrained from replying.

"I was punished for refusing to eat *hominids/people*, and then I was court-martialed. The court decided that my being crazy was an extenuating circumstance. Instead of killing me outright, they marooned me. But I kept the faith while I was on Green Pasture. They left me there because there are plenty of big apes on that planet. Hairy ones like the ones we had in our system before the wars; not smooth ones like you. They left me weapons for hunting, and said if I starved it would be my own fault, that their intention was to be merciful. Well, I never killed anything my own size on Green Pasture, just little things I didn't think God would mind my eating."

But it hadn't been enough. The Delphinian was seriously malnourished when it came aboard. It must once have been a massive creature to have survived without its necessary food for so many months.

"When your ship came, I was so happy. I thought it was a sign from God. If Delphinians wouldn't listen to me, maybe Earth would understand."

Steele didn't reply. Unfortunately, she agreed with the Delphinians. An animal cannot by act of will alter its physiology. A cow cannot resolve to live in the ocean; and, whatever the Bible said, lions cannot become vegetarians. Buttercup's peace plan would be suicide for Delphinus, and no species could accept peace on such terms. Every life form must fight for its own survival.

The prisoner groaned. Steele started. She'd forgotten that her thoughts would be read unless she made an effort to conceal them. "So it's all been for nothing. I'm just a foolish old *sow/woman.* I so hoped that there would be something practical in my idea that you could figure out." The prisoner's dying body sagged, and she clutched her blanket tighter.

"I'm sorry." There was something oddly touching about the prisoner's story. Her actions were simultaneously both heroic and pathetic.

"I want to ask a favor." The beady eyes blazed as Buttercup tried to see beyond Steele's thoughts into her soul. Her intense effort caused the telepathic voice to waver. "Captain, beg you. Please. I appeal to your bestiality."

Sensing an incongruous reaction, Buttercup tried again, groping for a way to express the concept in a form that the Earth captain would understand. "I appeal to your piggishness." Another miss. "I appeal to your humanity."

"I'll hear your request."

"I don't what to die on this ship. Recycling doesn't bother me that much. In the end, all flesh is recycled. But I know how it is in space. I know what goes on in the bilges. If it was for my comrades on *Boadacious*, it would be different; but I don't want to end up as food for your pigs. As you are a sentient life form, have the mercy on me my own officers had. Put me off your ship. Let me go dust to dust on land."

"I'm afraid that may not be possible. We're on course through a very barren sector of space. You are not expected to live long. There may be no land of any sort near enough."

"Will you promise me you will try. Leave me with some hope."

"Very well. I will try."

* * *

No one had ever tarried around Dead Red long enough to explore. A few energy irregularities were hinted at on the charts, but none of them were clearly marked. Steele ordered the lookouts to keep a sharp watch and to report even so much as a stray molecule of matter immediately. She took the ship on a course that would bring her close to the anomalies. The first was a thin dust cloud, hardly worth diverting for. The others seemed to have disappeared altogether; perhaps they'd never been more than mirages.

It took several hours to pass across the face of Dead Red. Steele took the ship close to its fading surface, curious about the star she had followed for so many months and probably would never see again. Close enough in, there was heat and light enough to flow into the sail plates, and the hull sweepers, for the first time in many months, found some bits of matter clinging to the ship. On impulse, Steele diverted the ship for another partial sweep across the star. Then, unexpectedly, in a close orbit where it was normally concealed by the aging star's corona, was a lonely satellite, perhaps the outermost of a series of planets and asteroids that had circled the star in Dead Red's younger days.

Steele stared at it in awe. It was a new world, one never before described or marked on the charts. Perhaps the Delphinian's foolish devotion had found favor with God after all. Steele briefly considered naming the bit of rock Buttercup, but realizing that would be difficult to explain to the Admiralty, settled instead on False Hope as she carefully entered the coordinates in the log.

Buttercup was taken to the planet wrapped in a space liner and died instantly as she was placed on the surface. The sailors carrying her in the gig cursed the random chill from the telepathized nonsense the Delphinian was too weak to control. It sounded like a combination of prayer and orders of the day: "All hands will be employed in dismantling cannon and fashioning them into agricultural implements, which will not under any pretence be used in aggressive action. Combat readiness exercises are permanently discontinued."

CHAPTER SEVENTEEN

"The course lies from Dead Red to Hubble and from thence to Enif." Steele had made that decision almost a year ago. Now as Christmas came and went, the stars that marked the ship's course remained the center of her attention, but the crew of *Lafayette* was absorbed by another of its annual rituals: Superbowl Monday.

In the twenty-first century, football divided into two distinct sports derived from the same root. The first combined the game played with a pigskin ball with demolition derby. These "football" games featured heavily armored players who used complex technology to batter each other's shells into rubble. The second version of football returned to the form of the game played early in the twentieth century with lightly padded amateur players who were required to be both scholars and athletes. Their contests appealed to a wide audience on Earth, and holographs extended the interest to all the Navy ships in space.

On the fourth Monday in January, two football teams competed for the Universal Championship. This game ended the cycle of games for the year, and a new series began in February. Ships ran the series several years after it was actually played, but for those in space the contests seemed immediate and compelling.

Like the illusions of twenty-four hour days and changing seasons, the illusion that football was real and important kept a warship's crew from focusing on what was objectively real and too frightening for ordinary minds to bear. More than five thousand hominids, designed by nature to live on a small planet circling a yellow sun, were confined within the walls of a tiny metallic object hurtling through an immense and mostly barren universe, travelling at a velocity at which no naturally created object could move, bending time, space, and every law of common sense.

On the bridge, sailors making observations imagined that the blackness into which they peered was the illusion, a flat black screen rather than a window into infinity. Reality was on the lower decks with its comforting suggestions of Earth space and Earth time. Only the captain never forgot where they were and where they were going.

As Hubble came into view over the bridge, Steele again became absorbed by navigation. In deep space, cutting even a nanosecond from the route translated to significant savings in energy. Taking sightings on the light of stars that had died aeons ago and from others that had not yet been born, Steele worked continually on refinements of the ship's course.

Was she merely doing her duty, or was this concentration pathological? The med/life officers, aware of the captain's growing abstraction, disagreed. Gordon insisted it was the nature of command in space to create personalities that appeared mentally unbalanced. The traditions of the Navy that gave the captain privacy beyond what any normal person could endure, far less desire, were designed to encourage exactly the sort of concentration on the needs of the ship that Parker was now fussing about.

Parker's view was that Steele was not concentrating on the needs of the ship as a whole but had developed an unwholesomely narrow focus on navigation. It was becoming an addiction, she insisted, and it was med/life's duty to intervene.

Yet the captain appeared to be functioning normally. She might be absorbed by navigation, but she attended to all her routine duties promptly. When Gordon, at Parker's insistence, questioned her, she admitted to having some fantasies. During night watches, she would sometimes pretend to herself that Captain Brook and the other officers were still alive, that they were asleep or at work somewhere on the ship, and that in an emergency they would come to their battle stations. It made her feel less lonely. Perfectly normal, Gordon concluded, and entirely harmless.

Meanwhile, the crew's concentration on Superbowl Monday mounted to a fever pitch after the last game of the regular season. For the first time anyone could remember, Navy would be playing in the finals. Annapolis won the Western division championship the week after the crew watched the University of Bangladesh trounce Johns Hopkins at Hong Kong for the Eastern division title. The excitement, near hysteria, that Monday night, brought many people into sickbay needing tranquilizers before they could sleep.

On the Thursday preceding Superbowl Monday, the universe outside the hull of HMS *Lafayette* took on an unfamiliar air of reality. A lookout spotted a ship. *Lafayette* shifted course to shadow it. The news travelled through the ship like fire, and before the watch changed, prize money was a hotter topic than the condition of the Navy quarterback's knees.

As *Lafayette* continued to shadow the unidentified vessel throughout the day with no effort to close the distance, some sailors who expected big cuts of prize money grew uneasy.

"She's got to let us fight, she's just got to." Petrov, Newcastle and most of the other gunner's mates nursed their ration of beer at a table outside the ship's store.

"Don't be a fool, Tattoo. We don't want a fight we can't win. There's no prize money if *Lafayette*'s the prize."

"What fight could there be we can't win, Coal? Tell me that? One ship, that's all that's out there. I don't care if it's the Delphinian flag ship, there's nothing in space we can't beat one on one."

Nodding heads confirmed the consensus among the gunners.

"But there's sometimes other things that make a difference when we fight. The funny, quirky things — you know, like getting popped by an asteroid so suddenly we're all working damage control and the enemy hasn't fired a shot."

"Yeah, but we wouldn't be holding this great distance because we're afraid of a random asteroid. Quirky things happen in a battle, but Brook would never have held us back because of that. You start to mix it up; then if something spoils it for you, them's the breaks."

"You know, there's something else it might be . . ."

"Chalkie, If you're going to say Steele is still worried that the gundeck can't hack it, you can forget it. Besides the plain fact that we've been working our butts off, we've been getting top marks. We're better than we've ever been."

"Yeah," Bitterschoen interrupted. "Hey, Tattoo, how'd you manage to teach your cowardly giant to load and fire like he's doing? Rambo used to get the shakes just getting close to anything that went bang."

"Role modeling," Petrov smirked. Waldo Bunyan was her personal triumph.

"Okay. Congratulations to everybody," Dover broke in again. "We've gotten so damned good we surprise ourselves. But what I was going to say wasn't that. I was thinking about the ship's energy stores."

"What do you know about energy stores, Chalkie? You been hanging around engineering in the dog watches again?"

"Where I hang around is none of your business, Pittypat. Anyway, it doesn't take inside info to know you got to figure energy stores before getting into a fight."

The gunners considered this insight. Rationing energy wasn't part of their job, but weapons being brought to bear and the ship altering course and pitch were the twin fundamentals of battle tactics. Nothing moved if the batteries gave out.

"How long since we refueled? Anybody here been paying attention?" The gunners looked at each other and shook their heads. Underway, drifting, or in a fueling orbit, it made no difference to anyone not on the bridge or in engineering.

"Well, I say, we find out. Grab someone on the bridge or in engineering who knows. God, I want to get some action after all these months in drill."

* * *

Watching the faint energy emissions of the distant vessel through the dome of *Lafayette's* bridge, Steele too longed for action. Among the larger ship's tactical advantages was the ability to see farther than smaller craft; the ship they were tracking could not see them. It gave her time to decide whether it was worth giving chase and forcing contact.

The bridge had enough data to identify the quarry. Definitely Delphinian, and probably a warship. Non-combatant vessels often disguised themselves as warships with faked weapons ports to discourage pirates. But it was difficult to imagine what purpose would bring civilians into the Great Void where there was nothing to salvage and no populated planets to sell to.

If the ship were what it appeared to be, it would be a magnificent prize. With over a hundred guns, the big frigate could in a pinch serve as a ship-of-the line. It was moving smoothly, as was *Lafayette*, on course toward Hubble. Steele wish she knew where it had been — and how long it had been since it had refueled.

A frigate had smaller energy requirements than a larger ship, but it also carried less backup fuel. What would happen if the frigate were challenged depended on how sure her captain felt about making it to Hubble. If the energy level was high, the frigate might head back into the void, forcing *Lafayette* to turn from the star to pursue. Steele knew her ship couldn't risk that, not for long. The batteries hadn't charged full since Twinkle.

She wished *Lafayette* had just a little more of a cushion. Nothing was sadder in the annals of space warfare than the loss of ships that fought to exhaustion. Winner or loser, it made no difference when power failed leaving the vessel adrift and lost in the pitiless vacuum.

Two days before Superbowl Monday, Steele still had not come to a decision. She studied the reports from med/life in the day's Important but Not Urgent basket. Inconspicuous austerities had already been imposed — the shipboard weather was unusually cold and overcast. Christmas was partly cloudy, and there hadn't been a bright sunny day since early fall. The full moon had not been visible since October.

Christmas dinner was traditional and festive. But before and after the holiday, the menu featured more mystery meat dishes based on the undifferentiated nutritional supplement than sailors normally tolerated.

Nothing further could be cut on the third-deck without declaring a state of emergency. Steele preferred keeping the sailors ignorant and happy.

Engineering reported all systems operating at peak efficiency. No wasted energy there. No way to reduce consumption.

Steele initialed the reports and tossed them into the Tinling file. One way or another, she must come to a decision within a few hours. Shadowing the unknown vessel had diverted *Lafayette* from her carefully plotted course.

She poked at the papers in the Trivial basket, looking for temporary distraction. A thick, rather grimy set of papers bore the fancy lettered heading HUMBLE PETITION. Yeoman Tinling had arranged this packet so that it was clear at a glance that virtually every sailor aboard had signed. Steele flipped to the bottom of the pile. The Marines too.

Wondering what kind of petition could produce such unanimity, Steele read through from the beginning:

> *If you please, Captain Margaret C. Steele, commanding HMS Lafayette, your honor, ma'am. We the undersigned, sailors and Marines of HMS Lafayette, are loyal subjects of the Queen and the Navy. We don't mean to be getting into what's none of our business. If we here have done so, we apologize and beg your pardon, and you don't have to read no further.*

Steele could imagine the kind of committee effort that must have gone into drafting this introductory paragraph. Some power brokering from distinct interest groups was evident. Representatives of various shipboard constituencies debating the fine points of wording and then insisting that the yeoman whose fine Italian hand produced the clean copy take dictation and not offer gratuitous suggestions on phrasing. The last bit of apology smacked of an effort to appease the Marines who were sensitive about any possible compromise of loyalty. But what was the point of all this?

Steele read the next paragraph.

> *Someone, we'd rather not say who, but it's someone who knows, told some others of us that Lafayette might be able to get some action soon and there could be a prize. We want to say that the main thing we are thinking about is NOT THE MONEY. We are all patriots and support the war effort and want to do good by our ship and the Navy.*

Marines, again. Steele still wondered what the point was.

> *The same someone who told us the other says that to have a fight we have to use more energy than when we*

don't have fights so maybe it would be good to have more energy reserves. In conclusion, and whereas all of the above, if the captain thinks it would help the ship, ESPECIALLY if it would help the ship to fight and take a prize, we sailors and Marines voluntarily volunteer to cancel all football games paid for by our ship's store so as to save the energy. Only if the captain thinks we don't really need to do this, then we won't cancel them. If we do cancel them, then we HUMBLY PETITION that when we get to port and recharge, the ship's store will get paid back so we can make up the games we miss. This volunteering is effective immediately and INCLUDES THE SUPERBOWL. God save the Queen!"

* * *

Lafayette responded to the helm handsomely with a grace and speed that did her designers proud. In open space, free of the need for sharp maneuvering necessary during the escape from Mantu, *Lafayette* was in her element. She ran down the prize swiftly and smoothly. By the time the enemy had sighted her and began to react, the frigate was under the dreadnought's guns.

She was the *Abomination*, easily identifiable now and listed in *Lafayette*'s most recent update of *Jane's Fighting Ships*. She had been around since the first war and still had her old-fashioned cigar shape design and tin pot bridge. Steele knew from her Naval Acadmeny studies precisely where the craft was strong and where she was vulnerable. Her captain had, no doubt, made personal modifications in the disposition of weapons and in rigging her helm, but the capabilities of the ship were limited by its fundamental design. She could roll on only one axis — *Lafayette*'s bell shaped mass could roll on an infinite number. It was checkmate — if *Abomination*'s captain was sane enough to realize it.

Unfortunately, *Jane's* was too out of date to be trusted to identify the commander. Delphinian captains were notoriously unpredictable; a significant proportion were quite mad. The Royal Navy never left its enemies in doubt. When a meritocrat commanded, tactics might vary, but the ship would be always be fought to its limits and would never surrender. Almost as certainly, a Navy ship would practice prudence and measure, no mindless and wasteful blasting away with heavy weapons when precision firing and surgical slicing might do.

Abomination's captain was not a lunatic. After trying a few textbook maneuvers in an effort to escape, some of which might have worked had *Lafayette* been a typically cumbersome battleship, the frigate cut its engines, ran out its silver sail plates, and prepared to resist boarders.

Steele breathed a sigh of relief. *Abomination* had not insisted on going broadside to broadside, a procedure that would have grievously damaged the smaller ship, leaving it much less valuable a prize. She hoped the enemy captain would be equally sensible when it came to boarding. The frigate could not escape. They'd have her eventually. It was the enemy's choice how many casualties they were willing to take. *Lafayette*'s boarders would fight to the death as they had been trained to do. The enemy had the option of surrender.

Steele put a red striper at the helm and left the bridge. This violation of Navy tradition and of *Naval Regulations* was now so routine aboard *Lafayette* that now she scarcely thought twice about it. She slid down the ladders to the launch docks where boarding parties were already assembled, waiting only for her signal to seal their armour and go out to grapple onto the enemy. In another violation of tradition and regulations the boarders would go out without a meritocrat to inspire them and control their excesses. This would be the real test of Rivera's drills. Steele reenforced the most essential points.

"That's our ship out there, our property. We're going to be very careful not to lower its value, right? Don't smash anything you can cut clean, and when you get where the pigs are remember that a dead Delphinian is good for nothing but recycling." She didn't have to tell the Lafayettes how much a live one was worth. A prisoner that lived long enough to be exchanged bought the life of a sailor or Marine now in the enemy's hands. The Admiralty placed an impressively high value on that when tallying up the worth of a prize.

"Take good care of your wounded. Never leave a live prisoner for the enemy. One for all and all for one! Lafayettes will live free or die!" The familiar slogans called up the expected heartfelt cheers. For boarding parties unit cohesion rested on the certainty that your mates would not leave you to the fate worse than death.

Kathy Clark went to quarters at the aft launch docks on the top deck of the third level. Her job was to get space armor and boots to sailors and Marines about to board. It was a really important job; the sailor who did it had to be a totally reliable person because if you got the stuff out too slowly or you got sizes mixed up, the whole boarding operation would be held up. Clark was very proud of her job. It was a lot of responsibility for a blue striper on her first tour and got her as close to the real action of boarding as a thirteen-year old could hope to get.

She grinned when she saw Waldo Bunyan's name on the list of sailors going out, and when she tossed him his kit with the triple extra large suit and the size sixteen boots, she flashed him a dumb sailor's sign: "Yo, Rambo! Keep safe and give 'em hell!"

Bunyan blushed and signaled his thanks. It still seemed funny to him when someone called him Rambo and this was the first time it had been done in Colonial sign. All the sailors knew the hand signals; they were useful in a lot of contexts — especially times like general quarters when silence was the rule. Kathy, who was still his "buddy," told him that in the telepathic language the word meant a weapon used by hunters to kill wild sheep, but really, she told him, Rambo was "a literary allusion." Kathy read books and knew about things like that. She couldn't remember exactly who Rambo was; she didn't think he was in the Bible, but it was someone from a long time ago who was a great warrior — "real wild and crazy."

It was Tattoo who had first called him Rambo — she did it during drills, especially when he did something she said was well done. When he asked her what it meant, she said she called him that because it sounded right; it rhymed with Waldo and it meant "someone who uses his head and butts hard like a ram." He watched her as she pulled on her armor, slapping down the seals automatically. As he put his on, he carefully recited the drill as she'd taught them to do, counting out each seal as he locked it.

Dover had command of *Gnat.* Steele inspected, he boarded his people and went off first. Petrov's crew then presented itself for inspection, holding helmets and weapons, ready to take out *Firefly.* Steele noted that Petrov had Waldo Bunyan on her team. That was good. The sooner the coward was bloodied, the sooner they could relax about him.

Bunyan stood between Petrov and a Marine sergeant who was almost as big as he was. It was a peculiar arrangement; Marines usually stood together and entered the launch last, but she wouldn't interfere with Petrov's methods. There was nothing wrong with interservice cooperation if Petrov could manage it.

"Ready to go, Chief?"

"Ready and more, ma'am!"

"Go aboard, then. Keep safe, and good luck."

Two more launches would follow *Gnat* and *Firefly* after the first two cleared *Lafayette*'s gravity orbit. Steele headed for *Bumblebee* as Petrov led her team toward the airlock. Bunyan, was right behind her until they reached the hatch. Then, abruptly, he balked. The Marine, gave him a shove, but he planted his feet and refused to take another step.

Petrov cursed viciously under her breath. Of all the times for Rambo to act up. She thought she'd gotten him under control. He was easy to manage as long as he didn't think too much, just get him to plod along, one step at a time, not thinking to step four before he did step three. She grasped Bunyan's arm, helping the Marine to urge him forward.

"No," Bunyan shouted, his voice echoing across the ramps. "I won't go. I changed my mind." The rest of the crew gasped and looked toward the captain, who turned slowly and deliberately returned to the dock.

"Shut your stupid mouth," Petrov hissed in Bunyan's ear. "We're at general quarters, you twit, and you just got a direct order. You heard the captain say to go aboard. This isn't a drill." She made another effort to get him moving, but Bunyan dug in his heels.

The captain was back. Petrov biting her lip in frustration, led the others in coming to attention. Except for Bunyan, ready to bolt, restrained only by the Marines who moved to block the way.

Steele moved deliberately down the line, confronted Bunyan and forced eye contact, wishing she understood what was going on in his head. Cowardice in the face of the enemy was on the short list for mandatory capital punishment. If Bunyan was going to come apart, he should have given notice sooner. It was too late now. Bunyan must obey, ready or not.

"Sailor, I order you to board."

"No, I won't go on that boat. You can't make me go."

Oh, yes she could make him — and would. Unfortunately. Even if it meant he went aboard feet first. Deliberately she reached for her sidearm. Too late, she realized the weapon wasn't in its accustomed place.

Abruptly turning on her heel, she strode across the deck, away from the launch docks, toward the main mast. Cursing the bad luck that let one skittish sailor hold up the entire operation almost as if it were one of Rivera's scripted exercises, Steele also cursed herself. Of all the possible displays of incompetence! She'd given the orders for general quarters, and then she'd gone to her station without her goddamn sidearm. Damn, bloody hell! If she'd ever done this while Captain Brook was in command, even on a drill, he'd have busted her on the spot. Now everyone had to wait while she went to get the blasted thing. *Gnat* out alone waiting for support; *Bumblebee* and *Hornet*'s crews twiddling their thumbs. Meanwhile the enemy was gaining valuable time to reenforce defenses, meaning more bloodshed for both sides.

One stupid mistake after another. Mistakes, mistakes, mistakes! She should never have risked letting Bunyan go with a boarding party. She should have told him to go below the minute she saw him and never have let him do anything dangerous until he proved his physical courage in smaller ways. Yes, Rivera would have put Bunyan in harm's way deliberately, as the best medicine for whatever ailed him, but she wasn't Rivera, damnit, and neither was Chief Petrov.

Bunyan should never have been shifted from going to quarters in engineering. That was the place for him, sweating over the lines where he couldn't see or hear anything but engine noise. She should never have let him go into general rotation with the gunners even though Brook and Rivera had both encouraged it.

Leaving him there had been a mistake. A terrible, terrible mistake. And now it was Bunyan who would have to pay for it. It wasn't fair, but that was how the Navy worked.

Tears stung behind her eyes. She held them until she reached her cabin. Then they flowed down her cheeks as she set her sidearm to charge and strapped on the holster. The Helmet tugged at the fringe of consciousness. With a sigh she surrendered to it. A Naval officer couldn't shoot a sailor in cold blood while awash in tears. It would send entirely the wrong message.

Open for access, the relevant memory banks in the Helmet released their contents. Like dream fragments unexpectedly remembered, they unfolded rapidly in interconnected sequences. Steele's conscious mind accepted the suggestion that this would not be the first time she killed one of her own people. Her heart still ached for Waldo Bunyan, but the tears stopped. Steele shuddered and exhaled sharply. The Helmet was in place. She ran the safety checks on the pistol, dropped it in the holster and returned to *Firefly*.

In Steele's absence, Petrov made her move. With clenched fists, she watched out of the corner of her eye until the captain disappeared at the main hatch. Then with a howl of rage, she threw herself on Bunyan, knocking the big sailor to the deck and pinning his arms.

"Help me, you fools," she screamed. "Sit on him! Who the hell has the first aid kit?" Two sailors and three Marines planted themselves on Bunyan's prone form as Petrov glared from one sailor to another.

"You! Stewart! I know you've got it. Hand it over. Now!"

The lanky man reluctantly pulled a pouch from a zipped pocket. Petrov grabbed it from him.

"Endorphins," Petrov muttered, pawing through the bag, "Where the hell did you stash the endorphins?"

"Tattoo," Stewart protested, "You can't do that. That stuff's just for medical emergencies. It's on the controlled list. I'll catch hell from the Director if . . ."

"Shut up." Petrov found what she was looking for and loaded two syringes. "Help me get his armor loose," she snapped and tugged at Bunyan's belt. "Give me some hip."

Stewart watched nervously. "A double dose? Tattoo, do you know how strong this stuff is? This guy's going to be higher than a kite."

"If he doesn't get this, he'll be dead. Where do you think the captain's gone?" Bunyan, catching sight of the syringes, was now roaring and thrashing harder than ever. Tattoo wished she could just slug him and leave him unconscious on the deck. But this hulking sailor was on her team and her responsibility. One way or another Bunyan was going out to fight.

"Rambo, goddamn you, I'm not getting my record smeared by some sorry excuse for a sailor getting shot for cowardice. Stop fighting me, or I promise you, I'm dumping you in a bag tagged KIA as soon as we're clear of the airlock."

Sweating and cursing, Petrov finally got access to enough bare flesh to force in a needle.

"Hold him still, you lunkheads. If this damn needle breaks off we're all in for it." Petrov emptied the syringe and waited a few heartbeats before driving in the second needle. Bunyan was already relaxing.

Petrov sat on the deck panting. The sailors and Marines slowly loosened their grip as Bunyan stopped struggling.

Petrov passed the empty syringes back to Stewart. "Wonderful stuff, endorphins," she said.

"It's meant to be used as a painkiller," Stewart said resentfully. He'd have to fake a report to explain the loss of two doses of a powerful euphoric.

"Sure it is." Petrov heaved herself to her feet and automatically checked out the seals on her armor. "Endorphins kill pain faster than morphine. But the stuff cures cowardice too."

"Courage in a needle," Stewart sniffed.

"Any kind will do in a pinch." Petrov squatted by Bunyan's disheveled form and gave him a shove. Bunyan slowly rolled over on his back, stretched and smiled.

"So, Rambo, if you've finished making an ass of yourself, tell me what came over you. Why did you freeze up after we've drilled this, over and over? Why did you clutch? Why now?"

"I'm sorry, Tattoo," Bunyan blinked and smiled shyly. "It was us going in a launch called *Firefly*. Becky Petrie told me if I ever went out in a launch named after a little flying bug, I'd be sure to get killed."

"Beautiful. Every launch on the goddamn ship is named after some 'little flying bug.' Why do you believe a ten-year-old kid who tells you something that stupid?"

"She didn't just make it up, Tattoo," Bunyan said seriously. "She was reading me from her fortune cards. She bought this deck from some Colonial in the hydroponic bay who painted these wonderful magic pictures. There was the Fool card, a guy with a blue dog, that she said was me, and then this other card with a big fly on it . . ."

"So your card was the Fool. Well, Hellcat got that right. Listen, Rambo, Hellcat was just fooling with you. She may have cards, but that doesn't mean she knows squat about telling fortunes. You want cards read, next time you go to the coven and pay Shadow. And stay away from Hellcat. She's what almost got you killed."

Petrov stood up, and gave Bunyan a hand to pull him to his feet. "What are the rest of you staring at? Get back in line and seal up your helmets. We're going to race to beat *Gnat* to that frigate, and I want us long gone before the captain gets a close look at Rambo's smiling face."

* * *

The *Abomination* was a splendid prize. Steele felt almost friendly toward her captain, now confined to his quarters for the duration of the voyage. So wise of him to surrender quickly. He'd put up only enough resistance to cover himself in the event of a court-martial — in the Delphinian Navy suffering a casualty rate as low as five percent was enough. Inspection of his food stores showed large stocks of emergency rations derived from the flesh of the non-intelligent Delphinian hominids that made up most of the food supply of the species before the First Galaxy War. It had been in the hold a long time. *Abomination* had enough in storage to make survival of most if not all of the prisoners distinctly probable even after the non-Delphinian meat was confiscated. Two other officers were taken in addition to the captain, officers who could be exchanged for meritocrats. They alone were worth as much as their ship.

Thanks to her captain's prudence, *Abomination* required little repair, and her batteries were surprisingly well charged. *Lafayette* drained them of everything beyond what was needed for life support and took the prize in tow. It would slow them down to travel that way, but with only commoners aboard as a prize crew, the frigate could not be trusted to accompany them in convoy.

The two ships moved as one toward Hubble, and before the end of March they were in orbit around the fueling star. The crew got its victory dinner on Easter Sunday, and to universal rejoicing, Navy beat Bangladesh in overtime the following evening.

"She owe us dinner, too," Parker said to Gordon as *Lafayette* moved away from Hubble for the final passage to Pegasus.

"We're not line, Parker. The victory dinners Brook gave were for the people who were fighting the ship."

"We also invited."

"Just out of courtesy. You never went anyway, so why are you so intent on the captain inviting us to dinner now?"

"This captain need company. All time sit alone with charts. Not healthy thing."

"Do you still think she's a navigation addict? Well, let me reassure you. Since we moved out of the Void, she's not on the bridge more than one watch out of six. She does her rounds, and then she's in her day cabin."

"I say still not healthy. Tell her have dinner. I go this time. We see her close up. Let talk like normal human. Be good for her."

Gordon shrugged. Parker never asked him for much. If she wanted him to do this, why not. He located an appropriate form, and scribbled out a formal request to be invited to the wardroom for a victory dinner.

The wardroom had not been used since the fateful evening when the *Pagan Queen* attacked. When Alice Little brought word to the galley that the captain was planning an officers' dinner, the crew greeted the news as though it signaled the end of a period of mourning. Chiefs McCarthy and McDougall fussed over the arrangements, but insisted that Little be involved. A captain's steward should know how such things were done.

Steele did not require wearing the full dress uniform traditional at these affairs. Little was disappointed. She wanted to see how her captain would look all dressed up in the Navy's finest finery. Steele explained she was honoring her guests' specific request; Doctor Gordon detested any kind of dressing up, and Doctor Parker did not own a full dress uniform.

The two physicians came to dinner in their dress blues, wearing decorations of which both had a good number. Steele had never seen Parker with a full display. It had somehow not occurred to her that the Colonial would naturally have earned recognition often during more than a decade of service.

"Room look nice," Parker took in the surroundings appreciatively. The determined efforts of bilgehands had removed every trace of organic soil from the furnishings. Third deck specialists repaired all other damage too. They had only one failure. Fatally traumatized, the mantelpiece clock would never tick again. Alice Little, with a good deal of supervision, had prepared the table, setting out fine linen and the ship's silver. The heavy silver bowl was filled with blossoms from the ship's fruit trees, now in full spring bloom.

"Yes, I suppose it is nice, Doctor Parker. I'm afraid it brings back too many sad memories for me to appreciate it."

Well, Captain, Parker thought, that's why I wanted you back in here. Build up some new memories to overlay the old and get on with your life.

"So tell me, Captain, what have you been doing with yourself lately." Gordon decided it was up to him to carry conversation at this dinner party. Parker was no conversationalist, and Steele seemed decidedly wilted.

Steele laughed. "Fighting Delphinians, for one thing. That's why we're having dinner, isn't it? Do the two of you want to hear the details of how we tacked and the enemy luffed and all that kind of thing?"

"God, no." Gordon turned his attention to his food and lapsed into silence. That was just the sort of tactical minutiae the line officers were always going on about, and it bored him silly.

Steele and Parker exchanged an amused look.

"Not ask doctor what do on third deck. He tell. Spoil dinner."

"What are you doing?" Steele couldn't help be curious; her own work had become very tedious.

"Casualty reports," Gordon replied. "It's time to get things in order before the end of the cruise. It's a short list this time, thank God. I don't know why you captains always avoid the Great Void; it seems to be a very healthy environment. If it hadn't been for the action against *Abomination*, there'd be almost nothing to report."

"Have one sad thing, Captain. Little girl. Like dancing. Have foot broke. Second time. Not can fix."

"Becky Petrie?"

"Yes, that's the one. Grommets are always trouble. This one broke an arch fooling around on the gundeck way back over a year ago. Then she got her hands in some filth in the barnyard and picked up a nasty dose of staphylococcus that almost did her in. No sooner did we get that cleaned out of her but she's back into the same stupid dancing around on the gundeck. God knows how she did it, but she rebroke the same foot. Looked like she'd been dancing with an ox. We couldn't save it; had to take it off. Petrie will limp for the rest of her life."

"That is a shame." Steele poked at her food. Thinking about Petrie spoiled her appetite. "I think it was probably my fault."

Parker gave Gordon a meaningful glance.

"Don't be ridiculous. How could it possibly be your fault? You haven't been dancing on the gundeck."

"I very much doubt that what happened to Petrie was an accident, Doctor. There's been rampant vigilante activity among the crew ever since the massacre. There was no way I could think of to stop it, so I didn't even try. If I'd made an effort . . ."

"Now you see," Parker said to Gordon. "I say captain too much alone. Have strange idea. Bet this not be only strange thought she have. You ask."

"How about it, Captain? Is Doctor Parker right? Is the isolation getting to you? What are you doing all that time you shut yourself up in the day cabin?"

"The same thing you're doing. Getting ahead on paperwork before we get to Pegasus."

"What kind of paperwork?"

"Nothing that concerns med/life."

"Nothing? A captain's final reports usually include references to med/life operations."

"They do. And mine will. But what I put in is none of your business. I take responsibility."

"There she do again. Take responsibility. See how she say that. Ask what for she take responsibility."

"Very well, Captain Steele. Doctor Parker and I would like to know for precisely what activities in our department you feel obliged to 'take responsibility' in that martyred 'the-captain-is-accountable-for-everything-that-happens-aboard-the-ship' tone of voice?"

Steele blushed. "I didn't mean to be patronizing you. I just didn't want you to worry."

"Goddamnit," Gordon roared. "Goddamnit, Captain, ma'am. We are worried now. Not about med/life — about you. I demand to know what you are taking responsibility for."

"All right, if you really insist on knowing. I've been preparing a bill of particulars . . ."

"See. Just like I say. She be brooding. All time think what be wrong. All time think her fault."

"Calm down, Parker." Gordon shouted, then realizing he was becoming agitated himself, attempted to take his own advice. "Let's approach this in a spirit of scientific objectivity." Gordon pushed aside his plate and folded his hands. "Captain Steele, if you please, describe one item that's on this 'bill of particulars' of yours."

"Very well. If you must know, it starts with one of the very first things I did after I took command, Doctor Gordon. I'm sure you remember. I knew it was wrong when I did it, but I did it anyway. The pirate. The one named Fart. I forced you to quibble on your oath. I forced you to kill."

"Now you are patronizing me, Captain. I am not a commoner, and I am not a child. I keep my own conscience. My conscience is a little sore on this point. I confess it. But it was my free choice. I would never obey an order I considered morally wrong. I am a meritocrat. I would disobey, go to the brig, accept court-martial, exactly as you would."

“No one else will be court-martialed, Doctor. I'm the only one with the power to bring charges, and I've made up my mind about what I have to do.”

“Now, see. See how bad she get. Captain mean charge self. Stupidness. No. Not allow. Captain, I say not do.”

“Simmer down, Anne,” Gordon growled. “I don't like this either, but you're getting perilously near demanding a court-martial for yourself — for insolence, and I'm a witness.”

“Not care. Captain, you say have list. Add new charge for self. Permit Colonial think-talk you. Talk you straight. Show you be damn fool.”

“All right, Doctor Parker. It can't make things much worse for me, and I suppose I owe you that much.”

“You hear Captain, Doctor. I have permission think-talk. You go. If be I insolent, you not be witness.”

“I don't suppose you two would consider taking time out and getting back to this after we've all had a chance to calm down.”

“I'd just as soon get it over with, Doctor. Do as Parker asks. Leave us alone.”

Gordon snorted, glared at both of them and left the wardroom, slamming the door. A fine state of affairs! Only three meritocrats left on the ship and two of them going at it as if they were premenstrual when he knew damn well neither of them was.

Parker's artificial voice could not carry the emotion that was fully evident in her flushed face. With Gordon gone, and the frustration of using the voice box lifted, Parker drained her water goblet to cool the soreness in her throat and wiped her face with a napkin before linking her thoughts to Steele's.

“Anne, I'm really sorry to have upset you. I . . .”

“No. I don't want your apologies.” Parker made the link and crossed her arms. “You gave me permission to communicate telepathically, and I mean to take advantage of it. You have the moral fiber to sacrifice your career for principle — well, so do I. Go through your so-called bill of particulars, these 'charges' you want to bring against yourself. I mean to argue you out of them one by one, and I'll stay here all night to do it if I have to.”

“Whew! Well, I guess I asked for this. Oh, Anne, I wish you could convince me. But I've thought about this indictment through a lot of sleepless nights. If there were any excuses I could find for myself, I would have found them."

"Cow manure! What makes you think you can see yourself so clearly? Recite your list of charges and let me show you how someone with a little more time in space than you've had would evaluate them."

"Oh, Anne, be reasonable. Your career in the Navy is all med/life. My whole time at Annapolis was learning the rules of conduct for command."

"Will you recite your list of charges?"

Amazing what a few months in isolation can do to a stable mind, Parker thought. Steele had, mercifully, decided she could not have been personally responsible for *Lafayette*'s capture by *Pagan Queen*, and nothing else she charged herself with carried a mandatory death sentence. But she had managed to find something to fault herself for in almost everything she had done or not done since.

"Then we have the case of the Delphinian prisoner. It had eaten our food and breathed our air, and the ship had a claim on the carcass. I not only kept it out of recycling, but used ship's power to put it ashore — a very expensive funeral for an enemy."

Parker's hatred of Delphinians was as great as that of anyone on the ship. It was fueled by knowledge of what the enemy had done to members of her family on her native planet. Steele's compassion for the animal she had been forced to pick up at Green Pasture seemed to her misplaced. But it wasn't criminal.

"I admit, I wouldn't have been so indulgent toward a . . . toward an individual of the porcine persuasion," she said. "Still, what you did was a legitimate command decision. If you decided we could spare the corpse, it was your right to do whatever you pleased with it."

"But as it turned out, we probably couldn't spare it. When I took the ship into combat, reserves were terribly low. Every little bit counts in space. That's basic. One two hundred pound cadaver plus energy for the launch could make a difference."

"But it didn't make a difference. We fought and we won. It doesn't take a degree from Annapolis to know that when you gamble and win, you don't get court-martialled."

"Well, perhaps Hawke will drop that charge. Look, Anne, it's getting late. I'm tired. Tired and discouraged. I know you mean well, but I know in my heart that I've failed the Navy. I should not have abandoned Brook's plan to fight our way to Pegasus. I should not have settled for survival. I should have met the standards. Whether or not one or another item in this bill of particulars stands is not the point. I was tried in the real test of space command, and I didn't meet the challenge."

* * *

HMS *Lafayette* recharged again at Enif and made contact with the fleet, clearing quarantine on the first day of June. Yeoman Tinling collected the paperwork from the captain and med/life officers, tied the packets with red tape and locked it all in a tooled pigskin pouch with a gold embossed Navy seal.

The gig carried *Lafayette*'s reports over to Admiral Christopher Hawke aboard HMS *Peacock* and returned with a written "request" that *Lafayette's* commander come aboard the flagship at 1800 hours — wearing full dress uniform, if you please.

Steele sighed. So Admiral Hawke meant to revoke her commission formally and with a flourish. He couldn't ask for her sword if she wasn't wearing one. It was his privilege to do it any way he chose, and she supposed she deserved it. Dishonoring herself, she had, by extension dishonored *Lafayette*, and you couldn't very well bust the acting commander of what was expected to be the new flagship by casually tossing her in the brig.

Alice Little, not being privy to the captain's concerns, was happy about uniform requirements for Steele's visit to the *Peacock*. She loved the beautiful white wool uniform and regretted never having seen her captain wearing it. She fussed over it as she laid it out and transferred the gold collar insignia.

Steele regarded it sadly. She wished she was still wearing the little sextant that was hers at the start of the voyage. She'd been performing well as fifth officer — at least Captain Brook seemed to think so. Now the center of force symbol of command he once wore must remain on her collar until she was officially relieved. It seemed to her now the badge of her failure and her shame.

The uniform hung on her body more loosely than it did eighteen months ago, when she wore it on that terrible Christmas eve. She cinched the sword belt in an extra notch to secure it properly. Automatically checking her appearance in the mirror, she was surprised to find herself looking better than she had expected. Her hair was completely white now, and her face was thinner than it had been two years ago, but the same glow of health that med/life maintained in the crew was apparent in her appearance as well.

Feeling much older and grimmer than she looked, Steele boarded the gig and was carried across star-spangled space to the *Peacock*. She was startled to see that her boat was not alone. Dozens of small craft were docked against the flagship's hull. Had the admiral called out the captains of the entire fleet to witness her humiliation? And, worse, had every one of them managed to report more promptly than she had? What was courtesy for calling on an admiral anyway? She thought being ten minutes early would have been more than adequate.

Lafayette's gig docked in a favored position, alongside the admiral's own. That was courtesy to the dreadnought. A pair of Colonials met her at the airlock, knuckling and signing that she was expected in the Admiral's day cabin.

Well, that was some relief. At least Hawke didn't mean to tear her down in front of the whole fleet. She slapped on her quarterdeck face, drew her body erect and entered the admiral's presence looking like the Annapolis product she was.

So, thought Hawke. This is the young meritocrat who brought a dreadnought across the Great Void. Only nineteen. It hardly seems possible. The whole crop of SOCRATES officers is something remarkable. Unquestionably the best group of new officers to come to the fleet in years, except . . .

"About this report you sent me, Lieutenant," he began carefully. He was still a bit leery of SOCRATES, never quite sure what button he might push and trigger a personality shift. Lieutenant Steele's expression was so rigid right now, that he wasn't clear whether she had a personality of any sort. "About this report. It won't quite do in this form. No, I'm afraid it just won't do at all."

"Yes, Admiral. I'm very sorry, sir."

"Well, it's nothing that can't be fixed up. Just a bit of rewriting is all it needs, I should think."

"Rewriting, sir?" She'd labored hard over the document, weighing every word. And she'd minutely inspected Yeoman Tinling's fair copy. Not a comma was out of place as far as she could tell.

"It's a matter of tone, actually. Yes, that's it, tone. It's all very well to be modest when you're putting in for a commendation. Lends a nice touch and all that. But really, Lieutenant Steele, this is excessive. Definitely, excessive. You have to be very great indeed to get away with being this humble."

Steele's eyes flew wide. My goodness, Hawke thought, this woman is still an innocent. Hard to remember with this SOCRATES crowd. One minute they carry on as though they'd been with the fleet for years, the next they're naive as new-borns. "Look here, for instance," he continued patiently. "At the end, here where you recommend that you be court-martialed. Now, really. We don't court-martial a commander who saves a ship for the Queen's service. At least, not very often, and certainly not when the ship is not only saved but comes into port with a full crew of healthy people towing a nice prize in its wake. If we were to do that, what would we have left for someone who surrendered a ship to the enemy? You see there's a difference, don't you?"

Speechless, Steele stared and nodded.

"Very good. Then I suggest you just dig around in the papers left by your predecessor and see how he put in for a commendation. Then you do it the same way."

Steele's quarterdeck face dissolved, and in its place Hawke observed a spectrum of emotions ending with a bright smile and a flash of dimples.

"Yes, well then." Hawke cleared his throat. Steele certainly had a personality. At least one. He rose. "Let's join the party, shall we? After all, you are the guest of honor. It's such a lovely evening, we've set up on the gundeck. The Peacocks do a marvellous sunset in June."